FATAL OBSESSION

FATAL OBSESSION

MICHAEL PAKENHAM

A DCI DANIEL APPLEMAN THRILLER

The Book Guild Ltd

First published in Great Britain in 2018 by
The Book Guild Ltd
9 Priory Business Park
Wistow Road, Kibworth
Leicestershire, LE8 0RX
Freephone: 0800 999 2982
www.bookguild.co.uk
Email: info@bookguild.co.uk
Twitter: @bookguild

Typeset in Aldine401 BT

Printed and bound in Great Britain by CPI Group (UK) Ltd, Croydon, CR0 4YY

ISBN 978 1912083 329

British Library Cataloguing in Publication Data.
A catalogue record for this book is available from the British Library.

To my darling Mrs Bond with all my love and thanks.

ACKNOWLEDGEMENTS

My thanks to Jeannie, my wife, for all the hours she has spent reading and editing and giving advice. To my daughter Caroline Wilson, Jeremy Thompson, Hannah Virk, Jack Wedgbury, and Philippa Illiffe of the Book Guild.

PART ONE
THE DISCOVERY

Let us then divert all other concerns on to the lesser
spirits; after all, after hurricanes the clear skies rapidly
follow.

Ovids, Art of love

1

Eliza Walker takes another drink off the tray of a passing waiter. She feels the eyes of her daughter boring into her back. She refuses to turn round – what business is it of hers if she wants to get plastered? *Every reason*, she hears a little voice saying in her head. Well, fuck it! The rehab clinic will always take her back. Well, that's a lie for a start, but nothing is going to stop her drinking today. She's watching her ex-boyfriend, handsome, hard-drinking, heavy smoking, exciting Tony Baker, marrying her best friend. Not six months ago he was on the point of asking her to marry him. And then she'd made the mistake of introducing him to Alice Winterbottom, the two-timing bitch. Friend! Okay, she was ten years younger, had a good figure and firm breasts, but you just didn't steal your best friend's boyfriend. Well, he'd soon find out how dull she was, and what a frozen bitch she was in bed, according to her ex-husband. But the sight of the two love birds cooing away at each other makes her want to walk up to them and throw her third glass of champagne all over her designer wedding dress. The only thing that gives her comfort is that once 'bastard Tony' discovers what he's married he'll soon be gone. Oh no, there was no way she'd take him back. Eliza Walker is not such a fool. She allows herself a satisfied chuckle. But the smile doesn't last long, for her pride has taken a terrible blow with the awful realisation that she is past her best and, oh God, men would soon pass her without a glance in her direction. She drains her glass and waves it at a passing waiter, tempted to say, "I've got two hands you idiot, so two glasses."

By the time she's downed four tepid glasses of rather too sweet champagne – Alice never did have any taste – she's in a belligerent mood. "Tony darling," she hears her ex-friend coo and she feels like throwing up. She starts to weave her way towards the disgustingly over-the-top couple. A kick in the balls will soon put a halt to the wedding night bliss. She feels a hand grip her wrist. "Mother, I think we should go."

Eliza turns to face her daughter. "Go! I'm not going yet. I'm going to kick the hell out of that man's balls and then throw my next glass of champagne all over that bitch's very expensive dress. After that I might consider going."

"Well, for sure you'll be thrown out if you don't leave, but you are going to do no such thing." Francine takes her mother firmly by the arm and drags her out of the marquee. Eliza doesn't resist. She smirks. She has her car keys tucked away in her bag, and if her uptight daughter thinks she's going to get her hands on them, she's got another think coming. Once outside Francine heads towards the hotel car park, holding tightly onto her mother in case she makes a run for it. "Give me the keys of the car, Mother."

Eliza's eyes light up. "No. I told you I don't want to go!"

"Mother!"

"Piss off, Francine!"

Francine feels the familiar pain of despair. If her mother doesn't stop drinking soon she's heading for an early grave, the doctor has told her. What continually came as a surprise was that she loved her and the thought of losing her was a re-occurring worry. She holds out her hand. "The keys now, Mother! If you refuse I'll let you walk back into the marquee and watch you make a fool of yourself in front of a lot of people. Do you want to be humiliated?"

Eliza's eyes fill with tears. She decides it's time to throw herself onto the grass. But Francine is quick to spot the familiar amateur dramatic bit, and forcefully drags her to a nearby bench before she has time to sink to the ground. Then she braces herself for the next act.

She's not disappointed. Tears flow freely down Eliza's haggard face, running in rivulets down her cheeks. She'd been beautiful once but alcohol and drugs have ravaged her once statuesque figure, and her soft pearl-like skin was now grey and rough. Her blonde hair is unwashed under her fading blue hat and her amber eyes have long lost their sparkle. Francine thinks she looks nearer eighty than fifty-seven.

"I've only loved one man. Jack Carpenter was perfect; the only man I felt I could trust," wails Eliza, saliva dripping from her mouth.

"I know, I know," Francine replies, forcing herself to control her impatience. This was ritual drunk-mother talk. Always the attributes of Jack Carpenter.

Eliza stamps petulantly on the grass. "You can never understand how much I loved your father. Jack was the love of my life and since his death all men have turned out to be wankers."

And there have been plenty of those. Of course, Francine knows it would only make matters worse if she says this. Instead she says, "I'm sure my father was a good man."

"A good man! He was perfect, Francine, in every way. Why did he have to die? We were days away from getting married and you were only a few weeks old. It was then I lost my faith in God."

"And it was then you started to slide into a life of binge drinking and drugs as you have so often told me. I'm lucky to be normal."

5

"Oh that is so unfair. I did my best for you. I worked my butt off to make sure you had new clothes, food and a roof over your head. Why have you always been so ungrateful?"

"I'm not ungrateful."

"I could have starved to death."

"Oh come on, Mother, your parents supported you, as they did me. Who paid for my education and medical school while you were bombed out of your mind? If it hadn't have been for my grandparents you would be sleeping rough and I'd probably be dead, not holding down a good job as a GP. Oh this is ridiculous, how many times have we had this conversation; but don't you ever expect me to feel sorry for you."

The tears flowed more freely. "You're cruel!"

"Home truths can hurt," Francine bites back, feeling a right shit as she always did during one of these confrontations. Your future husband suffers a major heart attack days before the wedding, leaving you to look after a six-week-old baby, leaving you with little prospect of getting a job and having enough money to make ends meet. What could be worse than that? Well, not everyone had a rich father, as Francine had told herself many times, but her sympathy had won the day and that was why she hadn't walked out on her mother years ago.

Eliza pulls out a large green silk handkerchief, badly in need of a wash, and dabs her face. She only looks a little more presentable after this. She stands up – sways – brushes down her dress, adjusts her hat, winces as she jabs her skull with a hat pin and smiles. Then she pulls out her car keys from her hand bag. She shakes them in front of Francine's face. "I'm throwing these in that lake over there if you try to grab them or in any other way try to stop me going back into the hotel. I'm not fucking joking. I hate you, Francine, hate you!"

Francine takes a deep breath. She knows her mother is not

joking. "Okay, Mother have it your way. Go back in there and make a fool of yourself. But don't expect any sympathy from me when your antics blow up in your face."

"Ha!" exclaims Eliza triumphantly. "Now watch me give that bitch a piece of my mind. I'll make her regret stealing that gorgeous hunk of a man from under my nose." It's on the tip of Francine's tongue to say, "Can you remember his name?" but she has to grab her mother's arm as she staggers towards the marquee. Only her vice-like grip stops Eliza from falling flat on her face.

★★★

Eliza never did throw a glass of champagne over her erstwhile friend, nor did she kick her ex-bed companion in the balls. She collapsed into a chair and started to get seriously drunk. Francine made no effort to stop her. Better that than making a scene. But there was no way she was going to sit and hold her hand and apologise for the vomit. There were friends, colleagues she wanted to talk to. Dance and laugh. Her job, and a demanding mother, allowed her little time to enjoy herself. Just for a few blissful hours she'd forget her mother. It was not until the happy couple had been waved goodbye just before it struck midnight, that she realised her mother was missing.

Twenty minutes after the last guest had left and Francine was growing frantic, a waiter found Eliza floating face down in the indoor swimming pool of the hotel.

2

Jack Carpenter moves cautiously in the bed. A light spring breeze is blowing through the open window. He rubs the sleep from his eyes and rolls over to stare at the woman lying next to him, her long blonde hair spread erratically on the pillow. Her amber eyes are closed; her soft alluring body is hidden by a thin worn duvet. He watches the swell of her breasts under the cover. She doesn't move and he sighs with relief. He has the urge to move on; the relationship has run its course. He's too young to settle down. Eliza Walker is beautiful, sexy and clever, but the spark has died. He wants out, but has he the guts to face her? Every day for the last week he has put off breaking the news. Well, maybe tonight. It doesn't occur to him that she might feel the same. He carefully crawls out of bed, shivers as his feet touch the bare floorboards. He grabs his work clothes and retreats to the shabby bathroom. In fact the whole house is shabby but there is no cash to spend on luxuries. This is where Eliza and he eat, sleep, argue and fornicate. No need for the clutter of furniture. Empty boxes of various sizes scattered round the room will suffice. He dresses quickly, fearful that Eliza will wake and she'll want to continue the painful argument of yesterday evening. He moves to the kitchen, grabs a slice of brown bread and bites into it. It is stale; there is no butter, so to work on an empty stomach. He looks at his watch; there is no time for coffee. He hurries to the front door and steps out into the spring sunshine. The street is coming to life, cars are being started, old bangers most of them: there are no millionaires in this street. Men hurry, shrugging on their coats, scowls on their faces; just another day of work lies ahead and Jack knows most of them would give anything to be somewhere else. He walks across the road to the bus stop. Two other men, one smoking, nod their usual greeting. Another shitty day awaits him, sweating his guts out carrying bricks on a building site in central London. His wait for the bus is short; it's never late. One day, he promises himself, as he smiles at the regular bus driver, he will own sites, and make his fortune. "And that, Jack Carpenter, is no dream," he says quietly to himself.

★★★

That evening he alights from the bus, bedraggled, tired, sweaty and fed up. He drags himself along the road to the dilapidated semi-detached house that he rents off a kind old lady who doesn't mind if he is late with his monthly payments and knows she's lucky to get anyone to pay rent for such a tip. He would rather be anywhere else. He reaches the door and opens it. It is never locked. There are no keys. The old lady had laughed when he'd suggested a key might be a good idea. "You've nothing to steal, Jack. Who would risk going to prison just to take a few boxes and a beaten-up settee?" She'd cackle then, showing her black nicotine-stained teeth. She's a forty a day smoker. Jack moves into the dark hall, which smells of damp and the fumes from Eliza's fags. "I'm home, darling," his voice sounding less than enthusiastic. He moves towards the kitchen, bracing himself for a familiar scowl and the question, "Why did you go without kissing me goodbye?" It's empty. He looks into the small front room: empty. He bounds up the stairs, goes into the only bedroom, expecting to see Eliza asleep on the bed. She's not there. He moves into the bathroom, his heart rate increasing. Her small bag of make-up, shop-lifted from various stores, has gone. He runs down the stairs to the kitchen and sees the note propped up on the table. He doesn't need to read it, he's already guessed Eliza has left him.

9

3

Francine sat curled up on what her mother liked to call *the lawn*, gazing wistfully at the River Itchen. "It's a Hampshire jewel and one of the finest chalk stream rivers in the country," her mother once told her. Francine had never had any desire to fish and nor had her mother, but the little three-bedroomed white thatched cottage on the water's edge was idyllic. It sat in a small unkempt garden which Francine had always called the wild garden. Her mother had never seen the point of mowed lawns and flower beds and since her mother's death Francine had not had the time or energy to improve things. It was on the outskirts of the village of Martyr Worthy, a few miles from the cathedral town of Winchester. Francine's grandparents had bought the house and most of the contents for their daughter, although Eliza had always boasted that she'd paid for everything. Francine had loved her grandparents and had promised to look after her mother when they died, and she'd kept that promise. Even though at times she'd been tempted to walk away and let her mother sort out the mess of her life. Her constant moaning about the little time Francine spent with her, her lack of money to buy alcohol, cigarettes and the odd spliff had grated on her nerves.

Today, the sun was shining from a cloudless August sky,

the heat was rising and midges were dancing over the tranquil river. She bent down and picked up Cat, as she called her ginger tom, who one morning, three years ago, had arrived at the front door looking decidedly worse for wear, and never left. "Not very imaginative," she'd laugh when anyone asked the obvious question. "But I never thought he'd stay so I didn't bother to think of a name. Hence Cat." She hugged him to her and watched the familiar figures of two slightly portly fishermen, called Harry and James – she could never remember which one was which – casting their lines on the opposite bank, and watched them waging a constant war against the small dark insects that hovered around them. She breathed in the warm scented air and, as she had done many times in the past, waved at the two men as they looked up. She forced a smile. The funeral of her mother two weeks earlier had taken its toll and guilt still hung over her like a damp heavy blanket. If she'd stayed by her mother's side she wouldn't have fallen drunkenly into the hotel swimming pool. She'd forgotten how to feel happy, but for a fleeting moment she was tempted to give her usual shout of welcome, with the offer of a cold glass of lemonade. It was a fleeting thought. Instead, she turned away and walked slowly back into the cottage. She'd promised herself that today she was going to sort out her mother's possessions. She'd bought a roll of black bin liners for the task at hand, the contents of which were either heading for the rubbish bin or to some grateful charity shop. Perhaps then, the ghost that was constantly standing by her shoulder, wagging a finger and whispering, *I thought you would keep an eye on me, Francine,* would disappear and she could kick start her life again.

★★★

Two sweaty long hours later the hallway was piled with black bags. Endless cups of tea had kept her energy up but now she would have given anything just to curl up in bed and go to sleep. However, there was one more room – *my room,* her mother had called it in a rather aggressive voice, as if daring her daughter to ever walk through the door when she was alone in the cottage. But Francine had dared, and once in it she had been left in no doubt that her mother's favourite colours were red and green, the paint splashed haphazardly over the four walls. Green curtains clashed with a bright red carpet. On the walls hung a collection of weird Indian paintings, which her mother loosely called, *my Indian period.* Though God knows what period she was referring to as she'd never stepped foot in India. Francine had long called the room Mum's Bazaar, but the décor was the last thing on her mind as she walked reluctantly into the room and stared at the large mahogany writing desk which her mother had kept locked. Now it was about to give up the secrets that Francine was certain were hidden in its drawers. Letters from creditors came to mind. Her mother never paid a bill until the final demand had landed on her desk and some she'd totally ignored, leaving Francine to pay the angry creditor. She fingered the key, which for years she'd known her mother kept in a china money box on the windowsill of the kitchen. At times she'd been tempted to take the key and sneak up to the bedroom and open the desk but fear had stopped her. She walked slowly towards the desk, mouthed, "Sorry, Mother," and turned the key in the lock. She pulled down the flap expecting to find unpaid bills, a stash of cannabis, love letters and packets of condoms. Her mother had at least had the sense not to become pregnant by one of *my many admirers* as she'd called them. But the last thing she expected was to find the desk empty. No letters, no drugs or unpaid bills. All the small apertures held no secrets. Puzzled, she unlocked the first drawer. Only dust and a half empty package of paper clips. By the time she'd pulled out the other five drawers only the paper clips lay beside her on the floor.

She stepped back and stared at the desk, puzzled. This was not what she'd expected. She knelt down on the carpeted floor and looked underneath. Why? It was a question she would ask herself many times in the coming weeks. Her curiosity was aroused when she saw something taped to the underneath of the desk. She reached underneath and carefully peeled the tape away. In her hand was a sealed faded white envelope. The colour told her that it had been there a long time. She moved to the kitchen and dropped into a chair before easing a knife under the sealed flap. She slid out the contents: a single folded sheet of paper. She stared at her mother's neat handwriting. Her heart started to pound and her hands shook. She controlled her breathing and started to read.

Darling Jack,

This morning after I heard you leave I asked myself what has happened between us? Why do you distance yourself from me? Why, why, why? I came up with an answer that made me cry. You don't want me anymore. I can't bear seeing you retreat from me. I don't want to watch our love wither away in acrimony. So, when you come home tonight I will be gone. I think that's what you really want. We've had good times and nothing lasts forever, so goodbye, Jack, I hope you do something worthwhile with your life other than just being a bricky. I know you have dreams and I have a feeling you will succeed. Whatever, have a good life. And fuck you, I'm pregnant.

Shock and disbelief hit Francine like a bolt of lightning. Her mother had lied to her for so many years.
Pregnant with me!
Francine sucked in her breath. She felt dizzy, nauseous.

She clutched the letter in her hand and stared at it for several minutes before reading it again. *Why did you never send it, Mother?* Could it be because she knew Jack would come to find her and offer marriage and then they would settle down to an unhappy family life? She suspected that her mother wouldn't have wanted that. But the only person to answer her questions had drowned in a swimming pool. Francine dropped the letter onto the floor. Her throat felt parched, she needed water. She slipped off the chair and hurried to the kitchen taps, found a glass and filled it with the cold liquid. She drank greedily. Her head began to clear, the nausea eased. She gathered her muddled thoughts. She moved back into the sitting room and pushed open the French windows. She walked out into the garden and dropped down onto the weeds. She had a lot of thinking to do and most of the thoughts were not pleasant.

Her mother had lied to her for over thirty years. Ever since she could remember she'd been told that her father had died of a heart attack, brought on by overwork. "And a love of gin," her mother would add, when in a particularly despondent mood.

"But it was all lies, lies!" Francine shouted up to the sky. And what of the tears, the protestations of undying love for this man Jack Carpenter that fell so easily from her mother's mouth? All bullshit! Every word about her father had been fabricated, and she'd believed it. Why would she ever have questioned her mother's words? Perhaps just as deceitful had been her grandparents' silence. They must have known the truth. "I can't believe that. How could they deny me a father?" Francine said out loud. A headache started to thump at the back of her head. She put her hands over her face. *Where the hell are you, Father? Dead, alive, an invalid, blind, suffering from Alzheimer's, married with children? Grafting to make a living or living in some far flung corner of the earth? I have to find out. I may cause waves but I have a right to know.*

14

Francine stood up, wiping daisy stains off her jeans, and hurried back into the house. Her laptop was on the kitchen table. A sense of urgency was flowing through her body. She powered up the laptop and went to Google. With shaking hands she typed in Jack Carpenter. A large list of Carpenters appeared on her screen and most seemed to be called Jack, so that was a dead end for a start. She knew he was a Londoner but not his birth date. She regretted never being more curious but she'd probably have been met with just another lie. So where to go now? Determined not to give up so quickly she thought of the letter. Her father had been a bricky, seemed to have ambitions, so could that be a line to follow? Construction, maybe? It was a very tenuous link but worth a try. She shut down Google and moved to linkedin.com. For over half an hour she scrolled through the website, most of which seemed to be offering jobs in America. She shook her head, she was running out of ideas. She moved back to Google and wrote in *construction companies in the UK.*

On the third line her heart leapt into her mouth.

Carpenter Construction Company stared up at her. She read the blog. Founded by Jack Carpenter in the East End of London. Yes, yes, this really could be him! London, construction! And he was very much alive. Wow! She read on. His date of birth could fit. He'd been awarded the CBE in 2010 for services to various charities and his help with disadvantaged teenagers. He was also in the top one hundred wealthiest men in the UK! Quite a man! And if that wasn't enough he lived not ten miles away from her with his wife and two children. So close. Yet so far away for how many years? Francine blew out her cheeks and felt the pain of tears. There was more than a good chance she'd found her father. *And I'm coming to see you, Jack Carpenter.*

She shut down her laptop, blinked and looked up at the ceiling. She had a strong feeling that her life was about to change. "Oh Cat, Cat, why can't life be boring and ordinary?" she said quietly, lowering Cat to the floor and filling his bowl with his favourite mess, as she called the tin of meat. For several minutes she stood looking out of the window as the sun twinkled on the water. In life, her mother had given her untold grief with her drinking, her drug addiction and the endless succession of mostly unsavoury men who came through the cottage door, all too willing to jump into her bed. But she'd managed to love her in spite of all these weaknesses. She'd defended her mother against those who'd criticised her, like a loving daughter, only to be rewarded with the one word that came to mind. Deceit.

4

Eliza is staring at her mother in disbelief. "Of course I must tell him I'm pregnant. How could you suggest anything else? It's our child. How cruel it would be not to let him know he is going to be a father."

Her mother takes a long draw of her cigarette and shakes her head. "Don't be so stupid, girl. Do you honestly think that a young man wants a child in his life at his age? No, a thousand times no. He's a penniless labourer. God only knows what you saw in him. He will never be able to support you financially. Come to your senses. You have told him the relationship is over, so stand by your word – forget him. You are very young – far too young to bring up a child. Rip up this letter you have written. He doesn't love you."

"How can you possibly say that?"

"Has he tried to get in touch?"

Eliza breaks eye contact and mumbles, "No, but I'm sure he would if he knew he was going to father a baby. I don't want my child to have no father."

"Well, if you feel like that, I think you should have told him before you walked out on him. Anyway, you won't have a child. You will get an abortion. It is the only solution. No other man will look at you with a child. You have your whole life in front of you. Don't ruin it. Get rid of it."

"It? No, no!" Eliza screams. "I want the child! You're so wrong. I still love Jack."

"Well, he doesn't love you, so see sense. Think of him as dead."

Eliza begins to shake. "You're horrible!"

"I'm right."

"You're so cruel!"

Her mother stubs out her cigarette and wags a finger at her. "Very well, I will have a word with your father. If he thinks I'm right then you are on your own unless you have an abortion. If he disagrees with me then I will reluctantly support his decision."

Eliza knows what she has to do. Her father has never said no to her. She glares at her mother and turns on her heels and rushes out of the room. She has to get to her father before her mother – it is her only hope. And the letter? Well, maybe her mother is right about that. Jack must be discarded. He'd make a terrible father – end of story. But something makes her decide to put the letter somewhere safe, where her mother can't find it, and who knows, perhaps one day she will send it. She walks into her father's study knowing that whatever the outcome of the next few minutes brings, her life will change forever.

5

"It gives me great pleasure to introduce Jack Carpenter," the mayor said, his flushed face beaming at his audience, his hands resting firmly on his protruding belly. This would do his re-election chances no harm, no harm at all. "Most of you here today will already know about this remarkably generous man, who has done so much for the youth of Hampshire, and supported many charities throughout England. And now he has stepped in and saved us from having hundreds of houses built on a greenfield site. To my mind, and apparently most of yours, Jack's plan is more than a good compromise and rids us of the annual fight and consequential loss of valuable income which could be spent on more important things. So without more ado, the floor is yours, Jack."

Jack rose from his chair – squeezed his wife's hand a little too hard and smiled as she winced. She'd whinged all morning about coming. "Why the hell you can't do this on your own, Jack, I really don't know. All those people looking adoringly at their saviour and wishing they were me. Makes me sick. Besides, I will miss my bridge morning."

You're like a stuck record, always the same pathetic excuses, he'd thought, shrugged and said, "You're coming, like it or not, but our chauffeur can drive you back once this is over. I've

19

got another meeting later in the day and I wouldn't want you hanging around, now would I?"

Sophie had glared at him, stamped her feet in frustration but knew it was pointless fighting him. Jack had thought, *Bridge, my arse! Huh! She's dying to shag her lover. Well, she's welcome to him, but on my terms, always on my terms. And the silly bitch doesn't even suspect I know.*

He took the microphone off the mayor and stepped to the edge of the stage. He smiled to his audience.

A generous smile, Francine thought, sitting at the back of the room. *And he's handsome as well.*

Jack coughed. "I can well understand that some of you still have reservations about my plan for this site but I think you will come on board when you see the finished product. As you know, this project has now passed through its final planning application. Several public meetings have been held over a long period of time and most objections successfully dealt with. Now it's time to move on, or," he gave one of his smiles that enchanted so many women, "I will be dead before the project is finished." There was a ripple of laughter in the hall. "Work is due to start in three months' time. My estimate is that within two years you will have something that this city can be proud of. An area where your children can play safely, and sports facilities for our local teams. Not to mention the six affordable houses that will be built on the perimeter."

"Never!" came a female voice from the audience. "It will be an abomination! You're no different than any other developer. Out for a profit and to hell with what people think."

"Sit down!" several voices shouted, followed by a burst of clapping.

Jack help up a hand. "You have every right to voice your opinion, madam, but let me finish and then you can shout at me as much as you like."

Francine laughed. *The man knows how to deal with a troublemaker. Been here before no doubt.*

"This project of mine will cost the taxpayer nothing."

"Oh yes! I've heard that before," came the same female voice.

"Nothing," Jack said patiently, fixing the middle-aged rather plump woman with his hypnotic eyes, and he got pleasure in watching her sink back into her seat. "My company, madam, will fund it. A trust will be set up for future expenses, like maintenance. The city will get a park, children's play areas, a cricket pitch, a pavilion and two football pitches. There will be a lake and plenty of space to relax. There will be no restaurants. There are plenty outside the park and I don't want to see anybody suffer. As I've just said, there will be six affordable houses on the perimeter and a clause in the contract with the city that no more will ever be built. From all the consultations that have gone on over the last two years I think this is what this city wants. Of course, we must have more houses but there are plenty more sites better placed and less controversial."

"Rubbish!" another voice interrupted. Jack took a deep breath; he knew he was on sticky ground on this one. As a builder of houses he knew that his site was the best for development. But he was also a romantic and still a dreamer. He wanted something to be proud of. Rows and rows of houses had never been on his agenda. He'd paid a fortune for the site. Houses would have made him a handsome profit but he was already wealthy. He looked at the young man standing up three rows back and saw the dislike in his eyes. He knew what he was thinking. "Think what you like, sir, I can see I won't change your mind. If you want a word with me later I'll be pleased to talk this through with you." Just as he'd hoped, the young man blinked, mumbled, "Thank you" and sat down.

A burst of applause shook the room. Francine was

impressed, even though she shared the young man's concern. Either Jack Carpenter was a very generous man with a lot of cash to throw around or he had a hidden agenda. *Like wind farms, and what was the other thing? Oh yes, fracking.* She didn't know the man well enough to make an on the spot judgement. *But I will find out.*

"So there you have it," Jack said once the applause died down. "No hidden agenda." *Had he read her mind?* "No call on a cash-strapped council and a guarantee that this park will forever be as good a greenfield site as you can get. Now, madam, any questions?" Jack said, pointing a finger at the first heckler. He was rewarded with a silent shake of the lady's head.

The mayor moved quickly to Jack's side, keen not to allow anyone else to threaten his big day. He took the microphone. "Now, there is food and drink put on for you, by our generous benefactor, in the next room, ladies and gentlemen. And Jack has agreed to answer any questions then. So it just leaves me to say that we must be one of the luckiest cities around to have attracted Jack Carpenter. He could have gone anywhere."

Jack took back the microphone. "There was never any doubt, Mr Mayor, that I would choose here," Jack assured him. "I live close by this beautiful city of Winchester and love this part of England. Every morning in the summer when I'm at home I wake to the sound of bird song and the unique smell of the English countryside. In winter I love the frosty bright days that seem to activate my brain." More laughter. "Let me tell you all that, for a man brought up in the East End of London, in a freezing old house and with little food to feed hungry mouths, that is a bonus that I never, in my younger days, expected to benefit from, and I will never waste it. This park is my thank you to God for making me so lucky."

Oh boy, you know how to play an audience.

★★★

As soon as Francine entered the room she knew it was going to be difficult to get near Jack Carpenter. She could just make him out at the far end, his head moving from side to side as he tried to satisfy his eager audience. She moved to a table and took a glass of white wine from a line of full glasses. She sipped. *This is not going to be easy.* But there was no way she was going to leave the room without introducing herself to Jack Carpenter – *possibly my father!* She started to weave her way through the crowd until she was close enough to smell his aftershave. A large red-faced old man was vigorously shaking Jack Carpenter's hand and mumbling words of thanks. It gave her time to study the man who so many people in the room seemed to be treating like a god. He was tall, she guessed around six one, slim, with a good strong head of hair which was completely white. His blue eyes seemed to sparkle as he spoke. His grey pin-striped suit fitted him too well not to have been handmade. *Made in London.* She couldn't see his shoes but suspected they were black and highly polished. His smile was generous. No doubt he'd had a lot of practice. She judged he was comfortable within himself. *It will be interesting how comfortable you feel after I've given you my news, Mr Jack Carpenter.* The red-faced man moved away. This was her chance. Dive in. She bumped against two women who had the same idea as her – apologised, but did not give way. She stood in front of him. He smiled at her. She smiled back and there was a catch in her voice as she said, "Mr Carpenter, please, a few words."

Jack saw an attractive woman. About five seven, he guessed. Auburn hair cut short. Smart black suit with a white blouse. Sensible shoes – none of the four-inch heels so popular with some women these days. No make-up. Her complexion was all natural. He liked that. He tried to guess her age. Maybe mid-thirties? She looked nervous. Oh dear, another whinger? He screwed up his eyes. She looked vaguely familiar. He looked at his watch. "I only have a few minutes left but what can I do for you?"

Francine took a deep breath. Suddenly she was filled with doubt. *Could this man really be my father? Am I making a terrible mistake? Will I perhaps disrupt his life? Well, that's one thing for certain if my research is right.* She gulped in air. But she was too far down the road to back off. She said, "I would like to meet you somewhere else but here. Oh, that sounds very forward – sorry. I promise I'm not making a pass at you but what I have to say is very personal. It will only take a few minutes of your time."

Shit, thought Jack. One of Sophie's lover's wives. Come to tell him to control the bitch and that he was a weak spineless shit who couldn't or wouldn't try and stop his wife fucking up her life. *What the hell do I do now?*

"Well, can you spare the time?" asked Francine feeling a rebuttal was coming.

Jack quickly collected his thoughts. *I'm trapped; might as well get this over with now.* "Can I have a name?"

"Francine Walker."

A curious expression slid across his face.

Does the name ring a bell? Francine thought.

But his voice was steady as he said, "Okay, Francine, why don't we meet at Caffe Nero in the High Street in say, half an hour? You do know where that is, I presume?"

"One of my favourite haunts."

Jack threw her a wide smile. She wasn't acting like an angry wife and she was most attractive. And the name Walker made him curious. He asked, "Can you just give me the smallest hint as to why it is so important to see me?"

"It's a family matter."

Jack Carpenter's face went white. He took a step backwards, almost colliding with one of the women who Francine had edged past. He ran a hand through his hair – tried to look

24

nonchalant, but his heart rate doubled. *Oh God, she is an angry wife! What the fuck has Sophie been up to now?* The scowl returned as he said in a wary voice, "Okay, see you at Caffe Nero in half an hour." He turned and walked away, ignoring the two women who had been patiently waiting to talk to him.

Francine made no attempt to follow him. *Oh dear, I've touched a raw nerve. Not a good start.*

★★★

Caffe Nero was only half full as Francine walked in. Young mothers with babies occupied half a dozen tables. She chose a vacant one, next to a red fire extinguisher, looking out onto the High Street. She wanted to spot him before he walked in. It was vital to look composed, even though her stomach was turning cartwheels. She ordered a latte and settled down to wait. The last time she'd felt so nervous was when she was taking a vital medical exam. Not only was there a chance he wasn't her father, but she'd also unwittingly implied a threat. Her latte in front of her, she seriously contemplated making a run for it. And then she saw him. *Too late! Shit!* She watched him walk through the door - look round – half raise a hand when he recognised her. He did not look pleased. *You're wishing I wasn't here.* She stood, her legs trembling, forcing a smile as he reached the table.

"Hello," she said holding out a hand. "Good of you to come."

He dropped into the chair opposite, ignoring her outstretched hand, and put his black briefcase down on the table with a resigned thump. His initials were embossed in gold on the leather cover. "This will have to be brief." He looked pointedly at his Rolex watch. There was a threat of anger in his voice. "Just tell me what this is about. My son got you pregnant? My daughter's tried to sell you drugs, or my wife is shagging your husband. Which is it? Either way it's not

25

my problem and I'm not partial to being blackmailed. So out with it and then I can go."

Francine gazed at him in horror. "Oh God, I'm so sorry. It is none of those things. I don't know your family. In fact, I think I've made a terrible mistake." She picked up her hand bag and jumped up from the table.

He grabbed her arm. "Oh no you don't. Whatever you have to say to me is obviously of some importance to you, so spit it out. I'm all ears. Francine, isn't it?"

She nodded and looked down at the table. She could feel his eyes boring into her. "I, I really don't know how to start this. I feel so foolish. I think I've got this all wrong."

"How about letting me be the judge of that?"

"Would you like to order a coffee first?" she managed to ask.

"Why not," said with the touch of a smile. He waved to a waitress. "Double espresso please."

Once the espresso was on the table, Jack sat back and stared at Francine. She looked terrified, her pretty face frozen like a mask, her mouth hanging open. This certainly didn't look like a come-on, but it seemed she'd got cold feet about something and wanted to extradite herself. He decided to rescue her. "Look, it seems to me that we have got off to a bad start. I've sounded angry and you look terrified. So let's start again." He laughed lightly. "So, unless you are thinking of enticing me into your bed or are going to try a spot of blackmail, I'm all ears."

"You don't honestly think that, do you? How awful."

"Actually I don't. So I'm very curious. Please…"

Francine fumbled in her bag. "I think this letter will explain everything. One way or the other this will tell me if you are the one I'm looking for." She put it on the table.

Jack took it – looked at the writing. It was vaguely familiar. And as he read on his heart turned a somersault and his eyes misted over. "Eliza!" he gasped. "Eliza Walker!"

6

He watches her get on the bus. Very pretty, looks flirtatious. Worth chatting up.

He waits for her to sit down three rows in front of him and then moves into the vacant seat beside her. "Hello," he says.

She ignores him, staring determinedly out of the window. But Jack knows how to operate. He's young, brash and handsome. Full of confidence, brimming with testosterone, walks with a swagger. A true East End boy. He knows how to strut his stuff and pull the girls. The direct approach has never failed. They just can't resist trying to put him down. And when they fail they get curious, and he's only two moves away from getting his leg over. He says, "Haven't seen you on this bus before. I would recognise a beautiful girl like you. Where you headed?"

She turns her head. This looks promising, he thinks. "What business is that of yours?" she asks. "Why can't you just go back where you were and leave a girl to her own thoughts?"

She oozes class – posh voice – out of my league? Definitely not. "You in trouble?" he asks.

"No. Now piss off."

"Is that the way to talk to a lonely man who spends every morning of the working week yawning through his journey to work? Do you blame me for wanting to talk to you? Look at the other passengers!"

She couldn't hold back a laugh. "Well, you could just read a book and mind your own business. Then girls like me could have a peaceful journey without being harassed by over-sexed men like you. Flattery will get you nowhere, Mr...?"

He holds out a calloused hand. "Jack Carpenter at your service madam."

She laughs again – an infectious laugh he decides. "I'm Eliza Walker," she says. "And that's all the information you're going to get out of me."

"That's enough," he says, boldly putting an arm around her shoulder.

"Get off!"

He makes no attempt to remove his hand. He knows girls, and she's liking it. "Tell you what," he says. "You doing anything this evening? Fancy going up west for a meal?"

"Boy, you really are a cocky bugger!"

"That's not an answer," he says.

She pushes his hand off her shoulders, turns to face him, her young firm breasts brushing against his chest. "I'm not a cheap tart, you know."

"Never thought that for one moment. I'm not up for a cheep thrill. Just want to spend time talking to a beautiful girl."

She slaps his face gently. "Okay, Mr Jack Carpenter, where shall we meet and let's see where, if anywhere, that leads us."

He smiles with satisfaction. Easy. My charm never fails, he congratulates himself.

7

Jack slapped the letter onto the table. He shook his head in disbelief.

Francine saw the shock register on his face.

"Christ, I didn't expect this!"

"So I've found the right person?"

"How do you mean? Tell me how you got hold of this?" Jack waved the letter in front of her.

"You're a suspicious man, aren't you? It was stuck to the underneath of my mother's desk. I was going through her things."

"Mother!"

"Yes."

"You're Eliza's daughter!"

"Well worked out. But you've not solved it all."

"How do you mean?"

"I'm *your* daughter."

"Jesus!"

"I don't think He's got much to do with it. Sounds as if you forgot the all important condom."

Jack just stared.

"Have you lost your voice?"

Jack shook his head. "This is taking a bit of time to sink in.

So, is Eliza going to walk in here at any moment? Are you the advance party, so to speak?"

"She died a few weeks ago."

"Oh that's terrible. She would be no age. How did she die?"

Francine saw sadness in his eyes as she leant across the table and said accusingly, "She drowned in a swimming pool and as you are the person referred to in that letter, I think you are partly responsible for her death."

Jack stared hard into Francine's eyes, held her stare and said nothing.

"And by the tone of the letter you were a bastard, Mr Jack Carpenter."

Jack moved uneasily in his chair. "I think that's a bit unfair. But tell me why it has taken you so long to contact me. And why didn't she send this letter?"

"Why she didn't send the letter I'm still trying to fathom out. Maybe she wanted you out of her life. Didn't think you'd make a good father. You were both very young. You know the answer better than I. As for me not getting in touch, the answer to that is that she lied to me as soon as I was old enough to understand. Told me you were dead. Died of a massive heart attack a year after I was born. Blamed it on overwork and gin."

"That was very cruel. How could she have lied to you?"

"Ask yourself that question. I have my own theory. But of one thing I'm sure, she loved you."

"But she left me."

Francine shrugged. "The letter quite clearly says that she knew you didn't want to stay but that she still loved you. It reads as if she had little choice but to pack her bags. We will never get to the bottom of her behaviour. All I know is that by the time she told me you were dead, she was already on the road to destruction. She was drinking heavily, into drugs and flirting with dozens of men, looking, all the time I suspect, to find a good substitute for you. She never found one. I think you broke her heart. It was not a happy environment to be brought up in. And until I read that letter I thought my grandparents were the bee's knees. They took care of me – supported me financially. I thought they loved me. Do you know what the worst thing about all this is?"

"Tell me."

"I think they deliberately robbed me of a father. There is no other explanation. And that destroys my love. and I'm hurting bad inside. Thank God they are dead because I would have to face them and ask the question."

Jack pushed back his chair, blew out his cheeks and shook his head. "Well, I certainly didn't expect all this. I think I need more coffee."

"And mine is a latte."

Fresh coffee in front of them, Jack cleared his throat and put his elbows on the table and stared at Francine. "I loved Eliza. We had a wonderful time together. I was a little in awe of her. She was educated, beautiful and came from a wealthy family. She was the opposite of a brash working class boy and yes, it gave me a kick to have her on my arm. But we were very young – full of lust – out for a wild time. And boy did we enjoy both. However, there was always that invisible divide. She was classy, I was rough. It made me feel uneasy. So once the lust and excitement began to fade I knew in my heart it was time to quit. I flunked telling her but she obviously read my mind. I was surprised how gutted I felt when I came back to an empty house. And as you now know, I never heard another word from her. At the risk of sounding brutal, I forgot her."

"And what would you have done if you'd known she was pregnant?"

Jack didn't hesitate. "I would have stuck by her."

"Yes, I think you would have."

"Thank you."

Francine wrinkled her nose. "I could be wrong, but something tells me you're an honourable man. Sorry, that sounds very old-fashioned. However, then I'm thinking you ruined my mother's life. To be honest, right this minute I feel confused. But then, I made a terrible mistake when I was young. So who am I to judge you?"

"How so?"

"I might tell you one day. But now is not the time. Tell me, Mr Carpenter, how do you feel about your new daughter or are you going to try and deny it? And if not that, do you see me as an intrusion in your life, a sort of interloper? Someone who wants to be in your life twenty-four seven and reap the advantages of your wealth? Would you rather I had never turned up?"

"I'm a little nonplussed, I can tell you. But when I come to terms with the fact that I have another daughter, I know I will want you in my life."

Francine laughed. "You could leap across the table, gather me in your arms and shout, whoopee!"

Jack chuckled. "I'm a retiring sort of man."

"I noticed!"

Jack reached across the table and squeezed Francine's hand. "But hey, it's how I feel. And I never want to lose you. We have a lot of catching up to do. You are family, Francine, and my children and wife had better get used to that."

"A son and a daughter."

"You've researched well. But I'm sure the information didn't say they are wasters, the pair of them. I'm sorry, I shouldn't have said that."

"That sounds a bit ominous."

"Like you have just said, let's leave that bit until later."

Francine nodded, and then asked, "How did you meet my mother?"

"On a bus."

"A bus!"

"Yep."

"Tell me."

He told her. When he'd finished he said, "You might ask what she was doing on a bus in the East End at that time of the morning."

"I might."

"She had been staying with a girlfriend who lived in the area. Car wouldn't start so she took the bus."

Francine smiled. "Well, you were a lucky boy. And I think you were a bit of a cocky young man. But the story is rather romantic. So where was she going when you captured her interest?"

"She was going to meet two other girlfriends. They had planned to see the *Mousetrap*."

"Really?"

"Yes. And she never saw the play! Did she take you?"

"She never ever took me to a play or the cinema."

"Well, maybe we should go and see it sometime."

"Sounds a good idea."

Jack said, "It's a date." He looked at his watch. "Shit, I'm late for my next meeting."

"You, better go. I don't suppose you got where you are today chatting up women in a coffee bar."

"No, but I'm not going to stop chatting up this one." He unzipped his briefcase and pulled out his phone. "Won't be a minute." He spoke briefly. "There, now I have all day. How about you?"

It was Francine's turn to glance at her watch. "I've evening surgery at five."

"You're a doctor?"

"GP."

He looked at his watch again. "Well, if you have surgery at five that gives us close on two hours to talk. Maybe by that time I will have got my head round the fact that I have another daughter."

"And me a father."

Jack chuckled. "Shall I carry on where I left off?"

"Where was that?"

"Meeting your mother."

"Okay, seems as good as anything."

"Well, we moved quickly I think you might say. After a great evening in the West End we met several more times before we decided to become an item. It was a brave move on her part – her girlfriends and parents were horrified, though she said her girlfriends were jealous! I rented what could only be called a hovel, from a very understanding old biddy who wasn't too fussy about having rent on time, and Eliza moved in with me. A whirlwind romance I think it would be called. Her parents, as you now know, had money, mine had nothing. Dad worked all the hours God gave him working in the London docks and Mum did cleaning jobs. We were opposites. I knew she liked me because I was rough, and *"because you talk funny,"* as she used to tease me, but what did I care, I was proud of being a working class boy and, anyway, I thought I was in love. We laughed a lot, we made love, and we didn't have a care in the world. She was beautiful, feisty, a laugh a minute and a wonderful cook! For both of us it was our first serious relationship. We got on really well. As time moved on I think her parents accepted me and my Dad said, "You lucky fucking young bastard. Don't go losing her." But I did – end of story."

"So what happened?"

"After a year, the excitement fell away and we grew up. Eliza and I discovered there was no such thing as a perfect world. We began to argue, we fought, and I began to hate being the kept man. I knew the relationship had to end. But before I could pluck up the courage to tell her, she read my thoughts and walked away."

"And you found another girl, married and fathered two children and became a very rich and successful businessman by all accounts."

"It sounds so simple. I can assure you it wasn't. I grafted because I wanted to prove to my parents that all their love and sacrifices had not been wasted."

"Quite obviously you succeeded."

"And Dad lived just long enough to see my feet on the ladder."

"I'm sorry."

Jack shrugged. "At least he got his dream."

"And obviously life improved for you. Let's face it, you don't get into the *Sunday Times* rich list without a lot of graft."

"I got lucky."

"I thought you might say that."

"I was twenty-three – shit scared that I would end up on the dole or even living rough. Going into crime was very much on my mind. Most boys of my age from our street were into crime. My Dad was very ill – lost his job – too many cigarettes. Mum was worn down by looking after him and trying to make ends meet. They were really struggling. Then one day Dad told me they might lose the house. I felt ashamed that I couldn't help them. Joining the criminal fraternity seemed the only option. I had plenty of offers but I knew that it would kill my dad. So I went to my boss and asked for a rise. He turned out to be a different breed to most of the builders, who just flogged their workforce, knowing there were plenty more suckers out there willing to take a miserly wage if anyone walked out. He said he saw my potential. I laughed in his face. I thought he was being kind before he sacked me. I was wrong. He gave me a desk job in the office and a fiver more a week. Fuck it, I was rich! It was like a dream come true. No more flogging bricks up and down ladders in all sorts of weather and being knackered at the end of each working day. The one thing I prided myself on was that I was a quick learner. If I found sites I'd be forever in his good books. So I went to work. And then, shit! He died, didn't he? Dropped dead one morning in the office in front of me. Massive stroke apparently. He had no family. Two days after his funeral I was sitting at my desk wondering where my next job was going to come from, as I assumed the business would be wound up, when a man walked into the office and introduced himself as my dead employer's solicitor. Stone the crows, Francine, the old bugger had left the firm to me!"

"And you've never looked back."

"At first it was a struggle. It was a small firm; the bigger vultures hovered over me, just waiting for the firm to die. The word put about was that a man of my age would never survive in such a cut-throat business. There were even threats. Bodily harm if I didn't sell up. It was then I discovered myself. I had brains! I had a hard streak. I had a nose for deals. I was obstinate and I had a sort of persuasive charm, so I was told. But above all else I wanted to succeed for my dad and mum. So instead of buckling under to the threats and the snide remarks, I borrowed money on the business, bought a semi for them and watched them die peacefully."

"And the business grew, obviously."

"Yes. But there were limits to how big it could get. So I started looking for other businesses. Invested, sold, reinvested and had a great run of luck."

"And now you're on the one hundred list of the wealthiest men in the UK."

"I guess."

"So, you're married with two children and to satisfy your ego you spread money about on good causes like confetti and bask in the glory."

"No! That is not how I am."

"So what motivates you to become such a large benefactor?"

36

"My early life, and there is only so much money you can spend unless you are very greedy. I knew what it was like to be deprived of nearly everything apart from basic needs and sometimes even those were in short supply. I saw my parents sacrifice everything for me. They were proud Londoners. Whatever the circumstances, they held their heads high and never let me know what fucking hard work it was to put food on the table day after day. From an early age my father encouraged me to be ambitious – take the odd risk, he'd say. I'd already decided there was no way I was going to end up like my parents, living from hand to mouth every day. When I'd made my fortune I saw it as a chance to help those who had never seen a green field, never had unlimited food, no sporting facilities, no holidays, and had never had the chance to get a good education. I don't pretend that I can save the world but I can help save some young people from becoming so disenchanted with their lives that crime, terrorism or suicide are the only options."

"Very noble."

"That's unkind."

Francine wiped a drop of latte from her mouth. "Ya, I'm sorry."

"I can understand your cynicism. But I guess you have never had to suffer the deprivation that goes with being poor. I can understand the terrible feeling of overwhelming despair that some of our young people feel today."

"I deserve the lecture."

"I didn't mean it to be. You just got me on my hobby horse. So how did you become a GP?"

"I had a reason. And let me tell you, Jack, I'm well aware of the struggles that some poor disadvantaged children have to deal with every day. Even here, in the so-called affluent south, there is still poverty among many families. I see a lot of it in my surgery and I do my best."

"How very noble."

They both laughed.

"And do you still have the original building business?"

"Yes. That is until my son Harry bleeds it dry."

"Oh. Do I sense a problem?"

"A problem, Jesus Christ, yes I have a problem, but I don't want to go into that right now. Let me hear a bit more about you."

"Okay. But first I must visit the ladies'. Four lattes play hell with my bladder."

"I'll wait."

Francine rose from her chair and made her way to the ladies' room. Once inside she eased the pain in her bladder and then moved to the washbasins. She looked at herself in the mirror. Could she see any features that matched Jack's? Maybe the eyes? No, the mouth. Yes, definitely the mouth. She washed her hands, ran her fingers through her hair and felt that this could be the best thing that had happened to her in years. The hostility that she'd felt towards him had vanished. It was too early to say she'd warm to him, but the hope was there.

"Feel better?" Jack asked as she slipped back onto her chair.

"Much."

"Good. Now, where were we before nature called?"

"I'm a partner in a GP practice in Twyford, just outside Winchester. I live in a small thatched cottage by the River Itchen in the village of Martyr Worthy. My grandparents bought it for my mother when I was four months old and it has been my home ever since. It is the perfect place to relax after a hard day at the surgery and I love it."

Jack shook his head in wonderment. "I don't believe this, it's extraordinary. I live just outside a village called Upham."

"I've driven through it! Jeepers, Jack, we are practically neighbours! How long have you lived there?"

"Twenty odd years."

"Oh my God, so close!"

Jack swallowed. "How cruel life can be. You know, missing out on your childhood."

Francine reached across the table and took his hand. She shrugged. "Maybe we can make up for all those missed years. What say you we start right now?"

"I hoped you'd say that! So, no doubts about me being your father?"

"They are getting less by the minute."

"Well that's encouraging, and do you like what you see?"

"I think you're probably a nice man, and you're in no way to blame for me being denied a father for all these years."

"Thank you. And I'm certain you are my daughter."

"Well that's a plus, no DNA needed," laughed Francine. She looked at her watch. "My God, I must fly."

"Time slips by when you're happy." Jack eased back into his chair and smiled. "But I wasn't certain it would work out this way."

"I tossed a coin."

Their laughter made several tables turn to stare at them.

8

Tom Jackson watched Jack Carpenter leave Caffe Nero. He was standing under the covered walkway by Boots the chemist in the High Street, sheltering from a heavy storm. Now, what was his boss doing there? Oi, Oi, what was this, a pretty young woman walking out beside him? "Bye Jack," he heard her call. Well, well, well, the boss plays away! Wouldn't Mrs fucking Carpenter be pleased with this tasty piece of information, the two-timing whore. No doubt he'd be rewarded in the usual way. Tom licked his lips in anticipation. Yes, she was getting a few wrinkles and yes, her skin was not as smooth as a younger woman's, but she was hot. Tom didn't give a second thought that perhaps his loyalty should be to his boss – loyalty was not a word in his dictionary. Tom Jackson lived from day to day. No long-term commitments, no wife or children to fuck up his life. And that's the way it would remain.

Mind you, he'd been lucky, no doubt about that. If he hadn't have been from the same street as Jack Carpenter he'd have no doubt that this lucrative and pleasurable job would never have materialised, and then he'd have just followed his father into nothing better than petty crime.

Slippery Jackson, as his dad was known, had been a small-time crook in the East End, his fingers in every pot of skulduggery. He was father of five children, who Tom suspected were not by the same woman, but what did he care? As long as someone put food on the table and bought him clothes, he asked no questions. He had been the only boy and it had been Slippery's fervent wish that his son would follow him into his nefarious business. But Tom, having dipped his feet in the pond, discovered that he didn't possess his father's cunning, so he'd gone out looking for a job-kosher or bent, he wasn't fussy. Then along had come Jack Carpenter, and life changed. He cut all ties with his father and mother and siblings without even saying goodbye. He was not one to share his good fortune with anyone except himself. Fuck the lot, he'd thought as he'd caught the train to Winchester. If his parents were now dead he couldn't have cared less. He had one hell of a life.

Tom gave his treachery little thought; he was not one to care about people's feelings. It was all about what was best for Tom Jackson. And a boss with a whore of a wife was an extra bonus, not to mention the opportunities of thieving from the family. He was twenty-seven and he had a cushy life to look forward to, never for one moment thinking that a moonlighting job that had come his way might cause a problem. He smiled to himself, pulled his coat collar around his neck, ran a hand through his dark hair and hurried off down the High Street. He was due to pick up his boss in just under an hour. And then perhaps he'd blow the whistle to Mrs Carpenter while he stroked her warm skin. Or maybe he'd wait until they were both exhausted. He wasn't sure how she might react when angry.

9

Harry Carpenter looked at the senior bank executive, sitting behind his desk, with disdain. Who was this man? Some jumped-up little prick who had worked his way to the top and enjoys the feeling of power that his position gives him? His suit was dark blue, tie to match, white shirt. Harry could swear he could smell the Persil. His dark hair was shining with health and his hands, which were resting on the desk in front of him, were manicured. He was the sort of man that Harry despised. "Please take a seat, Harry," this immaculate prick said.

Harry blinked. *Harry! For God's sake, have some manners. It's Mr Carpenter to you. Fucking creep.* But Harry bit his tongue. No point in antagonising the man. That could come later.

David Hennessey smiled across his desk. He knew Jack Carpenter well – admired him – felt sorry for him as he stared at this apology of a son. The one thing that got under his skin was a public school educated boy who thought the world owed him a living, and Harry Carpenter filled the role perfectly. He would prove a difficult client. His attire said a lot about him. He looked like a vagrant, with his long chestnut hair streaked with red highlights. *Ugh*! He wore a white T-shirt with, Who is the fastest man on wheels? emblazoned on the front and Vettel, stupid! on the back. His jeans needed a wash and his size ten Nike trainers had seen better days. He had at least a week's stubble and his eyes were dull. *Drugs?*

David Hennessey took a deep breath – the last he would risk taking unless he enjoyed the smell of unwashed humanity – and broke the silence. "Well, Harry, let me introduce myself. I'm David Hennessey from head office. I think we need to have a chat. I gather you rang yesterday."

"Too bloody right I did. I've had three cheques bounce in the last week. For fuck sake, don't you know who I am?"

Hennessey rubbed his hands together. It was unusual for him to gloat but he was looking forward to the next few minutes. "Indeed I do, Harry, but that makes no difference. If anyone goes well over their overdraft limit their cheques are bounced. I'm sorry if that has caused any embarrassment but you were sent a letter warning you this might happen. The contents of which you seem to have totally ignored."

Harry waved a hand disdainfully. "Well, just increase my overdraft – simple."

"I'm sorry, we can't do that."

"Why the fuck not?"

"Because we hold no collateral."

"But I have a trust fund worth over ten million quid."

"Oh come on, Harry, you must know that the Trust refused to lodge the assets with our bank. You're very lucky to have been given an overdraft at all, which I would like to point out, you wouldn't have got if your father hadn't agreed to be the guarantor."

"Well then, what the fuck's the problem?"

"Your father has withdrawn his support."

Harry nearly fell off his chair. "When?"

"Last week."

Harry's mouth felt very dry. His father had threatened to do this several times, but he never thought he'd carry out the threat. What was a million or two to him?

43

Hennessey allowed himself a few seconds to enjoy Harry's discomfort. *I know all about you, Harry Carpenter, waster, gambler, arrogant and immoral. You may be handsome, tall and have flashing blue eyes but if you think that will help you to get more money out of this bank you can think again. And what is more, your father agrees with me.*

"So, Harry, what are we going to do about your problem?"

Regaining his composure, Harry put his elbows on Hennessey's desk, who reminded himself to get the desk washed later. "What you are going to do, Hennessey, is unblock my account right this fucking minute or I will take my custom elsewhere. Got that?"

In your dreams, young man.

Hennessey did his best to hide a smile. "I'm sorry, *Mr* Carpenter, I obviously haven't made the bank's position clear. We will not increase your overdraft, and let me advise you that no bank will touch you. Your father has told me what your income is and you are overspending by nearly £70,000 a year. I think that that might be the reason why your father has withdrawn his support. So let me repeat; there can be no increase in your overdraft."

Harry leapt from his chair, causing it to tip backwards onto the carpeted floor. Pointing a shaking finger across the desk, he shouted, "You bastard!"

"You can call me all the names under the sun, Mr Carpenter, but listen to these five words – there is no more money. And on the subject of your overdraft, I must tell you that the bank wants to see a sizeable reduction by the end of the year."

Harry spluttered. "You're joking, for fuck sake. How am I going to live?"

"May I suggest that you sell your Ferrari, your Sunseeker boat and your polo ponies and stop lavishing incredibly expensive gifts on various young women? You haven't got the money, Mr Carpenter."

"You can't talk to me like that, you insignificant man. I will see you lose your job."

"I don't think I'm in danger of that."

Harry slammed a fist onto the desk. "My bloody father will release money from the trust just as soon as I have spoken to him. And then I will change my bank."

"That is not my concern," Hennessey said. And then he added (which of course he shouldn't have), "But I'll wager my year's salary that you'll be disappointed."

"I've had enough of this," Harry blustered. "Next time I see your face, Mr fucking Hennessey, I will want an apology. Is that clear?" Harry gave Hennessey the V sign and stomped towards the door.

"One more thing before you slam the door," Hennessey said. "Your account will be reopened but your credit cards have been cancelled. You're a lucky man. I wouldn't want you to starve."

Harry spat on the floor and slammed the door behind him.

David Hennessey heaved a sigh of relief. Did Eton teach you no manners? He pressed his bell and smiled at his secretary as she walked in the door. "I think I badly need a cup of coffee, Vanessa, and a damp cloth to clean this desk. And if we have an air freshener handy that would help cleanse the air. Please tell my next client that I'm running a little late. I need a few moments to compose myself."

10

Jack Carpenter looked at his son with utter contempt. How could he have reared such a total good-for-nothing, and that was being generous. He'd hoped that a public school education would have knocked some sense into a boy, who at ten was already showing signs of serious rebellion. "Waste of time you standing there swearing at me, Harry. I'm not bank rolling you anymore and the money from your trust is staying where it is. It cannot be released without my say so. Since you were twenty-two I have placed you in good executive jobs in two of my companies. Jobs that could have gone to more experienced people than you, who would have given their eye teeth to have them offered to them. But I took a gamble, and you fucked up. In the first you tried to seduce, to my knowledge, three of my female staff, with explosive consequences which nearly ruined the business. In the second job you were so idle that I lost three very lucrative orders. And when, out of sheer pity and fatherly love, I move you to my original business, you start milking the assets. I should have dropped you on a street somewhere long ago and told you to fucking well make your own way in life just like I have. That might have made a man of you, but I wouldn't be holding my breath. Look at you, Harry.

Unshaven, dirty clothes and playing with drugs and strutting your stuff in front of some very impressionable young women. God knows what they see in you. You stink! If it wasn't for that wallet and that ridiculous red car you keep flashing in front of their eyes, I suspect they wouldn't give you a second glance. I hate to say this but you embarrass me."

Harry blustered, "I'm your only son. You're only fucking son. How can you speak to me like this? I need money and I want it *now*. How can you refuse? Do you want to see me suffer? You brought me up. You're responsible for how I am now. I need three million quid – small change to you. So be a good daddy and pay me."

Jack clenched a fist.

"Yes, go ahead and hit me!" Harry shouted, pointing at his chin. "Go on, hit me!"

Jack let out a loud sigh. "I wouldn't give you the satisfaction. Now, crawl out of here and live on the money I pay you for fucking up my businesses. Count yourself lucky I haven't sacked you from the last one. But if I don't see you in the office when I get there this morning I think I will ask you to leave, and make you pay back the money you have embezzled."

Jack saw all the fight go out of Harry, to be replaced by a look of panic. "This tells me you're in deeper shit than you have told me. Oh Harry, Harry, you haven't been borrowing money from some shady characters, have you?"

Harry thought he saw his chance. His eyes filled with tears. "Yes, yes I have. I'm in big trouble, Father. I've been threatened with violence. I'm shit scared. Please help me, I beg you. I won't ask again – I'll change, I promise."

Jack folded his arms and shook his head. "Pathetic, that's what you are, Harry. What sort of idiot do you think I am? You're so transparent. It's no good playing on my goodwill. That was exhausted a long time ago. If you really are in some sort of danger then maybe a beating will teach you something.

47

Go out and face your creditors like a man because, I repeat, you won't get any more money from me. You must live on your income which, let me enlighten you, is a little over £500,000 a year after tax, for Christ sake. And that is pocket money. You live and eat here free. You fill that revolting car with petrol from the farm storage tank. Do you know what I was earning at your age? I was lucky to come home with £20 a week. So don't coming crying to me."

Harry was shaking. "Please, Father, I'm in danger. I'm not lying."

"You've made your bed, boy, go lie in it."

Harry staggered to a chair and collapsed into it. "Jesus, Father, you're a bastard. How can you do this to me?"

"I won't bother to answer that. Now, get out of my sight and sort your mess out. And turning up at the office might be a good start."

"I might be dead."

Jack was shocked by what he was thinking.

★★★

Jenny Carpenter met her brother as he stumbled out of her father's study. "What's up, Harry?" she slurred.

Harry stopped and looked at his watch. "Half cut already, I see. Back to rehab, is it?"

"Piss off."

"You'd better not let Father see you like this or the bastard will cut off your allowance. He's just thrown me to the wolves."

"Oh, that's it, is it? Has he finally seen sense and refused to bank roll you? Is that why your eyes are red, my poor darling brother?"

Harry pushed past her saying, "Why do I live with such a shitty family?"

"Because you're one of them, and you're the biggest arsehole amongst us. Let me tell you something, little brother, you won't last long on your own in this wicked world."

Harry whirled round. "Well at least I'm not a lush. Who are you to criticize me? What sort of life have you got? Out of your mind by midday, sleeping with whoever happens to be around, then by the evening you're anyone's. Why don't *you* get a life, eh, Jenny?"

"Oh sod off Harry," she spat, and put the bottle of vodka that she was carrying up to her mouth.

★★★

Jack heard this exchange outside his door and shook his head. How had it come to this? A useless son, an alcoholic daughter, who in her early thirties had already been in rehab three times, and a whore of a wife. It should have all been so different. He'd fallen in love with a knock-out girl from a "diamond family and good London stock," as his father had put it. Sophie had long soft auburn hair, legs up to her armpits, slim but not too slim, five nine and green eyes you could drown in. Not to mention the most superb breasts he'd ever set eyes on. He looked at her framed photograph on his desk and allowed himself a wry smile. He'd been flattered by her attention. She didn't come from a wealthy family, just good tradesmen stock, and she was a Londoner through and through. Like him she was ambitious. What was it she used to say to him in the early days of their relationship? *People like us, Jack, have the drive, the energy and an enormous desire to better ourselves and prove ourselves to our parents. We have nothing to lose. With no silver spoon in our mouth, no fear of losing the ancestral pile, we can forge ahead without fear. We don't need friends. We just need an appetite to take on the world, and if we fail and fall in the shit there is no one to care.* This had turned out to be all bullshit. He'd

49

worked his fingers to the bone and she'd worked at how to spend his money and get laid.

But he was ready to admit that he hadn't been at home enough. He'd failed to bond with his two children and Sophie had satisfied her growing appetite for sex by entering into various relationships with the ever growing male staff. By the time he realised he'd deserted his family for the success he so craved, it was too late. He reached for a packet of Camel filter cigarettes. He was fighting a losing battle to give up the habit. Who could blame him, surrounded by such a family? A family he was almost ashamed to admit was his. He gave a wry smile and drew the nicotine deep into his lungs and shook his head. So here he was, sitting behind his desk, fighting with his son, thinking he'd have to persuade Jenny to go back to rehab and wondering who was licking his wife's tits. Yes, he'd climbed out of the pit of poverty and yes, he was rich. But it was at times like this that he wished he'd never moved away from his roots. Poor and happy was much better than rich and miserable. And then two miracles had landed on his lap. The Winchester greenfield site and the arrival of Francine. Already he could feel new hope coursing through his veins, when only a few days ago he'd resigned himself to years of misery until he was lowered into the ground and his children went off to the nearest pub to drink champagne and celebrate with his wife. He was in no doubt they hated him. He stubbed out his cigarette into an ashtray and sighed. Much as he would like to say the same about them, he couldn't bring himself to hate them. Like it or not he was their father and a husband. As his father had once said to him, "Marriage is for life and if it runs into difficulties, remember that fifty per cent is of your doing." As usual, his father was right. So he'd stick it out. And by God, if his family tried any dirty tricks to drive Francine away, they would do so at their peril. As he rose from his chair and headed for the garden for some much needed fresh air, he mumbled, "And I deserve better."

★★★

Sophie entwined her limbs around his body. "Time for lovemaking," she whispered in his ear, her voice dripping with sarcasm. Why she still called it *love* made Jack want to scream. It was sex pure and simple; love did not come into it. For a split second he half-halfheartedly tried to pull away, but as she sank beneath the sheets he knew he was lost. He was virile, still horny – hungry for sex, even though he despised her. Things might have been different if he'd strayed. Temptation was always just round the corner. He knew there would be many willing bed companions. Fool? Some would say so, but Jack had seen the results of illicit couplings. As far as he could see they only brought unhappiness and made life at times intolerably complicated. At least with Sophie he knew where he was with her. She had sex with him because she believed he didn't know of her adulteress behaviour. He let her believe that: it saved a confrontation. *Weak stupid bastard.* He felt her tongue touch his skin and allowed himself to be swept away into a surge of lust. It would be short-lived and then he'd loath himself for being so weak.

When Sophie rolled off him he leapt out of bed, unable to bear her closeness any longer. He heard her laugh. That was the worst thing. She was so contemptuous. Not for the first time he was tempted to rip the bedclothes off her naked sweating body and pummel her with his fists. "Shit," he cried and bolted from the room. He ran panting into the bathroom and turned on a cold shower. Once satisfied that he had washed all trace of Sophie off him, he dried himself and moved into the spare room and slid under the cool crisp sheets, forcing all thoughts of the whore lying in the next bedroom out of his

51

mind. He lowered his head onto the welcoming pillow and thought of Francine. She could lighten his life. He felt a surge of anticipation but he knew he mustn't get carried away. It had only been one meeting. Did she really want to see him again? Or was she now having second thoughts. He was almost too frightened to find out. *Go on, you drip, you know you want to pick up the telephone.* He looked at his watch. It was past midnight. The urge was as strong as his lust had been an hour ago. He threw back the bedclothes and ran to the chair where he'd hung his suit. He took his mobile out of the inside pocket. He moved to a table by the window where he'd put his wallet. He pulled out Francine's business card. What had she said to him? *Ring me anytime except surgery hours.* He laughed and entered the number.

11

Jack looked at his watch impatiently. Did the damn second hand never move? His secretary, or PA as Janet Goodchild preferred to be called, threw a quick glance his way. She didn't need to look at the clock on the wall. Ever since he'd broken the news that he'd found a lost daughter, Monday mornings had become a time when he acted like an impatient schoolboy waiting for the schoolday to end. For a man who had always seemed so calm and in control of his emotions, this was something that Janet was struggling to come to terms with. Was it because another woman had entered his life, she'd asked herself. The irrational answer had been yes, however stupid she knew that was. She felt her heart sink as she gazed at this new Jack Carpenter: restless, seemingly happier than she'd seen him for years.

Standing five eight with her blonde hair cut short, her green eyes, long legs, neat firm breasts and welcoming smile, she reckoned she was still attractive at forty-one. But the only man she'd ever wanted had never cast a look her way. She'd fallen in love a week after Jack had employed her twenty odd years ago. She would never forget the excitement that had coursed through her veins when she'd got the letter offering her the job. She'd thought the pain of unrequited love would eventually pass, but it never had. Of course, she should have done the sensible thing and walked away, but just to be near him, to smell him, to listen to his voice had proved too strong an aphrodisiac and maybe one day… Her heart was his and always would be.

And did she want to return to her past?

Since the age of fifteen she had thought she was in control of her emotions. She'd suffered terribly once, entered a dark period of her life. And then at nineteen she'd read an article on Jack Carpenter. Two weeks later, when idly scanning her local paper, she'd seen his advert for a PA. Something had told her this was the change she needed, and the rest was history.

The only mistake she'd made was falling in love with her boss. Jack was an incurable disease. He had invaded her soul and that was threatening to open a past she was trying to forget. She fought the thought that she was obsessed, telling herself that even though he didn't know it he needed her by his side, always there for him whatever the crisis. She would never allow him to suffer. It was the only thing that made her life tolerable. And now he would need her more than ever because sure as hell the arrival of Francine was going to cause mayhem in the Carpenter household.

Jack was incredibly anal, scrutinising every contract, word for word, at times working long into the night going through builders' estimates and insisting on being present at every site to see material delivered. It was the reason he was so successful, and if he took his eye off the ball (which she had no doubt he was doing) she had to be there to keep the ship from sinking. She shuddered at the thought and, as she looked across her desk and said, "You have another five minutes before you need to go," she felt a guilty shock course through her whole body, because she was willing for the penny to drop that he needed her by his side.

Unaware of the turmoil he caused to his secretary, Jack

grabbed his briefcase and flew round his desk. "I don't need reminding, Janet. Getting a bit of a habit this Monday feeling."

"I have noticed, Jack."

She was rewarded with one of his engaging smiles as he made for the door. Her heart fluttered. *Stupid woman.*

★★★

Once out on Southgate Street, Jack quickened his step. He hated being late, still terrified that Francine wouldn't be there when he walked in. He hurried past Chaplins, the gunsmiths, where he took his Purdey twelve bore shotguns for a service after the shooting season ended, past The Hotel du Vin, where he took his clients, and ran across the road at the traffic lights, his heart rate increasing as he hurried down the High Street. By the time he reached Caffè Nero he was puffing badly.

Sitting at their usual window table with the fire extinguisher as her companion, Francine watched him weaving his way through the crowd of shoppers, tradesmen, and a block of Japanese tourists probably heading for the cathedral or the street market. She allowed herself a little smile. After their fourth meeting he'd confessed to her that he panicked every time he got near the café in case she had decided not to come. All her efforts to calm him had failed. "I have a mobile, Jack. I would ring you if I was delayed." But after three months her words seemed to have fallen on deaf ears. As he burst through the door and looked towards the window table she could see the anxiety drop from his face. *She's here, she's come,* she knew he was thinking. She smiled and gave a wave.

He rushed over, nearly tripping over his own feet. She stifled a laugh. He dropped his briefcase onto the table and threw his arms around her. She gently pushed him away. "Everyone is watching," she whispered in his ear. "Probably think I'm your mistress."

"Well, you have wicked thoughts, darling. Why can't I be a father greeting his daughter?"

"Because, Jack, peoples' minds don't work like that."

"Well, to hell with them. If I want to smother you with kisses that is what I will do." His eyes darted round the room. "Give these housewives something to gossip about anyway."

She laughed. "You really must stop worrying, Jack. I'm not about to disappear and I love our time together. I can't believe that someone who has gambled millions and built an empire can get into such a state over a date with his daughter."

Jack shrugged. "Businesses can come and go and life goes on. My life would end if I now lost you."

"Oh Jack…"

He cut her off. "Is that too dramatic?"

"It's a little sad, I'm thinking."

Jack looked surprised. "In what way?"

"You should have the world at your feet. Money, power, good health, a very generous nature I suspect, and a family. Yet here you are, telling me your life wouldn't be worth living if I disappeared. So what have you been doing for the last thirty odd years or so? It seems to me you've done pretty well without me. So why so desperate? Is this the right time to ask what's wrong?"

Jack rubbed his chin thoughtfully. "For various reasons my private life has not been easy. In fact it's been calamitous. By you appearing it has at least given me hope that life may well get better. Maybe desperate is exaggerating my concern, but yes, I am frightened I might lose you. After all, we are still in our trial period so to speak."

"Oh, that's rubbish. Look, I've missed a father for thirty-five years. I've lived with a paranoid mother. You seem okay so far, so I'm not just going to chuck this all in. Do you understand that?"

"I think so."

"Think so! Oh you really are insecure behind that smooth confident façade of yours."

"Maybe."

"I think there's no maybe about it, but come on, this is getting a bit too heavy. Let's enjoy our coffee and talk about the weather, like all true Brits do."

Jack laughed and waved to a waitress. "Espresso and a latte please." The young girl smiled. "I think I know that by now."

With their cups of steaming coffee in front of them, Sophie stared at Jack's troubled face. "Smile Jack. Come on, tell me what you would like me to call you. How about father, or do you prefer dad?"

He laughed. "I think I prefer Jack actually. My other children call me dad or father when they want something. Otherwise they just look at me and remain monosyllabic."

Francine shot him a concerned look before saying, "Okay, I have no problem with that. And this is going to be a short meeting, I'm afraid. I have a very sick patient to visit, but don't read that wrong. I'm not making an excuse to leave. I would much rather be sitting here with you."

Jack made no attempt to hide his disappointment. "Ah well, that's life I suppose. See you here next week?"

"Of course, but I still have a half hour before I go."

"Wow, that's generous!"

"Oh Jack."

"Sorry, that was uncalled for."

Francine decided to say nothing.

★★★

The half hour passed a little more awkwardly than either of them wanted. Jack was thinking what an utter fool he was and Francine was wondering if she would ever completely understand this man. Bill paid, Francine rose reluctantly from the table and bent down and kissed the top of his head. "Remember that I love you, Jack."

Jack smiled as he stood up. "I'll give it my best shot. Okay for next week?"

"Of course." And then she couldn't resist asking, "Maybe you should think of introducing me to your family, then we wouldn't have to have these meetings as if I was your mistress."

Bad mistake.

12

My therapist, an ugly bitch if ever there was one, once told me that my aggressive and violent behaviour would always be sitting at the back of my brain, waiting to explode if something happened to light the fuse. So, she would say, leaning forward and fixing me with her dark green eyes that made me think she couldn't care a fuck what happened to me, that control was the answer. Never allow myself to get into a position where the temptation to explode was threatening to engulf me. "Walk away." Then she would sit back, cross her rather fat legs encased in black tights, and say with a forced smile, "Remember this, my dear, and you might live the rest of your life a free woman."

Now, for the first time in many years, I feel what I can only describe as an itch tickling at the back of my brain. Is this what that stupid woman was referring to, I wonder and, if so, do I want to scratch it or ignore it? I confess that I'm excited by the thoughts that are swirling around in my brain and as the days have passed the itch has not gone away. I take a long slow breath and think back to my early days of violence and death and wonder if I can channel the itch into good use, and while fulfilling my aggressive nature gain a prize I would kill for and become a hero in most people's eyes. The thought excites me.

I have been thinking of a plan for some time now and this morning it is uppermost in my mind. It could work, yes it could work! No one would ever suspect this quiet, ordinary woman, the type no one notices in a crowded room, that I have become. Calm, always smiling, always ready to help, always allowing others to make decisions, and dressed in colourless clothes. But fuck that, I'm bored with this humourless persona. I smile up at the ceiling as I change into my work clothes, already feeling the adrenaline pumping. I look at my watch and see it is time to step out onto the street and walk to work. But this morning there will be a new energy in my steps as my mind goes into overdrive. I've come this far by cunning, now it's time to claim my prize.

The itch can no longer be ignored.

13

It was gone six when Francine pulled up at the cottage. Cat was sitting on the doorstep looking suitably annoyed. "Sorry, Cat, I was a bit delayed, I'm afraid. But saving a life comes before your evening feed." Cat did not look impressed. If he had had a watch Francine was sure he'd be tapping his wrist. She laughed as she bent and picked him up. He was as skinny as a rake and had bumps all over him. No doubt a legacy of his life before he came to stay. "Come on then, you'll get extra tonight," she said, as she ran her hands over his protruding ribs. No amount of food had put any weight on his body. With some difficulty she managed to get the key into the door and push it open, lowering a purring Cat to the floor, who flounced off into the kitchen. Francine put her medical bag and keys on the small hall table and followed him. Like him, she was hungry. Coffee didn't do much for the hunger pangs and she'd had little time to eat during the day. She gave a rueful smile. Didn't she tell her patients that three regular meals a day would lengthen their life span? She moved to the fridge where she kept the cat food and dutifully filled Cat's bowl before turning her attention to the other contents. There wasn't much. Half a cold roast chicken bought a week ago, so probably full of bacteria. Some rather shrinking vegetables, half a pint of milk, a can of fizzy orange juice and about six sad-looking strawberries. *What changes?* She wasn't going to get fat tonight.

As she straightened to stretch her back the silence around her suddenly hit her. The hum from the starving fridge, the noise of Cat eating were the only sounds. The cottage felt so empty. The drab surrounds of the kitchen, crying out for a facelift, did nothing to lift her mood. She was lonely. Not even a warm bath would help. She shook her head in bewilderment. A few hours earlier she'd been sitting at her desk waiting for her next patient, thinking of Jack. Happy thoughts. So what had brought this mood on? Was it Jack? How she would have liked him to be opening the door for *her* saying, 'Hello. Welcome home. Want a drink?' Memories of her mother flooded back. She had never greeted her with a smile or a drink in her hand and had never asked how her day had gone, and a meal had been completely beyond her. Normally it was just a drunken grunt. Since finding her father she'd hoped her loneliness was a thing of the past. In fact, for some reason that totally mystified her it had grown in its intensity. "Right now I'd give anything to see someone walk into the kitchen smiling," she said to Cat, who just stretched and walked out of the kitchen. "Well, you're a great help," she moaned.

She moved into the sitting room and stared at her mother's chair; she hadn't had the heart to throw it out with the rubbish – arms singed by dropped cigarettes. It was a miracle it hadn't caught fire while her mother sat staring at the television with glazed eyes. If you'd asked her what she was watching you'd be rewarded by a loud belch and an unsteady hand, shaking it for a refill. Francine shook her head. She let out a weak cry and fled upstairs to her bedroom, slamming the door behind her, but she found no relief. To her dismay the familiar ghosts were waiting for her. *What is happening to me? I should be so happy.* Her hunger disappeared.

Her stomach was churning. She shuddered and threw herself onto her bed, covering her eyes with her hands. "Why, why are you here now?" she cried, waving her hands in front of her face. Irrational thoughts swirled around in her brain. She must destroy the ghosts hovering over her. Now! "Go away, go away!" she shouted. She caught sight of her mother's picture on her bedside table. She lunged at it, threw it on the floor, where the glass shattered. She leapt off the bed and picked up the photograph before tearing it into little pieces. She threw them onto the carpet and started to sob. She moved to her chest-of-drawers and opened the bottom drawer and emptied the contents.

There it lay, untouched for years. A rather faded photo of Timothy Stafford. Handsome, tall and smiling at the camera. The backdrop, the sea off the pier at Brighton. It had been their last happy day together. He'd turned out to be a callous shit. She often wondered if he ever felt any guilt for ripping her heart out and yes, been complicit in a murder. She pulled the frame out of the drawer, some tears falling on the glass, and hurled it to the floor. The glass broke. She retrieved the photo and, like her mother's, tore it into pieces. Immediately she felt better. "You two will never invade my space again," she shouted. She dried her tears, controlled her breathing and headed for the door the glass crunching under her feet. She'd clear it up later. She opened the door and stepped out onto the landing. When she slammed the door, no ghosts followed her. She tossed her head defiantly and walked down the stairs and back into the kitchen, making a decision to spend some money on renovating it. Her hunger returned and she stared at the fridge. Well, damn the age of the chicken, the rotting vegetables and the mouldy strawberries. Somehow she'd make a meal out of the mess.

★★★

Jack fled to his study, locked the door and turned on the television. There was nothing of interest to him but it helped cut out the noise of his family fighting in the drawing room. He might have been tempted to have entered into the fighting and come out of it bruised and miserable. But he had Francine on his mind and nothing was going to be allowed to spoil the joy he felt. *So fuck it, you lot.* He smiled to himself as he relaxed in his favourite leather chair. Tears of joy were threatening to impair his vision. *For God's sake! I'm a grown man.* He rubbed his eyes with a hand and enjoyed the feeling of excitement that was flowing through his body. He had a normal daughter! A beautiful daughter! A daughter who actually had a worthwhile job! He would love her; God how he'd love her. No one would come between them and certainly not his other delinquent offspring. But there was the rub. He suspected they would not make Francine welcome and he knew from Francine's last words to him that morning that she expected to meet them soon. He picked his father's battered old silver cigarette case off the table by his chair and clicking it open pulled out a Marlboro. "The only item worth any money in this house," his father had said as he'd pulled out a Capstan. Jack chuckled at the thought. When his old man was sitting in a chair the fumes would always be floating round him. He scratched at an itch on his face, crossed his legs, fidgeted in his chair, lit the cigarette and inhaled. He looked at his watch and decided there was still time. With energy flowing he picked up his mobile.

★★★

Francine was on her fourth coffee, black and sweet. It was helping to wash away the taste of her supper. The strawberries had been particularly unpleasant. She was contemplating making a fifth cup when the telephone rang. "Oh damn," she muttered as she lifted the receiver. The last thing she wanted was an emergency call-out. "Hello."

"It's me," the voice said.

"Jack!"

"Yes, that's me." She heard him laugh.

"I thought it was going to be an emergency call," Francine said with relief.

"Well, it is. I'm avoiding my family, missing you and starving."

"Is that a subtle hint that you want to come over?"

"Well spotted."

Francine looked at her watch. "It's past eight. I have no food and I'm on call."

"Well, I can just about live without food and if you're on call you won't mind being kept awake a little longer."

"You think so?"

"Yes, I do."

It took only a second for Francine to make up her mind. "Okay, come over, Jack. It will do me good. Since we parted at lunchtime the day has been very stressful and I've been haunted by bloody ghosts ever since I walked into the cottage. Not to mention a supper of disgusting food. But I warn you, there is no wine or beer on offer."

"You sound very welcoming."

"Oh Jack, I'm so sorry. I would simply love to see you."

"Positive?"

"Absolutely, Daddy." She heard him chuckle. It was one of the things she liked about him, a sense of humour lurking beneath his rather suspicious nature.

"I'll be with you before you can say… what? Ah well, some long word."

"Great, see you then." She put the telephone down wondering if there was time to get to the pub to buy a bottle of wine. But then she didn't know what he liked to drink, so it would be a waste of time. With nothing to occupy her mind she started to pace up and down in the kitchen. The caffeine was kicking in. Her mind turned to the man who would soon be walking into the cottage. A man who, but for the letter stuck to the bottom of her mother's writing desk, she would have believed died years ago. It was a wonderful feeling, this love thing for a parent. Something she thought she'd been robbed of for good. Then a touch of panic struck her. Was she going to cause ructions within his family? It seemed likely from the small amount of information he'd let slip. What sort of relationship did Jack want to have with her? Absorb her into this family or keep her hidden like a mistress? She shrugged. What was the point in her worrying like this? It got her nowhere. Either way, she didn't want to lose him, but as she dropped onto a hard kitchen chair she realised that the thought of being hidden away like a mistress did not appeal to her.

She ran her fingers through her hair, then sniffed – bugger, she smelt of disinfectant. She needed a shower. She pushed back the chair, which narrowly missed Cat, and ran back upstairs. Carefully threading her way through the broken glass, she threw off her dirty clothes and ran into the bathroom. Turning on the shower she ducked under the cold water – it took her breath away but she resisted turning on the hot tap. She needed the stinging cold to clear her mind. Five minutes later she was back in her bedroom and heading for her wardrobe. She chose a pair of blue jeans, a white blouse and a beige cashmere jumper. Not very becoming, but Jack was her father, not a boyfriend. She slapped a little make-up on her cheeks, smeared on some lipstick and then dried her hair. As she turned off the hairdryer the doorbell rang. "Done it!" she shouted, shoving her feet into a pair of canvas shoes and bolting out of the room and rushing down the stairs.

She threw open the door, and there he was. Not a hair out of place and a gentle smile creased his handsome face. It was almost incestuous. He wore a light blue shirt open at the neck. *Thank God he's not wearing a tie.* His dark blue blazer fitted him perfectly. *Not bought off the shelf.* His beige trousers were pressed and rested half an inch over his polished black leather shoes. *No doubt the shoes and trousers were made for him.* He looked good and very reassuring. *If this was a boyfriend I'd be swooning.* She ran her hands down her jumper and felt decidedly tatty. "Jack!"

Jack shrugged his wide shoulders and threw her the infectious smile that she'd grown to love in such a short space of time. He radiated impressive health and confidence. Not for the first time she understood what her mother had seen in him. "Are you going to let me in?" he was saying.

"Oh, oh of course, come in. Sorry, my mind was distracted. I see you've brought your own refreshment."

Jack waved the bottle of Chilean Sauvignon at her. "I would have brought fish and chips as well, but that would have taken time."

"I'm glad you didn't do that. I would have been terribly embarrassed. Anyway, let's not stand here like two strangers sizing each other up. You go ahead into the sitting room. I'll take the wine and pop it into the fridge."

"I have an idea."

"And that is?"

"I take you to the Chestnut Horse at Easton. It won't take us long to get there and they serve food till late."

"That would be very spoiling."

"Well, if you don't mind me saying so, I agree that you look a bit stressed. Is this what having a father does to you?"

"No, of course not. It's just that – well, let's say I've had a tough day and leave it at that. One day maybe I'll let you into my secret but not right this minute. I don't want to spoil the evening."

"And would it?"

"Absolutely, so ask no more."

"Okay, I promise."

"Good. Now that's out of the way let's get moving. You must be starving and I could do with a refill. Six rotten strawberries and a piece of stale chicken breast have not subdued my hunger pains. I'll grab my keys."

"I'll drive," Jack said.

"We will have to go in two cars just in case I get called out."

"I can drive you back here."

"No, I would need to move quickly. Sometimes it's a matter of life or death."

"Okay. Then I'll drive to wherever you have to go."

"No, Jack."

He shrugged, "Okay. But no point me coming in. I'll wait here."

Five minutes later Jack was following Francine's car.

As usual the pub was packed, but there was a spare table outside and as it was a warm evening they were happy to take the barman's offer of the table, "Drink?" he then asked.

Jack looked at Francine. "Tonic water for me," she said.

"And I'll have a large glass of your driest Sauvignon."

"Fine," said the barman. "And I'll run a tab. Here are the menus. One of the girls will be with you soon to take your orders. Have a good evening."

They moved into the courtyard and dropped into their chairs. Francine let out a loud sigh. "God, that feels better," she said, taking a drink from her glass. "I'm sorry if I have seemed a bit unwelcoming."

Jack stared into her eyes. "Listen, will you please stop saying sorry. It's great to be here spending an evening with my daughter and not locked away in my study with my hands over my ears trying not to hear my dysfunctional family shouting at each other."

"Are you going to tell me about them?"

Jack made a face. "Let's just say they are a pain in the arse and that's being kind. My son owes money everywhere, my daughter is a budding alco, and my wife is probably thinking who's going to be her next shag. That satisfy you?"

"I won't ask again," Francine said apologetically, thinking that it was not the best time to ask: *so when are you going to introduce me?*

"Nothing more to say. Now come on, let's forget my family troubles and order. What's it going to be? I fancy a steak."

"You look like a steak man."

Jack explained. "When I was a young lad and starving most of the time, I used to read menus in restaurant windows. By the time I'd got to the desserts I was salivating. The one item that sent my stomach into a frenzy was the word steak. Fillet, rump, sirloin or rib eye, it didn't matter, I was prepared to kill for any of them. Once I could afford them I made a vow that I would never stop eating them until I reckoned I'd caught up with all the ones I'd missed. And I'm still catching up."

Francine laughed. "That's rather a sad little story. So you have your steak. I'll have the sea bass. Anything to start?"

"No, a steak will do me fine. I'll go and order at the bar. Otherwise we might be waiting here a long time."

Francine watched him move confidently back into the pub. She saw several women smile at him and watched him return their smiles. *Always the charmer,* she thought.

Once back at the table, Jack lifted his wine glass to his lips and stared at Francine over the rim. "I've had another idea."

"Full of them tonight, aren't we?"

"A holiday. I need one. You certainly need one, and I know the perfect place for us to go."

"Wow, that sounds a great idea, but I think you're forgetting that I've got a job. I can't just walk away. Besides, I took three weeks off after Mother died."

"But that was several months ago. I won't take no for an

answer anyway. You talk to your partners and two weeks from today I'll pick you up and off we'll go."

"Jack, Jack, I just can't do it."

"You can. I'm beginning to understand your dedication to saving people's lives but you can't do it if you're dead."

"Oh that's a bit OTT."

"Maybe, but I'm making a point. You look exhausted."

At that moment their food arrived. "Enjoy," said the waitress. Jack looked at his fillet steak and basket of chips and smiled at the waitress. "I'll enjoy this steak even more if you can bring me some tomato ketchup and English mustard."

"Tomato ketchup," asked Francine, wrinkling her nose.

Jack gave her an apologetic shrug. "I haven't lost all my common tastes."

"And that makes you more human," agreed Francine, watching a rather disapproving waitress put the two items on the table. They both laughed as she walked away. Francine watched amused as Jack smothered his steak with the ketchup. "Ugh," she couldn't help saying.

Jack smacked his lips. "Delicious; best way to eat a steak."

Francine did not argue. She boned her fish and said nothing. Jack was quite obviously in heaven; it would be bad to break the spell.

"Sorry," he said after ten minutes of licking the tomato ketchup off his lips and every now and then letting out a sigh of pleasure. "I can't talk while doing that." He crushed his mouth with his napkin and gave Francine a beaming smile. "Jesus, that was great."

Francine shook her head. "Do you always eat that quickly? Very bad for you."

"Yes, Doctor, always."

They both laughed.

★★★

Sophie Carpenter was in a panic as she turned the key to the front door of her small house tucked away in a quiet side street opposite the Royal Hampshire Hospital. She'd bought it as her brothel, as she jokingly called it, but even the thought of the young man's fingers playing tunes on her body just a short time ago did nothing to dampen the desperation stirring within her. It had never entered her head that Jack could be unfaithful to her. How many times had he told her that marriage was for life? She broke into a sweat. The implications of this new piece of information were too horrendous to think about, but thinking about them she was, and her imagination was running riot. Jack was about to leave her, cast her into the gutter and leave her penniless. She started to sob, oblivious to the looks of concern on the faces of passers-by. By the time she reached her six-month-old dark blue Mercedes Coupé she was convinced that Jack's next move would be to murder her. As she sank into the driver's seat and gazed at her smudged make-up she began to run over her options. There was no way Sophie Carpenter was going to take this insult lying down. As she exited the car park she nearly hit another car. She raised an apologetic hand out of the window and was rewarded with a torrent of invectives. "Manner, manners, you piece of shit!" she shouted back, before closing her window. "Calm down," she whispered and forced herself to stare determinedly out of the windscreen.

Once home, she rushed into the drawing room, letting out a sigh of relief that neither of her two children were there to witness the state she was in. Heading to the drinks table she poured herself a generous measure of Hendrick's gin, reluctantly adding a small dash of tonic. Then, with the glass clasped firmly in her hand, she dropped into one of several armchairs scattered around the large room and imagined Jack licking the woman's surgically enlarged boobs.

14

"If that offer is still open I'd love to come. I've squared it with the partners. Do you know, I don't even feel guilty?"

"That's the best news I've had in months. Away from prying eyes I can really enjoy the company of my lost daughter. I still feel slightly like a stranger."

"I know what you mean," agreed Francine. "You about to tell me where we are going?"

"Are you free for lunch?"

"Could make Bean Below. Do you know it?"

"The coffee shop at Twyford."

"That's the one."

"What time?"

Francine glanced at her watch. "Last patient around midday, so to be on the safe side let's say just short of one. I must be back in the surgery by two."

"Okay, I'll see you there."

★★★

"Tuscany! Whereabouts in Tuscany?" Francine asked.

"What's called the Tuscan Riviera. A seaside town called Viareggio. We fly to Pisa from Bournemouth in two days' time."

"You've been there before?"

"Several years ago when I was thinking of buying hotels."

"Did you buy any?"

"Two. We will be staying in one of them."

"Sounds wonderful," Francine said, controlling her excitement. "I have never been to Italy. Actually, the only place I've been is Brittany. Mother used to take me to a small pension every year at Easter until I was twelve. After that we both agreed to give up on Brittany for various reasons. One was Mother's dependence on alcohol, which made driving hazardous and gave her the ability to fall flat on her face in restaurants. It all just became too embarrassing."

"Poor Eliza. What brought this on?"

"I'm not too sure now. I thought it was your death!"

"Well, whatever, she managed to produce a well-balanced daughter."

"Thanks for the compliment, but to be honest I don't think it was any of her doing. Actually, Jack, can we draw a line under this please? I find it rather upsetting."

"Of course, I'm sorry I asked. Okay, where were we? Oh yes, I would have thought you were the type to travel a lot."

"I would have liked to have done, but Mother and work never gave me time."

"That sounds rather sad."

Francine shrugged. "I suppose. But you don't miss what you've never had."

"I don't know about that."

Francine laughed. "Oh well, that's my way of thinking." She glanced at her watch. "Look at the time! I must go. I'll have to pass on coffee, but the quiche was delicious."

"You're always going," Jack complained. "But it has been my pleasure. So, I will pick you up the day after tomorrow at two. Is that okay?"

"Wonderful, Jack, absolutely bloody wonderful. And in

case you suddenly think, oh my God I bet she hasn't got a passport, the answer is I have."

He threw her a broad smile. "That helps, so see you then." As she rose from the table he said, "Promise me that you won't be glancing at that damned watch every few minutes when we are on holiday."

"I promise. In fact, I might leave it behind." Francine went to move away, then stopped and turned. "You haven't told me how long we are going away for."

"Forever, never to return."

"No, seriously."

"One week."

"Bliss," said Francine with a smile as she walked away.

★★★

The Hotel Royal had been built in another era – Victorian – and so was rather old fashioned for some people's tastes. The ceilings were high and a large spiral staircase swept up to the bedroom floors. Looking around as Jack booked in, Francine understood why the hotel had caught his eye. Warm and welcoming, rather salubrious, its décor sombre. There was something very endearing about it, especially to older clients she noted, wondering if she would be the youngest. She knew that barring some unforeseen accident she was going to enjoy the week. She slipped a hand under Jack's arm as he moved away from the reception desk. "I can see what attracted you to this hotel. It's very conservative, and yet romantic. Rather like you, Jack."

"Is that how you see me?"

"Yes it is. You're very steady, set in your ways I suspect, and you give out an aura like one of those romantic film stars in the fifties used to do."

"Oh you're an expert on fifties' films?"

"I love that period."

"Well, I suppose I should take it as a compliment. I sometimes wonder though if I've thrown off too much of my East End upbringing. Underneath this facade I'm still a proud Londoner at heart, you know."

"I'm sure you are. But I like you as you are. Until I saw you up on that stage in the Guildhall I had formed the opinion that you would be brash, ruthless and not someone I would want to call 'Dad'. But I was so wrong. In fact it amazes me that you run such a very successful business. I know it's a tough world out there, especially in your line of work. Somewhere deep down your psyche there must be a hard streak."

"Oh I can be tough *and* ruthless if need be," Jack assured her. "That's how I survive. My father was a good teacher."

"Well, in the short time I've known you I've seen no trace of either of those traits."

Jack shrugged. "You haven't seen me at work or with my family. And by the way, well done with the watch."

"You noticed, then?"

"Not difficult. Now, come on, I want to go out. You ready for a tour or would you rather go to your room first?"

"A guided tour sounds good to me. The sun is shining, the air is pleasantly warm and believe it or not I feel like a drink."

Jack looked surprised. "I thought you said you never drank."

"Only when I'm working. Mind you, watching my mother do her best to drink herself to death was a bad advert for alcohol."

"I bet." Jack held out a hand and Francine took it. They moved out of the hotel onto the longest promenade Francine had ever seen. Cars flashed by and bicyclists passed more sedately. Across the street from the hotel she could just make out the sea behind a row of shops and restaurants.

"Oh Jack, it's lovely, and very different."

"And we can rent bicycles from the hotel and go where we wish."

They raced across the road, past the shops towards the sea. There were miles of white beaches covered with umbrellas of different colours, all laid out in neat rows. Raised Italian voices floated in the light breeze. *How soft their language is compared to ours*, Francine thought. Her heart sang. "I think I like being on holiday with my father," she shouted, as they threw off their shoes and started to run. The sand was warm, and they both felt they hadn't a care in the world.

Blissfully unaware of what awaited them back home they lifted their eyes to the sky and started to sing the Cliff Richard song, "We're all going on a summer holiday." This attracted a few stares, a few laughs and even cheers. "Ah matto Inglese!" was the shout. They smiled and waved to their audience.

15

Sophie was on a mission. It was time to find out if Tom Jackson was a lying little toad just trying to cause trouble, or if his news was correct. Knowing how trusting Jack was, she was sure that somewhere in the house he would have left a clue. It never entered his head that anyone would want to know his private business.

Well, she did.

Ever since the day they married she'd made it her business to search drawers, filing cabinets and various briefcases on a regular basis. She'd even searched his office in Winchester on various occasions when that snotty nosed secretary, Janet Goodchild, was out. She prided herself on knowing every little detail of his private and business affairs. If the time ever came for a divorce she'd be well briefed. Well, the time might have come, although no indication that he had another woman had come to light in her last search. But that had been a month ago. As she well knew, things could change at a flick of the fingers. So with Jack in Italy, visiting one of his hotels – or so he said – she had plenty of time to do a very thorough search. If he was cheating, then she'd be standing at the front door waving the name of the whore in the air and watching the guilt wash over his face. She would start, as she always did, in Jack's dressing room. It never occurred to her that she was being a riotous bitch.

She found the card in the inside pocket of the third suit she searched. "Bingo!" she screamed. She hurried to a window and collapsed onto the window seat. Her hands were shaking so badly that she nearly dropped the card. Fighting back the tears she read the name. Doctor Francine Walker. Below the name was a telephone number and the address of the doctors' surgery in Twyford. A doctor! She gasped for breath. Was Jack ill, so ill that he hadn't told her, or was he shitting on their doorstep? It made no difference that she'd been shitting on their doorstep for years. That was completely different. To think he was ill was bullshit; all the pointers were that the woman was his mistress. You didn't have lunch and kiss your doctor. She grabbed a pair of scissors that were lying on Jack's chest of drawers and ran back to the wardrobe. One by one she pulled out his suits and methodically cut them to pieces. It was slow work. A pair of garden shears would have made her work easier. It took the best part of an hour. By the time she'd finished she was sweating profusely and gagging for a drink. For several minutes she stood with hands on hips surveying her work. Jack would never wear any of the suits again. Her hatchet job had soothed her anger. She kicked away some cloth by the door and walked out onto the landing with dark thoughts descending on her.

★★★

Sophie sat across the breakfast table from her two children. The one thing she and Jack agreed on was that somehow they had made a bad fist of bringing them up. Her nose wrinkled as she smelt the vodka on her daughter's breath and she watched Jenny's hands shaking as she poured herself a cup of black coffee. Sophie wanted to shout at her but knew it would only lead to a painful row with nothing gained at the end. The girl was drinking her way to an early death; she was past saving. A stab of guilt hit her but quickly passed. Sophie was not one to worry too long about anyone but herself, even if it was her daughter. *Never wanted her anyway* was her excuse to herself whenever she bothered to think of her. She looked away and stared at Harry. Now, there was a different kettle of fish. Arrogant, rude, greedy and self-opinionated. The only trait he shared with his sister was his utter worthlessness. If she was pushed to decide which one she despised the most she would never hesitate to say *Harry of course*. Her mouth curled in disapproval at his dishevelled appearance. Quite obviously he hadn't washed for days. He was unshaven and his BO wafted across the table. And then she saw something on his face that said, I'm scared! She allowed herself a jab of satisfaction, before asking, "You in trouble, Harry?"

"Fat lot you care," Harry mumbled.

"Well, I asked," Sophie retorted, before heading for the dining room door. She had a pretty good idea what was scaring Harry and the more he pissed himself the better it would be. As she shut the door behind her she hunched her shoulders. Anyway, there were other more pressing matters to think about rather than whether Harry was in deep shit. She shook her head and put it out of her mind. She pulled Francine's card out of her trouser pocket and dialled Francine's home number. As she expected, she got her voicemail. So, storm the surgery. She had a terrible feeling that she'd be told Dr Francine Walker was on leave. *And where will you be, you little tart? Italy, of course!* She choked on the thought. She imagined them all cosy in bed. A surge of jealousy ripped into her. It was painful. "Bastard!" she shouted. She grabbed her bag from the hall table and ran out of the house. She raced to the garages shouting for Tom. As he came out she said, "My car – now – for fuck sake, hurry up!"

★★★

The receptionist looked up as Sophie coughed loudly. Used to all sorts of people asking questions, some stupid, some reasonable, the receptionist had learnt to smile at all comers.

"Good morning, may I help you?"

"I wouldn't be here if I didn't want help," Sophie snapped, fixing the young woman with one of her withering glares.

Oh dear, one of those, the receptionist thought. "Well, now you are here, dear, how about telling me your problem?"

Sophie swallowed. "Dear, I'm not your dear. And yes, you can help me, which, may I remind you, is pretty damn obvious. I want to see Dr Walker."

In a calm voice the receptionist asked, "Are you one of her patients?"

"No."

"Then may I ask why you need to see her? We have other doctors."

Sophie fought to keep her temper. It was obvious this woman was not to be intimidated. She changed tack. "I'm sorry if I have been a bit short. I just need to know if she's here. I would like to discuss becoming a patient in this practice, and I've been told she is the best."

"All our doctors are good, Miss, Mrs...?"

"Mrs Carpenter."

"Well, Mrs Carpenter, the first thing I must ask you is to fill out one of these forms and bring it back when completed." The receptionist passed Sophie a white form.

Sophie took a deep breath and did her best to smile. "Okay, if that's what I have to do, but can you tell me if Dr Walker is here?"

It was obvious to the receptionist that this woman was not going to budge until she had the information she asked for. Keen to get rid of this rude, tiresome woman, she said, "She's away on leave. She will be back next Monday."

"Thank you," Sophie growled, throwing the form at the receptionist. "I won't be needing this. I'm already registered with another practice."

Outside, Sophie stumbled into the car park. The shock was all consuming. "Rat, rat," she kept mumbling as she settled in the car seat. She didn't immediately start the engine. She needed time to gather her thoughts and shake off the panic. Once her breathing had returned to somewhere near normal and the desire to throw up had been controlled, she thought about her next move. Destroying Jack's clothes had given her a surge of satisfaction. *But now, Jack darling, the war really begins.* She knew where the two hotels in Italy were, she just wasn't sure which one he'd take this tart to. Ha! Of course, there was one person who would certainly know. Jack's doting, love-struck secretary. She gunned the engine and left the car park in a haze of dust.

Half an hour later she was striding into the Carpenter Enterprises office.

★★★

Janet Goodchild felt as if she'd been abused. It had been a very unpleasant experience. Sophie Carpenter, at the best of times, was hard to put up with, but in a rage she was quite simply terrifying, and it took a lot to frighten Janet. She had been stunned by the verbal abuse, which was quite unwarranted: a simple plea would have been enough. But it had been obvious from the start that Sophie was in no mood to be polite. Striding up to Janet's desk she had banged it with a fist and screamed, "Which fucking hotel is Jack staying at in

Italy?" Janet had opened her mouth to reply but had been cut short by another bang of the fist. "Don't try and fob me off, Goodchild, I know he's out there somewhere."

Janet had felt trapped and given her the name and number.

Sophie had stormed out of the office.

Now, Janet sat looking at the door, waiting for her heart to stop pounding. She prided herself on her loyalty, but under pressure she'd broken and without a doubt opened wounds that would never heal. Sophie would be after blood and Jack's new-found happiness was about to be shattered.

When later that day Jack and Francine returned to the hotel, a little worse for wear from too much wine at lunch, there were two messages waiting for him. The contents sobered him up quicker than a cold shower.

16

"I knew it was too good to last," Jack confessed to a silent Francine. They sat outside a bar on a sofa where they had drunk cocktails for the last four nights, watching mothers with their young children and lovers passing by, some walking, others on bicycles. Then, cocktails finished, they had moved a little unsteadily to a restaurant for supper. They had been so content with each other's company, both savouring the feeling of being wanted. Never in her wildest dreams had Francine ever thought she'd be so happy. Then an hour ago, the bombshell. Jack was right. It had been too good to last, as had everything else in her life.

Taking a large mouthful of her whisky sour she controlled the urge to scream at him and asked, "What are you going to do now, Jack?"

Jack raised his hands to the sky. "I have no idea."

Francine shook her head. "No, no, Jack, that's not quite good enough."

Jack was quick to pick up the anger in her voice. He couldn't blame her. His duplicity had come home to roost. He felt the first stirrings of alarm. "Okay, this is how I see it. We either stay here for the rest of the week and ignore my wife, or we try to re-book our flights and fly home tomorrow."

"Staying here is not an option, Jack. The sooner you face Sophie the better for us both. You should never have tried to keep me hidden away. Jesus Christ, I don't know why I went along with your deception! You should have been honest with her from the start. Now, according to your secretary, she thinks I'm your mistress. Well, that's something you will have to enlighten her about. I'm certainly not going to be branded a marriage wrecker or a whore. Our relationship is an honest one, Jack."

"It might be for the best if things remained as they are," suggested Jack, reaching for her hand.

Francine pulled it away and jumped from the sofa, knocking over the remains of her drink, which splashed over Jack. She did not apologise. She was seething. "No, Jack! You can't do this to me. I'm your daughter, for God, sake. Treat me like one."

Jack's head dropped into his hands. He could see how this was going to end. Sure enough, before he could think of a reply, Francine dug the knife in. "I'm leaving now. What you do is your decision. I'm confused by your behaviour, devastated and hurt. This crisis is of your own making."

Jack tried to intervene. "Shut up, Jack, let me finish. All through my life someone has come along and hurt me. I had hoped that things had changed when I found you. I felt I was important to you, and that you didn't need to hide me away like a mistress as Sophie believes. I don't want to stand around and be hurt by you again and again. So I'm walking out of your life. That way you can get on with it and I can try to rebuild mine."

"That's a bit dramatic."

"Think what you like, but I mean it."

"Please, Francine," Jack begged.

"You've lost me, Jack, and the sooner you accept it the better."

"You can't do this, Francine."

"Oh yes I can." Francine dropped back onto the sofa, fighting the desire to bury herself in his chest and sob. "Let me tell you one reason why. When I was seventeen I fell madly in love with another seventeen year old. It was at college. I loved him so deeply that all I could think of was the date of our wedding, even if it was years away. I was so sure he felt the same. Then one night we went to a party and got very drunk. We returned to our digs and fell into bed. Drunken sex followed and he forgot to wear a condom. I became pregnant. I was shocked but also excited. This would hasten the wedding I told myself. But when I gave him the news he looked at me in a funny way and I felt fear. To cut a long story short, he walked out on me, telling me I'd been careless, even though it was our agreement that he always wore a condom. When I reminded him of this he had the gall to say that maybe that was the case but it was always the woman's job to take precautions. I broke down then. I begged, I cried, I screamed hysterically. He didn't listen. He just walked away – packed his bags – and I've never seen him again. So I had an abortion. I never told my mother or grandparents. I couldn't even bring myself to confide in a friend. I was so ashamed. I felt like a murderer. And that, Jack, is why I became a doctor. I wanted to save lives and try to forget that I deliberately killed a life. I swore that never again would I put myself in the position that I could get hurt, and yet here I am, hurt. Do you understand that, Jack? I lost the man I loved and a baby. Now I'm close to losing a father, who I was growing to love, and I can't stand around and watch that love wither."

"Oh Francine, please no, that is not the case. My love for you will never wither. I can work this out and we can still be happy together."

"As your mistress, Jack. No thank you." Francine summoned enough strength to get off the sofa. "Goodbye, Father, have a good life."

Jack was so stunned that he made no attempt to follow her. Besides, he was lost for words because Francine had been right. He had thought the best solution was to confirm to Sophie that he had a mistress. Too late to say he was wrong, too late to say he'd sort it out as soon as he got back home. Just a few words, which had stuck in his throat. As he watched Francine disappear into the dark he had never felt so devastated.

When he got back to the hotel, and feeling as if his life was about to end, the concierge handed him a note.

It read:

Jack, don't try to follow me. I've left for the airport. The nice receptionist has found me a hotel nearby and I have sworn her to secrecy. I fly home tomorrow. Take care.

There was no signature, nothing to give him hope. Like Eliza all those years ago, Francine had thought it better to go, and as with Eliza he was frozen to the spot. He would let Francine go.

PART TWO
THE FALLOUT

17

It was the fourth Monday without seeing Francine and he was missing her like crazy. Mondays had become a day of deep despair. By lunchtime he'd be staring at his watch. He'd tried to concentrate on business, drank copious cups of coffee, thought of what his next venture would be, maybe contemplated asking Janet Goodchild if she'd like to have lunch with him, but it was all to no avail. The Caffe Nero was constantly on his mind, especially the little table by the window and the red fire extinguisher where he and Francine had sat watching passers-by and laughing at the boredom etched on some of the men's faces. He could even smell the coffee, and he had studiously avoided walking past its windows, which meant a long detour from the car park to his office. He'd telephoned Francine's home as soon as he'd got back, tried the surgery, whose receptionist had obviously been briefed to say she was not available. He'd written several letters, all of which had ended up in his dustbin. He'd even considered spending hours in his car watching her house, thinking that if she saw him he'd be forgiven, but he'd had enough sense to realise that a move like that would only make matters worse.

He still had hope.

He'd known her long enough to realise he'd made a

dreadful mistake, one she'd be finding difficult to forgive him for, and there was no hope of forgiveness until he'd faced Sophie and told her the truth. So simple, and yet so far he'd failed to get the words out of his mouth. The truth was that, as he lay sleepless, tossing the shattered dreams of his new life around in his head, he realised that he'd been quite happy with the statusquo, never giving enough thought to Francine's feelings. And that was why he couldn't just come out with the words, 'I have a daughter by another relationship.' What on earth could be simpler than that? What did it matter if Sophie threw a wobbly, or his children became hysterical? They hated him anyway. The only person who mattered was Francine. He'd been selfish. It was no good thinking he'd been trying to keep Francine out of the boiling cauldron that was his present life. He'd been looking after number one.

This morning nothing had changed, even though he and Sophie had had another traumatic fight the night before. She'd waved pieces of his suits in front of his face trying to provoke him. Laughing hysterically she'd danced around him half naked, throwing pieces of cloth into the air and screaming invectives at the same time. Then she'd started on the china! Jesus! What the fuck was wrong with him? Why couldn't he just pick up the telephone and tell Sophie he had another daughter? He slapped his forehead with the palm of a hand and swore silently. *What a prick,* he thought. Already his work was suffering, just at a time when he needed to be on the ball. The work on the site had begun, and as with every new project of such magnitude he needed to be focused.

Constant reminders from Janet that he had to go to a meeting or visit the Winchester site, or even eat a decent meal, made him realise he was on the edge of losing it completely. Francine was invading every minute of his life. It was time to pluck up courage and, as his father would say, 'Time to bite the bullet, young Jack.'

He looked across at Janet, who was studiously gazing at a letter on her desk. She knew her concern only irritated him. "Feel like a bite to eat today?" he asked.

Doing her best not to leap up from her chair and shout, 'You bet!' she shuffled with some papers on her desk, did her best to control her excitement and said, "I'd be delighted to accompany you. These letters can wait."

Jack suppressed a rare smile. He'd been aware of her crush ever since he'd employed her. "Good. Hotel du Vin okay with you?"

'Anywhere,' Janet was tempted to say, but instead she said, "Perfect."

Jack said, "You deserve a little pampering Janet. If it wasn't for you the last few weeks I think the business might be going down the pan."

It was music to Janet's ears. "And we don't have to pass the Caffe Nero," she couldn't resist saying.

★★★

The latest row had been spectacular, thought Sophie, as she lay in her bath, but it had gained nothing. She'd kept some of the remains of his suits just for such a confrontation, and her naked antics had not had the desired effect. "Bastard!" she screamed, kicking at the water petulantly. Thinking about it now it had all been a total waste of her energy. Even the throwing of glass ornaments and ceramic knick-knacks had had no effect. He'd just stood there, stony-faced with a self-satisfied grin on his face, dodging the missiles as they had hurtled towards him, and then he'd turned and walked out of the room. He had not denied her accusations, which was incredibly annoying. He had just said, "Think what you like Sophie, I really don't care."

She grabbed the soap and started to vigorously scrub her

body. It had to smell right for Tom Jackson. Actually, she was growing a little bored with the young man and this was borne out by the fact that the exciting feeling between her thighs was on the wane. A new conquest must be found, but a little of the excitement, stirred by what she had thought were secret affairs, had slipped away since Jack had disclosed that he knew of her extra-marital goings-on. There would no longer be that feeling of cheating on her husband that she enjoyed so much. Then a terrifying thought hit her. Could this signal the end of their marriage? Was this fucking doctor going to be a real threat or was Jack just happy to play around? It surprised her that she'd abandoned the idea of hunting her down and screaming abuse at her. It all seemed so utterly futile. She sank back into the warm water and decided her only option was to wait and see, and if possible control her temper. She didn't want to give up all the luxuries that Jack gave her, least of all the flow of cash. She accepted she had a lot of work to do to get him back into her bed, but there was a huge mental gulf between men and women as she had learnt many times. What was the title of that book one of her friends had given her for her birthday? Oh yes, *Men are from Mars, Women are from Venus*. Boy, how true that was.

She jumped out of the water and towelled herself down, splashed on a liberal amount of No 5 Chanel toilet water and walked back into the bedroom. She dressed in a very short skirt, no knickers, no bra. Just the way Tom liked her. If this was to be her last immoral act she was damn well going to enjoy it! Then she walked out of the house towards the garages. "Tom," she said seductively as she spotted him walking away, "have you forgotten it's time for our Monday lunch break?"

Tom turned to face her. "Sorry, doll, I've got other things to do." Then added, "What the fuck do you look like!"

Sophie stopped dead. "But this is how you like me."

"No more, doll. You're mutton dressed as lamb, as they say. Sorry, but your times up."

"What!"

"You heard. Time up besides, your husband sacked me this morning. I've got to be out of the flat by three this afternoon. So no more spying for you and no more sex. Fed up I was anyway. You're getting old. So thanks for the good times. For me there are plenty more fish in the sea. For you, I'm not too sure." With that he walked away, a satisfied smirk crossing his face. Which made a shitty day so far, a little more bearable.

Sophie frowned at his retreating back, struck speechless. This was not the way it was supposed to end.

★★★

Francine stared at her computer screen. She tried to concentrate on the patient's records. To her horror she spotted a mistake. There was no way she could bluff herself out of this one. She'd have to confess to the patient and then go to her partners and tell them she'd prescribed the wrong drugs a week ago. It didn't matter that the medicine was harmless, this was her third mistake in a week – a missed appointment in the hospital, a home call to the wrong house, and now this. She was all too well aware that if she went on like this she might put someone's life in danger. She'd either have to resign or take a break until she could get over this excruciating feeling of loss. She looked at her watch and saw the time was just gone one. The pain was always worse at this time on a Monday. She wondered if Jack was missing Caffe Nero as much as she was. She shook her head and swung round to face her patient. "I'm sorry, Mr Mitchell, I'm afraid I've made a mistake with your treatment."

★★★

Janet Goodchild was in the mood to impress her boss. Power-dressed in a black suit with a crisp white blouse, she sat upright behind her polished rosewood desk. The desk was bare except for a slim glass vase of six white tulips (her favourite flower), a small cardboard box full of pencils and pens, and a stack of papers in her in-tray left by Jack the night before. She wore a strong, slightly sweet-smelling scent, and her hair was freshly brushed into a pony tail. She was determined that Jack could not help but cast an approving glance her way as he walked into the office. Lunch the day before had not quite gone as she'd hoped. Jack had sat opposite her playing with his food and constantly talking about Francine. But today, if the invitation was repeated, she was ready for him. This might be her chance to make an impression. Jack needed love and understanding and she was ready to give him both.

She heard his footfall coming up the stairs. Her heart raced. She was rewarded with a drop-dead smile as he walked into the office. She moved out from her desk, stroking down her skirt, and waited. No compliment came her way. Just. "Morning, Janet, I'm away all day, so hold the fort, will you?" Then, walking over to his desk, he picked up the framed photo of Sophie and dropped it into the bin. "See you tomorrow," were his parting words as he headed back the way he'd come.

Janet felt as if she'd walked under a cold shower. It brought back memories of life as a child, constantly rejected by her parents. She looked up at the clock above Jack's desk. Seven hours before she would leave the office and head back to her one-bedroom flat on the outskirts of Winchester. Later, as she did most evenings, she'd sit alone watching the television with Jack, her ten-year-old budgerigar, for company, and eat a take-away curry or fish and chips, whatever took her fancy. But she could still dream, and as she picked up the first piece of paper from her in-tray she felt a new resolve.

It was time to trigger her plan.

She sat back in her chair and drummed her desk with her long fingers – piano fingers, her mother had told her, but life on the streets soon dashed any hope of ever playing one. She gave a loud sigh, eased herself off her chair and moved over to the coffee machine, remembering halfway across the room that Jack had said they needed more coffee. "Fuck," she murmured, reaching for her coat and bag. Costa Coffee was just round the corner. She stepped out into the street. The rain was pelting down. *What a shitty world,* she thought as she ducked her head and hurried off down the street. The one person who could make her happy was unaware of her love. He was her life. In fact she'd die for him.

18

Thomas George Henry Turnbull, commonly known as Tank, still cursed his parents for christening him Thomas. If he'd had any semblance of humour, he might have just laughed it off, taken it as a well meaning joke, but Tank did not possess a sense of humour and if he heard anyone calling him 'Tank' they would find themselves with an adjusted face. He was huge. Six foot two in his socks, biceps that did actually ripple, and tree-trunk legs. He had a shaven head, and a black drooping moustache that he hoped made him look a bit Mexican. His dark menacing eyes, set deep in his skull, said, 'Don't mess with me.' He was truly terrifying and he revelled in his notoriety.

He'd been raised on the same street as Jack Carpenter. They had been born ten minutes apart in the same hospital, their mothers lying side by side in the same ward. His father had been a docker like Jack's and they had shared the hardships that went with their job, struggling day after day to put food on their family's table. At an early age it was obvious that Tank was going to be a career criminal. He possessed not a shred of loyalty towards his parents. He scoffed at Jack's vow to make his father proud of him. "You're wasting your time, Carpenter," he repeatedly advised. "There's nothing out there for you. Better accept you've got no prospects. We are uneducated working class. Besides, why struggle to better yourself when we can live on welfare for the rest of our lives and do some thieving as a bonus?" Jack kept his own counsel in spite of thinking Tank was an idiot with few brain cells. It would only have enraged him and given him an excuse to thump him, even though he was probably the only so-called *friend* he'd ever have, and although Tank would never admit it, he had grudging admiration for Jack. So they formed a sort of partnership, looking after each other as they grew from childhood into wild teenagers. They had played footy in the street, drunk in the same pubs, fought side by side on many a Friday night against other gangs. Taken girls up against a wall. But as soon as Jack had left the street, Tank had vanished from his life. For Tank had lived up to his potential: stayed where his roots were and become a criminal. When asked what his profession was, he'd proudly say, "I'm a villain. And for as long as there is room for us villains in this world I intend to continue being one."

★★★

So for Jack to have witnessed his son tied to a chair in Tank's hotel room, with a razor-sharp knife threatening his manhood, would have come as something of a surprise, given that he had no idea that one of Tank's nefarious businesses was, to put it a little too politely, money lending. And Harry had made the mistake of borrowing money from him, before the bombshell that no more money was coming his way, and this had put Harry in a very dangerous situation, for Thomas George Henry Turnbull did not take prisoners. If you couldn't pay it would be wrong to think you had a future.

As Tank stared down at the sniffling wretch, he acknowledged that he had made a mistake. He had misjudged the son and Jack. The weeping creature in front of him had not come up with the readies – something that Tank had not taken into account because he had been confident that if Harry failed to keep up the payments, Daddy would come riding, like some white fucking knight, to the rescue, but there he was mistaken and the loan in mention was one of the biggest he'd ever negotiated.

A cool ninety thousand quid.

He glared at Harry, saw the wet patch between his legs and wrinkled his nose. The boy had no bottle. But then what could you expect from someone who had been spoilt since birth? "Oh Harry boy, you have greatly annoyed me," Tank began, holding his handkerchief to his nose. "I need full repayment within a week. If you don't pay up, this little meeting here will be the last polite one. The next one will lead to a slow painful death and a concrete coffin." He waved the knife in the air. "So, unless you are tired of this world, you had better come up with a solution pretty damn quick, as you toffs would say. Do I make myself clear?"

Harry nodded.

"Speak," ordered Tank's son, who was enjoying every moment.

Harry fought back tears and mumbled, "I have no money."

Tank roared with laughter, deciding there was no point in mentioning the Ferrari, the polo ponies, the expensive girls and the drugs. He had other ideas. "Did you hear that, son, this boy has no money. Oh dear, oh dear. You might as well slit his throat now." He tossed the knife to his son.

Harry began to snivel.

Son Terry, grunted enthusiastically. He was not a man of many words and if possible was even more violent than his father.

Harry felt he was going to shit himself.

This was what Tank feared, so he raised a calming hand.

"Tell you what, Harry, I have a solution to your problem. I've kept up with your father's rise to fame, so to speak, and I have followed his financial dealings with interest. Quite a clever man I must say. This is why I thought you were a safe bet. How was I to know your father had closed the bank? Come to think of it, Harry, why are you skint? Where has all that money gone that your father made over to you when you reached eighteen? Do you need me to enlighten you?"

Harry said nothing.

"Come on, Harry, this is no time to keep secrets from me."

Harry said nothing.

"I'm beginning to get annoyed, Harry."

"It's locked away in a trust."

"Speak up, Harry."

"It's in a trust, which I can't get to."

"Very wise. But what happens to the annual income?"

"I spend it."

"On cars, women and polo ponies, not to mention your gambling on the horses. I'm not amused, very definitely not fucking amused. How can I run a business when there are little arseholes like you about? I can understand how your father feels."

Harry said nothing.

Tank rubbed his chin. "Oh dear, oh dear, this is getting serious. And I suppose you're now going to tell me that you owe money to that crook of a bookie I've seen you with?"

"Yes."

"Oh you poor darling," Tank laughed. "Well, let me tell you, Harry, you chose the wrong one to mess with."

Harry said nothing.

"You might well be speechless. So what to do is the question I'm asking myself. I'm not going to tell you to grow up, sell your car, your horses, etc., etc., because I have a much better idea."

"Please, please, Mr Turnbull, give me a break. I'll get the money somehow."

"Ah, he talks! Of course you will raise the money, Harry, and I'm going to tell you how. Your mother holds twenty per cent of the value of the Carpenter businesses. So it's quite simple. You go back to her with your testicles still intact and tell her to make ten per cent of her investments over to me within two weeks and I'll cancel the debt. If she refuses, you will find yourself back here and son Terry will be sharpening his knife. Do I make myself clear?"

Harry almost choked on the bile that rose in his throat. "You can't..."

"I can," Tank assured him.

"She, she will never do that. And the amount would be far over my debt."

"Well, that's what happens when you don't pay your bills, Harry. It's called interest. And don't sound so worried. She just might want to save your testicles so that you can breed another piece of shit like you."

"She doesn't love me."

"Well, too fucking bad," interrupted Terry.

"My feelings exactly," added Tank. "So off you go and do your best with Mummy. You have two weeks to persuade her. Oh yes, don't think you can borrow from anyone else to pay me. I have put the word about to those who might be stupid enough to lend to you that you are a very bad risk indeed." Tank made a waving motion with his huge hands. "Now off you go, Harry, there's a good boy. And next time you come bring a nappy." Tank laughed at his attempt at humour. "Untie him, Terry."

★★★

Sophie stared at Harry in disbelief. "You owe a man ninety thousand quid?" she gasped.

Harry nodded.

"Does your father know about this?"

"He knows I owe money, but not to whom and how much."

"He'll skin you."

"He's already signed my death warrant."

"He's what?"

"He's refused to pay any more of my debts."

"So what are you planning? Leave the country?" said in hope.

Harry sucked in his breath, felt his heart turn a somersault and said, "Mr Turnbull will cancel the debt if you make ten per cent of your holdings in Dad's companies over to him."

Sophie nearly choked. "You're joking."

"No, Mother."

"And who is this Mr Turnbull?"

"He's a money lender and a few other things. Apparently, Dad knew him way back."

"May I ask how you got involved with a loan shark?"

"He came recommended."

"Did he indeed? You're a fucking fool, Harry. Look at you. A mess if ever there was one. A reckless gambler, a fornicator par excellence – excuse my French – an idle shit who has already fucked up two of your father's firms. And you stand here and expect me to pass over a shed-load of money, which I cannot afford to do, to a criminal. In your dreams, young man. Go back to this Turnbull and tell him to fuck off."

Harry gulped. "He'll kill me."

Sophie stared at Harry with disgust. She didn't love him. She'd never bonded with her children as her few friends had done with theirs. He was just an appendage she could do without. If he died she doubted she'd even bother to shed a tear. "Then run, Harry, and by the sounds of it move quick."

"Mum, please."

Sophie shook her head. "Not a chance, sunshine."

★★★

For the first time in her life Jenny Carpenter felt sorry for her brother. Sitting on the floor of her bedroom, with empty bottles of vodka as company, an unmade bed stinking of vomit, his face streaked with tears, he looked so unlike the cocky bastard who had tormented her all her life.

"You're in shit, brother," she said with a note of pleasure.

Harry's white face stared at her. "A fat lot you care."

"Christ, Harry, what are you going to do? Flee the country?"

"That's what Mother advises."

"Good advice. And really, Harry, did you ever expect our mother to help you? She'd rather see us dead than part with money."

"I hoped there was some kindness in that hard heart of hers."

"But not where ninety thousand is concerned."

Harry was close to tears. "Jesus, Jenny, what do I do?"

"Well, I suggest you slit your throat now. Or perhaps appeal to Father one more time. Have you any money at all? "

"I'm skint."

"Christ, you know how to blow it!"

Harry was lost for words.

Jenny shook her head so violently that the resident headache gave pain a whole new meaning. "You *are* joking?"

"No."

Jenny took a long swig from the bottle of vodka that was clutched in her hands. She belched loudly. "You telling me you've blown all that money Father gave to you three years ago?"

"The trust won't help me."

"But all that cash he gave you. Are you telling me you've blown it all?"

"Yes."

"Well, it was nice knowing you."

Harry pushed himself off the floor and picked up an empty bottle and threw it at Jenny.

She ducked, and it smashed against a wall. She levered herself out of the chair she'd been sitting in. She swayed. The room spun. "Get out!" she screamed and fell back into the chair, any sympathy she had for her brother evaporating.

Harry ran from the room blubbering like a three-year-old child.

★★★

Janet Goodchild lowered the phone and shook her fist at the telephone. Sophie always lit her fuse. Why couldn't she speak direct, to Jack? Surely they could have a truce over something as important as this? Why did she have to be the eternal go-between? "Thank you, Goodchild, I hope you won't forget to tell him. This is urgent," had been Sophie's parting remark. Goodchild! Why on earth did she insist on calling her that? Disdain, Janet had long ago decided. At first it had made her feel uneasy, now she just ignored it. Not for the first time she wondered how Jack could ever have married the bitch. But Mrs High and Mighty Sophie Carpenter had been right: her message was urgent and very disturbing. Janet looked at the clock on the wall of the office. It would be an hour before Jack walked in. In the meantime there was nothing she could do but fret.

★★★

An hour later Jack appeared. By that time Janet was imaging Harry without any testicles. "Jack, am I glad to see you!"

Jack saw the concern on her face. "Something gone wrong?"

Janet blew out her cheeks. "Your wife called. Said she'd rather leave a message than talk to you face to face."

Jack grimaced. "She's probably right there. We have nothing to say to each other these days – total breakdown."

"Well, if you don't mind me saying so, this is a time you should forget your problems and talk. Harry's in serious trouble."

"What's new?"

"Please, Jack, this is very serious. He's in debt…"

"I know that."

"Please listen."

"Okay."

"He's heavily in debt to one money lender, apparently has huge gambling debts and various other loans."

Jack shrugged. "I've told him to sell everything."

"I don't think that will be nearly enough. Sophie says he owes one man ninety thousand and no doubt interest is growing every day, and several thousand in gambling debts."

"Tough."

"And a loan shark called Turnbull is calling in the ninety thousand debt. Payment within a week or Harry will be dead meat. Excuse me, but those were Sophie's very words."

"Christ!"

"Harry says he can't pay."

Jack jumped up from his chair and started pacing the office. "Thomas Turnbull, my God! I thought I'd heard the last of that man years ago. He won't be bluffing."

"You know him?"

"Indeed I do. We were more or less brought up together. We haven't seen each other for years. Our paths took different routes. He became a career criminal. Broke his father's heart so I heard."

"He's threatened…" Janet reddened – "to cut off Harry's testicles."

"He might just do that."

"He'd never get away with it."

"Men like Turnbull can get away with anything."

"But not murder."

"Even murder."

"Dear God. There's more, Jack."

"Go on."

"Turnbull has suggested that your wife pay the debt."

Jack gulped in amazement. "How the hell can she do that?"

"By handing over ten per cent of her holdings in your companies."

Jack stopped pacing. "What!"

Janet repeated Turnbull's demand.

Jack shook his head. "Of course, she said she wouldn't pay."

"That's what she told me – rather forcefully. 'Tell my husband please Goodchild,' as she likes to call me, 'that I'm not paying a penny.'"

"Well, for once I agree with her. I don't want that man to be anywhere near my businesses." Jack moved to his desk and sat down, his shoulders hunched. "I can't say I have much time for Harry. He's blown a small fortune and that is why a few days ago I refused to lend him a penny more, but he didn't mention this debt. He's a waste of space. As you know, he very nearly did untold damage to two of my businesses, but he's my son, Janet. So I must shoulder some of the blame for the way he's turned out. I can't let him die. What amazes me is how Harry got embroiled with such a man as Turnbull. I thought he operated in London. But that is of little interest to me now. I will pay the debt."

Janet said nothing, just nodded her understanding as Jack hurried out of the room. She would do the same if she had a child… *But that is never likely to happen,* she thought with a touch of sadness.

19

Francine sat silently watching a blank television set with Cat sitting on her knee. It had been the same every evening since she'd returned from Italy. The good thing was she'd stopped crying, but the ache in her heart and the constant visions of Jack would not dissipate so easily. With a heavy heart she'd offered her resignation to the practice as she could not trust herself not to make another mistake. But it had been refused. "Take a few days off," advised James Smallbrother, the senior partner. So, with some relief, she'd taken up the offer and fought to get her head together, with some success. There were still sleepless nights and the odd panic attack, but on the plus side she was determined to repay the trust the other doctors had shown in her and return to work invigorated. It was the only thing that would keep her sane. *No more dishing out wrong pills, or I'm finished.*

She looked out of the window at the sun setting behind the chestnut trees that stood on the other side of the river, their leaves already beginning to show the signs of oncoming autumn. If everything was normal she'd be sitting outside enjoying the end of another day, in a much improved garden, thanks to Jack, a glass of elderflower cordial held in her hand (or if an off-duty weekend, a glass of chilled rosé wine) and

Cat wandering around imagining there was a mouse in every bush. If the fishermen were on the river they would wave, and if the fish weren't biting they'd come across the little bridge two hundred yards downriver and enjoy a glass of the sweet cordial. But she had no desire to move outside and she was frightened that she might burst into tears in front of the fishermen.

Her life had once more been turned upside down, and the fallout was painful. How utterly insensitive Jack had been. How could he expect her to accept the lie that she was his mistress? It mystified her that he didn't seem able to tell the truth. It was all wrong. No doubt there would be some people who would think she was being an utter idiot to walk away from a father just because of one word. It might seem trivial to some but she'd spent many years with a woman who didn't know the word truth, and this was all to do with lies. If Jack lied about this what other lies would he tell in years to come? She could not live with the ghost of her mother constantly invading her space.

She knew Jack was suffering too but there had been no letter telling her he'd changed his mind. She pushed Cat off her lap and brushed his hairs off her skirt. If she didn't eat something she'd fade away. Lethargically she walked towards the kitchen. *Oh Jack, you stupid man, why are you wrecking our lives?*

★★★

That was the very question Jack was asking himself as he drove to his temporary home. A small three-bed-roomed semi in the same road as Her Majesty's prison. He'd asked Janet to furnish it. Troubles were piling up. Harry's debt, Francine, possible divorce and Jenny. Jesus, what a family. It was time to show some guts. Tomorrow he'd sort out Harry and then?

107

He bit his lip – Francine. He moved uneasily on the dreadfully hard green sofa that Janet had bought and suddenly had an urge to get blind drunk. "Fuck the world!" he shouted.

Four hours later, with glazed eyes, and the beginning of a headache, he weaved his way across the city, climbed the steep hill to his semi and once inside collapsed back onto the sofa. He'd pick his car up in the morning.

20

There was surprise written all over Tank Turnbull's face as he saw the man walking towards him. He forced a smile but his heart missed a beat. Was Daddy coming to save his son after all? Would he be able to boast to his friends that he had the great Jack Carpenter at his feet, begging for his son's life? He licked the beer off his lips and raised a hand in welcome. "Jack, long time, eh? Welcome to my Hampshire abode."

"And I wish it had been a little longer," Jack retorted, ignoring the outstretched hand. "You're a bit out of your territory, aren't you? Living in a hotel? Not like you, Tank. And threatening my boy is not on."

"Now, now, Jack, no need to take that tone with me. I come to Hampshire quite a lot – got several business interests around here. Suits me to stay here in Alresford at The Swan. And let me remind you that this is a free country and I can go where I like. As for that toe-rag you call a son, I think we know where we stand. At the moment I have you over a barrel, as they say. So much so that if you can't be polite to me I might soon be in the mood to tell you to fuck off and I'll deal with that spineless individual that you call your son in my way, in my own time."

Jack rested a clenched fist on the bar top and gritted his

teeth. He stared into Tank's dark eyes and knew he wasn't bluffing. "Okay, Tank."

"Ah, that's better. So, want a pint, or now that you're a rich bastard with a posh accent would you prefer a white wine?"

"A pint of Guinness will be fine," Jack said evenly. He was not going to let this man antagonise him. He knew from their past relationship that Tank was never far from violence. He couldn't mess with him until the loan was sorted. After that the gloves were off.

Pints on the bar, Tank waved toward a table in an alcove. "I hate drinking standing up and I think we need a bit of privacy." Once seated he asked, "Is it a surprise to see me in your neck of the woods, Jack?"

Jack shrugged. "Nothing has ever surprised me about you, Tank. I presume there are rich pickings in this wealthy area and you are doing your best to redistribute some of it."

"Pretty well on the mark, Jack. But I prefer not to divulge any more information."

"I know you well enough to know it's not legit."

"Ah, you always did have a bad opinion of me, Jack. But let's look at it this way. We don't need to like each other, but we are both capitalists. We are helping reduce the national debt. You employ people, I employ people. Both of us are doing the unemployment figures a service and we are both redistributing wealth in different ways, right?"

Jack suppressed a laugh. "And you're still a crook. Now, Tank, I think it's time to get down to business. First, my wife will not be paying my son's debt. If you think I would allow you to become a shareholder in my companies than you are a bigger fool then I already think you are. So, I'm here to settle."

Tank visibly bridled. He wanted to smack Jack one. Jack saw the look in his eye. He'd riled him and that, as Tank was soon to find out, gave him an advantage. It was bad to negotiate when angry. Jack sat back in his chair, pulled out a large envelope from his jacket's inside pocket and put it down on the table. "Hopefully this meeting will be brief. I don't like the company."

Tank scowled.

"Take this, Tank, and thank your lucky stars I'm not a crook like you or you would be a carcass by this evening."

Tank leant across the table, eyeing the white envelope. "How much?"

"Open it."

Tank grabbed the envelope. And Jack saw the greed in his eyes as he tore it open and stared at the banker's draft. "A hundred thousand?"

"Interest and insurance."

"You're getting generous Jack."

"No. Just making sure you can't come back and demand more. I know your sort, Tank. I want you out of my son's life, and if you dare come back for more I warn you I can make a very bad enemy. I haven't forgotten all the things I learnt on the streets with you. I can still call on muscle."

Tank was tempted to say, 'old muscle,' but decided this was not the time to test Jack's patience. Instead he nodded and picked his mobile off the table. He waved it in Jack's face. "I'll ring son Terry and tell him to release Harry."

Jack clenched his fists under the table. "*You* have Harry?"

"Insurance," laughed Tank. "Yes, Terry picked him up early this morning."

"You really are a bast..."

Tank raised a hand. "Now, now, Jack, remember what I said about being polite."

Jack took a long pull at his pint, silently counted to ten, and said, "You haven't changed; still a tricky customer."

"That's the way I like it," beamed Tank.

"Okay, but before you leave me, just two things. I want a written receipt and I want your son to bring Harry here. Only then can you leave."

111

Tank sat back and roared with laughter. "Is that a threat, Jack?"

"Just a word of advice."

Tank shrugged. He'd never been a man to take a risk, especially if it meant bodily harm. "Okay, I'll ring Terry and I'll sign a receipt."

"Good man."

"You are an untrusting bloke, Jack."

Jack didn't bother to reply. His eyes said it all.

★★★

Harry stood very still, staring at the floor. He couldn't bring himself to look his father in the eye and the very sight of Tank sent shivers down his spine. He could feel Terry's breath on the back of his neck as he stood over him. He was terrified, sure that his father was about to cut Tank loose. His panicked eyes searched the bar as if hoping there was someone who would rush to his aid. It was a fleeting thought. No one in their right mind would want to be turned into pulp. By nightfall he was sure he'd be dead.

Tank spoke first. "Look at him, Jack, standing there shivering. Is he worth a hundred grand?"

"He's not worth a penny," Jack retorted, "but he's my son, and there is no way I'm letting you two thugs loose on him."

"Tut-tut," growled Tank, "that's no way to talk to two civilised gentlemen."

Jack gave a bitter laugh and stood. It was time to go. The smell was unbearable. He put an arm around Harry's shoulder. "Come on, let's get out of here before I puke!" Then turning to Tank he said, "You shouldn't have done this."

Not slow to hear the threat, Tank shrugged. "You can't frighten me, Jack, and I'm untouchable."

Jack pushed Harry in front of him. "Door," he hissed.

When they reached the door leading to the street Jack turned once more to face Tank. "You're on borrowed time, Tank." He walked out into the warm air and breathed in deeply. He reached for his mobile and rang the police. Then, turning to Harry, he said, "Now, get out of my sight."

★★★

By lunchtime the two Turnbulls were enjoying a tepid cup of coffee in the holding cell of Winchester police station on a possible charge of blackmail. At two o'clock a constable walked into the cell. "Phone call for you."

The call made Tank's blood boil.

By three o'clock he and Terry were walking free. In the car park Jack was waiting. As the two men approached he left his car and leant against the bonnet, hands folded across his chest. "You're lucky this time Tank, next time I won't withdraw my complaint. And to save you the pain of getting that draft out of your pocket it has already been cancelled."

Tank moved threateningly to within an inch of Jack's face. "You'll live to regret this, Jack," he growled.

"You can't frighten me with your threats, Tank. Better you forget this incident. I know how much freedom means to you, and the Hampshire police are aware of you now. One move against my son and any more visits to Hampshire to ply your miserable trade and you will be back inside, and this time I will press on with my accusation of blackmail. Accept you've lost and make yourself scarce."

For once in his life Tank was struck speechless.

★★★

Harry smirked at his sister. "Jesus, that was something else! Turnbull met his match there. Took the loss of a hundred grand without a whimper. You should have seen his face. Christ, Jenny, for a moment I actually admired my father. I'm still not sure I can believe it."

Jenny gave a drunken laugh. "A little shit like you doesn't deserve such fucking luck. If I was your father I'd have left you to Turnbull. But be warned, Harry, Dad won't protect you all the time. So treat this as a warning and don't carry on with your degenerate lifestyle. Dad is no pushover. Work hard for him – show him you can be trusted. Go to the office dressed like an executive not a slob. Stop snorting drugs, and shagging your girl grooms. Graft, it's called, bro, graft. Time you took that on board. "

Harry glared at her. "You're a fine one to talk, Jenny. Work my arse off for Dad? Christ, I'm Harry Carpenter, son of one of the richest men in England according to the *Sunday Times* rich list. Am I going to alter my ways? How dare Father try and tell me what to do. I'll live my life as I wish. Borrow more money and watch Father pay out to save my life. I've touched his weak spot. But do you know something, Jenny? If Father was dead it would solve a lot of problems."

Jenny said nothing.

★★★

Jack sat at his desk in his Winchester office and heaved a sigh of relief. He was alone. Janet had gone to lunch and the quiet of the room calmed his shattered nerves. He'd rescued Harry. How many more times was this scenario going to be replayed? How many more times would Harry stand in front of him, shaking, tearful and begging? Well, certainly this time would not be the last if he knew his son, and he'd play on his emotions. No doubt, right this minute, Harry was thinking that he'd got him right where he wanted him. Too true; no question about it. He shrugged. So no point in giving it more thought. He put his hands behind his head and sat back in his chair and thought of Francine. She had been the best thing to come into his life for years and he'd blown it. *So do something about it.* In a village not six miles away, there might be someone who could still bring back happiness to his life. He slammed his hands down on his desk and pulled out a piece of writing paper. He could have text or phoned but he felt a letter was more intimate and besides he feared he wouldn't be able to hold back the tears when he heard her voice. He picked up his biro, scribbled the date at the top of the paper and began to write.

21

They sat in stunned silence, staring open-mouthed at Jack. He leaned back in the armchair, folded his hands on his lap and waited. Jenny was the first to break the silence. "You have a daughter by another woman!"

Jack gave her his best smile. He was surprised how relaxed he felt, how easy it had proved to be to tell them. How stupid he'd been. "That's what I said, Jenny. You have heard all the details and I'm not disposed to repeat them."

"So this Doctor Walker is not your mistress as you had me believe," gasped Sophie.

"You jumped to that conclusion, judging me by your own low moral standards of behaviour. And this applies to you as well," growled Jack, waving a hand in his children's direction. Obviously you will need to digest this bit of news so I will let you get on with it."

"No!" screamed Sophie. "You can't just tell us you have an illegitimate daughter and then walk away. I want to know what you're going to do about her. Are you hoping she'll be welcome here, even become part of this oh so happy family? Am I expected to hug her to my breasts and say hi, nice to meet you at last?"

Jack looked at Sophie with distaste. "If you want to meet

116

her then that's okay with me but I don't think she'll want to bury her head in your breasts, Sophie, and say, Hi, Step-mum, hope we can get along."

"So you are ashamed of us?" Harry asked.

Jack stood up and pointed a finger one by one at his family. "You could say that. Look at you. A son who comes crying to Daddy, looks like a vagrant and doesn't know the meaning of soap. You're a spineless individual, Harry, and let me remind you your job is not permanent – I can sack you any time I like." His eyes swung to stare at Jenny. "And I'm ashamed of you as well. You're a drunk; you have sex with anyone, and you will probably be dead before you are forty. Yes, you may well snivel, but I'm in no mood to lie. And finally there's you, Sophie. An unloving, money grabbing, immoral woman, who humiliates me in front of our staff. Of course I'm ashamed."

Jenny ran from the room, shouting, "You never loved me! I hope you die, die, Father. You're a monster."

Harry just smiled. He didn't care a toss what his father thought of him. He now knew he'd found his weak spot. That was all he cared about.

Sophie moved within a few inches of Jack's face. "You're cruel, Jack Carpenter. I hope that this daughter sees the warning signs in time before you destroy her like you have us."

Jack stood his ground. "Think what you like, Sophie, I don't care anymore. You've got this house to yourself. I'm happy where I am. If you want a divorce you can have one. Oh yes, have no fear, you won't be short of money, but you may find yourself a bit short of young men to shag you. You're getting a bit wrinkled, you know."

"How dare you insult me like that, Jack."

"I'll say what I like."

Sophie spat in Jack's face.

He pulled out his handkerchief and wiped the spit away, before turning and walking out of the room towards the front door. He couldn't believe he'd said all those things. Cruel, heartless but true. He was past caring. If Francine could forgive him then she'd be his life from now on. If not? He didn't want to go down that road.

★★★

Francine didn't read the letter, it would only open the wound which was just healing. She stared at the familiar writing and cursed Jack under her breath. This was emotional blackmail. She reckoned she knew the contents off by heart, a begging letter asking her to understand. This had to stop. She moved to her desk and sat down and pulled out a blank postcard from one of the pigeon holes. This was going to be the most painful letter she'd ever written. Perhaps an email would be easier and more impersonal. No, it needed to be personal to get the message through. He had to see the words in her own writing and the stains from her tears. Then maybe he'd understand how much he'd hurt her. She picked up Jack's letter and tore it into pieces.

★★★

Jack was sitting at his office desk, drinking his first morning cup of black coffee, lovingly made for him by Janet, when the post arrived. As usual there were bills, always bills, three envelopes that would be replies to his quotes and two brochures about houses on the market in the Winchester area. He had considered distancing himself from his family, perhaps moving to Wiltshire. He had three small projects running there, but two things would keep him in Hampshire. Francine, and the one project closest to his heart up on the hill above the city.

And then he picked up the letter.

His brow furrowed, his heart rate increased. He was almost

too frightened to open the envelope. With shaking hands and an intake of breath he opened the envelope and began to read.

It had been a long time since he'd cried.

Janet heard him sob – cast a worried eye in his direction and then looked away. She longed to leap up and put her arms around his shoulders but she sensed he wanted to be alone with his thoughts. If he wanted her sympathy he'd ask. Of course, she knew he'd never ask. *So maybe it's time for me to make a move,* she thought. *To put my views to him.* To get Francine back should be his prime objective and bugger the rest of his family. What had they ever done for him? "More trouble, Jack?" she asked.

He looked up. Her heart went out to him. She could almost feel his distress. "Read this." He handed the letter to her.

★★★

It was another late evening as Francine turned the key in the cottage door. She was exhausted, hungry and feeling very low. She knew that by now Jack would have received her letter. As usual Cat was sitting on the doorstep purring. *Is this going to be my life from now on?* she thought, as she gathered him into her arms. *Coming home to be welcomed by a mangy cat?* She kissed his hairy old face and whispered, "Don't you dare wander off, Cat. You're all I have left, but if you want to leave a sinking ship I suppose I can't stop you." Cat gave her a perfunctory lick on her cheek before jumping out of her arms as she turned to shut the door. It made her laugh. Jesus, laugh! She'd forgotten how it felt. She put her medical bag down on the hall table and moved into the kitchen. The message light was flashing red. For a moment she thought, *Jack!* Then remembered her letter. Surely there would be no more calls from him. She picked up the receiver and pressed the message button. The voice was familiar. "Francine, it's Janet Goodchild. Could you ring me on this number as soon as you get this message? Don't worry if it's late, just ring please."

For a moment Francine hesitated. Was this Jack's way of still trying to get to her? She hoped she was misjudging him. Surely her letter had spelt it out loud and clear – no room for negotiation. Wrong word, she thought, but it would do. She looked at the telephone, turned away, looked back, hesitated, then grabbed the receiver. Before she really knew what was happening she found herself dialing Janet's number.

★★★

They met at the Holiday Inn outside Winchester, having decided it was wise not to meet in the city. No point in risking meeting Jack. Janet had suggested a light lunch. "More relaxing."

Francine wasn't sure about the relaxing bit, but she'd agreed.

Now, a day after Janet's call, they were sitting opposite each other in the hotel restaurant, picking rather unenthusiastically at cold chicken salads and both knowing that the small talk had to end. Francine swallowed the last of her chicken. "So, Janet, tell me what is so urgent. Is Jack using you as a messenger, because if he is I'm not staying for coffee."

Janet smiled. "I assure you I'm not a messenger. I'm here of my own free will, because I'm concerned."

"About what?" Francine flicked a piece of lettuce off her blouse.

"Jack's frame of mind."

Francine felt a slight touch of anger. "Well, that might be his fault. Listen, Janet, I'm not interested in his apparent shitty home life. What is eating me away is his refusal to tell the truth. I'd grown to love him. It was wonderful to have a father.

120

My whole life changed. Jesus, Janet, I miss him. But I won't be tagged as a homewrecker. Why should I be called his mistress? I'm his daughter, for Christ sake. What's wrong with that? Is he ashamed that I'm illegitimate, I keep asking myself."

"No, no it's not that."

"Well, whatever. My mind is made up. I cannot go on like this. I have my work and a home. I don't need Jack. All he had to do was tell the truth in the beginning. If his frame of mind is worrying you then he's only got himself to blame."

Janet put both elbows on the table and looked mystified. "I don't understand. Did you not get his last letter?"

"Oh I got it okay. I tore it up."

"You didn't read it?"

"No. Fed up reading the same old excuses."

"Oh dear."

"And what does that mean?"

"He's told his family about you. It was in the letter. They went ape I gather. Terrified that he might change his will. But at least it's all in the open now. And Jack being Jack, blames himself for everything. Must be blind," Janet finished.

"Oh God!" Francine reached for her glass of water. She brushed away a tear and smiled at Janet. "Then what am I waiting for? Where is he this afternoon?"

"He'll be in his office by three."

"I'll be there."

Janet was speechless.

"You didn't expect that, did you?" said Francine.

"No, I must confess I didn't."

"Pleased?"

For a split second Janet wasn't sure how to answer, but she quickly recovered. "Yes, yes, it's great," she managed to say.

Francine threw her a quizzical stare. "You sure?"

"Absolutely."

"Then let's not waste any more time. Get the bill and I'll

be off. Oh yes, if you see him before I get there please don't say a word. I want to surprise him."

"I promise."

Driving back to Winchester, Francine couldn't help thinking about Janet's reaction. She seemed disappointed.

As Janet walked up the stairs towards the office she could hear Jack talking on the telephone and this made her wonder if she'd done the right thing seeing Francine. *Now I will have to share him,* she thought. And the thought was not a happy one.

22

Tank Turnbull was staring out of his front room window, fuming. He didn't appreciate being got the better of, and Jack Carpenter had just done that. There was no way he was going to let it pass. He had his reputation to think of. This had been his manor for years and his word was law! He would lose all street cred if word leaked out about his humiliation in Hampshire. He imagined his so-called mates (so-called because he knew that if he slipped up they'd show him no loyalty) drinking their pints in the pub and laughing at his demise. "And guess who put him in prison? Young Jack Carpenter!" The laughter would reverberate round the room. Rage rose in his throat like bile. He slapped his thighs – revenge was on his mind. Moving back from the window he dropped into a chair and began to work out a plan. He allowed himself to imagine what form this revenge might take – a slit throat came to mind. No one made a fool of him and lived. Or maybe Jack should live and spend the rest of his life wishing he was dead – yes, that appealed. He gave a low laugh and rubbed his hands together. Tomorrow he'd set everything in motion.

The shuffling of saucepans from the kitchen snapped Tank out of his reverie. The aroma of roast leg of pork that Mildred was cooking for his tea made his stomach rumble;

he was starving. Mildred was his rock. She knew how to keep him happy, always had done. She'd fed him, given him a son Terry, now working out the way he'd hoped. She'd never complained. What more could a man want? He'd never strayed like so many of his mates, and was proud of that. The old mare knew her place was at home, always ready to satisfy his needs. Tank's world was male orientated, women were shackles. All this modern malarkey was shit. He belched loudly and strode towards the kitchen to put an arm round his plump wife's waist and give her the one kiss she was allowed each day. The first bite of pork was succulent and some juice leaked from his mouth. Licking his lips he gave Mildred a contented smile. What more could a man want? Pork crackling and the thought of what was to come.

★★★

Jenny Carpenter would have been the first to admit she was a mess. Life should have been so different. A good education, quite good exam results, pretty, sexy, so she was told, and a quick brain. "The fault of course lies with my parents," she would say if asked. Their constant fighting, ignoring the support a young girl needed as hormones raced round the body was enough to destroy any young girl's dream.

At sixteen Jenny had taken her first sip of alcohol and any hope of a normal life had vanished. Her useless parents (which she called them) were by then fighting most of the time and had been slow to spot the change in their daughter's behaviour. By the time they clicked that something was wrong Jenny was well on her way to becoming an alcoholic at seventeen, and when her father tried to warn her of the dangers she just shrugged and mumbled, "Yeah, yeah," and went on drinking. By the time she was forcefully sent to a rehab clinic she was beyond saving and she couldn't have cared a fuck and her parents had become hate targets. A friend had tried to console her by telling her that it was very difficult to differentiate between love and hate when there was blood involved. Jenny didn't listen. So, hate had fermented and now...! Some fucking little illegitimate whore had come on the scene. And her father would lavish Francine, or whatever her bloody name was, with expensive presents which she had never had. Jesus, he might even be tempted to change his will! Fuck, fuck, fuck! Life was shit.

As she swayed up Winchester High Street, past the Guildhall, heading for the pubs and eateries in Jewry Street at the top of the High Street, she waved at a few acquaintances who smiled at her, but Jenny did not stop to talk – she had a friend to meet. She'd been living rough for nearly three months. Surprised herself that her resolve to make a statement had so far held firm. Yes, there were moments when she was briefly sober when she wondered what the fuck she was doing, but once back into her inebriated state, the cold, the disgusted stares, the lewd suggestions from her fellow vagrants – and not all of them male – washed over her like the heavy rain that was soaking her now, and any idea of going home vanished, especially now that she had a friend. She almost fell through the door of Marks and Spencer's. It would not normally be a refuelling stop but this morning she was desperate. She bought two litre bottles of vodka, one for herself and one for her friend Taffy.

★★★

Taffy was a Welshman, Taffy was a thief, Taffy came to my house and stole a leg of beef. It was a rhyme Taffy had had thrown at him many times, and it was not always as a joke. He knew he was a Welshman but he'd never call himself a thief, just taking things other people had discarded to keep himself alive ever since he'd withdrawn from society and become a vagrant. He wanted nothing to do with the real world God had dumped him in – he wanted a world for Taffy and the only way to get it was to cut himself off from a structured life and rely on the bottle. But Taffy, if asked why he'd chosen such a degrading way to live, could not give an answer, because over the years his brain had shut down. Every now and then he'd be struck by a vague memory of horrors in his past but a good drag of vodka soon came to his rescue.

He was five foot six, stick-thin like in one of the characters in a Lowry painting. His once sparkling blue eyes were now sunk deep into their sockets. His balding head was covered by a black beanie hat and his bedraggled beard was home to a few unsavoury creatures. The few teeth he had left were yellow and the gums constantly bled. Mouth hygiene did not feature high on his list of priorities, survival took up all his time. He was a sad stinking mess. He would be lucky to live another ten years, although Taffy wasn't too sure about the word *lucky*. At some stage during most days, he wished that he had the guts to top himself. He believed he'd been homeless forever. He had no idea of his age; no recollection of any family or life before he came to Winchester. He knew he was Welsh because he'd been told he was; he knew he came from a place called Cardiff for that was what his rail ticket had said when the police had picked him up wandering aimlessly around the city on his first day. They had found him uncooperative, not for any bloody-minded reason, simply because his memory had called it a day. He'd been hospitalised, psychoanalysed, had brain scans, all to no avail. In the end he was just Taffy, another vagrant with a drink problem who blighted the streets of Winchester. He was nearly always drunk, sitting in the High Street with a battered old hat lying between his open legs, a few coins covering the bottom by the evening if he was lucky.

In spite of all the hardships he'd endured over the years,

he was a gentle soul. A heart of gold beat behind his rib cage, and that was why he'd formed a rather strange relationship with the girl whose life he'd saved. They were as different as chalk from cheese but soon they were feeding off each other's discrepancies. A down-and-out pauper and an alcoholic rich girl wearing designer clothes, albeit unrecognisable unless you read the label, expensive shoes, bedecked in bling, but smelling of booze.

It was two months since he'd found Jenny in the early hours of a weekday morning, lying in Winchester's central car park under a Toyota 4x4. If he hadn't have been suffering one of his half-sober moments, scavenging for cigarette butts and hopefully a bottle with the dregs of alcohol at the bottom, he'd never have seen her bare feet, and she almost certainly would have died from hypothermia. She was half naked, shivering from cold and very, very drunk. He'd pulled her out from under the Toyota, knowing that she was in need of urgent help. He had slapped her face and got some reaction. Enough to get her on her feet. "I'm not Tarzan, so do your best or die," he'd whispered.

It must have been a bizarre sight for anyone about in the small hours of a Wednesday morning. A small emaciated man, beyond middle-age, dragging a defenceless girl along the street. Luckily, at two in the morning, the streets were quiet and anyone who was about had felt it wise to walk the other way. He'd half-carried, half-dragged her to a shelter for the homeless he used frequently thanking a God he'd never had time for, that no policeman blocked his route. By late morning, as sober as she ever was, he'd sat down in front of her and warned her of the dangers she faced if she made a habit of getting smashed and choosing a car to sleep under.

She'd smiled weakly and then vomited all over him. A support worker had rushed to the rescue and, although the circumstances of Jenny arriving in the shelter were odd, she was happy to help one of Taffy's friends. Besides, it was not wise to ask too many questions from the inhabitants of the shelter. "That's how we do things here, dear," she'd explained to Jenny, who had expected to be thrown out.

"Where are we, and who are you?" Jenny had asked Taffy a few minutes after they had been left alone.

Taffy, by then fighting the desire to drink anything that would muddle his brain had again told her. His kindness, his acceptance that if she wanted to get pissed why the fuck not, touched a spot that had been sorely lacking in love and understanding for several years. So, as she told a fellow drinking companion later, "I've adopted the most lovely, sad homeless man, who in spite of his everyday struggle to stay alive understands me better than either of my parents ever will."

Jenny quickened her pace. If she didn't hurry she'd miss their weekly meeting and then he'd either have disappeared or be too drunk to help her. She turned into Jewry Street and there he was, sitting in his usual chair on the pavement, drinking a cup of coffee. To the restaurant owner he was part of the scene and, as he'd never caused any trouble and was always polite, he was welcome to a chair and a table before the crowd of shoppers and tourists arrived. "But remember, Taffy, only one free cup of coffee," reminded the owner. Jenny waved from across the street. He waved back and two minutes later she joined him. She plunked one of the bottles of vodka down on the table. "Your breakfast, sir," she said with a laugh.

Taffy gave her a broad smile. "Thank you, Jenny girl, most kind of you I must say. Going to join me for a tipple?"

Jenny dropped gratefully into a chair. She'd been hoping he'd say that. She badly needed to talk to him. "I'm having bad thoughts again," she stated.

"Oh Jenny, that should not be."

"I know, I know, but I can't get it out of my head. What happens if my father changes his will, Taffy, for Christ's sake. I'd be penniless and sure as fucking hell I don't do penniless. Jesus, I hate that whore who has come into our lives."

Taffy gave her a thoughtful look, tempted to say that if she was so worried about being dropped out of her father's will she shouldn't be walking the streets and living rough. You did not do homelessness for choice. Instead he gave a rueful smile. "Money, it's always money that you rich people think of and if that's the case perhaps you should go home and try to get on with your family. For this life doesn't protect you just because you come from money. No one could care a shit, and if they know you have money on you, sure as fucking hell, girl, you won't have it for long."

Jenny took the rebuke with a shrug. "I'm not going home. Final. Whatever I tried to do, love would not come my way. My father is besotted by this whore and my mother is shagging every moment of the day. They don't want me, Taffy, simple as that. So here I am, pissed, full of self-pity and hating the world. Living your sort of life may be a bowl of shit but it beats my home life I can tell you. I'm here to stay."

I very much doubt that, thought Taffy, but decided he might as well save his breath and he didn't want to lose his only friend. Instead, he nodded at the vodka bottle on the table. "Come on, let's have a go at this and forget the world."

Jenny held up her own bottle. "This will do me." She took a swig, then handed the bottle to Taffy. He took a long pull at the liquid and felt the familiar fire in his belly. He rubbed his tummy and half-smiled. "Who wants to be sober?" he said sadly, reaching out to touch her hand. It was cold and he noticed the veins sticking out. It told him a story and he shook his head sadly. She was a user as well as a drunk. He felt for this girl, a lost soul like himself. She was so young, so fragile, just like he was when he fell off the ladder. He'd suffered enough to know that Jenny would never last a year as a homeless waif. She was just not tough enough. "Listen to me, Jenny, while I can still put two words together. I never want to hear you say you'd want my life. Being homeless is degrading. Sucks all life out of you. You lose hope. Every day you're fighting to stay alive. You have to know who to trust and who to avoid." He ran a hand across his throat. "Or you're dead. It's a full-time job, which those who say we should be out finding work don't understand. You line up to eat; you constantly wonder where you're going to sleep. You hump your worldly possessions around on your back, hoping that some other poor bastard doesn't try to steal what little you have. When your clothes wear out you have to scavenge or beg to put someone's discards on your back. You're constantly exhausted, weak, always short of money. You long for a shower and if you can't find a bed for the night the fucking coppers come along and kick you off the streets. No, no, *no*, Jenny, this is not the life for you. However bad your life is, you have money, which means you can get out of this anytime you choose. I'd swap places with you before you could take another gulp of vodka."

Jenny scowled. "I thought you understood me?"

"Oh I understand you, girl. You're not in this for a long stretch. Either you will see that that other life is better than this or you will die. Simple."

Jenny gave him a weak smile. "Thanks for the lecture, Taffy, but I'll stick with what I've got and so die here in Winchester."

Taffy shook his head. "What a waste of a life." He took a sip of his cold coffee and decided he'd said enough. "So what you doing today?"

"Making a plan."

"Can you tell me?"

Jenny leant across the table and whispered in his ear. "I need money."

Taffy immediately knew what this meant. He shook his

worn-out eyes, staring at her in horror. "You're deranged. The vodka is talking. Going down that route can only lead to disaster."

She stood and gave a bitter laugh. "What do I care, my life is nothing, nothing, nothing. Can you hear me, Taffy, nothing!" She made to move. "You coming with me?"

Taffy looked down at his shaking hands. "No, I won't be coming with you. I'm safe here for the time being. You go and do what you want, Jenny, but remember I'll be here for you, drunk or sober. And you will come back to me, I know it."

"Okay, then, I'll see you later perhaps."

Taffy watched her walk away and a tear escaped from his eye and trickled down his face to disappear in his matted beard. No one had made him cry for years, and why should he care about some rich misguided female who would soon come to her senses? It dawned on him that those like Jenny, rich, greedy, spoilt, self-opinionated and up their asses, was perhaps one of the reasons why he'd walked away from society. But as he took another swig of vodka he knew he *did* care. She might be all of these things, even evil, but in many ways she was so like him. The problem was that her whispered words frightened the shit out of him. She would never survive on the streets. He took a long pull at his bottle, ran his hand through his beard, felt the dampness from his tears and wondered what to do. "One thing is certain, Taffy," he said to the table, "I'll miss her if she goes."

★★★

Harry woke, his sheets soaked with sweat, his hair matted, his tongue stuck to the roof of his mouth. He looked around the room in panic. The nightmare was still clear, so terrifying that as he tossed the sheets off his body he wondered if he could ever forget the decapitated head of his father leering

131

down on him, blood dripping from his mouth and splashing on his face. Involuntarily he swiped at his face, then looked at his palms for the sight of blood. He stifled a scream and ran to the bathroom. Turning on the shower he ducked under the cold spray and stood rigid, freezing. Slowly his mind cleared, his body stopped shaking and his eyes focused on his surroundings. The bathroom was as he'd left it the night before, nothing had changed. No blood anywhere, no corpse, no smell of death. He moved cautiously out of the shower and reached for a towel. Vigorously rubbing himself down he walked back into his bedroom and started to dress. He looked at the bed, the duvet lying on the floor, the sheets tied in knots and decided there was no way he could spend another night in this room. There were plenty others to sleep in. But would the same dream come back to haunt him wherever he chose to sleep?

★★★

An hour later, unshaven, his long hair uncombed and wet, Harry ran down the stairs into the hall. He crept past the dining room knowing his mother would be sitting at the table munching on a piece of brown toast, which had always got on his nerves. He risked a glance her way. Unlike him, she was immaculately dressed, not a hair out of place. How could she behave as if everything was normal? His lips curled in disgust and he hurried by. He opened the front door and stepped out into a sunny late-summer morning. He moved towards the stable yard, every step taking him nearer to the cause of his nightmare. He was met by a wall of silence. The loose boxes were empty, their doors open, the polo ponies all gone. There were no girl grooms laughing in the empty tack room. No firm backsides to slap. He kicked angrily at tubs of flowers in the yard and winced with pain. His Ferrari was no longer in the garage next to the loose boxes. Instead a green Mini, with number plates showing it was a 2004 model, was there in its place. This was the deal he'd had to strike with his father after he'd saved him from the clutches of Turnbull. He'd been a fool to think that his father would always come to his rescue without him paying the price in some way. "Let this be a lesson to you Harry," he'd said. "Next time you might not be so lucky."

"Well fuck you, Father," he shouted, as he walked into one of the empty loose boxes. The smell of horse dung still lingered. He breathed in deeply and felt his heartbeat slow – he had always loved the smell. He thought of his future. It looked bleak and that sent a shiver down his spine.

23

Francine had decided not to walk into Jack's office and say hello. She was not sure how to handle it. So once back at the surgery she'd found time to ring him. It had turned out to be an awkward five minutes but the outcome had been what she'd wanted more than anything in the world.

So here she was walking into Caffe Nero, around four in the afternoon, feeling nervous but excited.

"It will work out," she'd had to keep telling herself as she'd driven to Winchester, or she might have flunked it and turned back. She wasn't sure she could deal with rejection.

Nothing had changed, she noticed as she walked through the door of the coffee shop. She recognised several faces and saw the table by the red fire extinguisher was vacant. She smiled and moved to the table; it was a good omen. Her whole body was shaking. In a few moments he'd walk through the door and then… She breathed in, trying to control her heartbeat… He would be sitting beside her, no doubt wondering just like she was. Wondering if they could mend bridges. "We can, we can," she said quietly to herself. She fumbled in her bag and pulled out a handkerchief and dabbed at her face. She was sweating. She ordered a latte from a waitress and allowed herself to wallow in memories of all their meetings sitting at this table, laughing, as if they hadn't a care in the world. How she'd missed these precious moments, but maybe just maybe there would now be more than just moments. She sipped at the hot liquid, her eyes fixed on the door.

But ten minutes later the door had not swung open. He wasn't coming. She waved for a waitress and paid the bill, nearly dropping the money as she gave it to the girl. Unsteadily she rose from her chair and headed for the door, fighting the tears as she stepped out onto the street.

And there he was, only an arm's length away, looking flustered and unusually untidy.

They stared at each other, both frozen to the spot. "Oh my God!" Francine finally blurted out. "I thought you weren't coming."

"I got held up. Sorry."

"Not the best time to be late."

"I know. Can you forgive me?"

"Forgive you! Christ, of course I can forgive you. You look wonderful."

Jack laughed and moved aside to let a couple through the door. "You don't look too bad yourself. Coffee?"

Francine swallowed. "Anything."

Jack took her hand and squeezed it. "Been waiting long?"

"Long enough to drink a latte. Come on, let's stop standing here gazing into each other's eyes like two love lost teenagers. I can easily drink another latte."

Once back at the same table Francine dared to say, "Are we okay? Are we father and daughter at last?"

Jack leant back in his chair and put his hands behind his head. "Yes."

"So no more subterfuge or lies?"

"Cross my heart and hope to die."

"Fine, that's good enough for me. Double espresso with cream?"

135

He reached for her hand and nodded. "That will do me fine. So where do we begin?"

"Oh, Jack," was all she could say.

"Then we start from here."

"Okay."

"Good to see you, Francine Walker."

"Good to see you too, um, Father."

★★★

Francine sat stunned. All her energy had been sapped out of her. She'd watched him disappear into the crowd and felt light-headed. What has just happened? she asked herself. What am I doing? I must be mad. But if this was madness it could last forever. This was glorious and so unexpected. Where had all the anger and pain gone? "It's a mystery," she said quietly to herself, "and I have no intention of trying to solve it. It's happened and I'm happy and that's that." She looked at her watch and gasped. She was running late for evening surgery. She grabbed her bag and ran out of Caffe Nero.

★★★

He was going to be very late. There would be annoyance written all over their faces as he walked into his office. Not least from Tim Stafford, his site manager. But what did he care As he dragged himself back to his office all he could think of was the miracle that had just occurred. The most remarkable thing was the way he and Francine had sat and talked as if the last few months of separation had never existed. There had been no acrimony seeping out of her, no 'Why did it take you so long?' No mention of the pain he knew he'd caused her. She had smiled as if nothing had happened, drunk a latte, told him all her news and when he'd decided he had to leave she'd said, "Give me a ring tonight if you aren't too busy." Too busy! Jesus, he'd give up anything.

★★★

Janet Goodchild threw Jack a worried look. He wasn't concentrating and Stafford's news needed his full attention. Timothy was also aware that his boss's mind was elsewhere. He decided to elaborate a bit. "We're running into a spot of bother on the site, Jack."

Jack's head jerked up. "Bother, Tim, what bother?"

"Progress is stalled." He looked across the desk and thought he now had Jack's full attention. "If I didn't know better I would say we were being sabotaged."

"Sorry, Tim, what was that?"

Tim fought to suppress his irritation. He repeated his words.

"Sabotaged! Oh, that's a bit off the mark, isn't it? Maybe our suppliers are being a little slow and the weather hasn't helped with the buildings and the playing fields, but sabotage? No, Tim, forget it. Look, I don't blame you for being frustrated, my mind has been elsewhere. It's not often a man finds he has a daughter he never knew he had."

You're a stuck record, Tim thought.

"I know I haven't been to the site enough just lately and I'm sorry. But from now on I will give you my full attention. And I will sort out our suppliers in the morning. Okay?"

Tim knew it was the best he was going to get. "That's fine."

"Anything else, Tim?" It was Jack's way of saying the meeting was over.

"Nothing at the moment." He gathered up his files, stood up and made for the door, smiling at Janet as he left. It had been on the tip of his tongue earlier to ask her what was going on in Jack's head but he knew her loyalty to him would prevent her giving him an explanation.

137

No sooner was Tim out of the door than Jack was grabbing his leather jacket from the back of his chair. "I'm off, Janet. Having supper with Francine."

Janet forced a smile. "That's good. Made it up okay?"

"It's amazing Francine behaved as if nothing had happened. It was just like we had never been apart."

Janet stared at Jack, feeling the familiar jab of jealousy. "Wow!"

"That's what I thought. Right, I'm off; see you tomorrow."

Janet just stared at his retreating figure.

He ran out into Southgate Street and didn't stop running until he was opposite Caffe Nero. Out of breath, and with his heart pounding with excitement, he burst through the doors. The table by the red fire extinguisher was empty. His heart sank. He looked at his watch. Shook his head. *Bloody idiot*, he thought. She's got patients to see. There's no way she could wait around for over an hour hoping to see him. He laughed out loud and headed for the car park.

***

Three hours later they were sitting in the Chestnut Horse, a steak in front of Jack, a sea bass winking at Francine. She sensed his unease. "What's wrong, Jack?"

"Just can't quite believe this is happening."

"Well, thank your lucky stars it is. It could have gone the other way this afternoon. But as I said at Caffe Nero, all is forgiven. New slate, no hang-ups, no going back on your word."

"I promised."

"And I'm deliriously happy. A fool perhaps, but if that's the case I'm glad I'm a fool. I love you, Jack, and I never want to lose you. Okay?"

"I think I'm dreaming," Jack confessed.

"No, Jack, you're not. So listen up. Our troubles are behind us, end of story. Now shut up, eat your steak and relax."

Jack wanted to cry.

Francine saw the dampness in his eyes and felt a huge rush of love flow through her. This man was special to her, so bloody special, and between them they had nearly wrecked everything. Oh yes, she was happy to be generous. Suddenly she had an idea. "Look, why don't you come and live at the cottage? You're on your own in that small house and I hate being alone in the cottage. So, how about it?" Francine saw the startled look on his face. "I mean it, I really do. I think it's perfect."

For a moment Jack was struck speechless.

"Do you make a habit of saying nothing?" Francine teased.

"No, no, but you do have a way of surprising me! I certainly wasn't expecting this. It sounds wonderful. It's the best offer I've had for years. And thanks, Francine, from the bottom of my heart."

Francine put a finger on his lips. "What have I just said? All is forgiven."

24

Tank Turnbull spread himself out on the large white sofa and stroked the leather. He looked round the room and winced. The furniture had cost him an arm and a leg, and Tank did not like wasting money. Everything in this room was an insult to his fat wallet. Why on earth the silly mare had wanted to go to Harrods up the West End still mystified him. He could have got the whole lot off the back of a lorry. He hated the West End, felt out of place, just one of a crowd, a nonentity, and Tank hated being a nonentity. On his patch he was king. But there were times when he had to give way to the mare's wishes and trips to Harrods were mercifully few. Even so, as he felt the smoothness of the leather, he could still see the hole in his bank balance and that got him thinking about Jack Carpenter. The pain of losing the money bit deep. But he was already well advanced with his planned revenge. He gave a grunt of satisfaction as he thought of his request to a few who owed him a favour. The response had been positive, not that he'd expected anything else. No one said no to Tank when he was asking. Already he'd heard the Winchester project was in trouble but he still had his ace to play and one telephone call would sort it.

★★★

Janet Goodchild's mind was constantly churning, telling her that she was Jack's guardian angel. It would be a difficult undertaking, especially now that Francine was on the scene. Would she try to edge her out? She'd thought it through night after night, lying in her bed, in her cramped little flat, with ideas roaring through her head like the Eurostar speeding through the tunnel. Of one thing she was sure: Francine Walker had no idea of the vipers' nest that she'd disturbed. Only she, Janet Goodchild, was aware of the poison that threatened Jack. She had to move before the vipers struck and Francine got her feet under the table. She hadn't loved Jack for all these years to see his life ruined for any longer.

25

Jack was eating his breakfast with Cat as company because Francine had been called out early to a dying patient. He'd moved in six weeks earlier and hadn't regretted it for a moment, though Sophie had heard he'd moved and was constantly leaving vitriolic text messages on his mobile phone. He'd ignored them all.

He'd also learnt a few things about his new daughter, and one was that she was married to her job. There were no boyfriends and very little social life. Her partners in the practice seemed to be the only ones who asked her to their homes, and then he suspected they only talked shop.

She was like a machine – switched on in the morning and turned off sometime at night. He had no doubt that she was a very good doctor but why such lack of a social life? She was pretty – well, he thought she was beautiful – she could talk and talk and her smile was infectious. Yet she chose to curl up most nights in front of the telly or read a good book or sit outside in the garden and watch the sunset, all the time followed by a furry object named Cat, for Christ's sake! "This has to change," he confided to Cat. He stroked the soft fur and laughed. Now he was doing the same as Francine and soon Cat would be talking to him!

He looked at his watch. It was time to make for the office but he was tempted to stay and wait for Francine to return. Then he remembered that that was not an option. She'd told him she would be going straight into the surgery. "Ah, Cat, I have another idea. I'll drop into the surgery and suggest we go up to the site once she's seen her last patient." He pushed Cat off the table and chuckled. Six weeks ago if someone had told him he'd be talking to *and* sharing breakfast with a ginger tom of indeterminate age, he'd have said, "Don't be so ridiculous!"

★★★

They were sitting in his car, the windows open: they had discovered that they both liked fresh air when driving, even on the coldest day. Which was just as well as one of them would have been complaining they were getting frostbite. Today, however, there was no danger of that. The sun shone, the air was warm and they both felt content.

"Don't forget I've got to be back at the surgery by two at the latest, will you, Jack?"

"You know I promised you."

"But sometimes you forget the time."

"Only because I like talking to you."

Francine laughed. "Well, I'll make sure that mouth of yours doesn't get carried away."

"Thanks."

The site was above Winchester. Four years ago the fields had provided grazing for a herd of cows but then the consultations, the public enquiries, the arguments over the value of the fields and the reluctance of a farmer to sell unless the developers paid him a king's ransom had left the once green area a mess of old grass, brambles and rabbit holes. From the fields you could look down on most of the city, with the cathedral spire dominating the scene. Today, the city was shimmering in the sunlight. "It's beautiful up here, Jack. I can see why people got so upset about this being turned into a mini town. How lucky that you felt the same and put most people's concerns to rest. You are a very popular man."

"I didn't do this for my ego – I did it because I love this area and hated the thought of a large development springing up in this last rural area for miles. Okay, my plans will not suit everyone, but they are a lot better than a concrete mass."

Francine nodded as they pulled up outside the portakabin which served as the site office. Once out of the car she looked around. "Wow, this is quite something, Jack. I can see why you are so excited about it."

There was no line after line of houses being built, no sign of the foundations for large office blocks or shops. Just a vast area of new grass. Jack took her hand. "When finished, there will be a cricket pitch, two football pitches, low-level stands and a cricket pavilion. Behind this will be new trees, a children's play area and plenty of space for the good people of Winchester to come up here on a warm summer's day for a picnic. There will be some houses – I think they are called affordable houses these days, but no shops or restaurants. Nothing to take business away from the city."

"Oh, Jack, this is wonderful. So generous. It must be costing you a bomb. Are the council really paying nothing?"

Jack looked around him with pride. "Not a penny, Francine. This is my baby, my thanks to God for bestowing so much luck on my shoulders. Just hope He remembers when I get up there."

Francine chuckled. "I'm sure you will be well rewarded. I don't think I have felt so happy for years. Now, come on, show me around. It all looks very impressive."

"Okay, I'll just get my site manager. He's having a worrying time. We're behind on our hoped-for completion date. There have been long delays in vital material being delivered, which is very aggravating. It will workout okay but I pride myself on getting a job done on the date I promised. But that is no comfort to him. I think he's a bit like you actually – wedded to his job. Never relaxes. I keep telling him he's heading for an early grave."

At that moment the portakabin door opened and Timothy Stafford stepped out.

"Ah, Tim, at last a chance to meet my daughter; sorry I've kept her a bit of a secret." There was a startled cry behind him. Tim went white and the smile froze on his face. He stared at Francine in horror. Jack whirled round and saw Francine holding her head in her hands. "What on earth...?"

Francine's cry interrupted him. "Tim!" Then she turned and ran.

Jack looked at Tim. "What the hell?"

Tim found his voice. "Jesus!" was all he could say.

Jack turned and started to run after Francine. She'd got a good start and she was fit. He realised he'd never catch her but he kept running. She would have to stop when she reached the car, or would she? "Francine, Francine, wait!" he cried breathlessly. But if she heard him she kept running.

Panting hard, with his chest feeling as if it would burst, Jack ran on. As he saw Francine reach the car park he slowed down. She was standing by his car, but as he got closer she turned and ran away towards the road. On the road she stopped again and turned to face Jack. "Leave me alone," she gasped.

"No, Francine, we need to talk. Calm down please and tell me what is the matter?" He took a tentative step towards her, holding out a hand.

She never saw the car hurtling towards her.

Jack spotted it seconds before it would have cut her down. He threw himself at her, pushing her away from danger.

The car hit him, throwing him into the air. He bounced off the windscreen and fell onto the grass verge.

The car roars off.
Then blackness.
He doesn't hear her scream.

★★★

Tom Jackson drove the stolen Renault into a field, three miles from the site. Fingerprints were wiped clean. Then he took a last look round the interior to make sure he'd left nothing that could incriminate him. He'd read about how they could trace you from a single strand of hair. He slammed the driver's door, took off his yellow plastic gloves and shoved them in his trouser pocket and walked away. He'd failed: he'd seen Jack Carpenter fly into the air. How was he to know he'd be a fucking hero! His employer was a nasty individual at the best of times, would be mightily pissed off and that was not good for him, not good at all. He knew the man's reputation well. After all, he'd worked for him for three years. His job, as he called it, was to eliminate anyone, regardless of religion, sex or age, if they got in his employer's way. Like trying to take over his prostitution racket or, worse, his drug dealing. Tom liked to call himself the Terminator but his employer called him Jacko, which upset him somewhat as he saw himself as the best professional killer in the whole of the United Kingdom, and he thought he deserved better than Jacko. But he still called himself the Terminator, even though there wasn't a soul on earth who knew who he was. And that had always been a disappointment. He would have liked people to be afraid of him. Even those he killed never saw his face, as he always shot them in the back of the head and he always wore a green balaclava. Anonymity was vital in his line of work, so he had to be satisfied just to be a face in the crowd. Besides, he shouldn't complain, the money was great. And now that he'd lost his cover job as Jack Carpenter's chauffeur and Mrs fucking Carpenter's bed companion he needed financing.

He felt the damp under his armpits as he moved back onto the road and started to walk towards Winchester, to a flat that he'd bought as soon as he'd got the job with his employer. It was his hideaway in case of trouble. Full of enough tinned food to keep him from starving for a week. No one knew he lived there and no one had the telephone number. If he used his mobile he never rang from the flat. In fact, he was pretty sure he was as good as invisible. If, and that was a big if, he got back to the flat without his head being severed from his body, he could make plans. England wasn't big enough for him to hide. There would be a price on his head. His employer never kept a man or woman who'd failed him. He'd lie low for a week and then run. He swore under his breath as he started to walk. He'd always told himself that one day death would catch up with him and it wouldn't be peacefully in bed.

But he wasn't ready to die. Fuck you, Jack Carpenter.

PART THREE
THE RECKONING

26

He looks down on her, no pity in his eyes. They are cold and she shivers. It was not what she'd expected. Yes, it was a shock for him, but what about her? He hadn't got a growing embryo inside him. He wouldn't have the humiliation of having to tell his mother. He was a man and, as she already knew, men could walk away. She looks up at him as he stands over her. She pats the bed. "Please, Tim, come here. We need to talk." He looks at her as if she has some infectious disease and her eyes fill with tears. "Please sit with me," she begs. He shakes his head. "You silly fucking bitch, why didn't you take precautions?"

"Because," she cries, "we agreed it would be you to do that."

He laughs, a hard unfriendly laugh. "But you should have known that one night I might forget."

She wants to shout, 'How could I know, for Christ's sake, Tim? How could I know we'd come back from a party and make drunken love?' But she doesn't, because in a way he's right. She snivels and watches him recoil. This is not the Tim she loves: this is some monster she's frightened of. She whispers, "What are we going to do?"

His voice shows no compassion. "You get rid of it, of course."

"But it's our child."

"Wrong, it's your bastard. I want nothing to do with it. Get rid of it now."

"Why are you being so cruel?"

"Think what you like, Francine, but it has to go. I'm too young to be woken by some brat and change nappies in the middle of the night. Besides, I don't love you enough."

"You what!"

"I don't love you enough."

"Please, please say that's not true, Tim."

"I can't lie."

She looks down at her naked stomach, imagining the tiny embryo starting to grow. Something she imagined that at some time in her life would fill her with joy. Not this, not this rejection by the father. Her eyes widen in fear. "So what are you going to do?"

"Finish with you. We've had our fun and you've fucked up. Do what you like, if you must, with that thing in your stomach but don't come begging to me for support. Get rid of it Francine. It's your only option."

"Option!" she screams.

He doesn't bother to reply, just shrugs and turns away and walks out of her room, just as if he was leaving a stranger. All-consuming grief envelops her. She rests her hands on her stomach and wonders what it feels like to become a murderer. She rolls over on the bed and sobs.

27

Francine had always thought that nothing could ever match the mental torment that raged for months after the abortion of her baby. There had never been any choice once Tim Stafford had walked away. Her mother would have been incapable of giving her the support she needed and her grandparents would have turned their backs on her. She was eighteen and on her own. Now, after all these years, Tim had appeared like some threatening ghost from the past and immediately caused another serious crisis, which was close to being on-par with her abortion.

It should have been her lying in hospital with broken bones. Or more likely lying on a slab of concrete dead and naked, with various parts of her body being cut away for examination. Jack's quick thinking had saved her. The first twenty-four hours had been horrendous but now he was out of danger and the doctors had said he'd make a full recovery. The only damage would be that he'd walk with a slight limp. Francine sat in a chair by his bed, which she had hardly left since the accident. She'd spent the hours praying, crying and cursing Tim. She'd asked Janet Goodchild to move into her cottage to look after Cat, and made arrangements with her long-suffering partners to bring in yet another locum to cover for her. She wondered when their understanding would run out.

She heard footsteps outside the room and turned to look at the door. A tall slim blonde walked in with an air of superiority.

Francine stared at Sophie Carpenter. Sophie stared at Francine. The atmosphere was electric.

Sophie was the first to regain her composure. "You must be the long lost daughter, come to see Daddy, no doubt wondering if he's had time to change his will. I don't think I want you here. So please go."

Francine stood, thinking, *So this is the wife, living up to her reputation.* Her voice was low and calm; it was alien for her to be aggressive but her stomach was churning as she replied, "I was wondering when you'd find time to come, Mrs Carpenter." She pointed at the sleeping figure in the bed. "Your husband was close to death but did you care? I'm surprised you've found time to come and see him now. If he'd died, which was a possibility, would you even have bothered to have found the time to come and say goodbye? So I'm not budging. You can stay here as long as you like but you will have me for company, and if you want to stoop so low, you can ring a bell and make a fuss. I really don't care."

Sophie took two steps backwards. She was not used to being defied. She opened and closed her mouth like a fish out of water. Finally she spluttered, "Who the fuck do you think you are? You can't tell me what to do. I'm Jack's wife." She pointed dramatically at the bed. "I only have his word for it that you're his daughter. He says you're not his mistress but I suspect you're an imposter after his money." Then pointing at the door she shouted, "So get out!"

Francine folded her arms in front of her and moved to within a few inches of Sophie's startled face. She could smell gin. It was obvious that Sophie was up for a fight but Francine ignored the temptation to let rip, and said, "From what I gather, you are not part of his life anymore, and the only way I'm going to leave here is if security throw, me out. I've watched over Jack ever since he was brought in here and twice I've thought he was going to die. And where have you been? Not worrying about Jack, that's for sure." Then plucking up every ounce of courage she possessed, she said, "I think it's you who should go. This poor injured man lying here means nothing to you except for being a cash register. I suspect you might even have liked him to die. Okay, now call security if you want."

Sophie's cheeks reddened and she spluttered, "How dare you say that. I love him!"

"I'm sure."

"Bitch!" Sophie shouted. "I'll be back, and then you had better not be here. That man is still my husband." With that she turned on her heels and rushed out of the room.

Francine found herself shaking. She had no idea she had so much courage. She allowed herself a smile. In some way the confrontation had done her good.

But the feeling didn't last.

Timothy Stafford walked through the door.

Francine gasped, and glared at him. "God, another unwanted intrusion! This is not a good time, Tim; just go!"

Tim stood his ground. "I'll go once you've heard me out. There are things I need to say to you."

"What, that you're sorry for being so terribly cruel? That you're sorry you walked away and left me to kill our child? Are you going to say that, Tim? Are you here to beg my forgiveness? Because if so, this is not the time."

"So you didn't have the baby?"

"Oh what a shit you are. Did you never think to find out? Didn't you want to know if you were a father? What sort of man are you, Tim? Were you shaking in your shoes that I'd produce our off-spring out of the car when you saw me at the site?"

Tim looked down at the floor, his voice hardly audible. "Do you know I almost hoped you would?"

"Liar!"

"I think of you a lot."

"What, as one of your conquests no doubt, but never a thought about the baby. You never tried to get in touch. You didn't once wonder what had happened to that girl who loved you, did you? Don't try and deny this. You're soulless, Tim, bloody soulless."

Tim hung his head. "I'm ashamed, really ashamed, and I beg for your forgiveness. But that is not the only reason why I'm here. Another time, if you will give me a chance, I will tell you how I've suffered."

"Suffered? Suffered! Oh you poor poor thing! How can you say that! You don't know the meaning of the word. What the hell do you think I've done? So why don't you get down on your knees, right this moment, and apologise for being a shit?"

"The police think someone tried to kill you," Tim blurted out. "They want to talk to you and, when possible, to Jack."

Francine dropped back onto the chair. "What? Who would try to kill me? Come on, Tim, I'm a doctor. I may have a few wacky patients but none would go that far. It was a hit and run I agree, but not deliberate."

Tim shrugged. "Well, the police think otherwise. Thanks to one of our eagle-eyed workers he said the car was parked with its engine running and as soon as you came out onto the road it roared forward. If Jack hadn't reacted fast you would more than likely be dead."

"You don't need to tell me that." Then shaking her head she said, "I thought that at last Jack and I were close to being

156

able to live normal lives. Then you turn up and Jack nearly gets killed. He has a family who don't seem to care if he dies, and without a doubt they hate me." Her hand flew to her mouth. "You don't think…?

"Nothing would surprise me about that family. The police are looking into all possibilities and that is why they want to talk to you as soon as possible. They think you were followed to the site. The police think the driver was waiting for a chance to hit you or smash into Jack's car as you were leaving." He looked over at Jack. "How is he, Francine?"

Francine took a deep breath. "He's been lucky. His body took a fearful battering. He's covered in bruises and lacerations. Luckily his head struck the grass verge, not the tarmac."

"Sounds like he was *very* lucky. I can't see him dealing with paralysis very well."

"Nor me." Then she pointed a shaking finger at Tim. "You and I are to blame for this. If you hadn't walked out of that office I wouldn't have run and Jack would still be fit and well. We've killed one child and nearly caused the death of a wonderful man. We're poison, Tim. Please get out."

"I don't know what to say Francine, except to suggest that if someone was out to kill you they would have found another time."

"I think the police are wrong and now you've told me, I want you gone, Tim. Please."

Without another word Tim left. For a moment Francine stared at the door. The shock of seeing him again was still hurting. It was hard to take on board that he was working for her father. How strange could that get? She'd thought she'd never set eyes on him again, then fate had intervened and old wounds were opening. And… She felt a tremor pass through her. For a moment she'd looked into his eyes and realised how much she'd once loved him. She bit her lip. *No, no, don't go down that road, Francine.* She forced Tim out of her mind and

157

wondered what she'd done to deserve so many kicks in her guts. And had someone really wanted to kill her? She laid her head on the hospital bed and closed her eyes. She was desperately weary. A strange feeling of peace came over her as she felt Jack's warmth through the sheets. For how long she stayed there she never knew but at some stage a hand reached out and touched her face.

★★★

Taffy sat in his usual chair outside the restaurant. He had a copy of the *Hampshire Chronicle* in front of him. He would never waste money on a paper. After all, there were no goings-on in the world that interested him. If there was a nuclear war tomorrow and the whole world was destroyed, he'd be overjoyed, but he'd found the paper in one of the rubbish bins that helped to keep him alive. Normally, he'd have discarded it, but he'd caught the name Carpenter on the front page, so in curiosity he'd tucked it under his arm.

Now he sat sipping his coffee. He was stunned. Jack Carpenter was in hospital, the victim of a hit and run driver. The police were making enquiries. Taffy shook his head and wondered if any of his family were to blame; after all, Jenny had made no attempt to hide her hatred of her father. Should he mention this to the law like a good citizen? He gave what passed for a laugh. Him go to the filth! What a joke. Not fucking likely. What did he care if Jack Carpenter was dead or alive. His type cared shit for men like him. He scratched at his beard and shook his head, wondering what on earth had just passed through his mind. He mumbled to himself as he licked the taste of coffee off his fingers and looked up and down the street, wondering if Jenny might appear. He was already missing her. And then a rare stab of conscience hit him. If she didn't come to him then he must go and find her. Already she might be in a black bag, just another girl who had thought it was easy to make money off shitty, sex-starved men. He took a dirty handkerchief from a trouser pocket and dabbed at his eyes. He stood, swayed, hitched up his trousers with his frayed braces, belched and was ready for another day.

★★★

Tank Turnbull read the news and cursed loudly. It had been a fuck-up. No one was going to die. His plan had been to kill Francine so that Jack would suffer. How did he know that Jack was going to turn out to be a fucking hero? But the outcome was bad. His planned revenge had gone up the swanny. Jack had always been a thorn in his side, ever since their childhood days. Better at footy, braver in the street fights, and as time passed reminding him that honest people could succeed, and Jack had certainly done that. His success had really got under his skin and, if he was honest with himself, he was jealous. And now Jack had cheated death and ended up a hero – Jesus, was there no justice in the world? He'd have to put up with the media praising Jack and no doubt listing his successes and his rise from the gutter. Tank slapped his thighs in fury; well, there was one person who would not survive this cock-up. A cocky little weasel who he suspected was already on the run. He really would have to pick his assassins more carefully in the future.

★★★

Harry was disappointed that his father wasn't going to die. It would have solved most of his problems. No need to beg bastards like Turnbull for money. He'd be flush with the greenbacks, able to buy a new car, polo ponies and take girls on holiday. He walked slowly past a car showroom and stared at a shining new Jaguar. If only… "I wish you'd died, Father," he said quietly.

★★★

Tom Jackson hurried towards the Tesco supermarket on the Winnall Estate. He hadn't planned to break cover quite yet but he needed some vital provisions. He cursed his stupidity: anyone could have told him that milk wouldn't keep forever. So here he was doing exactly what he'd planned not to do: leaving his flat and walking openly in the streets. As he walked he kept looking behind him, telling himself at the same time that no one knew where he was – certainly not his employer. Nevertheless he was nervous as hell. Once inside the supermarket he hurried to the shelf where the milk was – grabbed three cartons of full milk, two blocks of butter and a loaf of Hovis brown bread. Then moved quickly to a checkout. "Made it," he said softly as he headed back to his flat.

Half an hour later he was climbing the stairs to his sixth-floor flat. As he reached for his keys he saw that the door was open. His brow wrinkled. *Idiot,* he thought. He walked into the small hallway and found himself staring at the large figure of Tank Turnbull. He was waving Tom's passport in his face. "Going somewhere, Jacko?"

Tom dropped the bag of provisions and said nothing.

Tank gave a throaty chuckle. He knew he was going to enjoy this a good deal more than Tom. "Didn't think I'd find you, eh?" he growled. "Well, let me tell you something before you leave this earth. You shouldn't have told that whore from the pub, who you have been shagging since you left Mrs Carpenter's bed, about your little hideaway. She couldn't wait to tell me when she heard there was money to be earned if anyone knew where you were. But you couldn't help yourself, you fucking fool, could you? You wanted to boast – probably suggested that you and she should come here one day and have a bit of you know what. As you are well aware, I can't tolerate failures. I wanted Jack's daughter dead. You cocked it up. You couldn't even kill your ex-employer. So I'm telling myself, if you can't be trusted to do a simple job like that, you are worthless to me. Anything to say?"

Tom looked down at the milk flowing out of the dropped cartons and fell to his knees. "Please, Mr Turnbull, please have mercy on me. How was I to know Carpenter was going to be a hero? How was I to know his head would strike the grass verge not the tarmac? I've served you well. I would never shop you, honest. Give me another job and I'll show you how loyal I can be."

Tank kicked at a block of butter and pulled Tom up by his hair. "Loyalty has got nothing to do with this. You knew the score when I employed you. Fail and you die. I'm sure you haven't forgotten that, you snivelling gutless rat. So stand up like a man and take your punishment."

Tom turned to run, but standing in the doorway was a huge man. "You're going nowhere," called out Tank. "Right Terry, out with him through the window. A drop of six floors should do the trick."

Tom screamed.

Tank laughed.

Terry heaved.

★★★

Jenny drained the last dregs of the bottle of vodka that she'd opened as soon as she'd woken, and it was only mid-afternoon. By night-time she'd be unconscious and hopefully on her way to a painless death. She was useless, a burden on society, there was nothing to live for, she told herself. She rested her back up against the wall of WH Smith on Winchester High Street and tried to focus on the people passing by, wondering if one of the men in the crowd could be the one who had slammed her up against a wall the night before. She'd driven a knee into his crutch and fled in panic. So much for her new career. She was hungry and bursting for a pee. But she wasn't sure she'd get the short distance to the public toilets without falling flat on her face and wetting herself. She crossed her legs and did the best she could to concentrate on trying to focus. But her eyes were misting over and her mind had already shut down. "Help!" she slurred, as she slumped to the pavement and urine flowed from under her skirt. She closed her eyes and hoped for death.

The next thing she was vaguely aware of was an arm being put round her waist. She tried to fight it off but the grip was too firm. She heard a voice whispering in her ear. "Come on, Jenny, let's get you out of here before the cops arrive."

Taffy had found her.

★★★

Janet Goodchild stirred the scrambled eggs in the saucepan and winked at Cat. She'd quickly learnt the way to his heart – food, lots of it. She was beginning to get quite fond of this mangy ginger tom. She felt a slight stab of guilt at the loss of her irritating budgy but she was sure he'd felt no pain. Anyway, what was she supposed to do? She couldn't have brought him with her, not with a cat about. So, left alone, he'd have suffered a prolonged death. She spooned out a quantity of egg onto a plate, buttered a piece of bread and sat down at the table. She had no appetite. Her visit to see Jack earlier in the day had been traumatic. She'd been slightly miffed to find Francine there; she'd wanted time on her own with Jack, to hold his hand, to kiss his face, to whisper her love, things which she'd never been able to do. Looking at him, all wired up, his eyes closed and both arms in plaster made her realise how deep her love was. She'd collapsed into Francine's open arms and sobbed.

★★★

That evening as she sat on the bench in Francine's garden waiting for her to return from the hospital, her mind began to race and it came as no surprise to her that if Jack had died, part of her would have died with him. Never to see his smile again… She choked back the tears. There was no guarantee that at some time in the future his life might not be threatened again, by illness or by an accident.

Time was being wasted.

She ran her fingers through her hair, looked across the river at a herd of cows grazing contently, their tails swishing in the air to keep away the flies, and wished she was sitting with Jack. Not alone, not angry, not plotting. Suddenly she jumped up from the bench and rushed panting indoors, ran up the stairs and burst into the spare room. She swore she could still smell Jack's scent. She shivered. She undressed and looked at her naked body in the mirror and wondered if it was good enough for Jack. With her body tingling with sexual arousal she moved to the cupboard where several of his shirts hung on hangers. She chose a white cotton one. She slipped into it and sighed. "Oh Jack," she whispered. She walked to the bed and slipped under the duvet. God, the smell of him! She wrapped the shirt round her and stretched out on her back. She began to shake. "Jack!" she screamed as a wave of ecstasy flowed through her body.

28

Detective Chief Inspector Daniel Appleman was not a practising Jew, in spite of his brother being a rabbi and his two sisters settled in Israel. His parents had moved to England from Tel Aviv before he was born. He'd never had much time for religion, certainly not as much time as he gave to catching criminals. From earliest childhood all he'd wanted to be was a policeman and in his teens he'd scarcely ever considered any other career. It was not the career that his rather autocratic father had planned for him. Another rabbi in the family would have suited him well and, if not, then a job in the city, where his son would make a bundle of money and give to the poor. There had been long arguments and tempers lost but Daniel could be as stubborn as his father and this was one battle he'd been determined to win. To give old Dad Appleman his due, once he knew he'd lost, he'd supported Daniel throughout his career, even to the point of telling his friends that he was very proud, "of my Jewish policeman".

Daniel was a DCI in Hampshire CID, where six years ago he'd met and married Police Constable Rachael Harris, a striking blonde beauty, tall and leggy, a smile to die for and a devotion to duty. Daniel considered himself a very lucky man, as he'd learnt over his years of service that to marry someone outside the police force could cause complications, which often led to divorce. It was difficult for a wife or girlfriend to expect a normal family life with someone who never knew when he might be called out. Often weekends were suddenly disrupted – even holidays had been known to be cancelled. So, to be married to a woman in the same career was a huge bonus and as he admitted to his parents, "a bit of a gamble".

At thirty-seven, and much to their surprise, Rachael had just given birth to Arty, a small gurgling bundle of fun, and was still on maternity leave. They lived in a three-bedroom house in the village of Morestead, only a few miles from Hampshire CID Headquarters at Tower Hill, Winchester. Much against his better judgement and his pride, Daniel had been persuaded by his father-in-law to accept a loan to buy the house. So, no mortgage and no time limit to pay off the debt. Sometimes he wondered what revenge his father-in-law might extract if he ever dared to leave Rachael. It was a white thatched detached cottage with a small garden overlooking fields where for most of the summer a small herd of Jersey cows grazed. Daniel, who had been brought up in a city environment, had soon grown used to the early morning mooing on summer days, the smell of the countryside when it rained, the aroma of the flowers in the summer evenings and the blissful peace that surrounded them. It was a haven, where for a few hours most days they could push work to the back of their minds. "And now," Daniel enjoyed telling his friends, "the arrival of our son has put the icing on the cake."

Daniel seemed to have developed a constant yawn. Arty had a good pair of lungs, especially in the dead of night, but he was not one to turn over in bed – he'd promised Rachael he'd be a hands-on father – perhaps he should have added, "as long as my job allows me". He stretched his six foot lanky frame, set his square jaw, pulled out a comb from his blue suit jacket pocket and brushed back his dark hair – no sign of baldness yet. He was good looking with a rather stern expression, which seemed to be saying, *don't mess with me and I will be fair to you.* If asked what she liked best about him Rachael would say it was his flashing blue eyes and his sense of humour. "But don't underestimate him," she'd add. "He's a copper through and through, and a very good one."

That was a judgement shared by his superiors and those who worked with him. New officers were told that "Appleman is a no nonsense copper. Universally liked and respected, and the sort of copper we would all like to be. And let me tell you he doesn't care a stuff for political correctness. He sees his role as keeping the streets of Winchester safe for law-abiding citizens." There were several men residing in Her Majesty's Winchester prison who would reluctantly agree with that.

This morning he'd risen early – downed a mug of black coffee and promised a sleepy Rachael that he'd do his best not to be too late tonight, but he wasn't feeling hopeful. There was a pile of files on his desk and several reports of the Carpenter hit and run. A funny one that. But today, he also had a personal concern nagging away at him. Rachael was getting a little like one of those police wives who felt deserted. Their weekend plans had been disrupted and she'd definitely been frosty when he'd given her the news that he'd be working, but she knows the score, he told himself. So what was eating her? He suspected it was Arty. She was tied to the house – a new experience for her – and always tired. The coming weekend with her parents was going to be a time when, for a few peaceful hours, they were going to take over, and Daniel had promised himself to take her out to dinner. As he sat down at his desk he realised it was a promise he should never have uttered to Rachael.

He picked up the report of the Carpenter hit and run from his desk and started to pace his small, rather drab office. He knew Jack well, might even call him a friend, though he had to be careful not to cosy up too much. He'd seen officers' careers cut short by getting too friendly with influential men. He'd done his homework on Jack Carpenter. He'd learnt it was useful to know a bit of history about prominent high-profile businessmen, who lived and worked on his patch. He admired men like Jack. Rising from a tough working class background he'd fought his own battles, never, as far as he knew, resorting to blackmail, bribes or coercion. According to those who knew Jack better than he did, Jack had battled against predators at the start of his journey to success, who thought he'd weaken under pressure. But they had underestimated the young man and, as Daniel knew, he was now running several huge companies, invested wisely, was wealthy and ready to share this wealth with those less fortunate than himself.

Pity about his family though. It was something Daniel knew he would never understand. How could you alienate your wife and children to the point they wished you harm? It just didn't seem to fit Jack's personality. But it was a fact and something that up until now Daniel considered none of his business. Not now. For the first twenty-four hours after the the car had hit Jack it had seemed reasonable to suspect one of his children, however improbable that might have seemed.

A call from a very hysterical woman confirmed his doubts. On reaching the block of flats on the outskirts of Winchester, he'd found the body of what turned out to be Jack's ex-chauffeur, Tom Jackson, and once he had been directed to the sixth-floor flat by the middle-aged Asian woman still on the verge of hysteria, it became obvious that Jackson had intended to either harm or kill Jack's daughter. The search of the one-bedroom flat had proved most enlightening. Under a mattress the search team had found twenty envelopes, each containing one thousand pounds in fifty pound notes, a passport, and a black diary listing the names of three men in London and Francine Walker. He had immediately contacted Scotland Yard.

The information received back left little doubt that Jackson was a hired killer, but who he was working for was an unsolved case and would probably remain so. The men murdered in London were Romanian drug dealers, no doubt trying to muscle on to someone's patch. So the link with Doctor Walker was a mystery.

But three hours later, sitting up in his hospital bed, Jack had no hesitation in pointing a finger at Tank Turnbull. "You know, Daniel, the man you had in custody for a short while along with his son."

Daniel nodded. "But why your daughter?"

"Revenge, for getting the better of him. He wanted to hurt me. And in typical Turnbull fashion he got someone else to do his dirty work. That's why he's still a free man."

"Any ideas why your ex-chauffeur is dead?"

Jack moved in the bed and winced – the pain was not allowing him to forget his lucky escape. "Because he failed to complete his contract, simple as that. Turnbull does not like failures."

"Wow, a hard man to work for."

"Worth the risk for the money I suspect. So there is your man, Daniel. You won't nail him because you will have no proof he was involved and a corpse isn't going to tell you anything. Interview Turnbull and he will smile, raise his hands and give you a hurt look. *'Now, Chief Inspector, please, would I do something like that? I'm a law-abiding citizen,'* he'll say, leaving you tempted to drive your fist into the man's fat belly."

★★★

Daniel lowered himself into his chair to wait for his PA, or as she was known in these crazy politically correct days, his management support assistant, Julia Sullivan. A rather quiet, plain, middle-aged lady, with short-cut black hair, and wide green eyes which seemed permanently to radiate a look of insecurity. She'd worked with him ever since he'd arrived in Hampshire, and was indispensable, making sure he never missed a meeting, always having his files in order by the time he came into the office. (He was known for his untidiness.) This morning, as she walked into his office with her usual smile of apology on her face, he knew she was going to give him news he did not want to hear.

"Good morning, Chief Inspector."

"Hello, Julia. Good weekend I hope?"

"If you want to know, it was shit."

Damn, thought Daniel, *I've put my foot in it.* Julia would not have had a good weekend. Her mother was ill, her dog had died the week before, and her long-time boyfriend (who Daniel thought she was well rid of) had walked away from their relationship. "I'm sorry," he mumbled. "I should have known better than to ask."

Julia shrugged, "No worries, it's all over now. Dog buried, boyfriend gone and Mother getting better, so not all bad news."

"Well, I was a moron nevertheless to ask. Now you are going to tell me I'm going to have a stressful day."

"Certainly this morning. You have a meeting with the chief constable. He's set up a press conference for midday and wants you with him"

"The chief constable! Why is he doing this? It's not normal for him to take a press conferences for an attempted murder."

"Well, I suspect it's something to do with Jack Carpenter. He's very much a celebrity in this area at the moment."

"Well, it's always the famous or rich who get the notice. Nothing changes sadly."

Julia Sullivan decided to say nothing. She knew Daniel felt that all victims had the right to the same amount of attention, not just the rich and famous. She said, "The chief constable is in the next room waiting for you."

"Okay, let's have the file and I'm on my way." Armed with the files, Daniel moved out of his office and walked into the one next door. "Sorry, sir, if I've kept you waiting," he apologised to Chief Constable George Blackwell, a large, ruddy faced ex-uniform copper, looking forward to his retirement in a few years' time. He had little hair left and he was going to fat. He drank little, but when at home he and his wife smoked heavily and when at work he smelt of tobacco. Daniel respected him. He was always ready to listen and give support if he thought it necessary. But above all else, what Daniel liked about him, was that he recognised what a very difficult environment his officers worked under these days.

"Morning, Chief Inspector."

"Morning, sir. Didn't expect you."

Blackwell smiled. "Well, you know how it is, Appleman, we have to show concern for those who help the city. I thought Carpenter merited my support."

Daniel said nothing.

Blackwell was not slow to pick up on Daniel's silent disagreement. If he'd still been in uniform he'd have felt the same. "Anyway, here I am," he continued, "and we've only got a few minutes before going into the lion's den, so fill me in just in case I've missed something."

And that's what Daniel did. "Looks like a dead case to me," commented Blackwell once Daniel had finished. "The perpetrator is dead so he can't shed any light on the case. Jack Carpenter seems to think he knows why his daughter was attacked. Ms Walker is still alive, Jack is going to recover and this man Turnbull has disappeared. Any family?"

"I'm told there is a son as bad as he is and a wife who would be dead if she shopped either of them."

"Looks like a dead case to me."

"My very thoughts, sir."

"Then let's go and tell the wolves this very thing. You lead, Chief Inspector. Looks as if I might be going to have an easy ride."

29

Taffy sat by the bed holding her hand. He couldn't remember if he'd ever held a woman's hand before. He felt awkward but nothing was going to make him let go. For the first time in his life there was someone who depended on him, or that's what she'd told him before she'd passed out. "Come on, Jenny, time to wake up," he slurred into her ear. He was not the only one who was getting concerned, and the decision to take her to hospital was getting closer by the minute. It terrified Taffy. He'd never see her again. She'd end up either dead or in prison being abused by other women. Oh yes, Taffy wasn't all dumb. He knew what went on in women's prisons to attractive young girls. Well, Jenny wasn't all that young but she was pretty.

"How's she doing, Taffy?" a voice asked over his shoulder.

He jumped, then turned his bloodshot eyes on the woman standing beside him. "Sleeping."

Mary Slater, small in stature, with short greying hair and green eyes, wearing a pair of blue trousers and a thick woollen jersey over a white blouse, was large on compassion. She'd worked in the shelter for the last five years. She'd watched her husband die an alcoholic at the age of fifty-six and it had almost broken her heart, but Mary was resilient, and when one of her friends had suggested volunteering for charity work, she'd opted for work in a shelter, rather than a tempting dose of sleeping pills. "After all, many of the inmates are alcoholics and there's not much I don't know about that," was her reply when asked why she'd chosen such a thankless task. Now, as she looked at Jenny she knew the signs. The pallor of her skin was serious cause for concern. A doctor was needed. Mary had discovered very early in her time at the shelter that drop-outs did not get much sympathy at hospitals. The view was that they clogged up the system, and their illness, whatever it was, was of their own making. So Mary had discussed this problem with Francine Walker, who had looked after her husband during the last year of his life. She'd shown a sympathy to the down and outs which Mary had not expected. It had been the beginning of a friendship that eventually had Francine promising that if she was free she would always come to Mary's rescue at the shelter, day or night.

Mary gently moved Taffy out of the way and bent over the bed. "I think it's time I called you a doctor, Jenny. Can you understand that?"

There was no response, not even a flicker of an eyelid. Action was urgently needed. "I'm calling a kind doctor, Taffy, so no need for you to get into a panic. Jenny here needs help."

Through moist eyes Taffy stared at Mary and nodded. There were not many people he trusted but Mary had told him one night, when she was sitting with him on a bed recovering his senses from a very heavy intake of vodka, about her husband and from that moment on, for some reason that he couldn't understand, he felt there was a bond between the two of them. Without uttering a word he moved away from the bed before taking hold of one of Mary's arms. "I don't want to lose her, I like her, she needs me. Please make sure she comes back to me," he begged.

Choosing her words carefully, for she could see that Taffy was on the edge of panic, she said, "I'll do my best, I promise."

She would have liked to have added, "But it will all depend on the doctors." She was close to tears as Taffy said, "I trust you."

★★★

It took Francine a little over half an hour to reach the shelter. She parked illegally outside its door, put the '*doctor on call*' disc by the windscreen, and ran into the hall carrying her medical bag. Mary Slater never rang unless it was urgent. The smell of food mixed with the pungent odour of unwashed bodies hit her nostrils but she was used to much worse smells. She saw Mary standing by a bed and hurried over. "Trouble?"

"Oh thank God you've come, Francine, this girl is very ill. She is drunk and has shown no signs of coming round. And look at her skin. Liver failure, would you say?"

Francine took one look and knew it was urgent to get this young woman to hospital.

"Yes, liver failure for sure. Do you know if she was on drugs?"

"No idea. I haven't seen her here before." Then pointing at Taffy she said, "This man here brought her in."

Francine glanced at Taffy. "Okay, can you ring for an ambulance?"

"Right away." Mary backed away and dialled 999.

Francine turned her attention to the man standing behind her, sniffing loudly. "You obviously know this person... I'm sorry, I don't know your name?"

Taffy wrinkled his nose; he didn't like telling anyone his name unless he trusted them, and he was suspicious of doctors. He shook his head.

Francine looked across at Mary who was talking on her mobile. She mouthed, *name?*

"Taffy," Mary whispered back.

Francine nodded her thanks and turned back to Taffy. "Well, Taffy, it would help if you could tell me as much as you know about her."

Taffy sniffed and stuck out his jaw. He was rapidly going off this woman. It had been cheating to ask his name off his friend. So there was no way he was going to give away confidences, but he knew Jenny was very ill. And he'd watched several inmates die in this room. He shook his head to clear his mind. Without making eye contact with Francine, Taffy mumbled, "I know nothing. Found her in a bad way – took her back here." There was no way he was going to divulge that they were friends.

Francine nodded. She needed a name but sensed she'd get no more from Taffy for the moment. She knew how secretive these people could be. "Thank you, Taffy. Very helpful."

"Ambulance on its way, Francine," Mary said.

"Good. Taffy couldn't tell me much, could you, Taffy?"

He shook his head again.

"Do you know anything about her, Mary? She doesn't strike me as a typical homeless. She looks well fed and her clothes are not the cheap variety."

"Taffy has brought her in here several times in the last few weeks. Always drunk, but then so is Taffy most of the time. I can tell you this is as sober as I've ever seen him. I think it's the effect of shock. He seems very close to this girl. They have formed a rather strange relationship. Unfortunately I only know her as Jenny."

Taffy was beginning to think he needed a drink. The thought of being sober was terrifying. He made a decision. "Yes, a friend." Then he blurted out, "She says to me one day. *'My name is Jenny Carpenter and my father is a right shit.'* Then immediately regretting letting out this piece of information he swung round and headed for the door. "Must go, getting thirsty." He already had the shakes.

Francine felt her heart leap into her mouth and she gasped. "Jenny Carpenter," she whispered.

Mary saw the worry lines on her face. "You know this woman, Francine?"

Francine struggled to find her voice. "If she's the one I think she is, I know of her, yes. She's my half-sister, but you don't want to hear about that right now. Later perhaps. And why she's in this state comes as no surprise from what I've been told, but the location does. It seems she might have left home. This is a big problem for me, Mary."

The sound of the ambulance siren didn't give her time to say anything more and her professionalism clicked in. She was a doctor and she had a patient who needed urgent attention. There would be time later for her to ask Jack if he knew his daughter was wandering around Winchester, and probably been sleeping rough for a few days at least.

★★★

Taffy's tears rolled down his cheeks as he shuffled along the pavement. He hadn't meant to blurt out Jenny's name. He was sure it would lead to trouble, and that was the last thing he needed. But worse, she might die and that would hit him hard. So giving her name to the doctor just might help save her life. She was too young to die and she'd brought something into his miserable life. He tripped on the pavement and fell against an unyielding brick wall of a house. He gasped with pain and tried to get to his feet but they had gone to jelly. He managed to push his back against the wall and stretch out his legs across the pavement. He'd have a short rest and then make the effort to stand. His brow furrowed as he realised what was happening: he was suffering the beginning of withdrawal syptoms, and if his last short spell of going sober was anything to go by he was in for a nightmare the likes of which he'd not wish on his

176

worst enemy. Already he could feel the demons in his head laughing. He slapped his face with his hands, saliva dripping from his mouth, and he moaned in agony. He knew what was coming. He made the effort to stand but his legs collapsed under him. He closed his eyes and felt despair. Once again the devil was grinning at him. His arms flayed in front of his face as he desperately tried to fight off the image. But his father would not go away. He was laughing and Taffy could feel the pain, he could see his mother trying to pull his father away, and he could hear his own screams as the pain intensified. He felt his father roll off the bed, but the pain did not die. It felt as if his head would burst.

"Taffy, Taffy, are you alright?"

He opened his eyes, but his brain was scrambled. Was this an angel looking at him? Was he dead? The angel moved a hand, it touched his face: it was warm, so inviting. Was this heaven?

"Taffy, what's wrong?"

He blinked and shook his head, winced with pain and stared at Mary Slater's face. An angel.

Mary realised that Taffy was terribly confused. His startled face told her that he'd visited some nasty place. Sadly, this type of incident was all too familiar to her. Fried brains dished up some terrible hallucinations. She kept stroking his hand, so cold, so scarred and she wondered how this poor man managed to stay alive or why he even wished to. *Foolish*, she thought, of course he wanted to be dead. For several minutes she sat beside him stroking his hand and slowly she saw recognition return.

"Jenny," he croaked.

"No, Taffy, not that friend; it's me, your other friend. Mary."

"Oh Jesus, I've been taken over by the devil."

"No, Taffy, you're safe, as I'm sure is Jenny." She looked at

177

the small crowd that was gathering. It was time to move before the police came on the scene: it would only complicate things. "So let's get you to the shelter. You're in no fit state to be on the street. Think you can make it?"

Taffy gave her a sly look. "If I have a drink."

Mary had long since learnt that it was a waste of breath trying to tell an alcoholic that he or she would be better off sober, especially in an emergency such as this. She'd also learnt that most were more accepting when drunk. She put a hand in her coat pocket and pulled out a miniature bottle of vodka and held it in front of Taffy. She heard a gasp from the crowd. *Well fuck them.* Taffy's eyes watered and he rose painfully from the pavement and held out a shaking hand.

"This is not yours, Taffy, until you promise to come with me."

"I promise."

"Say again."

"I promise, I swear on my mother's grave."

She passed him the bottle and heard murmuring in the crowd. She turned to face it.

"If you can do better you're free to have a fucking go. If not please fuck off, NOW!"

No one stepped forward; no one said a word. Within minutes the crowd had dispersed.

Mary put an arm around Taffy's waist and said, "Come on, let's get you safe."

30

Francine knew it was not the best time to break the news to Jack but she saw no alternative and yes, she was a little angry, but when she saw him propped up on two pillows trying to chew a grape, one arm in plaster and his black right eye going yellow, she managed to hide her anger.

He smiled as she came through the door. "I'm getting fed up being confined to this bed, I've recovered enough to move." Then he saw the frown on Francine's face and the anger in her eyes. "Something's the matter," he stated.

Francine said, "Jack, Jack, Jack, what was it we promised to do? Never tell each other lies or keep secrets." She dropped down onto the bedside chair.

"I've kept my word."

"No, I don't think you have."

"Enlighten me, then."

Francine did her best to control her voice. Anger was going to get her nowhere. "You've never told me that your daughter has gone off the rails so badly that she's now, for want of a better word, a homeless person, walking the streets of Winchester. I've just found her close to death in a shelter. She's now in hospital suffering severe liver failure, from which there is the possibility she won't recover."

"Oh my God! I had no idea, I promise you. I knew she was in a bad way but not this. I didn't know she'd left home. How did you find out that she was so ill?"

"I'm on call for that shelter behind the leisure centre. I have a special arrangement with them. I've just come from Winchester hospital. She's really bad, Jack. But how on earth could you not know? She's your daughter, for Christ's sake."

"Well, I've had a bad accident if you haven't noticed. No, no, that was unfair. The truth is that since I told my family that you were my daughter I've had no contact with any of them. After all, I don't live at home anymore. The news of your arrival on the scene must have pushed her over the edge. Does her mother know?"

Francine shook her head. "How the hell would I know? But I've spoken to Janet and she's going to try and get in touch with your wife. My God, Jack, how did you let your family get in such a mess? It makes me think there's another side to you that I still haven't seen."

"It's a question I've asked myself many times. I've spent hour upon hour trying to work out where I have gone wrong you know, like, do I have a cruel side? I really don't think I do. But obviously I've made mistakes, and the worst one was never being there for them when they were children. Work, not my children, was my priority."

"And Sophie?"

"She was useless. As far as she was concerned it was out of sight out of mind. They became feral, and so to try and make things up to them I lavished them with my new-found wealth. It only made things worse."

"Well, at least I'm beginning to think you're honest."

Jack stirred painfully in the bed. "Thanks. And here I am once again unable to help."

"This is not all your fault, Jack; my only meeting with Sophie in this room leads me to think…"

The door flew open and Sophie burst into the room, all scent, anger and high and mighty. She swung round to look at Francine. "I thought I told you not to come here again. But here you are, no doubt telling Jack that my daughter's illness is my entire fault."

Francine didn't flinch. Sophie was not slow to see the look of contempt that flashed across her face. "I think that that is immaterial at the moment, Sophie, given that your daughter may be dying. But let me enlighten you: if she hadn't made it to the shelter I have little doubt she would be dead by now."

"Shelter, what fucking shelter?" Sophie let out a sort of squeal.

"A shelter for the homeless, down and outs and drunks," Francine continued. "You had no idea, did you, that she wasn't at home, until Janet rang you." Francine's anger was beginning to boil. "You can't even tell me how long she's been gone, can you? And do you know something, Mrs Carpenter, I don't think you care. So don't come waltzing in here, smelling of some expensive scent, dressed as if you're going to Ascot and start accusing me of being responsible for your daughter's wayward ways. I think I'm entitled to say that you only have to look at yourself to know who must share at least half of the blame. But it is not part of my job to judge people. I'm a doctor and my only interest in your daughter is to see she recovers."

Jack clapped.

Sophie stood open-mouthed and ran from the room.

"She's making a habit of that," Francine said.

Jack clapped again. "Wow, Francine, that was spectacular. But if Sophie wasn't your enemy before, she most certainly is now."

"I think clapping is inappropriate."

"Yes, sorry." Jack reached out a hand and Francine took it.

181

They looked at each other in silence until a nurse walked into the room.

★★★

Once out in the hospital car park, Francine breathed in the fresh air and wondered where God was going to take her next. To say she was muddled was an understatement. She'd found her father, hit a high and then had stepped into a storm – she knew she'd have to be strong to withstand its fury. A near death experience caused by a man whom Jack had royally pissed off, a drunken half-sister lying in hospital, and an idle slob of a half-brother were only some of the worries that now assailed her. Life with her mother had never been as traumatic. As she unlocked her car door she wondered if it wouldn't be best to walk away from this turbulent family while she still could. "Shit!" she shouted as she slipped behind the wheel. "This is not what I expected." And then she looked up at Jack's window and suspected he was in shock after her revelations, which meant he needed her support more than ever. It was quite simple really, as she'd told the chief inspector. "Jack needs me and I want a father for better or worse."

Worse was certainly coming out on top at the moment.

★★★

Francine couldn't remember how many times she'd walked into Winchester hospital since becoming a GP but never had she been so nervous. As she hurried along the corridor to the ward, she acknowledged the odd greeting from nurses, without her usual smile. To her disgust she was shaking. Very unprofessional. She was not looking forward to the next few minutes, which could prove very explosive. She'd faced inebriated women before, some aggressive, some weeping, some shouting rape, and some just plain drunk after a night out with the girls. Apart from the latter, she'd felt concern, but she had a feeling Jenny would be something altogether different. If she was conscious and rational she would be hostile for sure. She found herself wishing that another doctor had been called to the hostel. She took a deep breath and pushed the ward doors open.

She was greeted by an agitated ward sister. "Am I glad to see you, Doctor!" Pointing to an empty bed, she gasped, "You'll never guess what has happened."

Francine eyes flew to the bed. "She's done a runner, sister?"

"That's about it. The most terrifying woman I've ever met, and let me tell you I've met quite a few of her sort, barged in here about an hour ago and demanded to take her away. Said she was her mother, waving a piece of paper in my face, which looked like a birth certificate, for fuck sake – excuse my language – and I thought the man with her was the father. I did my best to try and persuade them that their daughter wasn't fit to be moved, even called a doctor to tell them, but they wouldn't listen. 'I'm not having my daughter slumming it in a NHS ward,' this woman shouted at me. Then they more or less pulled the poor girl out of the bed, demanded a wheelchair and left."

"Well, for a start, it couldn't have been the father," Francine told the sister. "He's lying in bed at the Sarum Road Hospital in no fit state to go anywhere. So God only knows who he was. I'm a little surprised the daughter agreed to go with them."

"She was in no state to argue. That's what is so awful. She's very poorly. Sometimes people are shits, Doctor."

"It's not your fault sister, the mother is deranged, and I'm afraid I have no idea what her plans are, but I will try to find out what's going on and of course I will let you know. But remember, this is no fault of yours."

"I should have been more forceful though. She took me by surprise and by hesitating I lost my chance."

"It happens," Francine consoled her. "Now, I'd better go and try to find out what the picture is or I will have a dead body on my hands. I'll be in touch."

★★★

Jack shook his head in disbelief. "Say that again, Francine."

"Sophie waltzes into the hospital and takes Jenny out. I presume she's at home and I've contacted Janet and asked her to check. Hopefully she should ring any minute now. And tell me, Jack, who would be the man?"

"Probably some horny bastard keen to get into my wife's knickers. I expect he was on a promise."

"Unbelievable!"

"It's the way Sophie works: 'Do this and you get a shag!'"

"But this is her daughter's life she's playing with. Has she always been so self-centred?"

"Oh yes! So what do we—"

Francine's mobile rang. "Must take this, it's Janet."

Jack watched her face crease with incredulity. "I don't believe this. Thanks, Janet, I'll tell Jack."

"What, what?" Jack said.

"Well, to quote what Sophie said to Janet, *The ungrateful little cow has fucked off. And before you ask where to, I'll say I have no fucking idea and I don't care.* With that she broke the connection."

"We must find her, Francine; ring the police, they might help. Try everything please. Jesus, I wish I wasn't so immobile."

"I'll get onto it right away."

She wasn't the only person looking for Jenny Carpenter.

31

Daniel Appleman felt some sympathy for Jack Carpenter, who was obviously still weak and in some pain, and no doubt fighting his conscience. His face was drawn and he looked as if he could do with a good natural sleep – none of this self-induced stuff that Daniel disapproved of. By the look of him it was a bad moment to inform him that the police were up against a brick wall. "Your daughter is not a minor and she was only reported missing a few hours ago by her mother."

"Damn it, man," blurted out Jack. "She's been dragged out of hospital, taken home by an uncaring bitch, allowed to walk out the door without any attempt to keep her and because of this she might die. And here you are telling me that nothing can be done. Well, fuck you, Chief Inspector, go and do *something!* Is your budget being cut so much that you can't look for a woman in desperate need of care? Christ, man, she can hardly walk so I'm told. She shouldn't be that difficult to find! Think how you would feel if our roles were reversed and it was me telling you this while you lay incapacitated in this bed."

Daniel nodded. "I'm sorry." Then steeled himself for the next salvo to come from the bed.

Jack did not disappoint him.

"Sorry! Jesus, man, is that all you can say?"

Daniel gave an apologetic smile. "The thing is, Jack, she can't be classed as a missing person. She's a grown woman who left her home of her own free will. I know it sounds cruel but those are the facts. But if she doesn't appear in the next forty-eight hours I'll put out a missing person alert."

Jack scoffed. "But the thing is she didn't leave hospital of her own free will; the nurse on duty has confirmed that."

"But she left her house of her own free will, Jack, there is no argument about that."

Jack winced in pain and shook his head. "I can't believe I'm hearing this. Christ, Daniel, she could be lying in some gutter, dying."

Daniel could only shrug his shoulders. "I'm really sorry, Jack."

"If I hear you say *sorry* one more time I will roll out of this bed and hit you," hissed Jack. "And now you're going to tell me that your hands are tied."

His sarcasm was not missed on Daniel.

Jack's eyes moved to where Francine stood. "So what do we do now?"

Francine, who was standing by the door feeling more and more sorry for Jack, said, "I don't think you can blame the chief inspector, Jack, I'm sure he will do his best. And he has got a point: Jenny walked out of the house of her own free will. I suspect the last thing she wants is to be dragged back home."

"Or taken to the morgue," Jack bit back.

Daniel stood. "Look, I promise I'll do my best, Jack."

Jack stared at him in disbelief.

Thinking there was no point in carrying on a conversation that was only going to go one way, Daniel turned to Francine. "I'll keep in touch."

Francine gave him a small smile. "Thank you, Chief Inspector, you have my mobile. But one other thing, just before you go, I hear that you have given up on my hit and run. But let me ask you this: okay, the perpetrator is dead, but what if this man Turnbull decides he has unfinished business to attend to?"

It was a question that Daniel had asked himself several times. "I'm aware of the danger and all I can say is that we will be alert to the threat."

Jack snorted.

"As you advised me, Jack, we have nothing on him. You might say he's squeaky clean."

"Fuck him," said Jack.

Francine shook her head. "Find Jenny, Chief Inspector, that should be your main priority."

As Daniel closed the door behind him and stepped out into the corridor, he'd been tempted to say, 'There are other more important things for the police to do then go looking for a drunken young woman, who has only herself to blame.' He gave a rueful laugh – thank God his years in the police force had taught him there were times when you kept your mouth shut.

★★★

Taffy understood why Mary Slater had thought it wise to tell him that Jenny was on the wander again but part of him wished she'd kept her mouth zipped. The thought of Jenny wandering the streets concerned him deeply. So here he was shuffling around Winchester searching, searching. Evening was drawing in and he was exhausted and badly in need of satisfying his addiction. But he knew if he quenched his thirst he'd never be able to find her, and he didn't want to give up, so convinced was he that somewhere on a street in the city Jenny lay dying. For the third time that day Taffy reached the King Arthur statue at the bottom of the High Street and rested his weary back against the cool stone. He fumbled in his rucksack for the bottle of vodka that he had lifted the night before from a delivery van outside a pub. He smiled resignedly when he found it empty. *This must be an omen,* he thought; *I am going to find Jenny.* He put the bottle back in his rucksack; no one was going to accuse him of being a litter lout and he could still lick the last drop from the top of the bottle when he'd found her. He scratched the bald patch on the top of his head and tried to concentrate. He feared he couldn't go on much longer. He needed to rest, to eat food and there was no denying he needed some form of alcohol. Tears began to run down his unshaven face and he looked up to the sky and silently prayed for help, knowing it was a fruitless gesture. When had God ever helped him? He felt defeated, a useless drunk man who had been fool enough to allow his emotions to take charge. He closed his eyes, sank to the ground and thought of Jenny. "Where are you, where are you?" he whispered.

32

I'm sitting in the pub, waiting. I'm well aware that by now I'm not the only one looking for the drunken young bitch but I know her habits better than anyone. I pride myself on being a conscientious planner and I know that at around six on most evenings since her pathetic decision to try and become a homeless vagrant, for fuck sake, Jenny has turned up for a much needed visit to the ladies' toilets across the road and then join the old man for a shot of some sort of alcohol by the statue. However, I'm also aware that her pattern has changed since leaving hospital or she could already be dead. But I'm not one to give up easily so here I am back in the pub waiting. Anyway, there is fuck all else for me to do in the evenings except watch some banal show on television and eat yet another curry. It's getting dark and raining hard but the street lights mean I will still see her. I know I should be taking her to that nice policeman, Appleman, and then ringing Jack to tell him his daughter is alive. But Jenny is first on my list and I have no intention of saving her. I watch a copper stroll past the window of the pub – I take a long deep breath. *Don't come round the corner now, Jenny,* I think. But he's soon past, head down against the rain, no doubt thinking of a warm fire and a cup of tea. I heave a sigh of relief and take a sip of my water. No alcohol until the job is done; it confuses me.

I'm longing for a cigarette though, my one serious addiction, but I don't want to go outside because I have a perfect seat by the window and if I move I will lose it. I can already see three young men eyeing me with a look that says, *You should not be occupying a table for four.* Well, tough! However, I'm beginning to feel the onset of despair as there is no sign of Jenny. So maybe she will not be coming, maybe she has made another plan with the old man. I scratch irritably at my crutch I'm not good when things start to go wrong – my frustration builds – my anger seethes. Hold on, there is still time, but the excitement is draining from me.

I'm getting up to go when my breath leaves my body because there she is, weaving round the corner. Close one, I was about to move! And no sign of the old man. That's good; he could have been a nuisance, got in the way, wondered why Jenny had not come out of the toilets. But I must move quickly just in case he turns up. If he sees her, my plan will have to be aborted. She will be pleased to see me, I'm sure of that. I notice she's in a bad way, swaying, finding it difficult to put one foot in front of the other. The rain has flattened her hair against her skull and there is water dripping off her coat. It won't be long before she falls flat on that alcohol-riven face of hers. I'm buzzing again, my skin is tingling. Her eyes are searching the outside tables, no doubt looking for the old man. I throw on my waterproof mac, pull on my thin, black leather gloves and run out of the pub, hunched against the rain. She sees me. She smiles. I put a hand on her arm. I can smell her toxic breath. "Jenny, your friend hasn't come but I'm here. No need to be frightened. I want to help you." For a moment I think she's going to run. This is something I have feared, but she smiles at me again. "I'm a mess," she mumbles. *Not half as much of a mess as you will be soon,* I think. I'll help you," I repeat. "Come on, let's go and get you tidied up and then I will take you home." She stiffens – bad mistake; the word home is the last thing she wants to hear, but I can see she's desperate to trust me. I hold my breath as I put my hand on her elbow. She doesn't resist. I still have her confidence. Now I need to get away from here quickly. The road is quiet, the rain has put people off. I cover my face in my scarf, a precaution if a CCTV camera picks us up; if my planning has been correct I know where to avoid them but you can never be too careful. I walk her down the street towards the public lavatories opposite the King Alfred statue. Still no sign of the old man my luck is holding. I tighten my grip on Jenny's arm. I don't want her to run now that I'm so close to my goal. I lead her into the ladies'. It's empty. One hurdle dealt with. I slam the outside entrance door and hope that that will give out the message that the toilets are closed. Not a hundred per cent, but the best I can do. But if anyone comes in they won't be coming out. Nothing is going to stop me now.

I feel Jenny trying to pull away, she mumbles something, which I don't pick up, but I know I haven't much time before she starts to struggle. For a split second I release my hold on her and then grab her round the waist and ram her against the wall. She's too drunk to cry out or resist. She moans. I punch her hard in the stomach. She doubles up, spewing vomit over her shoes. I hit her again and as she falls against me I let her slip to the floor and then pull out my knife. She's lying on the floor, face down. She's breathing heavily. *Your last few breaths,* I think, as I put the knife between my teeth and bend down to roll her over on to her back. Her eyes are wide with fear. The smell of vomit is very strong. She flays her arms wildly in front of her face. I swipe them away and lunge at her chest. I feel the knife slice through fabric and then flesh: it feels like cutting into a block of fresh butter. I withdraw the knife and thrust

191

again. I'm laughing now, watching the blood flow from her mouth. She's making a weird gurgling sound. I pull the knife out again, tempted to make one last thrust, but soon she will bleed out and her life will come to an end. I'm feeling the urge to stand and watch her blood leave her body but I know I must get away before someone comes in and complicates things. I straighten up, wash the blood off my knife, remove my gloves and take off my waterproof. I grin. I've killed again. It's been a long time. I put the gloves into one of the waterproof's pockets and tuck it up under an arm. I walk out into the street, expecting at any time to be hit by remorse, but that's not what happens. Instead I think how exquisite I feel. I don't want to let the feeling go. I want so badly to be able to hold onto it. The joy of killing has not left me.

33

Jack was glaring at Sophie. He was tempted to slap her face. Her indifference staggered him. She was, as usual, immaculately dressed, and this made his blood boil even more. She was more concerned about her looks than about her daughter. He took a long deep breath, clenched his fists and limped towards her. "Why did you take her out of hospital, for God's sake, and having done that why didn't you keep an eye on her when you brought her back here? You must have known she might do something like this. She's going to die if she doesn't get treatment. Are you going to stand there smirking at me and tell me you don't care?"

Sophie turned her back on him, knowing that he hated that – she was in the mood to bait him. When she spoke her voice was devoid of emotion. "I took her out of that dreadful place because no daughter of mine is going to slum it in some filthy NHS ward or be treated by that slut you call your daughter. As for leaving here, well that was her choice. I would have seen her right." She ignored Jack's disbelieving grunt. "What happens to her now is her responsibility. So the answer to your question, Jack fucking Carpenter, is that I don't care all that much. If she dies, too bad, she will only have herself to blame. And now I'd be grateful if you removed yourself from the house."

Jack stared back at her in amazement. "I'm going nowhere. My God, Sophie, you've plumbed the depths this time. What's happened to you? She's our daughter – she's in desperate need of medical help and support and you stand there and tell me you don't care. She's become what she is because you and I have fucked up this parenthood thing. We are responsible, and if she dies it will haunt me for the rest of my life."

Sophie whirled round and jabbed a finger into Jack's chest. "Then don't waste time talking to me – get on your bike and find her. Now get out, Jack, this is no longer your house and I've got things to do."

"Like dropping your knickers," Jack spat angrily. "You're a monster, Sophie, and I hope you rot in hell."

"Oh piss off, Jack."

As he painfully walked across the drive to his car, Jack thought how churlish his remark about Sophie's knickers had been. But that's what Sophie did to him these days – made him retaliate with stupid digs at her infidelity. "Idiot," he mouthed as he eased himself into his car. He'd stooped to her level at a time when he should have only been thinking of Jenny. He turned the ignition and winced with pain, not sure if he had the strength to drive back to the hospital. A mile down the road he gave up and pulled into a lay-by, turned on his warning lights and dialled Francine's number.

★★★

At two a.m., with the rain still falling, Detective Sergeant Paul Flower pulled up behind Daniel Appleman's unmarked car. He was still rubbing the sleep out of his eyes as, head down, he ran towards the public lavatories at the bottom of Winchester High Street. He slapped his protruding belly, reminding him that it was time to go easy on the beer and chocolates. He was overweight for his five nine frame, and probably putting too much strain on his heart. He brushed back his dark hair – at least that wasn't falling out – rubbed his light brown eyes and took a deep breath. He was late. There were blue lights flashing from four police cars and an ambulance already on the scene. He knew he'd get the usual ribbing from his boss that recently he always seemed to be the last to arrive at a crime scene and perhaps it might be a good idea if he relocated nearer the city, now that he was distracted by the soft warm body of a thirty-something divorcee who lived in the flat below him and who was sharing his bed most nights. It made sense – as did most things his boss said – but he'd have to persuade the warm body to move with him.

"DS Flower, late again," boomed the voice of Daniel Appleman, causing Paul to forget the divorcee very quickly.

"Sorry, boss, I was out to the world."

"And your bed was a little too warm, eh?" Daniel quipped. "Well this should wake you up. Follow me. We've found Jenny Carpenter."

Paul blew out his cheeks. "Alive?"

"I'm afraid she's dead."

"So the drink got her in the end, did it?"

"No, someone with a knife did."

"Christ, who found her?"

"The young lady over there, talking to the police constable. Came in for a pee and wet herself when she saw the body and all the blood. Although hysterical, she managed to ring us. I'll make sure we get her home once she's given her evidence. We found Jenny Carpenter lying on the floor in a pool of blood, with three knife wounds to the chest. Definitely killed here."

Paul slipped on his over shoes and gloves and followed Daniel into the toilets. He stared down at the body and felt he might be sick. This had never changed over the years. 'You're a right softie,' Daniel had once said to him. And that he was – a man who cared about life and couldn't bear to see anyone cut down by some maniac. 'So, I'll go on being a softie,' as he'd told Daniel. 'And I'm not ashamed of it,' he'd added.

"What was she doing in here?"

"Probably either coming to ease her bladder or trying to get out of the rain."

"Or to trade drugs," Flower suggested. "Well, we don't have to put out a missing person bulletin at any rate," he added. "She hadn't gone far, had she?"

"Never thought she would, knowing the state she was in when her mother dragged her out of hospital."

"I hope her mother has a few sleepless nights," commented Flower.

"And the same goes for Jack Carpenter," added Daniel.

"So," asked Flower, "why do you think she was killed?"

Daniel didn't have time to answer, as at that moment Sarah Jones walked into the toilets. "You got here quickly, Sarah," he said, smiling a welcome at the forensic, a pretty middle-aged woman. Sarah Jones returned the smile. "Nasty business this," she said to Daniel as she knelt down beside the body. "At first glance it doesn't look as if the poor woman put up a fight. No bruises as I can see and her hands look fine, no blood under the nails."

"That means she knew her attacker," said Daniel.

"Unless she was so out of it she couldn't put up a fight," said Flower, giving the forensic an appraising look. He'd had a crush on her ever since he'd joined Hampshire CID. Sarah Jones was petite, athletic, had wonderful hazel eyes, and dark hair normally tied back in a pony tail. But he'd known from the start that he was not her type so had never made any attempt at dating her. He'd never been a gambling man. At forty-six he'd resigned himself to bachelorhood, which didn't worry him too much. He didn't care for children; he had a comfortable flat in a large country house eight miles from the city centre, a ten-year-old terrier and three tanks of tropical fish to keep him company. But then along had come the divorcee and his life had changed. Nevertheless, he couldn't stop himself staring at the forensic for a little longer than necessary. She was a knockout. He jumped as he realised Daniel was talking to him.

"This puzzles me," Daniel was saying. "Nothing of value seems to have been taken. Her handbag was on the floor, with her driving licence and credit cards inside, so the killer wasn't bothered about us identifying her quickly. Maybe there was a fall-out over booze that got out of hand."

"Or, as I've just suggested, drugs," said Paul.

"Excellent deduction, Watson," congratulated Daniel.

Sarah laughed, Paul grunted. *The bloody chief inspector making fun of me again,* he thought. But as usual he just shrugged it off and looked at Sarah. "So it was a knife?" he asked.

"A very sharp one at a guess."

"Then we must start looking for it. You never know your luck," said Daniel, turning to Flower. "Make sure the area around is secure, Sergeant, get the grounds searched in case the killer dumped the knife and while you do that I must go and see Carpenter. And here come your SOCO mates, Sarah," said Daniel, as half a dozen white plastic covered bodies hurried into the toilets. "They won't want us around in here any longer."

The two men nodded to the SOCO team and walked out into the rain. "Got any other ideas why she was killed, boss," asked Flower.

"Nothing that comes to mind but I've come to the conclusion that anything could happen in that family."

"Another revenge attack?"

"That would be a motive. No doubt Jack will scream Turnbull."

"Well, it can't be his own hand that plunged the knife in Jenny Carpenter's chest because he's in Spain."

"Another assassin, then?"

"Maybe, but if so we know there will be no evidence."

"Then at the moment we're well and truly fucked."

"As you said, Sergeant, fucked."

★★★

It was just gone four when Daniel pulled up outside Francine's cottage in Martyr Worthy. He was surprised to see lights still on downstairs. Had Jack somehow got the news? His thoughts were interrupted by the front door opening and Francine stepping out onto the drive.

"Chief Inspector," she said, shielding her eyes against the security light. "It can only be something serious."

Daniel closed his car door and took her arm. "Can we go in please, Doctor, and is Jack awake?"

The tone of his voice sent a shiver down Francine's spine. "Yes, yes of course come in. Oh God, I have a terrible feeling about this."

"Let's get inside first," said Daniel.

Without saying another word Francine led Daniel into the kitchen. "Sorry about the mess," she said, waving at the dishes on one of the worktops. "I've just got back from an emergency at the hospital and felt like a bite to eat. I have a feeling my appetite is about to disappear though."

Daniel rested a hand on one of the worktops. "Perhaps Jack should be here."

Francine's eyes widened. "It's about Jenny."

"Yes. So please, Doctor, wake Jack."

"And that can only be because you have bad news, Chief Inspector," Jack exclaimed as he walked into the kitchen. "Your voices woke me."

Daniel stared at Jack in his blue pyjamas, his dishevelled hair and unshaven face. "Jack," he began, "we've found Jenny."

For a brief moment Jack's face brightened.

"She's dead," Daniel continued.

"Dead!" Jack and Francine exclaimed in unison.

"Murdered, I'm afraid."

"Dear God, where?" croaked Jack.

"There is no easy way to tell you this," said Daniel. "In the toilets at the bottom of the city High Street."

"Oh Christ!" cried Jack as Francine ran to his side. "She must have got in with a bad lot. Fight over drugs, booze?"

"A possibility, but her purse had not been emptied. All of £150 cash and two credit cards inside. You would expect the homeless, the drug addicts, the alcoholics, to take the money and the cards. So at the moment I'm mystified. You got any ideas that might help?"

Jack rubbed his chin. "I feared you'd find her dead, but not murdered. Was she raped?"

"I'll know more when I get back to the station. I left SOCO at the toilets. But I don't think she was raped. She was fully clothed."

Jack's head dropped into his hands. "This is all my fault – poor girl, she thought no one loved her. I will never be able to forgive myself for deserting her. I suppose there is a possibility you may never find the killer."

"Yes," Daniel admitted. "It's a rough dark world she'd joined. And she would not have been streetwise. You live by your wits or you either die of booze, malnutrition, or you get killed. I would suggest that your daughter was an easy target. But the money still in her handbag doesn't add up."

"So why was she murdered?" asked Francine.

"That's a question I can't answer."

"Turnbull – it's got to be Turnbull!" growled Jack.

"He's in Spain," said Daniel, "so if this is his doing it's

another paid assassin and probably we will never find him. But we mustn't just assume its Turnbull."

"No, of course not," said Jack, "but if it's not him what the hell is the motive?"

"Do you know if your daughter had any enemies? Not to put it too politely she was a very wild girl."

Jack looked down at the floor. "I'm ashamed to say I know very little about her life. We did not communicate much and when we did it was normally to have a fight, ending up with her telling me I was a cruel uncaring bastard. She was an alcoholic, Chief Inspector, out of control and so more than likely did make enemies, but bad enough for someone to kill her, I doubt that."

Daniel turned to Francine. "How about you, Doctor?"

"Well, there is the old man at the shelter, where I was called to see Jenny. He was very protective of her. Apparently he'd sort of adopted her. They had been spending quite a bit of time together."

"Sexual attraction do you think, Doctor?" asked Daniel.

Francine pursed her lips. "I would very much doubt it. He's constantly drunk, doesn't know one day from another and he's old, but no one knows how old."

"Has anyone asked him?"

"Of course they have," said Francine. "They're not all fools at the shelter you know, Chief Inspector."

"I'm sorry, Doctor I didn't mean to imply that."

Francine smiled, "I'm sure. But it might be worth a visit to see if you can get anything out of him, though I'd be very surprised if he was your killer."

Daniel decided he'd got all the information he was going to get, so he closed his notebook and said, "Okay, let's leave this for the moment but I'm sorry to say, Jack, that I would like you to come to the morgue at Winchester hospital to identify her. Her body will be there by now."

"Will my wife know?"

"A counselling team, accompanied by a female PC, should have told her by now."

"She won't come."

"She will have been given the option."

"Fine, but there is no way she'll want to identity Jenny. She will expect me to do that."

"I'll come if you would like me to," assured Francine.

Jack rubbed his eyes. His pain visible.

"No, I must do this on my own. There is no way I'm going to put you through such a gruelling experience. No, don't object please. Wait here for me."

"I understand, but I'll come with you to the hospital and wait there. I think you might need me."

★★★

Jack had never bothered to wonder what the inside of a morgue looked like, let alone had to walk into one to identify his dead daughter. But as Daniel guided him through the maze of corridors at the hospital he grew ever more fearful that he would throw up.

"Nearly there, Jack," said Daniel, as they passed the pathology lab. "It's the next door. Are you ready for this?"

"Are you kidding, Daniel? I could never be ready for this."

"It won't be pleasant, I'm afraid."

"And my wife, any sign of her?"

"None."

"Good."

"Ready, then?"

"Wow," exclaimed Jack, "I don't know if I can do this."

"Do you want a cup of tea or coffee first?"

"No, no. I'm being pathetic. Okay, okay, I'm ready."

Daniel pushed open a door. The fluorescent lights made

Jack blink. The room was all glass, metal and tiles. Daniel slipped on plastic gloves, green overalls and rubber boots. "You must do the same," he said, handing Jack the clothes and boots.

"Brace yourself," Daniel warned as he inserted his security key to open the door to the main post-mortem room. It was dominated by two steel tables, one fixed, one wheeled, a blue hydraulic hoist and a row of fridges with floor to ceiling doors. The walls were tiled in green and the whole room was surrounded by a drain gulley. Along one wall was a row of sinks and a coiled yellow hose. Along another was a wide work surface, a metal cutting board and a glass-fronted cabinet filled with instruments. Next to the cabinet was a chart itemising the name of each deceased, with columns for the weights of their brain, lungs, heart, liver, kidneys and spleen. To Jack's right, two naked cadavers were laid out, one young man and an elderly woman, over which a young woman was bent taking stomach samples. On the left, Sarah Jones, dressed in a green gown, green Wellington boots and a green hat, plastic gloves covering her hands, was opening the door to one of the large walk-in fridges. Jack thought she looked a bit like a butcher. *Come to think of it, that is what she is,* he thought. She pulled out a tray on which lay the body of Jenny Carpenter encased in a white shroud. Jack shivered and swallowed bile. He felt his stomach churn. Any minute now he feared he'd vomit. He dragged his eyes away from the corpse and looked at Sarah. "How the hell do you remain sane?"

"Who said I was sane?" she replied.

Jack shook his head. "No more information please; let's just get this over with."

Sarah pulled back the white shroud.

Daniel asked, "Your daughter?"

Jack moved forward as if in a dream. He walked to the

table, aware that Daniel was gripping his waist, and stared down at his daughter.

His injured leg gave way.

He slid to the cold floor.

34

Sophie braked to a halt opposite Jack as he and Francine walked out of the hospital. She pushed open her door and practically fell out of the Mercedes. Her face was streaked with tears. Francine, who was gripping Jack's hand as hard as she could, stepped in front of him and waited for the torrent of abuse. Sophie ran towards Jack, hair blowing everywhere and shouting, "My darling is dead, dead! And you killed her, you bastard." Francine didn't move: there was no way she was going to allow this mad woman anywhere near Jack. "Leave him be, Sophie, he's in no fit state to listen to your tirade."

Sophie came to a halt and screeched, "You trying to tell me how to speak to my husband, whatever your name is?" Then swinging a fist she aimed a blow at Francine's face. Francine ducked, Sophie nearly lost her balance and the blow sailed harmlessly into the air.

"Enough, Sophie," shouted Jack, limping out from behind Francine. "This is not the place to make a scene."

"Well, fuck that!" Sophie shouted back, glaring at Francine.

"Calm down, Sophie, or I'll call security."

"Ya, ya, I bet," snorted Sophie. "Just what you would do, you bastard. And you can't stop me seeing my daughter, so get the fuck out of the way, Jack." Then suddenly all the fight went out of her and she dropped to her knees onto the tarmac and started to sob hysterically.

★★★

With a cup of builder's tea grasped in her shaking hands, provided by Daniel's PA, Julia Sullivan, Sophie shifted in her chair and crossed her legs and stared at the floor. It was three hours since the scene at the hospital and the sight of Jenny lying on the rolling table, her beautiful face looking so serene in death, had hit her like a blow to the solar plexus: she'd lost control, screaming hysterically, her mascara running down her face as the tears poured out of her. It had taken Jack the best part of a half hour to calm her down. Now, as she dabbed her eyes with a soggy silk handkerchief, she felt numb. Sitting behind his desk Daniel was aware that if he said the wrong thing Sophie would probably become hysterical again or, what seemed more likely, she'd start swearing at Jack. Neither option would get them anywhere. He had a murder to solve not a marital dispute.

Daniel rubbed his hands together. "More tea, anyone?"

"No thanks, we're fine," answered Jack.

"Tea! You call that tea," hissed Sophie.

"Oh for Christ's sake, Sophie, shut up!" growled Jack.

Sophie bit back a reply, realising that this was not the moment to have a go at her shitty husband.

"Please, both of you, fighting isn't going to get us anywhere," pleaded Daniel. "Out there somewhere is the killer of your daughter, so could you both calm down and listen to me. I quite understand your pain, Mrs Carpenter, and I feel for you, but I need some information urgently."

Sophie burst into tears. "My poor little Jenny, cut down in the prime of life. It's terrible, I'm devastated."

Of course you are, thought Jack, squirming in his chair. What an actress, what a bitch. He wanted to shout at her but what was the point? Sophie could play any scene without rehearsal. When he realised her dramatics were temporarily over he looked at Daniel and took the chance to ask, "Where do we go from here? Any theories yet, apart from Turnbull and the old man?"

"Are you ready for this, Mrs Carpenter?" Daniel felt obliged to ask.

Another burst of crying rent Daniel's office. "Ready?" Sophie managed to choke out. "Of course I'm not ready, you stupid man, but I have no choice do I?"

Daniel ignored her outburst and said, "I'm afraid no new evidence yet but there has not been much time to go into great details. So, Mrs Carpenter, as I have already asked your husband, is there anything that you can think of that would help me? Like, why was your daughter on the streets?" The moment the words were out of his mouth Daniel regretted the question.

"On the streets," exploded Sophie. "How dare you insinuate that she was a prostitute. She would never sell herself. That is pure conjecture on your part, Chief Inspector, and I take great exception to it."

Daniel forced himself to remain calm, realising that Sophie Carpenter had no idea where her daughter had been hanging out or what she had been doing. She could very well have been selling her body. Her mother was turning out to be all that he'd heard about her but there was no point in antagonising her further. "I didn't mean to infer that she was a prostitute but she had been wandering the streets and sleeping rough for several weeks before she was taken to the shelter. At this very moment my sergeant is at the shelter interviewing anyone who can remember her."

Sophie did her best to hide her amazement.

Jack shook his head. *She didn't know!* He swung round in his chair and said through gritted teeth, "Jesus, Sophie, what sort of mother are you? You come in here trying to make out you love our daughter and that you are devastated. But it's all an act, Sophie; you didn't even know she had left home after you had dragged her out of the hospital. And then what did you do? Nothing. If you didn't want to look after her why the hell didn't you leave her in the hospital? She was seriously ill. How could you dump her in her bedroom and leave the house? Christ, woman, you could have at least rung me. Once you got home and woke up to the fact that she'd done a runner did you ever think of going to look for her or ringing the police? No, don't you dare say a word, it would only be a lie. And if you'd behaved like a normal mum she might still be alive. She was sick, sick!" Jack shouted.

Sophie sprung out of her chair, her face reddening. "So where the fuck were you, Jack? Having an incestuous relationship with this bastard daughter of yours?"

"Oh shut up, Sophie. Can we be honest with each other for once? We are both to blame: we are shit parents and we have failed Jenny. That's why she's dead, for Christ's sake. And let me tell you something. You may not care, but I do, and I will never be able to forgive myself. I loved her."

"Loved her!" screamed Sophie.

"Yes, loved her."

An uneasy silence settled on the room. Daniel waited for Sophie Carpenter to throw herself at Jack. He found himself staring at her long manicured nails: they would hurt. He decided he was going to get nowhere with this warring pair. "Listen, I don't think it worth going on right now. It's obvious you can't be civil to each other. I suggest I talk to you individually."

Sophie turned to look at him. "Well, I'm done here, then,

so talk to my husband, Inspector, or whatever rank you are. If you want to talk to me get in touch."

Daniel felt a surge of relief. "Very well, Mrs Carpenter, please feel free to go. I had hoped this meeting might have shed some light on why your daughter was killed."

"Well, it hasn't, has it? So get on your bike, Inspector, and earn your salary." Sophie glared at Jack, spat on the floor and flounced out of Daniel's office.

There was a stunned silence, Daniel gazing at the spittle staining the carpet, Jack trying hard to get his heart back to normal. The silence was broken by DS Flower walking into the room. "Hope I'm not interrupting anything," he said, sensing the air of tension.

Daniel blew out his cheeks. "Not at all, Sergeant, Jack and I are just catching our breath."

"Mrs Carpenter?"

Daniel nodded.

Paul decided it was best to say nothing.

"So," asked Daniel, "I need some good news. Any luck at the shelter?"

Paul took out his notebook from his pocket. "Maybe."

"Tell me."

"I had a talk to a Mary Slater who more or less seems to run this shelter. The old man is called Taffy, by the way. He wasn't in the shelter – no doubt out begging somewhere – but Mary Slater told me he's Welsh and she has no idea of his age, but at a guess close to seventy. He's a mess, no recollection of who he is, drunk most of the time but non-violent. She doesn't think sex comes into it, but I think we should have a word with him. He comes back to the shelter most nights. According to Ms Slater he befriended the victim several weeks ago and got very agitated when she was taken to hospital. She couldn't tell me much more, but a drunken man getting attached to an attractive young lady got me wondering. She could be wrong."

"My daughter thinks the sexual bit is a non-starter," Jack said.

Flower made a face. "I still think a word is needed."

"I agree," said Daniel. "Let's speak to him. Perhaps go to the shelter when I've finished talking to Jack. You okay with that?"

"Fine by me," said Flower. "Give me a shout when you're ready."

Daniel raised a hand in acknowledgement and then quickly turned to Jack. "Look, Jack, I understand you can't tell me much about your daughter's activities in the last forty-eight hours and I'm not here to judge you, but if you think of anything that might help us in the next few days please get in touch. At the moment I don't really think we have a genuine suspect."

"Who's in the frame?"

"Only the two men I've already mentioned."

"As I feared. Looks like a random killing. I can't get my head round this. No sexual assault, no valuables taken. Jesus, Daniel. What the hell is going on?"

"I'm sorry, Jack, but I have no idea. I can only hope we have a DNA match and something from the CCTV cameras. I'll keep you informed. And, Jack, I'm very very sorry for your loss."

"Thanks, Daniel. I'll survive, but shit, how could anyone kill someone in cold blood apparently for no reason?"

"It happens," Daniel said, as he shook Jack's damp hand.

36

Mary Slater reluctantly led the two detectives into a large room with high ceilings, barred windows, wooden floor and lines of metal beds. It always reminded her of her first school's drab dormitory. It annoyed her to see the detectives wrinkle their noses. She was used to the aroma of unwashed bodies and other more unsavoury smells. She watched their eyes dart round the room and guessed they were thinking how could anyone want to spend time in a place like this, surrounded by the cloying smell and the feeling of hopelessness that wafted to every corner of the room. *Well, some people didn't have a choice, detectives.* Even at this time of day, when most people in Winchester were probably thinking about lunch, there were two men lying on beds, arms flaying and strange noises coming out of their mouths. Mary knew the demons were playing their sadistic games.

She fixed Paul Flower with a look that plainly said, *I don't like you,* as she saw him shake his head in disgust. She'd got his measure on his earlier visit. He would be the one to make no effort to hide his feelings. You didn't work in this job without being able to deal with people who lacked any understanding of the undignified plight of most of 'her family' as she'd come to call them. And she'd already worked out that the sergeant was full of contempt. But her father, a strong believer in teaching his children the pitfalls of life, had bred in her a kindness towards those less well off than herself, and a strength of mind to stand up to those who treated men like Taffy as scum. She had a suspicion she was about to have to draw on all her father's wise words.

"This is where my family live, detectives, and where they come for food and help. Sometimes we have as many as thirty poor souls in here at one time. Depends a bit on the weather. I try and keep beds available for our regulars."

"You run a selection system?" asked Paul. "Why give any of these useless, filthy layabouts preferential treatment?"

"I think, Sergeant, you are not knowledgeable enough on this subject to make such a statement," cautioned Mary, and then turned to face Daniel. "You have a question for me?"

"About one of your inmates."

"Ah yes, Taffy. Your sergeant here said you might want another word. So what do you want to know?"

"Do you see him as a sexual pervert?" asked Flower, smarting from Mary's earlier rebuff.

Mary put her hands on her hips and moved closer to this man she was coming to think was brainless and lacking any sympathy in his overweight body. "I wouldn't have any idea but I would be very surprised if Taffy ever has time to think of carnal matters."

"Carnal matters," sneered Flower. "I have another word for a sexual offender, Ms Slater. It's sex predator. And Jenny Carpenter was a very pretty young woman alone in a world she didn't understand. She would be extremely vulnerable to anyone's advances."

"But you told me, not an hour ago, that there was no sign of her being sexually assaulted."

"She fought him off, until he used a knife."

"Oh come on, Sergeant, I suggest you're entering the

211

world of make-believe. Will you tell me how an old man with an addled brain, who is drunk for nearly every hour of the day, can entice a person into a public toilet and knife them to death? Taffy can't even hold a fork, his hands shake so much."

"She might have been prepared to give him a blow job," Flower countered. "She could have gone with him willingly."

Daniel decided his sergeant had said enough and the look that Mary was giving him confirmed that. "You have a point, Ms Slater, and I agree it seems very unlikely that Taffy is our man. But he might know something. He was obviously close to Jenny Carpenter."

"And sexually attracted," growled Flower.

Mary composed herself before replying. "I could argue with you for the rest of the day about Taffy's character, and you, Sergeant, would just scoff. But he's a lost soul, haunted by a past he struggles to wipe from his mind. So he drinks. Most of the men or women who come here share an addiction to either drink or drugs, sometimes both, but they all have different characters. Taffy is kind and meek and longing for a friend. He recently found that friendship in Jenny. No, he's not a sexual predator, I'd bet my life on that. I think Jenny Carpenter gave him something that he'd missed all his life and it certainly wasn't sex."

"So what was it?" asked Flower, grudgingly beginning to admire this feisty woman.

"I think it was love."

"And that could lead to sex," stated Flower.

This time Mary decided to ignore him and said, "I think we are done here, Inspector. I have things to do and I'm sure you do as well. Are you arresting Taffy?"

"No I'm not," Daniel assured her. "Just a word, okay?"

"Can I bring him down to the station and stay with him

while you talk to him? He does get very muddled and since finding out about Jenny Carpenter's death he has gone on a blinder."

"Proof of guilt," stated Flower.

Mary felt like kicking him in a place that hurt men most.

Daniel dug him in the ribs. "You're welcome to be with him all the time. In fact your presence might help. So where is he?"

"Well, that was what I was about to tell you if your sergeant hadn't kept interrupting. I'm afraid I have no idea. I was just going out to look for him when you arrived."

★★★

Taffy was not far away. Grief had paralysed his limbs. His eyes were constantly full of tears and he felt as if his heart would burst through his chest at any moment. He thought he was dying, and the sooner the better. There was nothing left to live for. Only ghosts flitting around him in a constant effort to inflict pain. Now another ghost would always be dancing on his shoulder. Jenny would never leave him.

He was sitting with head bowed outside his regular morning stop, a cold cup of coffee staring at him from the table. He knew he would soon be moved on by the landlord. Kind as he was, a filthy drunk man hunched over a table did nothing for his profits. Taffy pushed back his chair and tried to rise in as dignified a manner as possible. When you are full of vodka, mixed with rum, and your heart aches with every beat, it is difficult to move your limbs. Halfway to standing he knew he wasn't going to make it.

Mary caught him as he fell back into the chair. It took every ounce of her strength to hold him upright. "Taffy," she said breathlessly, casting a desperate look through the window for the landlord. "Thank God I've found you. I need to take you somewhere and then we can go back to the shelter."

★★★

Taffy held Mary's hand, like a small nervous child, as he tried to make sense of what was going on around him. Two figures were floating before his eyes and something was telling him they were not friendly. He tried to focus on the room but the walls moved. He closed his eyes and vomited.

"Fucking hell, you disgusting old man, didn't your mummy tell you that it was rude to puke in front of people," shouted Flower.

"Enough," said Mary. "Can't you see this man is not well?"

"As if I care," retorted Flower. "I've a good mind to get him onto his knees and make him eat his filth."

"And if you do that I will give you good cause to arrest me, Sergeant. You're a very uncaring man."

Her words brought him up short. He had never thought of himself as uncaring. When he spoke his tone was softer. "I'm sorry, Ms Slater, that was uncalled for. I'm not an uncaring man. And I do realise this man has been through hell. I'll say no more. He's all yours, mate," he said with a smile, waving a hand at Daniel.

Daniel glowered at his sergeant. "Right, Ms Slater, can I suggest that you take this man back to the shelter? I don't think he's in any state to answer questions. I suggest that if we want to question him we come to you when he's sober, if that is possible. But I don't think he features in our search for the killer. I can't see him overpowering Jenny Carpenter, as I've said before. But I might like to ask him a few questions about her. Do you agree?"

"Thank you, Chief Inspector – it is Chief Inspector isn't it?"

"It is."

Mary continued, relief showing on her face. "I think that is a good idea. So are we free to leave?"

"Yes."

Mary rose from her chair and helped Taffy to stand. "Sorry about the vomit but I'm sure the good sergeant won't mind clearing up an innocent man's mess." She gave Flower a withering look as she made for the door.

Once the door was closed Daniel looked at Flower. "I think you met your match there, old friend."

"I think you're right, guv, and if that woman was a few years younger I might make a move on her."

Daniel laughed. "Don't kid yourself, mate, she'd eat you for breakfast."

37

Francine closed the door of her cottage with a sigh of relief. She was glad that Janet Goodchild had left. She was beginning to think she'd taken up residence for good, and she was steeling herself to ask her to go. There was something annoying about her and she wanted time alone with Jack to nurse him back to health. Janet breathing down her neck and looking disapprovingly at her every move was, to say the least, getting to her. She had witnessed emotionally disturbed people before and although maybe that was going a bit far with Janet there was definitely something about her that irritated her. She wrinkled her nose; was she jealous? No, certainly not. Janet had been Jack's right-hand man long before she'd come on the scene – loyal and not to be criticised, let alone suggestions that maybe she should seek work elsewhere. She shrugged her shoulders as she walked back into the kitchen, which Janet had left immaculate. Never had the worktops looked so clean, which sent a further jab of annoyance through her body. *Leaving a message,* Francine thought. Anyway, she was gone – good. Jack's voice cut into her thoughts. "Much as I value her loyalty to me I find her a little overbearing at times," he laughed

"She's in love with you."

"Oh come on, Francine, she's been with me for the best part of twenty years and we've never as much as exchanged a kiss."

"It's a woman's intuition, Jack. She's in love with you."

★★★

Janet walked back into her flat with a heavy heart. She'd enjoyed looking after Francine's cottage and had forged a bond with Cat, so much so that she was thinking of getting one for herself. As she walked into her sitting room there was no welcoming chatter from her budgy, Sean, named after Sean Penn, who, after Jack, was enough to make her heart throb violently. Perhaps it had been a mistake to give him to a pet shop. *Ah well, too late to have remorse,* she thought. No doubt Sean was by now very comfortable in a new home. But the silence made her realise how much she was going to miss Jack's company. It was the nearest she'd got to him in twenty-five years and it had had a profound effect on her. To hear his voice, to hear him shaving in the mornings, to hear him singing in the bath made her realise how much she loved him. "One day, yes one day, when that bitch Sophie is out of his life, he will turn to me," she said to the silent room,

She dumped her bag on the floor, moved across to the kitchen. At least the sound of the fridge would break the silence that was threatening to upset her usual calm. The kitchen smelt damp and looked unfriendly. She felt like a stranger. She sat down at her kitchen table, remembering why she'd bought the flat fifteen years ago: it was almost an exact copy of Jack's flat when he'd first employed her. Never mind that it was too big. She could sit there every morning and imagine Jack sitting opposite her. And that got her thinking about the supper he and Francine were enjoying only a few miles away. "Too much!" she screamed. She pushed her chair back, sweat

217

starting to run down her face and rushed upstairs. In a drawer of her dressing table she pulled out a blue handkerchief that she'd taken from one of Jack's pockets several years ago. She rubbed it against her face, immediately feeling better.

★★★

Jack watched Francine drive off to work with a sigh of relief. He hadn't told her that Tim Stafford was coming to pick him up within an hour and if they met it would only upset her further. She'd suffered enough already. He hobbled back into the cottage and sank into an armchair in the sitting room. It was only a few seconds before Cat was on his lap demanding his morning attention. Absently, he started to stroke the soft hair, oblivious of the constant purring of delight. His mind was on other things. Who had killed Jenny, and why? What was the motive? Who was this man Taffy? Had he the energy to see his latest project above Winchester through to its end? And what should he do about Tim Stafford? His head started to spin. So many questions, and no certain answers. He felt spent.

He heard the car pull up outside the cottage, eased Cat off his lap and was horrified to find himself thinking that his life had been much simpler before Francine had entered it. By the time he stepped out of the door and waved a welcome to Tim he realised that he had no right to be thinking that. Francine had nearly died for loving him and for a brief time he'd never known such happiness.

★★★

Tank Turnbull was in a very dark mood, and when he was in a mood Mildred knew it was best to leave him alone. Come to think of it she rather enjoyed these silent brooding moments:

218

it left her in peace. It had given her time to ring round to a few friends and plan a day up the West End. She got fed up staring in silence at Tank's growing belly.

But now the West End was only a dream.

Here they were in some dump of a villa where he'd fled, *"for insurance purposes,"* he'd informed her, stuck up in the mountains above Marbella in Spain, with only the odd snake or cockroach to keep her company. Their flight from London had left her no time to even pack her necessary essentials and for sure there wasn't a damn place to replace them here. "One case only," Tank had barked. And Mildred had known there was no point arguing.

She stretched out her short legs on the worn sunbed and gazed down over the valley. She could just make out the sea shimmering in the strong sunlight, which made her long to dip her feet in its warm waters. Why the hell couldn't Tank at least have rented a villa with a pool? She looked across to where her son Terry was lying on the other overworked sunbed, fiddling with his fucking mobile. She was surprised his fingers weren't stuck to it. She moved her head so that she could see Tank pacing up and down behind the glass doors in a room which passed as the sitting room but which she called a fucking tip. All she could do was pray that soon he'd find a villa good enough for her to live in. He'd promised, and he'd better keep to that promise or an anonymous telephone message might be flying back to the filth in the UK. She had more brains than Tank gave her credit for, which might one day be his downfall. Come to think of it, at this very moment, as another black fly decided to stride across her cheek, a call might be a good idea anyway. Mildred slapped at the offending creature and silently made a vow.

One day she'd go back to her friends and Tank would be on his way to a very long holiday.

38

Francine sat on the grass, her legs curled under her. Surgery had finished and she was not on call but the relief she normally felt was absent. She swatted away a fly determined to annoy her, and looked across at the two fishermen casting their rods. There had been a decent rain the night before and their concentration was solely focused on the water: fish should be rising. Anyway, she was in no mood to wave and smile. It was a warm muggy evening and she should be enjoying her usual off-duty glass of Merlot, content and relaxed. Cat, who was oblivious to his mistress's mood, prowled the garden with enthusiasm. The garden came alive with things to stalk at this time of the evening. He pounced, shook a small mouse and proudly advanced towards Francine. She pushed him away and he flounced off with a look of disdain. Even Cat could not change her feeling of desperation. Then she felt the light touch of a hand on her neck and looked up at a smiling Jack. She patted the grass. "Come and sit here. I was beginning to have disturbing thoughts."

Jack eased himself down beside her. "Penny for them, Francine."

"There's more than one penny. Which one do you want to hear?"

"That bad?"

"Afraid so."

"It sometimes helps to talk to someone."

"Oh Jack, Jack, I've been talking to you ever since we met and look where that's got us. It's a mess: none of this would have happened if I hadn't come on the scene."

"I don't want to ever hear you say that again."

"But it's true. And there is nothing we can do about it. The damage is done. And just to make matters worse, Tim Stafford turns up. I never thought I would set eyes on him again. And do you know, Jack, I'm disturbed that I still feel something for him. Yes, I know that's crazy and it frightens me, but I can't deny it. When he left me I thought I'd hate him forever, but when I saw him my heart didn't just turn over because of shock, there was something else. I remember whispering secrets in a warm bed, holding his naked body tight and thinking how lucky I was to have such a man lying beside me."

"Do you want him to go?"

"I don't know."

"Would you like me to make up your mind for you?"

Francine laughed. "No, Daddy, I'm a grown-up now."

And for some reason, that neither could explain, the atmosphere lightened, and as the two fishermen came opposite the cottage Francine stood and waved. They looked up and waved back. "Drink?" she shouted.

39

"You look a bit of a mess, mate," commented Daniel with a chuckle. "That pretty little divorcee overworking you again?"

Flower scowled at his friend, took in his clean white shirt, blue tie and well pressed trousers and polished black shoes and did his best to smile.

"I don't have a wife to do the laundry. I live alone, I have little time to buy clothes as you work me too hard, and if you must know my little divorcee, as you call her, was away last night. So I had one too many beers and fell asleep halfway through a porn movie. That satisfy you?"

Daniel slapped him on the back. "Okay, don't upset yourself, but honestly, Paul, a clean shirt and a tie would help."

"Point taken – sir," he added with a wry smile.

"Wow, you are grumpy this morning. Hope your little divorcee comes back soon."

"She's not the only thing that is making me grumpy. I really thought we had a suspect. Two witnesses saw this Taffy bloke hanging around the statue the night Jenny Carpenter died, and I thought he fitted the bill just perfectly. But the timing was wrong and anyway I must agree that I don't think he has the capabilities to kill a young woman, much as I would like to pin the murder on the wretch. And what really pisses me off is that he lives on benefits paid for by hardworking men like myself."

"He's really got to you, hasn't he? But you're wrong about the benefit thing. Mary Slater tells me he draws nothing from the state. In fact they don't even know he exists. Recently, Jenny Carpenter has been feeding his appetite for alcohol and before that I assume he got enough money from begging. So how about zipping that large mouth of yours?"

"Okay, okay guv. For the second, and hopefully last time, I've got the message."

"Good. Now I'm off to the shelter. I've just had a phone call from Mary Slater and apparently Taffy is relatively sober."

Flower bit his lip. "I think it might be wise for you to go alone; I would find it difficult to be polite. You will get more out of him if I'm not around."

Daniel managed to hold his silence as he walked out of the room.

★★★

If Daniel had hoped that Taffy would feed him some vital piece of information he was disappointed. He might have been a little more sober but policemen were not his friends, and however much Daniel tried to assure him that he would come to no harm if he had information that might help catch Jenny Carpenter's killer, he seemed incapable of putting two words together. After a half hour of sipping coffee, wrinkling his nose at the smell emanating from Taffy, and casting looks of frustration at Mary, Daniel finally decided to surrender.

"I think I'm wasting my time, Mary. He knows no more than when he came to the station. That he's shattered by Jenny's death is obvious but that doesn't mean he had any part in it. And look at him – he couldn't kill a mouse. Okay, he was in the area of the toilets that night, but at the wrong time.

Also, there are no fingerprints and no signs of sexual activity, no semen, no DNA. No, he's not a suspect."

"I'm sorry, Chief Inspector, that he can't help you."

Daniel smiled his thanks. "I didn't think he would be able to, but I must follow up on the smallest crumb. At the moment the killer has got the better of us. No motive, no leads. Whoever he or she is they are very clever. We have a tough job ahead of us."

Mary took his hand. "Goodbye, Chief Inspector, thanks for coming alone, if you know what I mean."

"Sergeant Flower?"

"You got it in one."

40

Jack's heart is racing as he breaks to a halt outside the imposing red brick mansion, walking distance to a village and five miles from the city of Winchester. He's been looking forward to this from the moment the particulars of a house with a small farm had come through the post. He looks at the climbing roses, the manicured lawns, and knows this is the house for him. Okay, he understood fuck all about farming, or for that matter country life, but he'd always fancied himself milking cows and walking across his land with a gun tucked under his arm, and then walking on Sundays to have a pint with a few mates in the local pub. Perhaps going to church first was a bit of an ask. His land! God, what a wonderful word that was. His land! If only his father had lived to see this day. A smile would crease his wrinkled face, he'd light another fag and probably shed a tear. He looks across to the passenger seat where Sophie sits and beams. "It's beautiful, Sophie, it's beautiful, isn't it? He reaches across to her and runs a hand down her long stockinged leg. She breathes in and turns to face him. "Yes, it's lovely, you romantic fool. But don't go mad: let's see around first and then discuss it."

But he's already made up his mind.

★★★

225

How time changed things. Today his foot wasn't pressed down on the accelerator pedal, his heart wasn't beating with excitement and his mood was very different to those heady days. This is what Sophie had done to him: ripped the joy of living out of his life. As he stepped out of his car he felt appalled to find himself thinking that he was a stranger in the place he had loved and cherished: his reward for hard graft. He stood on the drive and looked at the garden he had planned on the first day they had moved into the house. Even after only a few weeks of absence he saw weeds in the herbaceous borders which would never have been there if he'd been at home. He was tempted to start weeding. Reluctantly he pulled his eyes away and trudged towards the front door and walked into the hall. Not so long ago he would step into the house and feel warmth embrace him, but not even the painting of his father, looking rather severe, could lift the feeling of gloom that now hovered over him every time he entered the house. He remembered the old man's reluctance to sit for hours, while a young painter, who was costing a fortune, tried to make him sit still and forgo chain-smoking his beloved Capstans. 'It will be rubbish, rubbish. You're wasting my time,' the old man complained time and time again.

"Morning, Dad," Jack whispered, feeling his stomach turn. "Glad you're not alive to see the mess I've made." He heard footsteps behind him. Hunching his shoulders he turned to face Sophie. There was nothing to be gained by uttering futile greetings and the shortest time he had to spend in his wife's company the better.

Jack took a deep breath. "I think we need to talk about Jenny's funeral."

★★★

Daniel stood under some trees that overhung the cemetery of St Mary's Church, Upham. He stood well back from the family as Jenny's coffin was lowered into the ground. Jack had insisted on a family only service so there were no more than ten people standing round the grave. He couldn't help wondering if one of them was the killer. He saw few tears, which got him thinking how strange families could be. He knew he would crack up if one of his children died. He focused on Sophie Carpenter, standing well away from Jack. She interested him: up her arse all the time and unable to show any emotion. He was tempted to think the unthinkable. Looking at her now, apparently taking little notice of the proceedings, he'd have sworn she was relieved. Not for the first time he felt a touch of pity for Jack. Was she really as hard as she seemed? Was she capable of what he was thinking? His eyes swivelled to Janet Goodchild, standing on Jack's left in a dark blue outfit, no hat. He suspected there was unrequited love there. On Jack's other side stood Francine Walker, looking the exact opposite to Sophie Carpenter. Her face, under the large green hat that she was wearing (no doubt to try and hide the tears), looked white and drawn. He had liked what he'd seen of Jack's daughter, poor woman. What a family to get involved in. He'd witnessed the professional side of her but the events of the last few weeks must be taking their toll. He wondered if she was wishing she'd never found her father. He moved a little closer so that he could study their faces better. He'd learnt that facial expressions could give a lot away and he was particularly interested in that creep Harry Carpenter. *Another loser,* he thought, as he watched him picking his nose and chewing what he assumed was gum. He was wearing a faded green T-shirt, a pair of black jeans and brown brogues. *No respect at all,* he thought, glad that he wasn't downwind of Harry. He wondered if Harry had a reason to knife his sister, or did Sophie Carpenter kill her in a fit of rage? Surely not, but as Flower would no doubt say to him when they met later at the station, "Everybody is capable of murder."

41

Jack had learnt an important rule when he'd first started out in business on his own, that you trusted people at your peril. So that was why he was heading for Lincoln's Inn Fields in London to alter his will, rather than walking into the office of his regular solicitor based in Winchester. He had chosen to walk from Waterloo station and was hot. He wiped the sweat off his forehead, fiddled nervously with his tie, and walked into the offices of Stanford, Elliot. As he moved up to the reception he was aware that he might be putting Francine in more danger. But he *so* wanted to give her back something for all the love and support she'd shown him through such horrendous times. He'd given it a lot of thought, realising that it would be the last thing she would expect, but his heart had won over pragmatism. He hesitated momentarily before smiling to the receptionist.

"Can I help you, sir?"

"Yes, I have an appointment with Charles Stanford."

The die was cast, no going back now. He followed the receptionist up the winding oak stairs, with pictures of the firm's past partners decorating the walls. Jack had always thought they looked rather superior, staring down their noses at you as you climbed the stairs. It had surprised him that a working class boy, such as Charlie, had fitted into this public school environment. But then Charlie had always been able to surprise him, not least when he became senior partner of one of the most admired and feared litigation firms in the city of London. However, there was one thing that even being a respected lawyer of some repute would never change. It was his bedraggled appearance. The heavy mahogany door swung open to reveal the five foot four diminutive carcass that was standing by its desk, beaming its usual infectious smile and wearing a crumpled grey suit, a blue shirt open at the neck, and scuffed black shoes, which no doubt at some time had been handmade. His wild ginger hair reached his shoulders. He looked like some half-cut yob, and he couldn't have cared less.

"Jack, me old mate," he boomed in a surprisingly deep voice. "Terrible news about your daughter. Nowhere is safe these days. Come and sit down; have a cigar before I take you out to lunch at the Savoy Grill. You look as if you need a bit of cheering up, and who better to do that than yours truly?"

42

From my hiding place I watch Harry Carpenter ride out of the stable yard onto the lane. I can hardly contain my laughter. He is no longer mounted on a shining polo pony, just an old grey cob. The girl riding with him falls short of his once beautiful companions. This is a girl from the riding stables where Harry now hires a horse. There is no way he's going to see me; anyway, he's too engrossed in chatting up the girl beside him. She is about eighteen, but Harry likes them young. I don't move a muscle. I'm going to kill him in a few days' time.

Once they are out of sight I move. I push through the roadside hedge and walk to my car. I press the unlock button on my remote and open the driver's door. On the seat is my kitchen knife, sharpened and ready. It feels good to be holding it. I gently run a finger along the sharp blade and smile at the small drop of blood that appears on my finger. I suck it off. The thought of this second kill gives me a rush of adrenaline. My hand will be steady. Like Jenny, Harry will at first be pleased to see me. And once he realises he's facing his last few seconds on earth it will be too late to put up a fight. My brain is clear. Remorse there is none, because shit like Jenny and Harry Carpenter don't deserve to live. Dead, they can no

230

longer inflict pain on Jack. Very soon, if all goes well, Harry Carpenter will be rotting under the earth and joining his sister in hell. I slip into the driver's seat, turn the ignition key and drive off. I'm so hyped up that I feel like turning back. I could smash into the horse and then run over Harry as he lies stunned on the ground. Oh what joy that would give me. But I mustn't let my enthusiasm get the better of me; there is the girl and I would have to kill her. I draw in a long breath and slam my hands on the steering wheel. I think of looking into Harry's eyes as I drive the knife into his chest. I cannot wait.

43

Janet Goodchild was feeling out of sorts. Yesterday, Jack had informed her that tomorrow morning he was going to London to see a solicitor about making a new will.

"I can't trust our friend, John Winthrop: his office leaks like a busted bucket and I don't want the whole of Hampshire knowing about my new will."

"Would you like me to type it out for you?" she'd asked. And much to her surprise he'd said rather gruffly, "No thank you, I'd rather go to London," and that had really hurt. Jack didn't trust her. She'd concealed the stirrings of anger, a feeling she'd never had before towards Jack. But now with Jack in London, alone in the office, tired and irritable from a sleepless night, she could contain her anger no longer. She swept the contents of her desktop onto the floor – and stamped angrily over them. A picture hanging on the wall of Jack and Sophie smiling at the camera was smashed by a paperweight thrown with great force. The noise of breaking glass broke her anger and her heartbeat eased. The storm had passed. But as she sank to the floor to clean up the mess, flashes of her past danced proprioceptively in front of her eyes. If these were the old demons rising from their slumber she'd have to tread carefully. This was not the time to slip back into her old ways.

Nothing must be allowed to shatter her dreams.

Mickey Dunn had supplied Jack Carpenter with anything from a screwdriver to steel girders ever since Jack had built his first house. He acknowledged he'd been lucky to have been brought up as a child in the next street to the Carpenters, and as everyone knew Jack favoured those who had lived in his area. Mickey's business had grown substantially thanks to Jack, and his standard of living was way above what he'd expected when he'd got his first job as a street cleaner. But the problem with Mickey was that once he'd held cash in his hand he wanted more – in simple terms he was greedy, and that was why he'd got involved with Tank Turnbull. Bit by bit he was sucked into Turnbull's various illegal operations and Mickey's finances flourished.

Then one day Turnbull told him it was payback time. "I've had a little rumble with Carpenter," Turnbull informed Mickey, one evening over a pint, "and I'm asking you to do a small job for me."

Mickey's mouth had fallen open because he knew the word *ask* was not in Turnbull's vocabulary. It was always "I'm ordering you to."

And that had been the beginning of Mickey's downfall. Jack had not taken kindly to his supplies being cut off or delayed. It put his contracts at risk, especially his site above Winchester. So an email had been sent to Mickey Dunn, company director, cancelling all further orders and informing a fuming Mickey that Carpenter Enterprises would no longer be dealing with him.

Slowly, Mickey's company sank into receivership, only to be rescued by Turnbull buying into the company. Now, short of cash, no longer his own boss, furious that he'd been treated so badly by a man he'd thought his friend, Mickey was out to get some revenge, although he knew he could not touch

Turnbull – well, he could shop him even if he was soaking up the sun in Spain, but he'd not live to see the filth putting on the handcuffs. However, Carpenter was a different story. He felt he could ruin his new venture without too much risk and as luck would have it he was aware of the Turnbull/Carpenter fallout. So surely Harry Carpenter was still short of a bob or two.

Now, here he was sitting in the bar of the Swan Hotel in Alresford, a flourishing small town near Winchester, waiting for young Carpenter to arrive. As he'd hoped, Harry had taken the bait. He ordered a pint of local ale and moved his overweight frame to a table by a window. His brown weasel eyes surveyed the room, which at midday was beginning to fill up, he ran a hand over his bald head and patted his jeans' pocket just to make sure the money was still safe. To say he was nervous would have been wrong, for Mickey had never been nervous in his life, but he had to admit to being a little apprehensive. He was parting with cash he could little afford, but the thought of doing Carpenter a shed load of damage had become like a drug. He took a pull at his pint and waited.

As always, Harry was late, time meant nothing to him, and Mickey was getting worried that he'd chickened out, when he strolled through the door. Mickey waved and Harry came over. "Long time no see," Mickey said, thinking this was the sort of language Harry would use. "Take a seat."

Harry eased himself onto the seat. "What's all this about, Mr Dunn? Thought I'd seen the last of you. I'm not after money anymore."

Bet you are, thought Mickey, wasting no time in pulling out his brown envelope and waving it in front of Harry. "You going to turn down ten grand? I'm not going to talk to you long, Harry, I don't like your sort, so if you want a drink have one after I've gone. Now, here's my offer. I will pay this to you – he waved the envelope again – if you do some serious damage to your father's new project. Interested?"

Harry looked suspiciously at the man who the last time they had met had threatened all sorts of injury if he didn't pay up on a debt. He'd paid but hoped he'd never see the man again. And yet here he was offering him money in advance to do damage to his father's property. He did his best not to show his excitement but his eyes said it all.

Got him, Mickey thought.

44

The blast shattered the portakabin windows, blew in the door and hurled Tim Stafford out of his bed. He landed on his back, the breath driven from his body. For several minutes he lay on the floor stunned, gasping for breath, his ears ringing from the noise of the explosion. He rolled over onto his back and stared with horror at the stars. The roof had been blown off. Panic threatened. But his survival instincts clicked in. His brain was saying check yourself before moving. He moved his toes. All well there. He could move his legs, he could feel sensations in his fingers and he could see. Nothing seemed to be broken. He pushed himself into a sitting position. Christ, his back hurt, and his pyjamas were shredded. He stood, swayed and looked around. The roof had collapsed onto the floor, just missing his bed. He felt sick. He started to shake. He looked across the newly laid football pitch to the flames shooting into the air and saw the cricket pavilion ablaze. The wail of approaching sirens galvanised him. He became aware of his nakedness. By the light of the fire he found a pair of trousers and a shirt lying amongst shards of broken glass and twisted pieces of metal. He tore off what remained of his pyjamas and struggled into the trousers and shirt. Unable to find shoes he stumbled out onto the damp grass. Shivering from a combination of shock and cold he limped towards the blazing cricket pavilion.

★★★

Jack woke to the sound of his mobile ringing. Rubbing his eyes he jumped out of bed and stumbled to the table where he'd left his phone the night before. He had a premonition that something must be wrong. No one rang him at this time of the night, unless it was Sophie playing her stupid games again. But the voice was Tim's.

"Jack, disaster here. Come down quickly. Cricket pavilion alight. Must go as I'm on a police phone." The line went dead.

The first thing that came into Jack's mind was that yet another disaster had struck. "Jesus, when is this going to end?" he shouted to the ceiling. He threw some clothes on, yanked open the bedroom door and hurried down to Francine's room. He didn't bother to knock. He threw open her door and shouted, "Francine, wake up, wake up. Trouble on the site."

Francine woke with a start, sat up in bed and stared at a frantic Jack. It only took her several seconds to work out that this must be an emergency. She shook her head in an effort to clear the fog of sleep from her brain. "Jack!"

"There's a fire at the site, Francine. The cricket pavilion is alight. Tim has just phoned me. It sounds bad, but he's okay. Can you come with me?"

"Of course. Give me a few moments."

★★★

They stood in awed silence watching the flames eating their way through the pavilion. Soon it would be a pile of rubble. The firemen were fighting a losing battle – the pavilion had at least ten large cans of diesel stored on the premises by the building contractors.

Francine was gripping Jack's hand as he talked to Tim Stafford. He was relating the event as it had unfolded. "And that's about it, Jack," he said. "Must be arson. Who the hell would do this?"

"I have an idea, and if I'm right we will never prove anything. I know—"

At that moment a huge blast rent the air. "Jesus, what now?" shouted Jack.

Tim yelled, "It's the football changing rooms!"

Still holding Francine's hand, Jack ran towards the new blaze.

★★★

By early morning the fires were out, though still smouldering. The fire crews had managed to save part of the football changing rooms but the cricket pavilion was a total loss. Jack was rooted to the spot, staring at the singed grass, the blackened skeletons of the new trees, and the devastation all around him. Nearly a year's work had gone up in flames and he was very angry.

Daniel Appleman moved to his side. "Arson, I'm afraid, Jack. Any idea who hates you enough to do this?"

"It has the signs of Tank Turnbull written all over it."

"Last heard of he was in Spain."

"He'd never do a job like this on his own. A telephone call to a mate would be enough. You'll never find out the truth, waste of time."

"Perhaps we should suspect him for the murder of your daughter."

"Look, Daniel," Jack stated "we have no way of ever finding out if he was responsible for this mess. As for putting out a hit on Jenny, well I think that's going too far. If he's implicated in this and the hit and run, my bet is that he'll be satisfied. Of course, I don't want to ask you to dig no further, but you could be wasting valuable time and resources. "Catching Jenny's killer must be your priority."

"And that is what I will keep in my little black notebook Jack."

★★★

Tank settled down on a large white sofa with a glass of Pol Roger champagne clasped in his hand. It was his favourite drink, as it was with Winston Churchill, and that made it all the more enjoyable as he liked to compare himself with the great man. Fighting a large enemy with small well-trained resources. In fact, he was sure that Winston would have made a very good criminal. He patted the place next to him. He was in a particularly good mood. News had just reached him about the fire and the death of Jenny Carpenter. Someone else had it in for sodding Jack Carpenter. He gave a loud belch and patted the sofa again. "Come here, mare, and celebrate with me," he said, pointing to a glass of lemonade on a table by the sofa.

Mildred took the glass and dropped down beside him. She smiled with little enthusiasm as they clicked glasses. "Is this all ours?" she asked, waving a hand around the vast room.

Tank thumped his chest triumphantly. "All ours. A pool, a large villa and sunshine and it cost me nothing thanks to a man called Mickey Dunn. What more could we want?"

A lot more, thought Mildred. *My friends, my house and my visits to the West End,* but forcing a smile she said, "I've got to hand it to you, Tank, you think of everything, but who is this Mickey Dunn?"

Tank patted her knee. "Now, you know not to discuss

business with me, mare, just be grateful for a friend's generosity."

Mildred knew if she pressed him for more information, he'd smack her one.

"So, why don't we go down to Marbella tonight and have a few jars with our friends?" Tank suggested.

Mildred nodded. It was the last thing she wanted to do. Friends! A new life of crime beckoned. She gave a sigh, *The sooner I get away from here the better,* she thought, even daring to think, *without Terry or Tank.* It brought a smile to her face.

★★★

"As I see it," said Daniel, the next morning, sitting behind his desk and talking to Paul Flower, "the common denominator in all this is the Carpenter family, but how these events tie in beats me. It seems we can agree that the hit and run and arson attack was revenge for Jack getting the better of Tank Turnbull, and it would be easy to assume that Jenny Carpenter's death is linked to this desire for revenge. But I don't think that. This has stepped up the ante and Turnbull doesn't fit. So, if I'm right, what is the other motive for killing Jenny Carpenter? Was this a random killing? If Jenny hadn't been in the toilets would another woman have been killed? Or was Jenny the target and someone was waiting for her?"

"Another of Turnbull's mates? That might explain why none of her valuables were taken," argued Flower.

"I just can't buy into that, mate, but maybe we will know a little more when all the tests come through. Let's keep Turnbull in mind but agree there could be another reason. Like drugs, a sex attack disturbed or just a plain falling out between two drunks. It's possible, but if so why were none of her valuables taken? Also, a random killer normally leaves a clue somewhere. It's done in a panic, probably regretted soon after and the killer runs. But the site is clean, not a hair, no semen, no footprints, nothing on CCTV, nothing. This has the makings of a very well planned attack. If so, why?"

"Family feud," suggested Flower.

"That has passed through my mind. Sophie or Harry. Both seem very unlikely killers."

"Another contract job?"

Daniel shrugged. "I have a feeling about this case and it's not a good one. So come on, let's have some ideas from that brain of yours, unless of course it is frazzled by love."

Paul chuckled. "You can't leave it, can you; just like a stuck record. But I admit this great brain of mine is blank, but it has nothing to do with love. However, I do have a suggestion."

"Which is?"

"We ignore the random killing idea. I don't think it fits. If you push me, which you are, I'm inclined to go along with a family matter or a serial killer. But then I'm thinking a serial killer likes to take a trophy, but no trophy here, as far as we know. I can't back this up with any hard facts, but this family have fought for years. So is money involved, or is just plain hatred boiling over?"

"I don't think I'm at the state of definitely pointing my finger at the family, just thinking aloud," Daniel said.

"But you think we should look close to home."

"At the moment I think it is our best bet, but I want to dig into Jack's past, see if he seriously upset someone in his early days when he was building up the business, other than Turnbull. However we look at it, for there is one thing for certain, this is the work of a truly screwed up person. As well as that, we take a close look at those who work around him now. We may well upset a few people but we've done that before."

"Agreed," Paul replied. Then adding, "Pity we couldn't screw that filthy old man."

"Sergeant!"

"Sorry, guv, out of order."

"Zip it, okay?"

"I won't say another word."

"Unless you come up with something worth saying."

Paul shook his head. "I have one more thing to add – rather an unpleasant thought, but I'm thinking is it possible that Sophie and Harry Carpenter could be in danger? That we might be about to have a very serious situation."

Daniel rubbed his chin vigorously. "And that would blow my family feud theory right out of the fucking window."

★★★

The incident room was alive with voices as Paul and Daniel entered. "Hey, Flowery," a voice said from the back of the room. "Is that divorcee keeping your nuts warm?" There was a buzz of good-natured laughter, which soon died when they saw the scowl on their boss's face. "This is not the time to act like adolescent teenagers," Daniel snapped. "Leave the sergeant's private life alone." And then added, with one of his smiles that made him popular with his team, "At least until we get to the pub. Which, I would like to point out, may be some time unless we all knuckle down and solve this case. So let's get to work."

There was scraping of chairs as the team sat down feeling suitably ticked off. Then, when the room was quiet, all eyes focused on Daniel.

"Right," he said, "on the whiteboard we have all the people we think are in some way involved in this murder. You will note that I have not included Tank Turnbull. We have gone as far as we can with him for now, so don't waste time on him. This morning, Sergeant Flower and I have decided that we should cast our net further afield, so I'm asking you, Constable Andrews, to dig into Jack Carpenter's past, especially the time

242

when he was starting to be successful in London. I'm looking for anyone he might have royally pissed off. I know how much you enjoy reading thrillers, so here's your chance to see if you've learnt anything useful from them."

"Okay, guv, onto it now," said an attractive five seven Jane Andrews, her hazel eyes flashing with excitement as she stood up behind her desk, brushing back her long brunette hair from her eyes. She was new to the team and knew this was her chance to make a mark. "Thank you," she said in a low voice, which Daniel acknowledged with a nod.

"I also think," continued Daniel, "that we need to take more interest in the people around Jack Carpenter. Such as his workforce, Tim Stafford and Janet Goodchild in particular. They are the closest. Okay, I see a few raised eyebrows, but remember this. There have been cases where the person coming under the least suspicion has turned out to be the culprit. So watch, listen, ask questions if you need to. We are a team trying to find a killer and maybe prevent further deaths. We are not here to be nice or frightened of upsetting someone. We are here to solve a visious crime. Sergeant Flower will lead this side of the enquiry."

"What about the arson?" asked a constable.

"As I've just said, if you'd been paying attention, Constable, instead of picking your nose, the hit and run and the arson attack have nothing to do with the murder, so let's get busy; we have a lot to do before this case blows up in our faces."

As Daniel walked out of the room Flower touched his shoulder. "Thanks, mate, for giving me the chance to make amends for my rant about the old man. It is much appreciated."

Daniel turned and smiled. "How long have we known each other?"

"Several years."

"And how many cases have we worked on together?"

"Lost count."

"Dozens and dozens. At least seventy per cent have led to a result. If you think one rather childish rant is going to end our partnership and friendship then I suggest you don't know anything about me. You're good, Paul – too fucking good to be thrown out of the force. There would be those, in this politically correct environment that we have the misfortune to live in, who would like to hang you out to dry for your outburst about the old man, but not me. Now, go and do what you do best. I need your intake and I have a feeling we haven't much time."

As Daniel watched Flower walk out of the room he could have sworn he saw a tear.

45

I'm concerned by the interest the police are taking in people around Jack and that is concerning me because I have no cast-iron alibi for the night of the killing of Jenny. I must be careful not to underestimate Chief Inspector Appleman. He is astute and that makes him a dangerous adversary. Tread carefully I tell myself as I walk down towards the town centre feeling excited. My mission has become much more exhilarating. I must be aware that Appleman will no doubt keep an eye on me, as he will the Carpenter family. I stop outside Marks and Spencer and decide to buy a fish pie and some yogurt. As I stand at the check-out behind some aged old biddy, unable to find her credit card in her overlarge bag, I'm tempted to reach out and take a bar of milk chocolate winking at me at the beginning of the counter. My hand reaches out – I'm inches away from breaking one of my rules no chocolate until my task is complete. I pull my hand away just as the old lady stops yacking to the attendant. Doesn't she realise others have work to do? And I contribute to her pension! Finally, with bag in hand (bought for a ridiculous ten pence), I head for home to sit in front of a blank TV screen and plan how to keep below the chief inspector's radar.

46

Francine did her best not to show how ill at ease she was feeling, after assuring Jack that she was happy to have Tim Stafford stay at the cottage temporarily. It had been a spur of the moment offer, which she was now regretting big time. Not because she couldn't stand to be anywhere near him, but because he still managed to make her heart skip a beat. And now, as he walked into the kitchen, all fresh from a shower, smiling at her and Jack, and smelling of a familiar aftershave, she felt a familiar thump against her ribs.

This is so weird, so damned weird. What is happening to me? This is the man who made me have an abortion; for Christ's fucking sake! And yet here I am looking at that SO handsome face and thinking how much I'd like to be in bed with him! No, no, get away from me, Tim – just go and never ever come back – I hate you!

Francine dropped the saucepan into the sink, ran her hands through her hair and screamed. Then, without saying a word she fled the kitchen – grabbed her car keys from the table by the front door and fell out onto the drive. Jumping into her car she managed to start the engine with shaking hands and hurtled away from the cottage. Only when she reached the surgery did she realise that she hadn't the faintest idea how she'd got there.

In the kitchen Jack and Tim exchanged worried glances. "What the hell was that all about?" said Jack.

Tim knew only too well.

★★★

"I'm so sorry, Jack, I don't know what got into me; well, that's not really true, I knew what was happening and I didn't want it to happen – no way. That man cannot come back into my life. Do you hear me, Jack, he can't come back."

Jack had caught up with her during her lunch break in what he now called, 'Francine's bolthole'. She'd been sitting at their usual table in Caffe Nero, staring at the red fire extinguisher as if it contained all the answers. He knew that she was feeling really bad. "Look, Francine, don't apologise to me. I should have never suggested that Tim come and stay in your cottage. But it's no longer a problem. Tim is moving out right this moment as we speak and I have told him to find a new job."

"But you'll be lost without him."

"There are plenty of good men out there and, besides, you are my prime concern. He goes."

Francine experienced the oddest feeling. Faced with the imminent departure of Tim she should have been relieved, even delighted. She'd been telling herself that she was in no mood to get involved in a very complicated relationship, ever since she'd fled her cottage. But as she was about to find out, emotions could mess up everything. "I don't want him to go," she heard herself say.

"You what?" gasped Jack.

"I really don't want him to go," she said in a quiet voice.

Jack sat back in his chair and stared at his daughter. "Do you know what you're saying?"

Francine gave a weak smile. "Not really, but it's how I feel – I think."

"You think. Is that enough? You might be facing a life-changing decision here and all you can say is, I think."

"I know I sound crazy, and yes, this is making me crazy. But you see, Jack, I realise that I have never stopped loving him. Oh, I know what you're going to say. He walked away from his responsibilities and you lost the baby. But we were both young and, however shitty he was, time has made me realise that he was right. Neither of us were ready for children. Over the years, I've cursed him, hated him and missed him in equal proportions. And if he hadn't have walked out of that portakabin, I would have left it at that. But the devil is at work here, Jack, and if Tim wants me to go back to him I know in my heart I will, even though one part of me is saying, *he killed your child*."

Jack shrugged. "Well, you're grown up enough to make your own decisions."

"And some of them have been right and others have been wrong."

"That happens to all of us during our travels through life."

"I suppose. And what do you think this one is: right or wrong?"

"Perhaps it is a good time to let you know how Tim feels."

Francine laughed. "Oh, I'd almost forgotten he had a say in this. Has he mentioned anything to you?"

"Plenty after you left."

"And?"

"He's as crazy as you."

"Oh wow, this is a life changer indeed."

"So does he stay?"

"He stays working for you, Jack, but he does not sleep in my cottage – not yet anyway. I need to tread slowly, as I'm sure he does. I need time to think how crazy I am and be sure that the craziness lasts. This won't be easy with all the other things that are happening at the moment. Will you speak to him for me? Please do, Jack. I don't think I'm quite ready to beg."

"I think it should be him to beg. To beg your forgiveness, for a start. What he did was appalling, however young you both were."

"Are you saying you think this is all wrong?"

"No. As I've just said, you must go the way your heart takes you, Francine. There is one thing I've learnt about life. Love is a very funny thing – dangerous, but the best feeling in the world. And when it hits you, all good sense goes out the window."

"Well, you should know. And thanks for the fatherly advice." Francine looked at her watch. "Oh God, here we are again talking too much and I'm going to be late for my first patient. I'll see you tonight, and Jack?"

"What?"

"Thanks: and I love you."

★★★

Harry Carpenter was aware that to splash about his payment for services rendered might well lead to some awkward questions from his father. But the temptation to go out and blow some of it on a brand new motor was so strong that he wondered how long his resilience would last. He'd walked past the car showroom many times and each time he gazed in wonderment at the shining new silver Jaguar proudly sitting in the showroom window, but he'd known he was a few bob short, until Mickey's readies had landed in the palm of his hand. This was his fifth walk past in four days and each time he'd edged nearer to the glass entrance. Then fate intervened. As he stared through the window, a young man beckoned to him from behind a desk. It was all the encouragement Harry needed. He was hooked.

47

I know where he's going, so I can hang back a bit and blend in with the morning walk to work. I would prefer if he doesn't see me. I see him stop and stare at the window, look round and walk into the showroom. I know what is going through his mind. He's weak: he will give in. Nothing and no one has ever stopped Harry spending money. And I know he's got a wad of it burning a hole in his pocket. I followed him to the Swan Hotel in Alresford. I could see him through the window, no doubt striking some dodgy deal, with a small weasel-like man. I watched him pass Harry a large brown envelope. The grin on Harry's face confirmed my suspicion. A wedge of money for some dirty deal. Harry's greed knows no bounds. I'm certain he torched Jack's project, the little creep. He'd do anything to hurt his father. And what's this? Oh Harry, Harry, have you no control over your urges? I watch him drive out of the showroom in a silver Jaguar convertible. That must have cost him a bob or two. Well, you won't have time to enjoy this reckless purchase for very long. My plans are complete and the adrenaline is pumping. Goodbye, Harry Carpenter. This world will be better off without you.

48

Janet Goodchild was running late for work and she'd never been late for work in her life. Not even the excruciating pain of her menstrual cycle had stopped her being in the office an hour before Jack. But this time she'd had other things on her mind and lost track of the time. She was exhausted. She'd had little sleep. She couldn't stop thinking about Jenny Carpenter. It was playing on her mind. She parked in her usual spot behind the office and was relieved to see that Jack's Range Rover was not in its usual place. She opened her door and stepped out into the cold air. She'd have his coffee ready for him after all – black with two sugars. As she climbed the stairs to the office she wondered how many cups of coffee she'd made for Jack over the years. Come to think of it, how many sandwiches had she bought him? He must have kept the little delicatessen down the road in business on his own.

She unlocked the office door. The room was cold. Thank goodness she'd arrived before Jack. She hurried to the thermostat and set it at twenty-one degrees, the temperature that Jack felt comfortable with but which she found a little too hot. But what Jack wanted Jack got. Then she moved to the kettle, filled it with water and pressed the switch on the wall.

She could have done all this in her sleep. She laughed then – well, she practically was. She fussed around until she heard the kettle bubble, then moved to the cupboard where the instant coffee was kept, set out Jack's mug – the same one he'd used for years – and moved to her desk. He'd always insisted on making his own coffee. She dropped into her chair, brushed her green skirt down and, as she had done every morning, almost from the day Jack had employed her, dreamed of the day she would be Jack's wife.

★★★

But Jack was going to miss his coffee. He'd decided to visit the site first. Talk to Tim about the problems that beset the whole operation. Not only the fires, but also the late deliveries of essential material. Finally, if he thought Tim was in the right mood, he'd broach the subject of Francine. His inclination to end his employment was still on his mind, but who was he to ignore his daughter's wishes?

He was looking at the wreckage that had been his dream and wondered if he had the willpower to start all over again. Then he thought of the obstacles he'd met on his way to being one of the most successful businessmen in the UK and gave a wry smile. He would not allow himself to be defeated by the likes of Turnbull. He turned away from the depressing sight and saw Tim walking towards him. He raised a hand in welcome. "Hi, Tim, you coping with all this?" he asked, waving a hand at the desolation.

"More or less," Tim replied. Then looking Jack in the eye he said, "Mind if I say something which is not relevant to all this?"

Sensing what was coming Jack said, "Not at all, but if I'm right I think it is *very* relevant. Let's say, your job could be on the line."

Tim nodded. "I had a feeling you might be going to say that."

"Well then, let's hear what you have to say."

Tim cleared his throat. "I've had time to think of Francine's behaviour, and what you said to me that morning. As you know, I haven't seen her since and, frankly, I'm in a muddle. Tell me Jack, what would you do?"

Jack took a deep breath. "Look, Tim, I'm not into counselling. What I think is not relevant this is your call. What decision you and Francine come to is nothing to do with me. But it may surprise you when I say I cannot condemn you for your past behaviour. We do lots of very stupid things when we are young. In some ways it was what happened to me, though, unlike you, I didn't have to make the decision to break up with Francine's mother. She did that. Nor did I know she was pregnant. I understand why you walked away. The difference is that I never had to make a decision to either stay with Francine's mother or walk away. What I would have done if I'd known she was pregnant is something I ask myself quite often, especially since finding my daughter. So I'm in no position to play the high and mighty with you. But if you will allow me, I would like to give you a word of advice."

"Go ahead."

"If you really think you still have feelings for Francine then I don't think you should just walk away again without talking to her. But if you hurt her I will probably kill you. Got that? So what I'm saying is, talk and then make the decision together. You may well break Francine's heart a second time, but at least you will not live the rest of your life regretting not talking to her. She loves you, Tim. Why, slightly mystifies me. But if you still love her and think you can make her happy, let me tell you she's up for it. The ball is in your court, young man. Now, before we both end up in tears, hugging each other and assuring each other that we will be buddies for the rest of our years on this earth, we need to get down to the business of rescuing this disaster. I have told the local council that there is no way we can meet our proposed deadline. They accept this, but I have a mountain to climb, with or without you. One good thing is that now Turnbull is off the scene we might get our deliveries on time. However, loyalty is very strong in the criminal circle that he rules and he just might get someone to keep bothering me. I've never used violence at any time of my life but there comes a time when a man can take no more, and the Turnbull family have pushed me close to the edge. So I have sent a warning to what I call his clique, through channels that are still open to me. *Back off. No more shenanigans or there will be serious trouble. You will be making a huge mistake if you think I've gone soft.* And to reinforce my determination to start afresh I have withdrawn all my business with the firms I think have been playing to Turnbull's tune. Wherever he is, I know that that message will reach him."

★★★

On his own, eating a tuna sandwich for lunch, Tim Stafford was thinking of what Jack had said three hours earlier. It would be wrong to gamble. He had to be sure of his feelings before talking to Francine. Okay, hardly a day had gone by in the eighteen years since they'd split that something or somebody hadn't reminded him of what life might have been if things had worked out differently. But that didn't mean he was ready to try to reignite the love he once had for her. It had never entered his head to try and get in touch and when he'd seen her as he stepped out of the portakabin it was not a rush of love that had enveloped him, just pure panic, then to be replaced by guilt. Could he deal with his guilt? That seemed the overriding question. Would it haunt him every time he saw her? Could they get together again as if nothing had happened? Could he come to terms with the undoubted fact that he'd been instrumental in killing an unborn baby? He'd failed so far, so how could that change? He'd be devastated if he lost this job. This massive project was as close to his heart as it was to Jack's. But he had to face the real possibility that he'd have to leave. There was no way he could work alongside Jack, unless he and Francine were an item – friendship would not be an option. He looked across the grass field that would soon be a cricket pitch and saw Jack organising the placement of the new portakabin. He munched hard on a piece of brown crust and came to a decision.

★★★

Daniel Appleman was drinking his third mug of coffee by the time a rather weary looking Flower walked into his office. "How did your interviews go today?" he dared ask.

Flower shook his head. "Bloody awful and not very useful. I drew a blank wherever I went. Sophie Carpenter was quite something. At one point I thought she was going to attack me. But she's got a rock solid alibi. Excuse the pun. She was in bed with a new lover. I've spoken to the man, well, almost still a boy – twenty would be my guess – who looked close to fainting when I put the question to him. I don't know if he has a girlfriend or whether it was just sheer embarrassment at having to admit he'd slept with a woman old enough to be his mother. Whatever, he corroborates her story. So the only way she could have killed Jenny Carpenter was to hire a hitman. Of course, the lover and her might be in cahoots, but I very much doubt it. He's the new under gardener – not on the scene for long enough. Then I had a word with that arsehole Harry. He couldn't have done it – he was in a dodgy club in Winchester which apparently he frequents several nights in a week. I was tempted to bring him in and throw him into a cell until we had corroborated his story. After that I dropped in on that secretary you were on about the other day. You're right about her being in love with Jack, but why would she kill one of his family just as the opportunity to step into Mrs Carpenter's shoes might be on the cards? I gather the divorce is well advanced. She claims she was in bed all night, and at the moment I accept that. So I think we can assume, at the moment, that unless there is new evidence we will have to look elsewhere for the murderer. And that, as I said the other day, means we are fucked. We don't seem to have a single worthwhile lead."

Daniel shook his head. "I agree with all that you've said. We seem to have hit a brick wall, unless Constable Andrews comes up with something."

"And if she doesn't?"

"We can't just sit on our hands – the detective super is getting into trouble with the assistant chief constable who's getting it in the neck from the chief constable. Jesus, everyone seems so impatient. I had a nasty look from the ACC this morning as we passed in the car park. Arsehole didn't even say good morning. He's like a dog with a bone. I wouldn't put it past him to soon bring in the London boys, with their smart suits and *we know best* attitude. It would help if we could come up with a motive. I'm mystified."

"So, what's your take on this, guv?"

"I think we're running out of suspects too damn quickly."

Flower rubbed his unshaven chin vigorously, hoping that Daniel had not spotted it. It would only lead to another good-humoured dig about the divorcee. And it would have struck home. He'd once again dallied too long and he would be the first to admit he looked scruffy. "Nothing has made me change my mind that this murder was premeditated. It's the lack of evidence that makes me think that. It was well planned and all evidence was wiped clean. The killer knew where the CCTV cameras were positioned. A random killing would have left a fingerprint, a piece of hair or clothing, and the same goes for a mugging or an attempted sexual assault. Maybe a serial killer is amongst us, but why target Jenny Carpenter? I'd wager that we are missing something and maybe the killer is closer to us than we think."

"I go along with you on that," Daniel said. "Oh, and by the way, I don't think a beard is going to suit you."

★★★

Taffy lay on his bed in the shelter. He hadn't had alcohol for days and any strength he'd had was draining fast from his body. He was feeling too weak to get up and go outside in the cold rain to beg all day. Even then, his takings might not come to enough to buy his longed for bottle of vodka. Everything in the room swayed before his eyes; every limb ached; his head hurt whenever he lifted it off the hard pillow; and he stank. It was easier to foul himself than stagger to the toilet. Within his muddled brain he was aware that the ladies of the shelter were trying to help him, to make him more comfortable before he died. The trouble was they all thought he'd be happier if he died sober but he didn't want to die sober. He wanted to be pissed out of his mind and sink into an alcohol, induced coma, feeling no pain, and wake up in heaven, to be greeted by Jenny. He felt a warm hand touch his forehead. He knew the touch; he tried to smile.

"Don't waste your energy, Taffy," said Mary. "I need to get you out of this bed and clean you up. Are you going to cooperate?"

Taffy shook his head.

"Why won't you help me, Taffy?"

"Because you won't get me a drink."

"You have water."

"Well, fucking great."

"Listen, Taffy, this is for your own good. It's been all of ten days since you had alcohol and you are making progress. I promise that soon you will feel better and then life will improve. Now come on, be a good boy and get off that bed."

"Fucking do-gooder," Taffy growled, gripping the sides of the bed with his hands. "I want a drink and I'm not moving until you get me one. Otherwise I will die and then you can drag my carcass off this bed and clean up the filth."

If he thought he was going to bully Mary he was in for a shock. "Listen up, Taffy, I've seen the likes of you so many times that nothing can faze me. You're not dead yet and the reason is that you are sober. So you either get out of bed now or I will call for help and we will drag you off the bed. The room stinks of your shit and urine. So what's it going to be?"

Taffy started to shake. The thought of hands running all over his body brought back the nightmares – the cloying hands of his father – the wetness on his skin – the screams of his mother. His hands flew in front of his face, desperately trying to push the ghosts away. He started to scream, and before Mary could act he was on the floor thrashing wildly at the ghosts floating in front of his face.

Mary watched in horror as he tore his stinking shirt off his body with his urine-stained hands. Then he rolled over onto his back and started to sob. Long painful sobs that tore at Mary's heart. She was certain he was about to die. Swallowing the bile that rose in her throat she dropped beside the writhing body and began to rub Taffy's bare chest. "It's alright, Taffy, I'm here with you. No one is going to hurt you."

"Get off, get off!" he screamed, slapping his hands on his dirt-encrusted flesh. "Get off me, Dad, leave me."

It was all Mary could do not to burst into tears. She'd witnessed one other homeless man who had been abused by his father as a boy, screaming the house down as a doctor tried to inject him with a sedative. The needle never got near the man and she'd watched him die in mental agony. "But you're not going to die on me, Taffy," she said firmly, pushing his hands away and gently rubbing his chest. "No way are you leaving me. Do hear me, Taffy? This is Mary talking. Not your father, not your mother, just me, Mary Slater." She held her breath, waved away two women who had come running. "I'm okay," she gasped, silently praying to the Lord for help.

49

So Harry Carpenter is the arsonist. I suspected him all along, the rich little shit. He deserves to die for hurting Jack so badly. Boy, am I going to enjoy getting rid of him. I scratch an itch behind my ear and wait.

It's two in the morning. Harry should be coming up the lane anytime soon in his silver Jaguar XF. He is so predictable: three nights a week at the Winchester club and always one was a Saturday. If he wasn't so arrogant and didn't have money in his pocket no one would want to know him. As usual he'll be drunk and he will use this rat-run to get home. Come on, Harry, I'm getting impatient.

I'm never described as impatient, just boring, polite and perfect, that's me. Huh, if only they knew! I take the knife out of my pocket, it was raining. I run my fingers slowly across the cold steel. The excitement is unbearable. I'm shaking. I must stay calm. Breathe deeply, slowly, slowly. Wait. Come on, Harry! I check the position of my car across the lane, the bonnet is up. Harry will not be able to pass.

I can hear a car. Please let it be him, otherwise my plans will be fucked. My heart is pounding so hard it hurts my chest. Calm, keep calm. A car hurtles round the bend and screeches to a halt not three feet from where I stand. Close! It's him. I watch him fall out of the car in his drunken state. "What the fuck are you doing here?" he slurs at the top of his voice, as he staggers towards me. "Who the fuck are you?"

"Oh Harry, it's me. Thank goodness it's you. I was scared." I squint, his headlights are blinding me. I throw up my hands to shield my face from the glare, and smell his rancid breath. "I've broken down, something wrong with the engine. Can you help me?" I'm such a good actress, if I was on the stage I'd win an Oscar.

"What the fuck are you doing out here at this time of night?" he barks.

"I had a little errand and I broke down – been here for hours." It wouldn't have mattered what I'd said, he wasn't interested. I might just as well have told him I was waiting to stick a knife in the first driver who came along.

"Oh for God's sake, I need to get home," he mumbles impatiently. "Let me take a look. I know how stupid you women can be."

It's not in Harry's nature to be polite or helpful but even he has worked out that if he doesn't try to help me he won't get home. He staggers towards the open bonnet.

"Thank you so much Harry, you're so kind," I say sweetly.

"I'm crap at this sort of stuff," he slurs, as he whacks his head against the bonnet and slumps forward onto the engine.

"You're fucking crap at everything, Harry," I hiss as I push the knife deep into his back. I pull it out and lunge again. The sensation of the knife cutting through his flesh is ecstasy. The knife goes deep into his back – I pull it out and lunge again – I love the feeling as it cuts through the flesh. Harry cries out and slips to the ground. As he hits the ground he rolls onto his back. I swear his eyes are looking at me in amazement. I hear a gurgling noise – I watch the blood flow from his body in the glare from his lights. I'm transfixed to the spot. How I like to watch them die. My body starts to shake – a message that it's time to move. I close the bonnet, hurry to the Jaguar and turn off the headlights, then back to my car, open the driver's door, slip onto the seat, take off my leather gloves and insert the key into the ignition. I drive away, biting back a shout of triumph. Not quite time to celebrate – I have more work to do.

50

Jim Smallbrother had been delivering papers in the area for as long as he could remember. Come rain or snow he prided himself on never failing to get through to the most isolated houses, even if that meant he had to walk. This Friday morning he had no such worries, as the weather was clearing, after three days of continuous rain, and with luck he might see the sun by the time he'd finished his rounds. He'd be back home in time for breakfast and sit down in his favourite chair to read *The Sun* newspaper and listen to Alice, his wife of thirty years, pushing the hoover over the green carpets in the hall.

As he swung round the bend his day changed.

★★★

By eight o'clock the lane was sealed off, yellow tape flapping in the breeze. SOCO swarming everywhere. Jim was still shaking as he talked to a constable, who had kindly given him a mug of tea from his flask. "Terrible, terrible," he kept repeating, looking at the white plastic sheet that covered Harry Carpenter's body. "It was such a shock. Gawd, I nearly threw up!"

The constable nodded in sympathy and gently patted him

on his back. "You'll be home soon, Mr Smallbrother, once the chief inspector or the sergeant has had a word with you. Then I suggest you take the rest of the day a bit easy. Not nice to see a dead body, is it?"

"Bloody awful! Will it be long before someone sees me?"

"The sergeant is coming over to you now."

"Mr Smallbrother," began Flower, holding out his hand, "so sorry to keep you waiting. Just a few words and then you can be off home, but I would like you to come to Winchester station later and make a statement."

"Gawd, Sergeant, I've had a terrible shock. Feel a bit queasy. I'm not used to finding bodies lying in the road." Jim forced a smile. "Quite ruined my day this has."

"I'm sure, and I won't keep you long. Just tell me in as few words as you can what you saw as you came round the corner."

Jim cleared his throat. "A fucking dead body, that's what I saw."

★★★

Daniel Appleman looked at Sarah Jones. "Cause of death, Forensic?"

"Stabbed in the back three times. He was killed here."

"How long since death?"

"Difficult to say at this precise moment but my guess is around five hours."

Daniel looked at his watch. "So, in the early hours?"

"Definitely."

"Harry coming home from one of his Saturday nights out," said Flower.

"Someone who knew his route well was waiting for him," added Daniel.

"Indeed, guv. So this points to a local person even more."

"And the same person who killed Jenny Carpenter."

"Looks like it," said Flower. "Let's hope the SOCO team find something for us to work on this time. You never know, the killer could have been careless."

"In your dreams," said Daniel.

★★★

It was a job that Daniel never got used to. For all the years he'd been a policeman it had never got any easier. He'd watched families break down, women and men crying, children looking bewildered and the looks that said, *why couldn't you have stopped it?* This was almost certainly what Sophie Carpenter was going to say once she'd got over her shock. Whichever way he looked at it, it was going to be a very unpleasant hour or two. He was certain she would thoroughly overplay her emotions. Perhaps he was being unfair but he wasn't sure she cared about her children too much.

As he drove he could imagine the pain he'd be feeling if any of his children were murdered. *I would never recover from such a blow,* he thought, as he braked to a halt outside Sophie's house. "No turning back, Jane," he advised Constable Andrews who he'd brought with him for moral support. "Brace yourself. This won't be pleasant."

Andrews swallowed, relieved that she hadn't had time for a big breakfast. She was still trying to get used to dead bodies, but it wasn't proving as easy as she'd thought. And now a grieving mother. "My day can't get much worse, guv," she said.

"Prepare for a surprise, then," said Daniel, with a touch of a smile, as he opened his car door, then adding as the front door of the house flew open, "You haven't yet met Mrs Carpenter."

There stood Sophie looking distinctly worse for wear.

"Saw the car," Sophie croaked, making no effort to invite them in. "Well, well, if it's not the good chief inspector. Come to tell me you've caught the person who butchered my daughter, have you? No, no, of course not, I can see by your face that you have come to confess you are no further on with your enquiry, so I'm still a suspect I suppose."

Daniel was sure she was going to fall flat on her face at any moment, and once she got the news of Harry he felt that's exactly what she'd do. "Do you think we might come in, Mrs Carpenter? I have something to tell you."

"So I'm correct, am I, no further on, eh? Still a suspect, ha, knew I was right. So say your piece here and then go – I really don't rate you, Appleman. You're wasting my time."

Daniel bit his lip. Jesus, what was it with this woman? "Mrs Carpenter, please, I have some bad news and it would be better if I told you inside."

"Well tough, this is as far as you and your little girlfriend get."

Realising, short of pushing past her, that he and Jane were not going to get into the house, he took a deep breath. "I'm really sorry to tell you, Mrs Carpenter, that your son was killed in the early hours of this morning."

Sophie's hands flew to her mouth and she staggered forward, falling into Daniel's outstretched arms. "Dead!" she screamed, managing to push herself away from Daniel. "Harry's dead?"

"He was killed on the lane by the stables."

"Killed, how?"

"He's been murdered."

Sophie sank to her knees sobbing.

"It must be a terrible blow. I'm deeply sorry. Constable Andrews will stay with you if you wish."

Sophie made no effort to hide her disgust. "No thank

you!" she spat, her voice rising several octaves. "Do you think one of your officers would be able to comfort me? For fuck sake, you're clueless and incompetent. Why, why, why didn't you give Harry protection?"

Andrews stared in amazement. The boss had warned her, but this… One minute the woman was having hysteria and the next minute she was ranting on about police incompetence. She wondered how her boss was going to react.

But Daniel was prepared – it was ironing out the way he thought it would. He gave Andrews a quick glance and bent down to offer his hands to help Sophie get up. She swatted them away and a sort of low animal growl came out of her mouth as she leapt to her feet and flew at Daniel. Before he could move away, her long well-manicured fingernails ran down each side of his cheeks. "You haven't answered my question," she screamed.

Then she turned away, staggered back to the door and slammed it in Daniel's face.

"Wow," exclaimed Andrews. "What now, guv?"

"We leave, that's what we do. Let Mrs Carpenter wallow in her own grief, if she has time for that. We've done our job."

Andrews felt relief – she hadn't been looking forward to holding the woman's hand.

For a few moments Sophie stood rigid inside the door, listening for the car to drive away. Then, as she heard the engine start, she crumpled to the floor, tears pouring down her face. Suddenly the awfulness of the situation hit her. Two children brutally murdered. Even though there had been times when she'd thought she'd have been better off without them, to have them torn from her by an evil killer was something different. She rolled over onto her side and curled up into the foetal position, stuck her thumb into her mouth and moaned, realising there was no one to give her sympathy.

She was alone, no family, no close friend to lean on, and she was terrified.

★★★

"Jesus, mate, those scratches look sore," said a concerned Flower as he gazed at Daniel's cheeks. "It looks as if she reacted a touch badly."

"It was quite a show," Daniel said, as Flower handed him a mug of coffee, bought from Costa Coffee on his way back from the murder site. He knew how much Daniel hated the station coffee. Daniel took the coffee and slumped behind his desk, pointing to a chair for Andrews. "Do you know something, it never ceases to amaze me how differently people react when told of a death in the family, but Mrs bloody Carpenter was something else. One minute she was on her knees crying hysterically, the next she went berserk, tearing at me with her nails and sobbing violently. Started to rant about how we should have guarded Harry. If I was a cynical person, I'd say she didn't care too much about losing her son, more interested in giving me a mouthful."

"She certainly changed very quickly," interrupted Andrews. "Grief didn't seem to last that long."

"Grief is shown in different ways, Constable," said Flower.

"I'd like to think she was devastated," said Daniel. "She slammed the door in our faces and turned the lock, so I can't say more than that. I'll go back this afternoon and find out if she wants to come to the morgue to see her son. In the meantime it's time we told Jack Carpenter."

"Done it, guv. And Doctor Walker," Flower assured him.

"How did they react?"

"It was painful to watch. I said I'd pick Jack up later and take him to the morgue to identify Harry. Beoming rather a habit, the poor man said."

"What the hell is going on, Paul? Does this mean Doctor Walker and Jack are in danger? Do you think this might be an attempt to kill off the whole of the Carpenter family?"

"It's a possibility, and random killing can be taken off our list. This is a well thought out crime."

Daniel shook his head. "Whatever, it's making me feel very angry – I don't like a killer to be laughing at us and this one most certainly is."

"Likewise."

Daniel gave a weak smile. "You make tracks for home, Andrews; this could be your last evening meal at home for some time."

"Thanks, guv, and you two?"

"I think long hours have already begun," said Daniel. "And a word of advice. If you want to stay in the force, stay single. If not, resign. Marriage and coppers don't mix."

"I'll take that on board, guv," laughed Andrews as she moved towards the door.

"A good girl that," said Daniel, once Andrews was out of the room.

"That was a bit hard on her, boss," said Flower.

"Better to know the truth now, before a kid and a moaning boyfriend or husband force her out," argued Daniel.

"Well, I just hope she ignores you." And what's brought this on? Trouble at home?"

Daniel looked at his sergeant, wondering how much of his private life he could trust with his friend. Station gossip was hard to contain, but he felt he knew Flower well enough to know that he was not a person to rush straight to the incident room and say, 'Guess what the guv has just told me.'

"You could say that," he confided. "How many times in the last few weeks have I gone home, sat on the sofa drinking a glass of wine and talking about our newborn son? How many times have I put him to bed? How many times have I fallen out of bed when he's woken us crying in the middle of the nigh? Jesus, I'm lucky Rachael is a copper. Anyway, enough of that, no time to wish I was in another job, we have work to do. The detective superintendent will be waiting and you know how she hates anyone to be late."

"Makes you think though, doesn't it?" Flower commented as he joined his superior out of the room.

★★★

The incident room was crowded as Daniel and Flower walked in. DS Joyce Hollis was standing by the whiteboard, hands on her considerable hips. When he'd first met her and he was single, the thought used to pass through his mind what it must be like to be trapped between her thighs. In fact, she was quite pretty, he thought, with her flaming red hair tied in a bun, her blue eyes flashing confrontationally as she talked to you. She was now in her mid-forties and Daniel had known her since he'd been a DS. She stood around five nine, which made her quite a formidable woman to disagree with. He'd heard she had quite a reputation as a wild one in her teenage days. Now she was a down-to-earth copper, good at her job, but as Daniel had learnt on his first case with her, she had no sense of humour, which was immediately borne out by her, "Good of you to turn up, Chief Inspector."

Daniel knew better than to point out that he and Flower had had a rather busy morning. "Sorry, ma'am," he said, as he joined her by the whiteboard where pictures of the Carpenter family were stuck up along with ones of Francine Walker and Janet Goodchild. He looked across the room. There were no smiling faces, just an air of gloom. He knew the signs – this had the makings of an unsolved case. They needed encouragement; pessimism must not take hold.

"Okay," began Hollis, "what have we got so far?"

Daniel cleared his throat. "This morning, ma'am, we had another murder in the Carpenter family."

Hollis waved her hand impatiently. "I know that, Daniel, move on please, I haven't got all day."

"Yes, ma'am; right, what have we got that is positive so far?"

There was a groan around the room. He held up a hand. "We still have the report from SOCO to come but we do know that the knife wounds almost certainly prove that the same weapon was used for both killings, so reasonable to assume that the murders were carried out by the same person and who is local, or anyway knows the area and the Carpenter family well. The lane was a perfect place for an ambush at so early an hour and no CCTV. It had been well chosen. So what would we expect to find? Tyre marks, footprints and blood. Well, the blood is Harry Carpenter's. The tyre marks and footprints were as good as washed away by the heavy rain so we can't expect much there. This killer plans every detail very carefully. Like the rain. I have no doubt he or she was waiting for a wet Saturday night and there have been plenty of those this month. Not much to go on there. Then we come to motive – well, any ideas would be welcome. Both Jenny and Harry Carpenter were not your usual level-headed young people. One was an alcoholic, the other a drug user and deeply in debt among other things. So quite possibly there is someone out there desperate enough to want to kill them. Let's say a drug dealer, a money shark or, very unlikely but worth mentioning, a pimp. That, however, would seem to exclude the same killer. So let's have some ideas."

"Could it be a serial killer?" asked a voice from the back of the room.

"It depends what you call a serial killer," interrupted Hollis, "but for the moment let's settle on that word. Carry on, Daniel."

"Yes, ma'am. No doubt the media, with its desire for sensationalism, would love to use the word, *serial*," Daniel continued. "I think we should delve into Jack Carpenter's past. See if we can find out anything that might have happened before he became wealthy that might give us a clue. So I'm going to ask you, Constable Andrews, to spend every hour God gave you digging into the past. Contact the Met; they might know something. You okay with that?"

"I'll be on it right away, guv," beamed Jane Andrews.

Another hand flew up at the back of the room. Sergeant Tower was a hardened copper and was nicknamed Google by the squad because of his abundant knowledge of the local Winchester area, its shady inhabitants and illegal goings-on. Over the years he'd built up many reliable sources. Okay, they wanted rewarding and it had cost him a bob or two but the rewards had been worthwhile. He liked to think that several cases had been solved on his evidence and the gratitude of his superiors made up for the little money he'd paid out. No one asked too many questions as to how he'd obtained the vital piece of evidence.

"Yes, Sergeant?"

"Shouldn't we look close to home as well, guv?"

"Definitely," interrupted Hollis again.

"I'll be on it right away."

"Good," said Daniel, wishing Hollis would shut up. "Now, one more thing. I know we are stretched for officers but we must ensure that we keep a close eye on the two Carpenters and Doctor Walker. It won't be easy and will mean long hours. Sergeant Flower will organise a rota as best he can. Married officers better warn their better halves," Daniel said with some feeling. "Okay, ma'am?"

Hollis smiled, looked across the room. "Let's go; meeting over. Remember, I'm looking forward to some results before we meet again. The media are already behaving like a pack of hounds."

And you're one of them, thought Daniel as he put his notebook in his coat pocket.

51

The killing of Harry was risky. I'm sure that Appleman will have worked out that the killer is local and even knows the family well, but of course this was a risk I was well aware of, so why am I sitting here on my arse, drinking a mug of tea, worrying about it? What I need to do is plan my next move, not sweat about a possible knock on my door from a smiling Appleman. I get off my kitchen stool, stretch and look at the knife on the worktop that has now rid the world of two wasters. I see a small spot of blood still stuck on the blade and smile – Harry's. I pick up the knife and lick it clean. I'm getting the taste for blood, better than a boiled egg any time. I laugh at the comparison. I look out of the kitchen window and think about my final task, a task that will make me a hero. I will be able to explain, and I will be understood. I know the media are branding me a cold-blooded killer. Idiots! I'm killing so that one man's life can become gloriously peaceful. I'm sure that when I explain my reasons in detail for ridding the world of such trash (which I will eventually get a chance to do), I will be understood, even praised. Those who are trying to hunt me down will never catch me, and when I face them at a time and day of my choosing, they will see me in a different light. It's time to bring my diary up to date and then scribble down a few

ideas in my little black notebook. And then suddenly I have it!
I need to create a diversion. One to throw the police off the
scent so that I can complete my mission.

★★★

Two hours later, my diversion is planned. An innocent man
will die. But I couldn't care a shit. I'm focused, any lingering
thought of pulling out gone. I must be more careful. No
stupid moves, a mistake many killers make. Pity, because I
enjoy playing games. I tear two pages out of my notebook that
I had written likely victims on and slowly eat them. Taste is
disgusting, but the best way. I have come to the conclusion that
I must try and sow doubt into the good chief inspector's mind.
I will leave my intended target alone for a while and strike
at my diversion. This might really fuck up Appleman. Yes,
yes, I like this idea: another game. Then, while the police are
rushing around like headless chickens, I will strike at my real
target. I clap my hands; frankly, I'm amazed at my cunning. Or
is it God guiding me? I rush back to my bedroom and throw
myself on the bed. I start to pant, oh how this killing game
excites me; I begin to sweat, to breath heavily. I know then that
ecstasy is not far away. I close my eyes and wait. The build-
up is ecstatic. Then I scream, writhe on the bed panting, and
for one glorious second I'm transported into another world.
Why does it have to be so short? Finally my breathing steadies.
Calmness returns. Time to work out my new plan, nothing
left to chance. I imagine feeling the knife pierce flesh. The
cry of pain, the rush of blood, the body, already nearly dead,
sinking to the ground. I throw myself off the bed and run back
into the kitchen. I need a glass of wine. Fuck my intention
not to drink. I raise the glass to the ceiling. "For you, Jack
Carpenter, this is all for you!" I shout.

52

Sophie had thought that grief would soon evaporate, helped of course by a few good slugs of gin and some virile young man whispering sweet nothings in her ear. But it dawned on her that the one emotion that was not going to leave her was fear, deep, deep, ever present fear. Whatever the time of day, whatever she was doing, fear sat on her shoulders like a heavy sack. "It's fucking tearing me apart right now," she confided to her hairdresser in desperation, who, not used to his client worrying about anything except where her next shag was coming from, was lost for words. Taking this as a sign of sympathy, Sophie burst into tears and buried her head in her hands which made his hand slip. "Now you've fucked up my hair!" she screamed as water mingled with her tears.

★★★

Two hours later Sophie was leaving the hairdressers, swearing that she'd never come back. It had done her good to let her temper rip at the man and she dared to think that the fear had left her, but as she clicked the locks on her Mercedes and slipped behind the wheel it returned – like icy water running down her back, making her gasp with despair. With shaking

275

fingers she charged up her mobile and was surprised to see a text from Daniel Appleman. What the fuck did that wanker want?

Please come to the station as soon as you can.

Her heart pounding, she started the car and eased her way into the flow of traffic. She was not used to doing what men asked but something told her that this was urgent. With her tongue stuck to the roof of her mouth, a sign that her next gin was due, she fought the desire to head home and feel the cold liquid of a Hendrick's gin and tonic slip down her throat.

★★★

Daniel rose and held out a hand as Sophie was shown into his airless office. She ignored the hand, sniffed and forced a smile. "Well, here I am, Appleman, what do you want?"

By now Daniel had got the measure of her outbursts, so he ignored her, just smiled and looked calmly at her, waved at the chair and said, "Make yourself comfortable, Mrs Carpenter, and I will talk to you in a moment. But first, I have a very important telephone call to make, which is not for anyone's ears but my own. So excuse me while I go to another room. The constable here will get you a cup of coffee." With that, Daniel walked out of the room, leaving a rather uneasy constable to deal with Mrs Carpenter, who for once was struck speechless.

"Tea or coffee, madam?"

"Fuck off, you little man, I want nothing, and anyway I'm sure your beverages are disgusting."

The constable nodded and put his arms behind his back. Well, she was right about the coffee. He deemed it wise to say nothing to this pathetic woman. He almost smiled as he watched her crossing and uncrossing her legs, wondering if the station gossip was right. Mrs Carpenter uncrossed her legs rather a lot.

It took Daniel half an hour to walk round the station twice, go to relieve his bladder, and walk out into the car park for a much needed smoke before he judged he'd tested Sophie Carpenter's patience to the limit. It was time to address the subject of protection with her. DS Hollis had been right. "Time to take her off the suspect list," she'd advised, "and put her on the life in danger list." Much as he despised the woman, he'd agreed. It was his job to defend anyone in danger as best he could, and he was quite sure that Sophie Carpenter could well be in grave danger, so what to do with this foul mouthed woman? As he walked back into his office, now smelling strongly of her scent, he waved the constable away and smiled apologetically at Sophie's glaring face. Not giving her a chance to swear at him he said, "Let me begin by saying I know how much you must be mourning the death of your children."

"Save your breath, Appleman. I don't want sympathy from you. I consider you incompetent and I think I'll put my views to the chief constable when I next see him. So, what do you say to that?"

Bitch, thought Daniel, fighting the urge to stand up and slap her face. "You're free to do what you like but I didn't ask you here to defend my actions, so let's not waste time swapping insults. You're here because I think we should give you security. This may be a little intrusive, but it is for your safety."

"What does that mean?"

"Tight security means a WPC will be with you day and night. I don't want to frighten you but I think you could be in danger."

"You just *have* fucking frightened me, you idiot man. And pity you didn't think of that before my darling son was killed."

Daniel took a deep breath, deciding to ignore her last remark. "I'm sorry, but I want to keep you alive. I would like your cooperation by not going out alone at nights."

"What!"

"Stay at home, Mrs Carpenter; it is for your own safety. I know it will not be easy for you but I will make sure the WPC's make themselves as unobtrusive as possible."

Sophie's face went white and her voice was not as aggressive as usual. "You think I'm in real danger, don't you?"

Jesus, how many times does this woman want me to say, yes you're in danger? he thought, sighing loudly. "Yes, Mrs Carpenter, you're in danger, and the police will do their level best to protect you, but you must cooperate. There is only so much we can do."

Thinking that there was no mileage in annoying Appleman further, her attitude suddenly changed. "I understand – I'm sorry to have been rude, but I'm scared. Do you really think the killer might come after me?"

"It's a chance we must prepare for."

"You don't beat about the bush, do you, Chief Inspector?"

"I must be honest."

Sophie visibly shook in the chair.

★★★

Francine opened the cottage front door and nearly slammed it in Tim Stafford's face. It was on the tip of her tongue to tell him to get lost, even though she'd invited him over. *Very bad mistake,* she thought, forcing a smile. "Tim," she said almost in a whisper.

Tim leant forward to kiss her but she stepped away. *Hang*

on, I'm not ready for that. Don't rush things. He held out a hand and she took it. "Shall we go into the cottage?"

"Good idea, bit cold to talk out here all night."

In your dreams, Tim. She swallowed, took a deep breath and controlled her voice as she said, "Yes, a bit cold. Come on follow me. There's a fire in the sitting room."

She controlled a laugh as he gave her the impression of a naughty schoolboy come to be disciplined by his teacher. "Relax, Tim, I'm not going to eat you. You go on into the sitting room and I'll get us a drink. Beer or wine?"

"Red wine if you've got it, Francine, and I'll come into the kitchen with you. Don't want you to be alone."

Pity you didn't say that some years ago, Timothy Stafford. "Okay, I'd like that." *And I mean it!* she thought.

Glass of wine in hand, Tim stood awkwardly in the middle of the kitchen. He stared at Francine's back as she tossed something that smelt delicious into a frying pan. He was a bundle of nerves and unable to read Francine's vibes. He could only think that she was regretting asking him over, and there was no Jack to give him moral support. Driving to the cottage he had rehearsed what he was going to say, but now, watching the stiffness in her back, his confidence leaked from him. Did she not want him here? He wouldn't blame her. Was she thinking she'd been right when she'd told him it would be better if he packed his bags and left her alone? Was trying to rekindle what had been a happy and lustful relationship impossible? It crossed his mind, as he put his half drunk glass down on the worktop, that he'd broken her heart once and that he couldn't risk doing it again, in spite of what Jack had told him.

Before he could say he was leaving, Francine swung round to face him. She was holding the frying pan in one hand and for a second he thought she was going to hit him with it. Realising this she laughed, and after a second's hesitation he

279

joined in. "You thought I was going to clock you one didn't you, Tim?"

"I did. And I think I'd better—"

Reading his thoughts Francine said, "No! Don't go. I have things to say. I should hate you, Tim – always thought if I ever saw you again I would want to smash your face in. But surprise, surprise, I find myself still thinking you're the most handsome man I've ever met. And Jesus, this is hard to say, I still have feelings for you. It's crazy, crazy."

"I, I—"

"Hang on a minute, let me finish. No running off this time."

Tim rested his back against the worktop. He didn't dare raise his glass to his lips, his hands were shaking too badly.

"I'm not going to bang on about how much you hurt me when you did your disappearing act. I think you're well aware of that. Have you ever thought how much I suffered? You broke my heart, damn you. The one good thing that came out of that dreadful time was that I eventually became a doctor. It was my way of trying to make amends for taking a life – well that was how I saw it. I've lost count of the number of people's lives I have saved or helped others to save. I think, if God can ever forgive me for aborting our baby, I've done my penance. So tell me, Tim, did it change your life?"

"Not as dramatically as yours."

Francine gave a light laugh. "No, you're dead right there. Did you just shrug, tell your friends I was a careless scrubber and go on living your life as if nothing had happened? No don't interrupt. But it HAD happened, Tim – I was pregnant!"

"No, I told no one."

"Not even your parents?"

"No one."

"Ashamed, were you?"

"It grew on me, yes."

"Nothing better to think of, eh?"

"Please, Francine, it was not like that."

Francine put the frying pan back on the stove. "Okay, okay, let's leave it there. So tell me, how did you get involved with Jack?"

"I went into my father's firm and became an architect like him. We didn't agree over the way the firm was going so I decided to branch out on my own, ending up being hired part-time by Jack. After a year he offered me a full-time job and here I am."

"And once again you are messing with my emotions."

Tim hung his head. "I know."

"And damn you, Tim Stafford, I wish I'd never set eyes on you again."

"So why am I here?"

"Because I wanted to see what you were like all these years on. I wanted to try and work out why I fell in love with you."

"And?"

Francine hesitated. "I can't answer that. I don't think I will ever be able to work that out, just like I'm wondering why I was so mad to ask you over tonight." She laughed again. "And don't be tempted to say it's because I love you! Oh shit! Now look what I've done, I've burnt the fucking Dover sole. Well, that means no supper, I'm afraid. Just have to do with the wine."

Tim smiled.

Francine thought, *God, he looks great!*

For a moment neither spoke and it was Francine who eventually broke the silence. "Look, Tim, when I saw you walk out of the portakabin my heart missed a beat and I panicked and to be honest I feel a bit panicky now. I'm standing here looking at you and only seeing a kind man; bloody fool, I'm telling myself. But emotions have a way of taking over, emotions that can lead to big mistakes. And I think that's where I am now. On the edge of a big mistake."

Tim sighed and drained his glass.

"A refill?"

"I don't think so."

"Time to go, Tim?"

"It might be for the best."

"I don't think I want you to walk away into the sunset."

Tim blew out his cheeks. "I don't want to do that."

"So?"

Tim flashed a smile. "In that case…"

At that moment Jack and Daniel Appleman walked in.

53

Suddenly, Sophie is surrounded by police. I can only blame myself for that, but it is going to present me with a few problems when the time comes to strike. The last few nights my dreams have become macabre. Blood, sliced breasts, knives being driven into a body time and time again and then a face appears, rotting, crawling with ants. It is then that I have woken, dripping in sweat and screaming. Not in disgust or fear, no, just a strong desire to taste human blood. As I dress I'm aware that I'm close to being addicted and as with all addictions you fight them or you let them control you. I have no fight in me.

I'm not hungry but I must eat. Well, you stupid cow, why not eat the sandwich which you bought yesterday for just such a reason? Once in the kitchen I head for the fridge and reluctantly open it. Staring at me is the beef sandwich. Yuck, it does nothing for me. I chuck it in the waste bin. I'd like to eat Sophie's flesh, warm and dripping with blood. Amazing what imagination can do. I make no attempt to force the thought out of my mind. The pleasure is overpowering. Come on, come on, this is no time to dwell, I have things to do. And, Mr Appleman, what's in your thoughts? Am I still ahead of you? I think I still know your every move.

I'm shaking now, as I start to think of Sophie again – her face as I raise the knife, her eyes radiating fear for the split second before I drive it into her chest and her miserable life comes to an end. I pour myself a glass of cold water. Then, my thirst satisfied, I move towards the door, shrug into my thick coat, grab my car keys and move out of the flat. I'm a little scared. This will be my greatest test but I will succeed. Otherwise the other killings will be for nothing and I will end up a lonely spinster. Familiar adrenaline begins to pump. I might even be tempted to cut a bit of flesh off Mrs fucking Carpenter. Depraved? No, just doing what I have to do to save a man from a miserable life. And what's wrong having a keepsake?

I'm driving carefully out of Winchester; I don't want the police to pick me up for speeding but this twenty mile an hour restriction is annoying. Nevertheless, I'm a law-abiding citizen. Well, that's a laugh. I'm heading to Sophie's house to see how many police cars are outside. It will give me some idea of the number that guard her during daylight hours. Though I'm thinking I will strike at night, as I know that there will be a reduced number after dusk. How good it feels to have an ear to most of the inspector's plans.

The downland, today bathed in sunshine for a change, that faces the house is the perfect place to stop. It is a good vantage point and no one can see me from the house. I see two police cars, so maybe only one at night, but how many arrive in the car? That is something I will only know once I'm in the house. Dangerous, but oh so exciting. I'm shivering with the thought, and utterly confident that I can outwit the police. So my mind is made up. A night attack. It is my best chance of sending the bitch to hell.

Now I'm driving back down the lane and heading towards Winchester, thinking of only one thing – the demise of Sophie Carpenter. I hit the curb – *shit, concentrate, you fool, or all your planning will be for nothing.* I'm taking slow deep breaths to control my excitement.

★★★

The next morning dawns wet and dull. Back to the usual. I'm awake, planning my diversion. It is tempting to strike at Sophie now but my gut feeling is still to create a diversion. It's my insurance policy, I'm telling myself, as I jump out of bed, all nerves and a strong desire to get moving. In the bathroom I splash my face with water. No time for a shower or I will be late for work and I can't risk being late. I'm feeling good. As I'm walking towards my car I hum a tune by Diamond; I'm confident I'm nearly there.

54

Detective Superintendent Joyce Hollis had called a progressive-review meeting for early morning and the incident room was strangely quiet as Daniel moved up to the table to stand beside her. He was feeling particularly low this morning. There were two women demanding his attention, one because of his job and the other because he loved her. Right now he had to concentrate on Hollis. He ran his hands through his hair and looked round the room at the glum faces, before turning to Hollis. "I'm sorry to have to report, ma'am, that we have made little progress. The forensic reports that have trickled in have been of no help and frankly I don't think we can expect much from the ones yet to come through."

"Okay," said Hollis, "let's add up what we've got so far." She glared at Daniel. "Anything, Chief Inspector, or am I wasting my time here? No DNA, no camera footage, no blood match, no footprints, not a clue anywhere. Looks to me as if the killer is a ghost. So that answers my question I think." She turned to tap the whiteboard. "We can remove Mrs Carpenter from our suspect list at least. Can any of you in this room improve my day?"

Even before she asked the question, Daniel could tell there

was no good news about to come from his officers. "This is getting me down, ma'am," he confessed. "It feels as if I'm sitting on a time bomb, which at any moment is going to explode. Look at us," – he waved a hand around the room – "all sitting here, notebooks in front of us, looking miserable. We need a break, ma'am, but I can't see where it's going to come from. I'm scratching my head so hard that I'll soon be bald."

Hollis forced a smile at Daniel. "Look, I understand how you feel, and I know everyone in this room is working overtime to find something positive but I'm under as much pressure as you are. So, no point in wasting time sitting here sipping tasteless mugs of tea and coffee. Go out there and dig and dig into Jack Carpenter's past, for I have a feeling that that is where you might find something, and, Chief Inspector, I expect a more upbeat report the next time we meet. Get to it!" With those words ringing in Daniel's ears, Hollis strode out of the room. He hoped that she hadn't heard the sigh of relief that went round the incident room before she closed the door.

"She doesn't change," commented Flower as he joined Daniel at the table. "Must think we're a load of magicians."

"I expect she's getting it in the neck from my friend the ACC. He'd love to see me fail. Do you know something, right at this moment I don't think I'd care. Rachael is moaning at me, the chief constable is getting frustrated, keen to see progress, our liaison officer, that infuriating David Stone, is moaning like hell as to what he's going to say to the media next. Pressure is building, mate, and to add to my troubles man-power is stretched to the limit guarding the depleted Carpenter family. No clues, no suspect, an unhappy wife and the dread that someone else is going to die."

"Well, we can't solve a case without any evidence, and as for motive…"

Daniel shook his head. "I'm as mystified as you. Oh shit,

287

I've just remembered that I've got a meeting with Carpenter in half an hour. Could you visit his missus and check all is well there? If we lose her I think I can kiss my career goodbye."

"Lose her boss?"

"Murdered is the word, mate."

★★★

Jack Carpenter did nothing to improve Daniel's mood. The moment he walked into his office Daniel guessed that Jack was about to explode – he was not to be disappointed.

"What the hell is going on, Daniel? Two of my family killed and you seem to be walking around like a headless chicken. Surely the killer has left something that you can work on?"

"Look, Jack, I'm not going to waste my time making excuses but policing is not like running a business where you can plan ahead for problems. You can't plan ahead for a murder."

"Don't state the obvious, Daniel," said Jack. "I'm not a fool, I know a murder can come and hit you in the face without warning, but don't try telling me that with all the resources the police now have to hand you can't find the smallest piece of evidence to work on. All killers make mistakes."

And who are you to know? Daniel thought, furious that his efforts were being ignored. "Are you trying to say we're incompetent?" he asked through gritted teeth.

"I think you're looking in the wrong places. Bothering my secretary, for example. Christ, man, she couldn't kill a fly. Okay, she hasn't got a cast-iron alibi for the night of Jenny's death but her word is enough for me and so it damn well should be for you. Move on, Chief Inspector, and leave my friends and staff alone and be aware that if anything happens to Francine I will never forgive you and will haunt you for the rest of your fucking life. Clear?"

"And Sophie?"

Jack waved a hand in the air. "And Sophie."

Daniel felt anger stirring inside him, but knew to lose his temper would only make Jack think less of him and, in spite of everything he'd just said, there could come a time when he might need Jack's cooperation. But to stay in the same room a moment longer was not an option. He glared at Jack, shook his head and walked out of the room. "Bastard, bastard," he kept saying to himself as he walked to his car.

★★★

"By the look on your face, things didn't go too well," said Flower as Daniel walked towards his office.

"Need a word, Sergeant," said Daniel as he stepped into his office.

Flower grabbed his notebook off his desk and followed his boss into the office. Daniel slammed his briefcase down on his desk and shook his head. "You could say that, Sergeant. Jack called me incompetent, told me to stop the team hassling his staff and then told me he'd haunt me for the rest of my life if any harm came to Francine. Jesus, man, he didn't seem to care a damn about his ex-wife. It was a very undignified performance and left me wondering what sort of man Jack Carpenter really is. Okay, we know he has no time for his wife but to more or less tell me that he doesn't care if she dies is unbelievable. I was tempted to give him a piece of my mind, I can tell you, but we might need his cooperation at some time so I decided the best thing to do was walk away."

"He's suffering, boss," said Flower. "Evidence points to his son being the arsonist – his room had a singed T-shirt and pair of jeans smelling strongly of petrol in a drawer. Very careless, but then he assumed we'd never suspect him. Probably right, if he hadn't been killed and we searched his room for any clues. Now both his children have been brutally killed. That's enough to send anyone crazy, I reckon."

"That doesn't give him the right to tell me how to do my job or show such disregard for Mrs Carpenter."

"I agree, but I'm sure he's cursing himself right now."

"Maybe, but he well and truly got under my skin. Anyway, no point in taking up more valuable time, we have work to do, as Carpenter would say, but I'm starving and need a drink. How about we remove ourselves to the Green Man for a pint and a bite to eat, and we can sit down with no danger of being interrupted and, as Hollis said yesterday, add up what we've got so far?"

★★★

Daniel had always liked the Green Man in Southgate Street. It was opposite the cinema, not far from a car park and the food was good and reasonably priced. Before Arty was born he and Rachael would drop in after a film for a drink and a steak. As he pushed open the door and walked in he couldn't stop himself from thinking that it had been several months since he and Rachael had been able to take an evening off. It was time to change that, but when, that was the question. Work, Arty and sheer fatigue would have to be sorted first.

Pints and steaks ordered, Daniel's rare, Flower's medium rare, they moved to a table with comfortable armchairs and collapsed into them. For several minutes they sat in silence while their brains relaxed and the atmosphere calmed their ragged nerves. Daniel took a long pull at his beer. "Ah, that feels better, and here come our steaks."

The two men set to and it didn't take long for them to clear their plates. "Wow, that was good," said Flower, smacking his lips.

"And now to business," said Daniel, wiping the mustard off his mouth with a paper napkin. "So, what have we got? Two dead bodies, almost certainly killed by the same person. Suspects: Janet Goodchild, Doctor Walker, Jack Carpenter. The old man. Motive, your guess is as good as mine. Random killing? That looks unlikely as well. Same knife almost certainly used both times according to forensics. Maybe a serial killer or someone who has got the taste for killing. This is quite usual in rape cases, but this is definitely not tied to rape. I think this is something to do with way back when Carpenter was building up his business. The two murders have been well planned, hence no evidence. The killer has had time to clean up, avoid any CCTV and walk away. So we have fuck all. Anything to add, mate?" Daniel asked.

"Right, suspects first. Doctor Walker has a cast-iron alibi for both nights. Two emergency calls at the time of death. Jack Carpenter in my view can be excluded, as can Mrs Carpenter, and we know the old man is incapable. Pity about him. That leaves the PA. No alibi for both nights. But why would she want to kill off the family? It seems very implausible to my mind. What would she have to gain? As for motive, well, my thoughts are the same as yours, but one thought you left out. Is this the end or is there another death planned?"

Daniel rubbed his chin, finished his pint, thinking that another one would go down a treat but forcing himself to ignore his thirst. "If this is a serial killer, he or she will almost certainly strike again and it's reasonable to think that Sophie Carpenter is the most likely person to be in danger."

"Not Doctor Walker?"

"My way of thinking is that she's come on the scene late, so not connected to any of Carpenter's early business dealings in London. Of course, we are dealing with someone who enjoys killing so we cannot be sure of anything. I think we must dig and dig into Jack's past, and Goodchild's perhaps.

At the same time we must be aware of a really dangerous threat to Sophie Carpenter. So, time to get off our arses, Sergeant and get back to the station. We have work to do."

★★★

That evening, Tim Stafford sat outside the replacement portakabin as the evening shadows spread across the newly laid cricket pitch. He could hear a cock pheasant cackling away in the distance and somewhere a pigeon was cooing as another day drew to a close. Everything was coming together nicely. There was no trace left of the fire, the new pavilions were well on their way, new trees had replaced the burnt ones and the football pitch had been re-sown. With a bit of good fortune the project would be finished by early summer, only six months late, which a few weeks ago had seemed like a dream. But Jack could always work miracles, and with new builders and suppliers the project had been put back on track. He hunched his shoulders against the biting late November wind and knew that he would never find a better man to work for, which made his decision to leave all the more painful. Thinking about it brought tears to his eyes but it was for the best. Late into the night that he'd been with Francine in the cottage, and when Jack had finally gone to bed he and Francine had drunk the best part of two bottles of red wine and looked into each other's eyes and knew, in spite of emotions pulling them in all directions, what the answer should be. He'd explained to her that the guilt would never leave him and there was no way he could go into a long-term relationship knowing that that guilt would haunt him every time he looked at her or saw a young child walking down a street or playing cricket or football or even sitting with their parents in a park. Tears had been shed and hugs had been exchanged, but they were realists. They would stay friends, which Francine told him she would never have contemplated a few weeks earlier, but that she shared his views totally. The parting at the front door in the early hours would remain with him forever. So here he was on his last night on the site – his life in tatters, alone, because years ago he'd made a terrible mistake. He turned to go back into the warmth of the portakabin, when he heard a familiar voice call out his name.

He smiled with relief. A bit of company was just what he needed.

55

It is the perfect time for me to strike. I know how he's feeling. Devastated. Well, Timothy Stafford, I'm about to help you out of your misery. I see him look towards me through the gloom and I shout. He raises a hand and I know he would like my company. I laugh, ha, company! Little does he know. As I walk across the damp grass I'm thinking of why I've chosen Stafford to be my diversion – I'm rescuing a woman from the attention of a wicked man. Just like saving Jack from Sophie's clutches. Stafford does not deserve to live. That is my justification. I feel the usual adrenaline surge as I near the portakabin. Very soon now, Stafford's blood will be flowing on to the floor and I will dip my fingers into the warm liquid and lick them. The thought makes me shiver. I feel the cold steel blade of my knife tucked into my belt and walk on. He's standing waiting for me, a smile on his face. He holds out a hand, I take it. It's cold, the skin feels rough. He leads me into the portakabin. I'm offered a drink, I ask if he has any beer. He nods and walks towards a fridge and pulls out two bottles of Beck's beer, not my favourite but it would be rude to refuse a condemned man. After all, it won't be long before my knife is slicing into his flesh. So what's it matter if I dislike the brand? He points to a well-worn brown leather chair and I sink into it, making sure the knife doesn't cut into my ribs as I sit down. I steer him onto the subject of Francine. (Not difficult, as I sensed this is what he would want to talk about.) Even the sadness in his eyes does not change me. I'm doing this distraught man a favour, as well as administering justice. I stand – he thinks I want another beer – I accept. He turns his back on me. My heart is threatening to burst through my chest. My excitement is at its height. My armpits and thighs are wet. I take out my gloves from a pocket in my coat and put them on. One last deep breath. I slip off the chair, draw the knife out from under my coat, hold it firm, and say, "Tim." He turns, I lunge. The knife cuts through his shirt and sinks into his flesh. His eyes widen in surprise. He drops his hands, desperately trying to wrestle the knife from me, but he is already growing weak. I pull the knife from his chest, slash frantically at his arms and lunge again. His mouth opens, I suspect to scream, so I slam a hand over his mouth and heave. He slips to the floor with the knife in his chest. I quickly bend down and pull it out before driving it in again. Surely this will kill him. He gurgles, blood runs from his mouth. His eyes are wide open. His mouth moves as if he's trying to speak but no sound comes out. He coughs and his blood hits my face. I feel the warmth and laugh. He's dying, my job is done. He's died without a fight and is off to meet his Maker. I waste little time staring at the blood-soaked shirt or the pool of blood oozing from his chest. I would like to stay and watch him bleed out but know that that would be foolish. I bend down and dip a finger in the pool of blood and put it to my lips. I savour the warm taste. I see a blue hand-towel on his bed. I take it and rub my face, then roll it up and push it into my coat pocket. I leave the cabin, struggling with my feet in shoes one size too big – another ploy to put the police off the scent. I will soon be back in my flat and then I must wait to see if the hoped for mayhem breaks out. Surely, officers will be taken from Sophie's house, and then I will move. Time will not be on my side. It won't take long for the detective to realise that something doesn't fit. But he will be too late. It sounds so simple, but I'm well aware this next killing will test me to the full. Every ounce of my body is ready for the challenge to come. Not for the first time, I know that killing Sophie will be the most dangerous adventure I have so far undertaken.

Also the most exciting.

As I'm walking back in the growing darkness I nearly trip over a body. I can make out it's a man lying half hidden by the long grass on the verge of the road leading to Winchester. My heart thumps – I have an idea. I bend down – my fucking glasses slip from my nose – shit! I swear loudly, but as I pick them up off the grass I'm relieved to find they are not broken. I feel panic growing; I'm wasting valuable seconds but this chance is too good to turn down. I pray that no one will have chosen this spot for an evening walk or a quick fumble. Though I'm pretty certain it is too wet for a dog walker or an oversexed couple. I fight the panic, count silently to a hundred and then look at the body. It has not stirred. It's snoring that irritates me. It's alive. I kick at it none too kindly. It grunts then begins to snore again. I bend down and smell an unwashed body and the strong aroma of alcohol. Although the light is bad I think it's the face of an oldish man, but what do I care? I move fast. With my gloved hands I rub the knife on this stinking body, forcing myself not to breath. Then, I tuck the knife under my coat. My diversion has been better than I could ever have expected. This will really focus the police and hopefully, for a little while at least, this stinking individual will find himself the suspect for three murders. How can the good chief inspector ignore Tim Stafford's blood on the man's clothes? How can he not think that this man killed for money to buy booze or drugs? I don't expect him to think he's the killer of Harry and Jenny but it will hopefully take his mind off these deaths long enough to relax the security surrounding Sophie. Time for me to move and kill her. I look up at the sky and walk away humming Bocelli's *Time To Say Goodbye*. Very apt, I'm thinking, as I reach my car. I feel no guilt at killing an innocent man. I slip into the driving seat, turn the key and head for home. Just one more detail to clear up.

56

It was just gone eight the next morning, with rain lashing across the cricket pitch, that Jack got out of his car to pay a much needed visit to Stafford, especially to talk over his decision to leave. There were important things to discuss. Matters which he should have dealt with several weeks ago. *I've been a bit distracted,* he thought ruefully as he swung his briefcase in annoyance. "But thank God Stafford has seen to everything," he said to the rain-filled sky.

Then his eyes widened in horror as he saw the body of a man lying not a metre from where he was standing. He dropped his briefcase on the grass and moved quickly, bending down to stare at the unshaven face, the body covered in rags and what looked like blood on his chest. He sank to his knees, convinced he'd stumbled on a dead body, but then a groan told him the man was alive. He reached out and shook him, only to be rewarded by another groan. Jack reeled back from the smell of sweat and vomit, fumbling in his pocket for a handkerchief. Then, holding it to his face with one hand, he shook the body again. Apart from another groan there was no new reaction. Jack made a decision. This man, who at first glance looked well on the way to death, needed urgent medical attention. He pushed himself to his feet, retrieved his briefcase, fumbled for his mobile and ran towards the portakabin. As he burst through the door he was met by a sight far worse than the body by his car.

★★★

Half an hour later the portakabin was a major crime scene. Two police cars, an ambulance, the SOCO white van and Sarah Jones' red Renault were parked on the grass. Jack was sitting on the battered leather chair, his head in his hands. *Where on earth is this going to end?* he thought. *How many more people close to me are going to die?* A cough made him look up. Daniel Appleman was standing by his side. He jumped up and shook his head. "My God, Daniel, this, this is unbelievable. I don't think I can take much more of this. Why would anyone want to kill Tim? Can you explain this?"

Daniel, who was expecting another burst of fury, took several seconds to reply. "I can't, at least not this minute. I thought that if there was another murder planned, Sophie would be the target, not Stafford."

"But it follows the pattern. Someone close to me," croaked Jack, rubbing at his red-rimmed eyes. "And a good friend, who I will never be able to replace. He's given his heart to this job. He's loyal, understanding of my rather crazy moves. Gives me gentle warnings when he thinks they are due. And how is he rewarded? Murdered because of me. Jesus Christ, I'm a living time bomb." He stared at Tim's body, not yet covered by a sheet, and Daniel watched the tears flow. He was in no doubt that Jack was near the end of his tether and at the moment he was powerless to do anything about it. He put a consoling hand on one of Jack's shoulders. "I'm lost for words, Jack, I never expected this."

Daniel could sense that Jack was having difficulty in keeping his anger in check when he said, "The killer is laughing at you, Daniel. And what of the man by my car?"

"What man?" Daniel asked, a worried look crossing his face.

"Jesus!" Jack exclaimed. "Coming across Tim's body drove the thought of the man out of my mind. I was about to contact the emergency services. How the hell could I forget?"

"Where was this man, Jack?"

"By my car. I'm surprised you missed him."

"He's not there now. I'm parked beside you."

Jack looked puzzled. "He was alive, but he didn't look as if he'd move far. He looked pretty far gone to me. I think there was blood on his chest. I was going to ring emergency services as soon as I got here."

"Don't blame yourself," said Daniel heading for the door of the portakabin. "I'll get an officer to go back to our cars and search, but I have a feeling your half-dead man made a recovery."

"How could I forget, how could I? My mind is going crazy."

"We'll find him. The question is, was he in any way connected with Stafford's death."

"He must have been the killer."

"That's possible, I suppose, though from what you have just told me it sounds unlikely. We will know more when we find him, as I'm sure we will."

Jack cast a doubting eye in Daniel's direction.

Not slow to see the look, Daniel repeated, "We'll find him." And before Jack could reply he continued, "If his condition is as bad as you say he won't get far."

Jack made no attempt to hide his disbelief. "For God sake, man, of course he's the killer. Probably killed my two children as well. What the fuck do you get paid for, DCI?"

Daniel looked across at Flower. "Tell him, Sergeant."

Flower looked at Daniel, thinking, *thanks very much, boss, drop me in it.* He said, "Look, Mr Carpenter, I promise you we are doing our best but at the moment we have nothing to go on except you finding, in your own words, this old man looking half dead. He has now disappeared. The chances of him being the killer of Mr Stafford seem very remote because no valuables have been taken, and would a man in his state be able to overpower a fit man? The killer of your children is very clever and I suspect this is his or her work, not this man by your car. Both the DCI and I are extremely sorry for your loss, Mr Carpenter, and let me assure you we are working hard to find the killer, but you must understand it is proving difficult because apart from the knife we have no evidence at all."

Jack blew out his cheeks. "Oh I shouldn't have said that. I'm sorry for my outburst," he said looking at Daniel, "but—"

At that moment Sarah Jones hurried into the portakabin. "Sorry to interrupt, guv, but the body is about to be moved. For your information I would say that the knife used is the same as for the other two killings. A smooth-bladed knife. Also, five stab wounds each time to the chest. No sign of a fight, which leads me to believe that he knew the killer just like we think the killer knew Jenny and Harry Carpenter. It is my opinion, for what it is worth, that this is the same killer."

"We think the same," growled Daniel.

"What now?" Jack asked.

"I think you should go home," said Daniel. "You've had a terrible shock. We will keep in contact. And if you can think of anyone who would like to do you serious harm, please let me know."

"I've already given you a list."

"Yes, but please think again – it's very important."

"I understand, and once again I'm sorry for my behaviour, it's just that—"

"No need to apologise," said Daniel. "You're having a bad time and we all say things we don't mean when stressed. Look, would you like a driver to take you home? I can arrange for your car to be delivered later."

"No thanks, I'm okay. I will go to the office and contact Francine. I would like it to be me who tells her."

"Of course."

A second later Francine burst into the portakabin. Eyes wide in horror she stared at Tim's body lying on the floor in a pool of blood. "No!" she screamed.

Jack rushed to her side and held her tight. She fought her way out of his hands and rushed to look down at Tim. "He's dead, he's dead, isn't he?" Then she turned to Daniel. "What, what has happened?"

Seeing no way of making the scene any less horrific than it already was, he replied, "I'm afraid so."

"How?"

"I'm afraid he's been killed."

Francine dropped to her knees, fighting back the tears. Then looking up at Jack, she sobbed, "Do you know something, Jack, there are times when I wish I had never found my mother's letter."

Then, resting a hand on Tim's forehead she collapsed beside him.

★★★

At seven thirty, Mary Slater was busy pouring out tea from a battered old urn for those who had slept rough. At least fifteen regulars came to the shelter every morning. Eleven men and four women but today there were five more bedraggled customers on account of the wet night. Apart from Sundays she was there to serve them, even though she found it hard to get out of bed in time to be standing behind a trestle table with urns of hot water and teabags in front of her, doing her best to smile at people who had forgotten how to smile. She'd learned, early on, that it was useless trying to persuade some of these hardened homeless people to take advantage of the shelter's beds, even on a bitterly cold night. They were set in their ways, preferring the fresh air and what they called "our freedom." At least three of the men had been coming for their breakfast and a cup of tea for as long as she'd worked at the shelter. Five years – years that had tested her compassion to breaking point, and yet she'd never once thought of giving up on her *charges,* as she called them. She tried not to think of the ones who had disappeared. No doubt some had died and she'd come to accept that death had probably come as a relief. She'd soon learned that most of these homeless were eagerly awaiting an early release from their hell.

Suddenly there was a commotion at the end of the queue. Individuals were backing away, trembling, mouths hanging open. She put down the mug she was holding and hurried round the table. Standing in the middle of the room was a wet, shivering, filthy Taffy. He was a dreadful sight. But what had broken up the queue and filled everyone with fear was his blood-soaked clothes.

Oblivious to the danger she might be putting herself in, Mary rushed towards him but stopped a few feet away when she saw the look in his eyes. She'd seen it before and knew it could spell danger. His eyes half closed glared at her as if daring her to come closer. Spittle was running from his mouth. He reeked of whisky. Mary reached for her mobile to call the police but Taffy saw her and lunged towards her. The small crowd that had gathered melted away they knew Mary was ringing the police and police spelt trouble. Mary side stepped Taffy's outstretched hands and quickly put her mobile back in her skirt pocket. The call would have to wait. Controlling Taffy was her priority. In as calm a voice as she could muster given the circumstances, she held out a hand. "Taffy, where have you been the last few days? A right state

303

you're in," she said. "Come here and let's see what I can do for you." Taffy didn't move. She took a deep breath and inched slowly towards him; she had to somehow get his confidence. He moved a hand, Mary froze, Taffy dropped his hand, Mary was a foot away from him. Seeing her chance, she grabbed one of his arms. She felt no resistance. Instead, Taffy started to cry, large tears staining his grime-covered face, and Mary sensed that any danger to her was over, at least for the time being. She put an arm round his waist and led him towards a bed.

She had grown fond of this lost old man and had hoped that she'd successfully weaned him off alcohol. *Well, that's turned out to be a bit optimistic,* she thought, as she drew Taffy towards her, at the same time fighting the desire to throw up from the smell. "Let's get you onto a bed, eh? It looks as if you could do with some sleep. When you wake I'll make you a nice meal and clean you up. You don't look as if you've eaten for days." He made no effort to resist or speak but Mary knew from past experience, that it would not be long before he became agitated, and when agitated he became a problem. She reckoned she had about five minutes – valuable minutes that could not be wasted. She led him to the nearest bed and covered him with a blanket, making no attempt to remove any of his filthy clothes. "You sit there, Taffy, I'll be back in a few minutes." Then, spotting Flo Lawrence, one of her middle-aged helpers, dressed as usual in multicoloured trousers and a baggy grey jumper that had seen better days, she whispered, "Call the police, Flo, and say it's urgent. Then try and calm the rest of our friends here down. Some are in a right state." With her long dark hair flowing behind her, Flo Lawrence, a tough druggy in her youth, had seen it all before. And she was quick to realise there could be a dangerous situation brewing. She pulled her mobile out of her jacket pocket. "Thanks," croaked Mary as she turned to hurry back to Taffy. As she'd feared, he had fallen off the bed and was shaking on the floor. When he saw Mary he started to shout, "I've killed someone, I've killed someone, Mary. It was the devil."

There was a rush of feet, the sound of mugs being dropped on the floor. Within minutes the last homeless person had fled from the shelter.

★★★

Low clouds hung like a blanket over the city. The traffic was nose to tail as Daniel drove away from the site and onto the main road to Winchester heading for the homeless shelter. He felt depressed. He had never got accustomed to viewing a murder scene. He'd lost count of the numbers he'd been called out to to witness the result of human inhumanity. He always thought he'd get used to it and yet, each time, he lost something inside that affected his emotional balance. The outcome had always been to sharpen his senses and fill him with a determination to track down the perpetrator. Suddenly, a red light glared through his windscreen and he slammed on his brakes. His mind had been concentrating on other things, not too good an idea on a wet morning in the rush hour. He shook his head angrily. He would be no good to anyone dead. He accelerated away as the lights turned green and continued towards the shelter where he knew Mary Slater would be urgently awaiting his arrival.

When the call had come through from the station he'd made his excuses to Jack and run from the portakabin, leaving Flower to manage that end. From what Mary had told the station, one of her homeless had walked into the shelter covered in blood and screaming he'd killed someone. By the time he reached the shelter three of his officers were already there, standing by the main door. Their relief at seeing Daniel was palpable. He spotted the small figure of Mary, her hair matted by the incessant rain, standing beside the officers.

Daniel was the first to speak. "I'm sorry it's taken me so long to get here but I was up at the Carpenter site. I'm afraid there has been another murder."

Mary's hand flew to her mouth. "Another murder?"

"Afraid so."

"Well, I might have some answers for you in here. You know the man Taffy already, and I know you had eliminated him from your enquiries, but about an hour ago – I'm afraid I have lost track of the time – he walked in here covered in blood, stinking of alcohol and screaming he'd killed the devil. At this moment he is under a bed having a fit."

Daniel hunched his shoulders against the rain and hurried into the shelter, followed by Mary, who waved Flo away. "Leave this to me; two of us will scare him to hell." Flo nodded her understanding.

"Please go easy, Chief Inspector," begged Mary. "And it would be best if it was just you and me; Taffy does not like Flo Lawrence. This is a very dangerous situation. Taffy's moods can become violent."

Daniel nodded. "You lead on, Mary. You know him better than I do."

As they approached the bed they could hear Taffy moaning. An eerie sound that sent shivers up Daniel's spine.

"He's been like this for some time now, Chief Inspector. I'm really worried. His constitution is not strong. In fact, given the state he's in, I can't see how he could hurt anyone, let alone kill someone as he claims. May I ask who's dead?"

"Jack Carpenter's site manager was murdered last night."

"Dear God! And you suspect Taffy? I don't think he would be capable – he's been missing three days, probably hasn't eaten and, knowing him, drunk a few bottles of booze if he could get his hands on them. But how he got covered in blood I can't explain and I doubt if Taffy will be able to either. Come and see for yourself."

Daniel hesitated. "Before I question him could you tell me if he goes wandering – I mean, leaves the city?"

"He has been known to. Why do you ask?"

"Because I think he might be the person who Jack Carpenter found lying in the grass up at the new site. You know where I mean?"

"Yes."

"Could he walk that far?"

"In three days I suppose he could, but I can't explain why he would be there."

Daniel scratched at his chin. "Well, I think there's a good chance he's the man we are looking for, but I'm inclined to agree with you about his inability to kill anyone, let alone a fit youngish man."

"I doubt you'll get much out of him."

"I must try."

"Of course."

Once they were standing over Taffy's writhing body Mary dropped to her knees so that she could see his face. His moaning was grating on her nerves. To her disgust she was on the verge of losing her temper. She took a deep breath, before laying a hand on his shoulder; he began to shake. She whispered in his ear, "Taffy, it's me, your friend Mary. I will help you but you must stop making these noises. It's going to make you ill. Please, Taffy, just for me, calm down and listen." She sat back on her haunches and waited. The next move had to be made by Taffy. It was not long in coming. He violently pushed her away, knocking her backwards. The breath was driven out of her body. She saw Daniel lurch towards Taffy. "No!" she managed to shout, pushing herself into an upright position. "Leave him. I'm fine."

Daniel reluctantly drew back. Taffy's next move was to sit up and belch loudly. His deep-set eyes glared at Mary. His cracked lips opened wide to show his rotting teeth. Mary knew that this was the moment he'd either launch himself at her again or he'd stay calm. To her relief he seemed to have calmed down. She judged it was the moment to risk letting Daniel speak to him, but as Daniel dropped down beside Mary, Taffy staggered to his feet and fled down the room.

"Leave him!" screamed Mary to Flo, knowing how dangerous Taffy could be. Flo stepped back and Taffy, arms flaying, flew past her.

"He's making for the door!" Mary shouted at Daniel. "We must stop him."

"My officers will do that," he replied fumbling for his radio.

But it was in vain. Taffy burst through the door onto the street – bounced off one officer and threw himself into the busy road, screaming that he'd killed the devil.

The young man in a black BMW had no time to brake. Taffy was thrown into the air, his head making contact with the windscreen before his body slipped off the bonnet and landed like a bundle of washing back onto the road.

By the time Mary and Daniel reached him he was dead.

★★★

As Daniel headed for the interview room his mobile buzzed. It was a cryptic message from Rachael, demanding to know if she was going to see him today. 'Or are you still stuck to your fucking chair in your sodding office?' He knew he had a lot of making up to do in that department, or soon he might be watching the television on his own. No doubt she was remembering her father's warning words, and right this moment Daniel had a nasty feeling she'd be wishing she'd taken his advice. He put the phone back on voicemail. No time to eat humble pie.

57

At a few minutes after four o'clock the same day, Detective Superintendent Joyce Hollis was waiting for Daniel and Flower as they walked through the door into the incident room. The atmosphere was electric. Daniel looked at the expectant faces and felt his stomach churn. He was tired, longing for something to eat and worrying about Rachael.

"Another death," said Hollis, giving Daniel a look that clearly said, *When the hell are you going to give me some good news?*

"I know what you're thinking, ma'am, and I wish as much as you that I had something positive to report."

"So nothing on the old man?"

"He's dead, and the footprint found outside the portakabin does not fit his shoe – I say shoe because he only had one pair and they were nearly done for. So, although we have no idea why he was lying on the grass by the site, he is definitely not our killer. Even if we hadn't got a footprint I would be extremely doubtful that he could kill anyone. He was weak, drunk and starving. However, the footprint is the first bit of evidence left by our killer."

"And what does that mean?" Hollis asked.

"I know it is a mistake to work on hunches, ma'am, but I have a gut feeling about this footprint. Care to hear it?"

"I'm listening."

"That it was deliberately left by the killer. "

Hollis snorted.

Undeterred, Daniel continued. "I think the killer thought we were getting a bit close."

"And?"

"So the footprint is designed to put us off the scent. Make us look elsewhere. I just cannot believe that a person who has been so careful to leave bugger all clues, who has avoided all CCTV, suddenly plants a footprint right outside the portkabin for us to find. To my mind this doesn't add up."

"Are you saying that Stafford was killed deliberately to put us off the scent, Chief Inspector?" Hollis asked.

"That, ma'am, is exactly what I'm inferring."

"Well, if that is the case we are dealing with someone who is not only clever but pure evil. However, I'm not sure I can buy into your theory, but it seems that that's all you have got at the moment, so work on your hunch but don't let your team close their eyes to another theory. This is a huge case and someone is cocking a snoot at us."

"We will do all we can to find the killer."

"And now," said Hollis looking at her watch, "we have a very difficult press conference to go to."

Daniel hid his surprise. "You want me to come with you?"

"You and Sergeant Flower, and I'm sure your friend the ACC will want you to field most of the questions."

Daniel inwardly groaned.

"You alright with that, Chief Inspector?" Hollis asked, giving him a knowing smile.

"If you say so, ma'am, of course."

★★★

An hour later Daniel walked into his office. He felt battered. The press conference had not gone well and he knew the ACC had enjoyed watching him squirm under the persistent questioning of an ever frustrated press corps. There were no leads to report and they wanted results, gory details about Stafford's death and an immediate arrest. They got nothing. Disbelief hung over the room and only the interruption of the chief constable calling time saved Daniel from any further loss of face, but he knew his reputation as a policeman who got things done had taken a knock. He sank into his chair, rested his elbows on his desk and closed his eyes. He might have fallen asleep if Julia Sullivan hadn't walked in. He looked up and smiled.

"I'm sorry, boss, but I have a bit of bad news?"

"What now?"

"Your wife, sir, she's on her way right this minute to see you."

As if on cue Rachael stormed into the office looking angry and carrying Arty.

Daniel leapt up from his chair and moved round his desk. "You look very beautiful when angry," he said.

"Don't pull that one on me, Chief Inspector, I'm not in the mood. How about offering me a chair?"

Daniel helped her to a chair. Rachael sat down with Arty on her knees. "So, what have you got to say, Daniel? When Arty was born we agreed certain things. None of which you have honoured – not one bloody thing! No, don't interrupt; okay, I accept you've done the odd night, but not very many. I've given up work, which I miss, although Arty is a joy. But you promised to help and where have you been? Sitting here brooding over a case you can't fucking solve. I doubt you even know what your son looks like."

"That's unfair, Rachael. I know I have not been the husband I should have been but I'm up to my eyes in a serious murder enquiry and I don't think the killer cares a damn how you feel. What do you expect me to do? Cuddle Arty while you go swimming to get back your figure, have lunch with your mother, and shop?"

Rachael jumped from the chair, almost dropping Arty. "Now look what you nearly made me do, you uncaring bastard. That is below the belt. I would give anything to be back here helping you to solve this case. I know what this means to you, I know you don't like being beaten but I need you every now and then to come home, kiss me and Arty and hold me in your arms. As for my figure, well, I didn't think it was that bad. And lunch with my mother! You must be joking. You know how I try to avoid that! Fuck you, Daniel, yes fuck you! I'm just trying to be a good mother."

"This is all wrong." said Daniel. "I should never have said those things. I'm tired, feel defeated and worried sick that someone else will soon die. I'm so, so sorry, Rachael, but please try and understand. I will do better when this case is solved, I promise."

"Don't make promises you can't keep, copper. We both know what will happen when the next case lands on that fucking desk of yours."

Daniel hung his head and said nothing. She was right.

Rachael glared at him. "I don't know why I bothered to come here. I should know you're married to your work and if I want to stay with you I must put up with it. After all, as a copper, or probably an ex-copper – yes, don't look so surprised – I'm quitting – I should be more understanding. There is no room for two coppers in the same family. Arty needs me but he also needs you and in case you've forgotten I need you too. I love you, Daniel. Just try your best to show you love me back. That's all I ask."

Daniel saw the tears in her eyes and could only mumble, "I'll be home tonight."

"You fucking better be, or Arty and I might be tempted to go to Mum's, and, boy that should tell you how neglected I feel." With that, she stood, glared at Daniel and walked out of the room.

Daniel made no attempt to follow her. He knew he'd let her down and that probably she hadn't been joking about a trip to her mum's. Arty needed a father and she needed a husband. He would forget that at his peril. Whatever happens today he had to be home by seven to put Arty to bed. "You've made a big mistake, whoever you are," he said to the empty room. "You're messing with my family and I'm coming to get you." But even as he said these words doubt was circling in his brain. "Damn you, damn you!" He whirled round and angrily swept the files off his desk, kicking at the trash can at the same time, which flew across the room and hit the door as Julia Sullivan walked in. The mug of coffee she was carrying flew out of her hand and smashed on the hard floor.

Daniel stared at the mess and mumbled, "Sorry, bad day."

"No worries sir, the coffee is shit."

58

I watch the reporter on lunchtime local television interviewing Chief Inspector Appleman. So this was the old man I fell over. A drunk homeless, totally unable to wield a knife, let alone stab a young fit man in the chest. What a fuck up. There goes any chance of Appleman thinking the murder was unrelated to the other two killings. But watching Appleman's face as he tries to explain that there are no new leads to a hostile reporter cheers me up somewhat. With luck, when all this has ended, he will face serious questions from his superiors. I would love to see him crawl because it's dawning on me that I'm facing a very canny policeman, who if I'm not careful could fuck me up considerably, and that would be catastrophic now that I'm so close to the end of my mission. Well, I can't hang about any longer watching Appleman squirming, I have matters to attend to. I press the television remote. His voice is beginning to grate on my nerves. I can feel depression coming on. My head is thumping. I need to refocus: work out if this cock-up will force me to change my plans. I close my eyes. (I think better with them closed, always have.) I see Sophie Carpenter baiting Jack, laughing at his unease, staring at him with those wicked eyes, no doubt about to strike him with a well-manicured hand. And that does it. I open my eyes full of new energy. Depression gone. Nothing has changed – stupid of me to panic. I never had much confidence that the diversion would work, so focus, focus and don't let that bitch ruin Jack's life any longer. I force the homeless man and Appleman out of my brain and settle down to make a plan. "You're as good as dead Mrs Sophie Carpenter," I shout to the television, nevertheless aware that I have said this before. I feel hungry, thirsty, in need of something tasty. Well, that's a laugh, the only food I have in the fridge is two Mars bars, a half-used packet of smoked streaky bacon and a pint of whole milk.(None of this semi-skimmed rubbish for me.) I have a loaf of brown bread, butter and honey and a jar of instant coffee. What more does a starving person want? I give a resigned laugh and move to the kitchen. God, how drab it looks. But soon all this will change. I feel relaxed as I turn on the kettle and pick up my phone to order a pizza. I start to hum, tunelessly, my mum would say. Fuck her! I'm going to be someone soon. A person people will look up to and treat with respect. Pity the old hag isn't alive to see the transformation. And then a thought strikes me. I'm no longer the person I have spent so much time in constructing. I'm thinking and doing things my old ways, the bad ways. I rub my head, knowing that what was up there has changed, meaning I have changed along with it. Going backwards. And this is not how it should be. My past must not be allowed to enter my soul or all my plans will be of no use. It will not be easy but it's a challenge I will win.

★★★

Another day, and work calls. It's just gone seven as I move out of bed and head for the bathroom. Sleep was hard to come by – my mind was working overtime. I can hear the rain beating

315

against the bathroom window. I strip and walk under the shower, turn on the cold tap, and feel the biting cold water wash away any affects of the Pinot Noir. I dress quickly in my working clothes. It is important not to change my routine (I can't allow any suspicion to come my way). I move into the kitchen. I wrinkle my nose as I see the half-eaten pizza. At least three flies are enjoying their breakfast. I shoo them away and dump the pizza in the rubbish bin. I turn on the kettle, grab a piece of brown bread, stuff it into the toaster, move to the fridge for butter and then gaze out of the window until the kettle boils. Then I take my mug of coffee and toast to the kitchen table and sit down. I chew and drink and think. I reckon Sophie's got about ten hours left to live.

★★★

I think I've just endured the slowest eight hours of my working life. I don't know how many times I looked up from my desk and could have sworn the clock on the mantelpiece was broken. I fight the urge to run from the office for some much needed fresh air. Recently I've learned that when an urge gets its claws into you, it can be very difficult to ignore that urge. But I fight and win, thank the good Lord. Now, at last, it's time for home. I wrap myself in my thick fake fur coat and realise I've been sweating. Nerves, excitement, danger? None of these three: it's frustration. I need to see blood, to taste it, to watch it pour from Sophie's breast. Jesus, I really must get a grip!

Out on the street it's still raining; will it ever stop? But right now I need it. It will make my next move safer. I'm going to stake out the house (television jargon, but it sounds good).

I need to see what security Sophie has around her. I'm not kidding myself in to thinking that I will see every copper but I will be able to get some idea by the number of cars.

My heart turns a cartwheel – I'm so very close. I will watch and wait. I have three days off, so I must make the best of them. I start my car and pull away. The swish, swish of the wipers is getting into my brain and I need to be fully focused. I can't turn them off as I know I will be quickly blinded by the water. I beat at the steering wheel in frustration – concentrate, concentrate. This has always been a problem – I am easily diverted. I decide to pull in at a lay-by and sit quietly for a moment. I must not underestimate the policeman. I'm sure he is no nearer suspecting me, but one slip-up and I might be in the frame. I like this game – me against him. Of course, I will win and the winning will be so satisfying. But I have to admit that outsiders have been known to buck the odds, so no room for complacency – I mustn't blow it.

The rain has stopped, so I'm on my way again. I'm driving past the house. There are two police cars parked on the drive. My intuition is telling me to be suspicious if there are no police cars visible because there is no way Appleman will pull security completely. I risk driving past one more time and then accelerate away. To hang around will create suspicion. It's not as if this lane is busy; only a few cars pass the house during the day.

I'm back in my drab kitchen, with the radio turned down low to soothe me. I move to the fridge; I have forgotten to restock. Angry, I slam the door shut. It's getting to be a habit to have an empty fridge: too much on my mind. Well, a walk to the fish and chip shop will do me good. I'm in need of some exercise. It will help clear my mind.

59

Arty gurgled happily as Daniel lowered him into his cot. He pulled up the side of the cot and shed a tear, as it dawned on him that this was only the third time he'd put his son to bed since his birth. *The miracle of birth is passing me by,* he thought, as he straightened up. His mind had been on other matters, and he had not forgotten Rachael's words in his office. He blew a kiss to Arty and turned to walk out of the room. Rachael was downstairs cooking supper. He'd have a quick shower, slip into his favourite pair of jeans, T-shirt, garish pair of yellow socks and brown slippers and try to force the thought of the killer out of his mind – at least for the rest of the evening.

But half an hour later, as he hurried into the kitchen, he was met by Paul Flower, a rather sheepish smile on his face, holding a bottle of the local Upham ale and munching on peanuts.

Rachael turned from the stove, smiling. "Thought you and Paul could fill me in over supper, Daniel. I'm curious to know what keeps a man away from home when he has a loving wife and son to greet him as he walks through the door."

Daniel understood Rachael well enough to know this was a hidden rebuke but also an attempt to defuse their disagreements. He swallowed his surprise, thinking that

Rachael read his mind too easily sometimes. She knew that they would talk about the case all night, so why not hear out the two men most involved. Besides, he knew she was genuinely interested. Once a copper, always a copper, the saying went. He gave a weak smile and nodded to Flower. He had to admit to being a little disappointed – he'd hoped for some time alone with Rachael.

Rachael was not slow to see the disappointment in his eyes. She knew what he was thinking, but there would have been no way that Daniel was in the mood to whisper sweet nothings in her ear and stroke her face, which she loved so much. When Daniel was on a case she was beginning to accept, albeit reluctantly, that she and Arty took second place. "Now, off you two go and mull over this case, because once the food is ready I don't want to hear another word about it until supper is finished. You have been warned, Daniel."

The two men exchanged glances, nodded and left the kitchen.

"You're upsetting her, Daniel," observed Flower, as they walked into the sitting room.

Daniel gave a rueful smile. "I know, and I haven't got a solution."

***

"Okay," said Rachael an hour later when plates had been put in the dishwasher and coffee and two glasses of brandy rested in front of the men. Since the birth of Arty she had not touched a drop of alcohol and she was beginning to think her drinking days were over. No more girls' nights out and getting smashed. "Let's have your line on this case that seems to be consuming you all."

Daniel took a sip of his brandy and cleared his throat. "To put it bluntly, we have three deaths and not a single lead. There

319

seems to be no motive and no definite suspects, although we are keeping an eye on Jack Carpenter's secretary, but she seems a very unlikely killer."

"So tell me," questioned Rachael.

"The big one is motive, and all the rest follow on from that. We are as certain as we can be that the killer is the same person. We think the murder of Stafford was an attempt to put us off the scent. We know he or she is very clever and that each murder has been carefully planned. Now the victims. Jenny and Harry Carpenter and Timothy Stafford. Murder weapon, a sharp knife, probably a kitchen knife. Why were these three killed? Family feud? Revenge? Something murky from Jack Carpenter's past life? Random killing? A serial killer who just enjoys killing and the Carpenter family happens to be in the wrong place at the wrong time? I'm pretty certain this is not the case, as even Stafford is linked to the family, so they are being targeted for some reason. Stafford's killing, as I've said, I think was an attempt at a diversion to put us off the scent. So, does that mean we are closer than we think? Answers, answers are badly needed, because I have a dreadful feeling that this person is still active and that means that Sophie and Jack Carpenter and Doctor Walker are in danger."

"It sounds nasty," said Rachael.

And then the baby alarm sprang into life. Arty was exercising his vocals.

Daniel leapt up from his chair. "I'll go." And before Rachael could say a word he was halfway up the stairs.

Rachael smiled at Flower, who looked at his watch. "Getting late, Rach, I think this is a good moment to call time. There's nothing more to add to what Daniel has just said. Don't be too hard on him – he's hurting."

"I know. I just wish he didn't think this was all his fault. His moods are difficult to deal with sometimes. And I'm so tired, so I know I'm not giving him my usual support. It's funny really, before we married, Daniel was so honest about the strains put on a couple working on the force, and my father warned me constantly about the dangers of family life, but I ignored them both. I told myself that as we were both in the police we would never have a problem. But I didn't pencil in children. Arty is a full-time job and I would like Daniel to be part of that job, but in my dreams, Paul. Oh, we will work our way through it, because we love each other but I can understand why there are so many unhappy marriages around in this line of work. Take my advice, Paul, keep your love affair with the divorcee a part-time adventure, then you'll have all the fun and none of the marital worries."

★★★

Next morning Daniel woke with a start. He'd actually slept. *Jesus, that was a change*, he thought. He threw himself out of bed, realising that Rachael was already up and feeding Arty. He was running a bit late, but sod it. He quickly showered – a morning luxury he had not been able to enjoy for some time. He fell into his dark blue suit and rushed down to the kitchen, still fiddling with his blue tie. Rachael was feeding Arty on her knee. "Thought I'd let you sleep, Daniel. I think you needed the extra hour."

Daniel gave her a kiss on her cheek and waggled a finger at Arty. "I needed it," he confessed, "but must go now. I'll have coffee in my office."

"Okay, but don't forget to eat something. Your mind works better on food. See you tonight?"

Daniel played with his tie. "I'll do my best."

"I know you will. And Daniel."

"Yes?"

"Don't worry, I'm fine again now. Last night was good."

Daniel gave her a broad smile. "Thanks, and yes it was."

As he reached the kitchen door Rachael said, "Daniel."

He turned.

"Love you. See you tonight."

"I love you too."

Rachael believed he meant it.

★★★

Francine looked across the kitchen table at Jack eating his fruit and fibre. It was not often they had breakfast together but she'd planned this. This was a game-changing day and the sooner she got over telling Jack the better. She sat silently looking at him until he'd finished his cereals, realising for the first time how much the last few weeks had sapped his energy. He looked drawn and his once bright eyes stared across the table at her with a look that she could only call despair. She took a deep breath, aware that her hands were shaking and her heartbeat racing. "Jack, I have something to say."

He picked up his coffee cup and said, "Go ahead, then."

"I've been thinking."

"Haven't we all?" he interrupted.

"Please, Jack, hear me out. This is important."

He shrugged. "Okay, I'm listening – well, sort of."

"Please, Jack, don't make this any more difficult than it's going to be."

"I know what you're going to say."

"Then tell me, clever clogs."

"You're thinking of leaving."

Francine drew in her breath. "Jesus, am I that obvious?"

"I'm right, then?"

"Yes," said in a weak voice. "I really don't think I can take much more of this. My work is suffering, I can't sleep and I'm convinced that all this is due to me."

Jack reached over the table and squeezed her hand. "I can't believe I'm hearing you say this."

"Well, I'm sorry, but look at it objectively. I find you, causing Sophie to go berserk and you leave her. Your two children hate you even more than they did and then they get killed. Finally, Tim plays hell with my emotions and then gets himself killed. For heaven's sake, Jack, if that's not enough, to add to it all the killer is still loose. So who is next? You, me, Sophie, Janet Goodchild? Come on, Jack, I'm a Jonah. I'm the one who is responsible for causing all this mayhem. I should have walked away sooner. Then maybe all this misery could have been averted."

"Don't you dare say that, Francine. None of this is your fault. I know we are living a nightmare but it will end and then you and I can get on with our lives, and I want you around. I don't want to lose my only child."

Francine bit her lip, fighting back the tears. "I know, Jesus, don't I know. I desperately want us to be happy but I don't think we are any nearer that than the first day I met you in the Guildhall. I'm not the sort of person to show much emotion – my mother drained me of that years ago. Of course I love you, Jack, but I think there will always be something between us that will fester. I come along and wham, you lose a family. I won't be far away and I have no intention of never seeing you again. But our relationship will be closer if I'm not here. You may not agree, but my mind is made up." Then she whispered, "I think."

Jack hung his head. "I didn't think it possible that things could get worse."

"Oh God, Jack, you are making this so difficult."

"Do you blame me?"

"It's difficult for me as well, you know, and I would have thought you'd want to feel I was safer away from here."

Jack pushed back his chair with a crash. He was visibly

shaking. He stood the other side of the table, staring at Francine with damp eyes. "You've just succeeded in doing something that the loss of my children failed to do. You've made me wish I was dead." He turned and rushed out of the kitchen. A few minutes later Francine heard the front door slam.

He was spared the sight of the tears rolling down her face.

★★★

Sophie stretched her aching body and threw an arm over the man's naked chest. He'd been excitingly athletic. It was the best two hours she'd had since that ungrateful little shit Tom Jackson had walked out on her. Maybe things really were getting back to normal. She rolled out of bed and moaned as the muscle pain hit her. It came as a shock to realise that she was getting old and lonely. Men, like whatever this hulk of humanity liked to call himself, would soon be passing her by without a glance. She had to admit she was losing the battle of holding on to the image of youth. Not even the regular visits to the gym could hide the wrinkles and the ever so slow gathering of flab round her middle. She was discovering that it was confidence-shattering to grow old. She staggered to the bathroom, turned on the shower and stepped under the warm water. She gasped, letting the water ease her pain and revitalise her body and mind. She turned off the shower – grabbed a towel and dried herself. She was in a hurry now. Keen to get away from the house before the man woke and wanted more exercise. She gave a derisory laugh. Who the hell did he think he was? A one-night stand was a one-night stand, not a marathon.

She dressed in a blue tracksuit – brushed back her hair and tied it into a bow – slipped her feet into a pair of Nike canvas shoes and quietly moved out of the bathroom onto the landing. She gave a sigh of relief when she heard the snoring coming from the bedroom. The man was heading for a big embarrassment when her unsuspecting maid came in with her cup of morning tea.

60

I'm ravenously hungry. The fish and chips have long since left my intestines. I realise I haven't eaten food for at least ten hours. Not surprising I feel a little worse for wear. I really must get myself together or I will be too weak to carry out my mission. I move out onto the street and walk into the local coffee shop, buy myself a jam doughnut and a cup of strong black filter coffee. I look at my watch – I have all day free, so I order another jam doughnut and a coffee refill and begin to feel energy flowing through my starved body. My plan is to drive once more past Jack's house. (I still call it that.) I've heard that security has been tightened. I wipe the jam off my mouth, drain the cup of coffee and move to the counter to pay. I get to my car, put on a pair of glasses, pull a cloth cap down over my forehead just in case Sophie is out as I drive past. There is a second when I'm exposed to anyone standing on the drive. I turn the ignition and feel the excitement begin to flow. It dawns on me that I will miss this sensation after Sophie's death.

I decide I have time to drive to the Tesco store at Winnall, to replenish my dwindling store of provisions. I park and get a trolley. The store is humming. I suddenly fancy a curry. I can almost smell it as I hurry towards the correct shelf. I will make a pig of myself at lunchtime – perhaps have a nap and dream of the time that I can watch the television and know that someone else is going to be cooking my meals. I find the green Thai chicken curry, drop the package into my trolley, grab a pint of milk, a loaf of brown bread and a ready-made fish pie, then hurry to the checkout counter. I smile at the young woman, ask for a bag. Ten pence: daylight fucking robbery. I breathe in as I leave the store and head towards Upham.

★★★

I'm back in the flat now, sitting on the sofa, staring at the television screen, my curry on my lap. I scroll through the Sky Sports programmes and soon grow bored. A growing unease is stirring in my body, taking away the pleasure of a Saturday afternoon. Was I spotted as I passed the house? I can't get that off my mind. I then do something out of character; I hurl my plate of curry at the television. It smashes against the screen, shattering it. There is a flash of electricity and then silence. I run my hands through my hair. I'm very confused.

★★★

I find myself lying on the floor, the room is dark, evening has arrived. I slowly stand up, mystified as to why I was on the floor. I feel my way to a light switch on the wall, and look round. I see the television, the smashed screen and plate, the curry staining the floor. I frown. Did I do this? I move to a chair and sit down. The room moves; I shake my head; there is a pain behind my eyes. What is going on? I feel a growing sense of panic. Have I a brain tumour? Then a more rational assumption hits me – I'm dehydrated so I fainted. I'll stick with that. I carefully ease myself off the chair. I stand still, allowing my eyes to focus before moving towards the kitchen.

Once there I fill one large glass with water and another with milk. I drink slowly. I feel better, so I drink another glass of water. Already I feel my strength returning. I look at my watch and am shocked to see that it is nearly ten p.m. I got back from driving to the house around five, so I have lost nearly five hours. I can't afford to allow myself to be like this again. I must look after my health. I don't want to die just as I'm reaching my goal.

61

Francine woke early, as she always did on a Sunday; lying in was not for her. It was the only day she knew she could have a leisurely breakfast and, with seven-day surgery being proposed by the government, it might soon be a luxury of the past.

But today she was not going to enjoy her breakfast and a browse through *The Sunday Telegraph* and the *Stella* magazine, a zany product that normally made her smile.

As she added a few items to the suitcase, tears began to run again. She wondered if she'd ever stop crying, but she'd made her decision so tears were not the answer. She'd had enough – cowardice? Maybe, but she couldn't do her job while under constant strain. And strain there was in bucketfuls. So here she was, on the morning she'd been dreading for a whole miserable week, leaving the home she'd grown up in, in which she'd fought with her mother, sat in the derelict garden and watched the fishermen, and come home these last few months to a smiling Jack. A good friend, who had suffered untold misfortune, had once told her that life could change rapidly and take the breath out of your body. She closed her wardrobe shut the one suitcase she was taking. She'd return and pack up the rest of her belongings later. (This was her chickening-out clause, just in case she had a change of mind.) She cast one last look round the room that was so full of memories, and with a heavy heart moved as quietly as she could out on to the landing, praying that Jack wouldn't wake in the next bedroom. Creeping down the stairs she opened the front door, walked slowly towards her car and pressed the unlock button. The heavy rain beat against her head and she quickly put her case and handbag onto the back seat. Leaving the door open she retreated back into the house to find Cat. She found him stretched out in his bed by the cold fire in the sitting room. He made no move to jump away as she bent down and took him in her arms. He purred and nuzzled into her chest as if he knew she needed comforting. Once more she moved to the front door, stepped out and silently pulled it shut. A stab of pain passed through her body. She took a deep breath and put Cat into his travel bag next to her suitcase. Now beginning to panic that Jack would appear at any moment, she hurried to the driver's door and slipped into the seat. For once she didn't curse the late November rain as the noise might hide the sound of her starting the car. As she moved away she saw a light go on in Jack's bedroom. She smothered a moan and put her foot down hard on the accelerator and the car lurched forward onto the lane. She felt desolate that she might not see her father again. *This isn't how it was meant to be,* she thought, gripping the steering wheel and staring out at the glistening wet tarmac.

★★★

Jack had woken with a start. He'd fumbled for the bedside light switch, and sat up dazed. The vital seconds it took for his brain to register what was happening took away any chance of running out to try one last time to persuade Francine to stay.

Now he sat in the kitchen, nursing a cup of black coffee,

feeling utterly defeated. He wondered what he could have said that might have changed her mind. It was a waste of time going down that road. Francine and Cat had gone. "The cottage is yours for as long as you want it," she'd told him the night before, but right now all he wanted to do was get out and never come back. No way could he live here without Francine and that bloody cat. He munched unenthusiastically on a piece of brown toast and tried to think clearly. As he stood up to make for the telephone to try Francine's mobile he realised that he was already missing her. *Do all fathers miss their daughters as much?* he wondered, as the ringtone turned to voicemail. He decided not to leave a message. He had to leave her to get on with her life. This was a re-run of all those years ago when he'd walked into his house and found Eliza gone, and this time the pain of loss left him breathless.

★★★

The rain made driving difficult, as did the irritating pain in her stomach, and she knew she had to stop before she had an accident. She pulled into a lay-by on the Hog's Back in Surrey and cut the engine. Closing her eyes she thought of the monumental decision she was making. *I'm deserting Jack* was the constant thought going through her mind and the more she thought of it the more of a shit she felt. A rat leaving a sinking ship passed through her mind. She heard Cat purring in his cage on the back seat and turned to smile at him. "Just you and me now, Cat. Alone again," she mumbled.

★★★

Francine turned off the A3 into the small village of Effingham with a mixture of excitement and fear. *I'm about to start my new life,* she thought. She drove carefully, fighting to control her emotions which stubbornly refused to go away. She risked a look at her watch. *I'm late*, she thought. The traffic through Guildford and on the A3 had been heavy but no doubt estate agents were used to clients being late. She drove slowly now, watching out for the white cottage that she'd rented for a month, hopefully to give her time to adapt to being away from Jack and her job, and work out her next career move. "You can't miss it," the agent had said. "Three houses down from the pub on your right as you come into the village." She sighed as she thought of the understanding reception she'd received from her fellow partners when she'd put in her resignation. "There will always be a space for you here, if you ever want to come back," said Paul Tyler, the senior partner.

Would she ever be ready, she wondered, nearly missing the pub. She slowed to a crawl and a few minutes later saw the white cottage. *Here goes*, she thought, as she turned into the drive with a beech hedge on either side. A blue Ford Mondeo was sitting by the front door and a woman of around five seven with blonde hair down to her shoulders was leaning against the bonnet. She braked to a halt behind the Mondeo, turned off the engine, took a deep breath and opened her door.

★★★

"God damn the bloody woman," exclaimed Jack, throwing his mobile onto his desk and looking up at Janet Goodchild. "Sophie's gloating, fucking gloating. She's full of viciousness. Can't just say, I'm so sorry that Francine has gone. She hopes I'm suffering, and Jesus she's got her wish."

Janet had never seen Jack in such a state and her heart went out to him. *Why did you ever marry that bitch?* she thought. She said, "It's no good working yourself into a state, Jack, you

332

know what she's like. Don't give her the pleasure of knowing how upset you are. She's not worth it. You'll soon be rid of her and, who knows, Francine may have second thoughts. You're her father and I know she loves you."

Jack slammed a fist down on his desk. "You're right about Sophie but wrong about Francine. She's taken Cat and that means no return."

Well, fuck the cat, thought Janet. She said, "I don't think you should read too much into that. And in my way of thinking, if she's taken Cat she will return. Cats are notorious for not settling down in new places and she would hate to lose him. I think it's good that she took Cat. It means her mind is not yet made up."

Jack forced a smile. "Well, if you're right I'll give you a big kiss, Janet."

Janet had great difficulty in not leaping across her desk and shouting, "why not give it to me now?"

★★★

Daniel Appleman was sipping a gin Martini and playing absently with the olive stick. On Sunday evenings Rachael spoilt him with his favourite tipple, and a Martini normally worked magic with his moods. But she could sense his tension and knew there would be no fun in bed tonight, which was a bugger because she knew there would be no other night that Daniel put his mind to sex. It wasn't because he was bored with her, it was just that work had to come first. After all, she told herself, they wouldn't have a nice house and a good living if it wasn't for his job. Recently, however, weekends seemed to have been jinxed. On each occasion when she'd been hoping for an exciting romp and then a quiet day just talking, Daniel had been called out. She so wanted to discuss the new décor she was planning for the sitting room. Samples of wallpaper, colours of carpets, and curtains were strewn over the floor and he didn't seem to notice. At this rate she'd never get the sitting room done before the New Year. Some wives would be moaning by now about the disinterest their husbands were paying but she was a copper's wife and she'd been a copper too. With a loud resigned sigh she plopped down on the sofa next to him, leant over and kissed his neck. "Something more gone wrong, Daniel? Before you nod that head of yours I know something new has come up and I can tell it's not good. So come on, out with it."

Daniel took another sip of the ice-cold drink and stared into Rachael's eyes. How magical they were. She was *gold standard*, as he liked to say, and his love for her was as deep as it had been the day they had first met on a freezing cold beach in Cornwall, the wind sweeping her long blonde hair out behind her. They had accidentally run into each other while on an early morning run, heads down against the sting of the driven sand. And ever since then he'd done his best not to upset her by making excuses.

"The problem is, nothing new has turned up," he began. "We are still in the dark and I'm terrified time is running out on us. I can feel it in my bones."

"Feel what in your bones?"

"Another death. And I've got no idea how to stop it. Jesus, Rachael, how I hate being like this. Do you know, I've even been thinking that I don't want this job any more. I have nightmares about it."

"You needn't tell me that!"

"I'm sorry."

"No need, love. Just let me say one thing before I mix you another cocktail. You're a top-dog copper, much respected and envied. Look back at the cases you have solved. Believe you me, you will work this one out in the end."

"Unless my end comes first. Redundancies are coming."

"Oh for fuck sake, Daniel, if you go on like this you'll be a nervous wreck. No one is going to sack you. Believe in yourself – this will come right. Now, I'm going to work the cocktail shaker again and then we are going to have an early night. Tomorrow is the time to start worrying again."

62

Daniel walked into the incident room feeling decidedly jaded. Two Martinis had swiftly become three and now he was nursing a headache that two paracetamol were finding hard to shift. It had been worth it though. Rachael had spun her magic – covered his body with kisses – and he'd soon been transported into heaven, but the morning alarm clock had soon brought him back to reality. "Morning, Sergeant," he said to Flower as they met outside the incident room. "Good Sunday?"

Flower licked his lips. "Does that tell you anything, mate?"

Daniel slapped his friend on the back and pushed him into the room. "Well, hope it did the concentration a bit of good. We've a tough day in front of us and it seems as if the team are expecting that." He looked round the room at his team, none smiling, just waiting for him to explain why they had all been called in so early. "Morning," he said. There was a mumbled greeting.

Daniel knew his team. Three had been in the Hampshire police force for as long as he had, and the new additions were working in well. He knew he had their respect, which was just as well as his briefing would carry no encouragement. He gave a thin smile, dropped his hands by his side and cleared his throat. "Our investigation seems to have stalled."

A groan went round the room. He raised a hand. "I know, I know. I've said these words so many times these last few weeks that you must be sick of hearing them, but the truth is, I have nothing new to report. But it's not the first time that I've been in this situation, and we mustn't give up hope. Out there is a killer and unless we work our butts off it won't be long before we have another murder. However, it is my opinion that the killer could be a little rattled, as the killing of Stafford seems to show. So out there somewhere is a clue we are missing, which has encouraged me to suggest we work a new line." He looked over at Jane Andrews. "Nothing come up yet from your enquiries, Constable?"

She shook her head. "Still digging, guv."

"Good. Because I think the clue is right here at home. We are missing something, and that something is right under our noses. So, back to the drawing board. Go back and interview everyone you have spoken to already. If they look as if they are hiding something don't be afraid to suggest that they are lying, and inform them that you will have to bring them to the station. Bluff, I know, but it has worked before. Talk to the locals and anyone who has spoken to Carpenter recently. Ask, ask and ask until you are sick of the word. It is our only hope. Okay, that's the easy bit. The worst is yet to come. In twenty minutes, myself and Detective Superintendent Hollis have another press conference planned to keep the hungry sharks at bay. Anyone like to take my place?"

There was general laughter around the room and every hand was carefully tucked away out of Daniel's sight.

★★★

Charlie Murray gave Daniel a welcoming smile as he walked into the room. "Didn't expect it to be me, did you, Daniel?" said the Chief Constable.

You're one better than your assistant, thought Daniel, as he took the outstretched hand

"Bit of a surprise, sir."

"I'm sure, but I thought it was time for you and I to have a little chat where no ears are hopefully flapping. We have a very difficult press conference coming up within the hour and I wanted you and I to decide how we are going to deal with it."

"Are you going to take it?"

"You sound surprised."

"Just a little, sir."

"Well, I know that you and the assistant chief constable don't always see eye to eye, so to avoid the chance that disagreements surface at the conference I decided I'd come with you instead."

"Thank you, sir."

Charlie Murray smiled. "I don't want your thanks, Daniel, what I want is for you two to patch it up and stop behaving like two squabbling schoolchildren. I do not like two of my best officers to be at loggerheads. Understand?"

"I'll do my best," Daniel lied, thinking that his boss was deceiving himself if he thought the ACC was a good officer.

"Right. Now let's get to work and decide how we are going to explain to the press why we haven't moved forward since the last conference. They are going to be rather antagonistic, so our liaison officer has just informed me. But we've dealt with that before, eh, Daniel?"

"Indeed we have."

"Is there nothing new we can tell them – not the smallest crumb?"

"I think our best line will be to say we are exploring a new lead but we can't say more than that for the time being."

"Are you exploring a new lead?"

"Only that I'm now convinced the killer is a local."

"On what basis do you make that assumption?"

"Because the killer knows a hell of a lot about Jack Carpenter's daily business."

"Well, that's a plus I suppose, and it brings me nicely onto another matter. I think we have reached what I call the treading water stage of this investigation. I know you have interviewed everyone you can think of – studied CCTV footage until you are bog-eyed all with no result. As you know, our resources have been cut to the minimum and I can't let you have every officer in the county working for you. So, you have forty-eight hours to come up with something to persuade me that you can keep your full team. Otherwise, I will have to cut you to the bare minimum."

Daniel groaned. "And allow this creature to kill again."

The chief constable shrugged his shoulders. "It's called austerity, Daniel, and I'm sure you, Joyce Hollis and Sergeant Flower can work things out with a reduced team. In fact I'm banking on it or my arse will be on the line."

And what about mine? Daniel thought.

63

My unease will not go away. Yesterday, I had another visit from a young WPC asking me the same questions as last time. Where was I on this night and that night? I did my best to keep calm but it did send alarm bells ringing. I know they are asking Jack about his past life and it has dawned on me they might do the same to me, which would not be a good idea. I hope I put the WPC's mind at rest. There wasn't very much for me to say, just that I was in bed at the times she asked. What I really wanted to do was shout, "Fuck off, you nosey bitch, I know your type!"

I'm so close to the completion of my mission, but I know Appleman is beginning to put two and two together and that is seriously annoying me. If he was off the case my life would be a good deal easier. He is too shrewd. I'm sure he senses that the killings are not over and, worse, I'm sure he thinks Sophie could be the next target, for what the local press are now calling, 'this serial killer amongst us'. Well, I am amongst you but I'm no serial killer. And that reminds me of reading a book about a killer, who had to kill and kill again just to get to his intended target. Well, that is not me; I see myself as a saint, come to the rescue of a man whose life was about to be ruined by a greedy money-grabbing family. Of course, this will become clear to everyone once they know my reasoning, and I will be exonerated for my actions. I will be hailed as a hero, not as a killer. So perhaps to try and silence Appleman is a bad idea, tempting as it may be. I have already eliminated one man I had at first not intended to target and I do not want to end up branded a psychopath. So, Appleman, you might reach old age, though I would love to stick my knife into your no doubt hairy chest and watch you bleed out.

I'm eating more sensibly now, which is a plus among many negatives. The truth is, I never imagined it would be so difficult to finish my mission. Security around Sophie is tight. I presume this is because Francine has fled the nest, and that leaves more officers available and one less likely victim. But I hold a trump card because I know something that I'm sure the police don't know. It is the cellar grill at the back of Jack's house. It is not secure. It has been like this ever since Jack bought the house. No one cared, and only one person used it. That whore, to let in her lovers (though I have another name for them). I would prefer to kill her outside the house but I can see that that is now impossible without taking a bigger risk than I'm prepared to take.

So tonight I'm on the move again. I'm in the garden fifty yards from the house. I search the area in front of the grill with my night-vision goggles (bought on eBay) and see nothing but shrubs – no movement that might be a policeman. I creep forward over the damp grass. I feel the touch of cold water through my woollen trousers; waterproofs would have made too much noise. I reach the grill, I touch it. It moves, it has not been fixed. I stifle a cry of joy. This will definitely be my way in, but once in, I step into the unknown. I move away, out of the garden, onto the lane and walk back to where I have hidden the car. I'm ready to strike.

I decide I'm too hyped up to go back to the flat and sleep, so I'm heading for the motorway. I will drive to the Basingstoke slip road and then come back to Winchester. By then I know I will have calmed down and I will be able to sleep, for sleep is very important. Tired, I could make a terrible mistake. As I drive and my heart rate eases I lick my lips and imagine that I'm tasting Sophie's blood. I can see her face as I drive the knife into her inflated breasts – God, that makes me feel good. I nearly miss the slip road – concentrate, you silly bitch. Being dead will do no good at all.

64

At nine a.m. on the sixth day of January and carrying his mug of coffee, Daniel Appleman left his office, rubbed his bloodshot eyes and made his way through the security doors towards the incident room. He was feeling frustrated, the investigation had stalled and he was nursing a headache brought on by too much alcohol the night before, which had led to a long discussion with Rachael about the planned new decorations in the house and the possibility of a puppy. By Easter, he'd promised. He gave a rueful smile as he walked into the incident room.

All thoughts of new carpets and a puppy peeing everywhere were quickly forced to the back of his mind as he stared at the silent faces of his team, huddled together in the middle of the room. It was obvious that the threatened cuts had filtered through to those present.

"Is it true?" asked Flower, breaking away from the group.

"Afraid so, unless we can come up with something pretty damn quick."

"So we're being disbanded," stated Flower.

"No, definitely not, but our manpower is going to be cut. Or, as the chief constable said, we are at the treading water stage. I managed to persuade him of the dangers of cutting us too short of officers at this time and he agreed to hold fire for an unspecified time. However, my take on this is that we might find that fewer officers are on call at any time day or night. So we will be stretched but definitely not disbanded."

There was a groan around the room. "We're pretty stretched already," said WPC Jane Andrews.

"I know, but I can't challenge those upstairs when we have zilch to give them. We are in a spot, there is no doubt about it, but don't give up. I've learnt that a killer, however clever, leaves a clue in the end."

"Well, let's hope it's before someone else dies," said Flower. There was a murmur of agreement round the room.

"And that's what worries me," confessed Daniel. "My time as a copper has taught me that someone who has planned every killing meticulously will strike again. So we must be aware of that. The addiction is now so strong that even if they want to stop, there is no way they can fight the urge to kill again. It might be hours, days or even months but they will continue their killing spree at some time. I'm not talking about a passion killing or a robbery here, I'm talking about a mind so evil, so calculating, so caught up in the feeling of power that they just can't let it go. However, I have not wavered from the thought that if there is to be another murder, the target this time will be Mrs Carpenter. It fits the profile."

"So we tighten security around Mrs Carpenter?" suggested Flower.

"Like a ring of steel," Joyce Hollis said as she walked into the room. She nodded at Daniel before continuing. "Every angle must be covered. Thin on the ground we might be, but we can only do our best. I have great faith in you all. This cutting of officers is not because the chief constable thinks we are incompetent, it's policy. I don't want to see morale drop, is that clear?"

There was a collective nodding of heads.

"Good. And I believe you and Sergeant Flower are off to see Jack Carpenter again, Chief Inspector," said Hollis.

"Yes, ma'am."

"And with a bit of luck you'll come back with a new lead to follow."

In your dreams, thought Daniel.

★★★

They walked thoughtfully towards the patrol car, both wrapped up in their own thoughts. Not until they were in the unmarked patrol car and Flower was driving onto the main road did he speak. "You sounded a bit worried back there."

"I don't like failing, mate, and this has all the hallmarks of a case that won't be solved. It's a terrible thing to say but unless we have another killing, this person may well get away with these heinous crimes, and that sticks in my gullet. We are no nearer catching this bastard than we were after the first murder."

"This pisses me off something rotten, I can tell you. I hate defeat as much as you but this person must be one very clever individual."

Flower waved Daniel to silence as he navigated his way around the Winnall roundabout and headed towards Martyr Worthy. "Unless Carpenter comes up with some useful info I think we are in the proverbial shit," he eventually said.

"Well, we knew when we joined the police it was not going to be all milk and honey," Daniel replied.

"I know that, but the pay stinks and the political correctness which has crept in makes me sick. And now we are never left alone to get on with our job. Results, results is all the top brass want. Now look where we are, being cut off from officers just when we need them."

"It's not what it was like when I first joined," agreed Daniel. "All we seem to get is flack from the media and the fucking government. I'd like to see some of them get off their arses and work the hours we do. Not to mention the dangers we face nearly every day."

"But would you like any other job?"

"Right now I can think of a few."

Flower gave him a dubious look. "Well, if you were looking for an easy job, boss, I think you chose the wrong profession."

★★★

There was a frown on Jack's face as he opened the door of Francine's cottage. "You better come in I suppose. Let's go into the kitchen and you can tell me why it's been worth my while hanging on here waiting for you instead of seeing to urgent business in the office."

Feeling distinctly uncomfortable, Daniel cleared his throat. "I'll be honest with you, Jack—"

"And so you bloody well better be, Chief Inspector," interrupted Jack, making no attempt to hide his frustration. "It seems to me you are up against a brick wall. Is that all you and your sergeant here have come to tell me yet again?"

Daniel gave a weak smile. "I don't think I could have put it better."

"Well, at least you're honest. Look, here I am alone – no Francine, two of my children dead, Sophie under threat if I can believe you, and you have absolutely fucking nothing to report! Why not? So why are you here?"

"We just want to run over a few things again," said Daniel, his heart threatening to burst through his ribs.

"Okay, fire away, but I think you are wasting my time." Suddenly Jack slammed his fists down on the work surface. "In fact piss off, both of you, and don't come worrying me until you have some useful information. I think you know your way out. Good day to you both."

★★★

"Wow, that was not quite the way we wanted it to go," said Flower as they drove away from the cottage. "He's not best pleased with us."

"Why should he be? We're like a team of blind idiots wandering around wondering where we are," said Daniel.

"I would have liked to have questioned him though," said Flower. "He must have a past before he became a big man in the pool. Out there must be someone who hates him."

"He would say, not enough to kill his family. We have to face it, we are up against a brick wall and unless we have a lucky break we're going to go on struggling."

Daniel scratched at an itch on his face. "Well, Jack Carpenter might not like it, but I'm in the mood to think the unthinkable and when we get back to the station I'm going to get Constable Andrews to go on digging into Jack's past until she falls asleep at her desk. And I want every officer on the team to question his staff again and that means everyone, especially those close to him."

"But Andrews has already dug and found nothing."

"Then she must dig deeper. We must put a microscope on all their lives, and while we're at it I want you to get in touch with the Met and ask them if they know where Turnbull is. I suppose it's possible we eliminated him from our enquiries too quickly."

"Very well, job as good as done."

65

"I thought I'd never sit by this fire extinguisher again, " laughed Francine a little nervously, patting the red metal as she slipped into the seat opposite Jack.

"And I thought you'd gone for good."

"I would always have come back to see you, but I'm sorry, Jack, it was cruel of me to go. For the sake of my sanity I just had to get out of here. But a couple of weeks sat in a cottage in Surrey, talking to no one but Cat and missing the buzz of my job, gave me time to take stock of my life, and the two jobs I looked at were not what I wanted. I began to realise how lucky I was to be working in such a happy environment at the surgery. Also I was furious with myself for being such a coward and walking away from you at such a difficult time. So, here I am back in your life, ready to face whatever comes your way. My partners have yet again shown incredible patience and offered me my job back, and the father I love is sitting opposite me. I came to the conclusion that I'd be more miserable away from you staying in Surrey, and it would have been a crime to desert you."

"Jesus, Francine, I've missed you. If this terrible business ever comes to an end at least I will know that I have a daughter who loves me. This is a new experience for me and I won't fuck it up. Oh, I know you may think that I will get too possessive but I promise that you will be allowed your own life. Perhaps, dare I say it, get a boyfriend. I won't step into your space. All I want to be able to say to people is that I have a daughter I'm proud of."

Francine leant across the table and kissed his out held hand. "I wonder how many times I've done that," she laughed. "And am I forgiven for running away?"

"Of course you are."

"Well, that's probably more than I deserve. Now, tell me what's new. You look tired and I bet you've lost weight. Those handmade suits are looking a little too big."

"I must confess to not being in good shape. I never thought I could be so worried about anything as much as I am about these terrible killings. I don't sleep very well at the moment and Daniel has been questioning me about Janet, and she thinks Daniel has her down as a suspect. I have done everything I can to calm her down and assure her this is not the case."

"That means he's desperate."

"I flew off the handle at him the other day, unkind, but I feel so frustrated that the police can come up with nothing. I'm scared, Francine. I think our chief inspector is beginning to fear that this might be one case that defeats him. He hasn't said as much to me, but when you start questioning the innocence of someone who has been a loyal servant for years it doesn't take too long for one to realise that the case is taking its toll."

"He might as well suspect me. How on earth could he point a finger at Janet? She's like a little mouse and she loves you."

Jack chuckled. "Everyone seems to tell me that these days. Yes, of course I've been aware of her love for years, but I've never given her any encouragement. It may sound unkind, but she's not my type."

"Well, I should watch out once Sophie has left. And talking of her, how is that going?"

"The divorce is through, and in three days' time she will be on her way to London. New house, new life and plenty of money to burn."

"Is she happy with that?"

"She can't wait to leave. She's scared out of her wits and with good reason. She hates being followed everywhere she goes by the coppers and she will feel safer in London. Not to mention access to horny men. She won't miss me and I certainly won't miss her. It's funny how you can fall in love and think you will be together for the rest of your life and then without warning it all blows up in your face."

"She isn't a nice person, Jack. So, you will be moving back into your house once she's left?"

"Only if you want me to."

Francine stared into his eyes. "I think I would. Better for both of us."

66

I'm standing under the barren branches of an oak tree, the rainwater dripping on my waterproof hat, which I'm using for two reasons. One, to keep this bloody rain off my face and two, to hide it. Which is also the reason why I'm standing some way back from where the old man's coffin is being carried from St Mary's Church to his burial spot. A flash of pity makes me draw in my breath, but it's swiftly gone. The old man should not have been lying there in the first place. A gust of wind blows water over my clothes and reminds me of the times my mother, my elder sister and I used to walk in the warm summer rain on Brighton beach. I smile as I remember the laughter. How happy we were to be away from our father, the filthy stinking piece of shit. I wipe away a tear as I think of my mother dying of malnutrition, which left my sister and I to roam the streets, and our terrible falling out. A movement to my left makes me jump – a cat. Bad to have all these memories floating back – they make me jumpy. But as I watch the coffin lowered into the grave I think of my father. Did he ever come looking for us? If he wasn't already in hell I'd hunt him out and drive my knife into his stomach. I stiffen – I see movement again. Fuck off memories, this is not a good time. I'm not here to reminisce, I'm here out of curiosity. I want to see who is saying goodbye to this sad old man. There are no surprises. Only six people walk away from the graveyard. Jack, Francine and a lady I presume to be a Mrs Slater from the shelter. And of course the two policemen. Curiosity satisfied, I step behind the tree and move carefully back to the road. I have half a mile to walk to my car, and I look up into the leaden sky and smile at the rain. The time to complete my mission is close and then maybe, once more, I will be able to laugh in the rain with someone I love.

67

Daniel Appleman woke with a start. The room was dark, the wind was howling outside. He fumbled for the bedside light and managed to switch it on without knocking over his glass of water. He turned to look at Rachael but she was not there and it dawned on him what had woken him.

Arty.

He looked at the clock on his bedside table and saw it was five in the morning. Just the time that Arty thought he should be having his breakfast, and Rachael was struggling to wean him off this annoying habit. Daniel stretched his arms above his head and began the process of coming wide awake – hard when he'd only been in bed for four hours. Thank the Lord he'd fought off the temptation to take a sleeping pill. Rolling out of bed and thinking bad thoughts about his son, he hurried naked to the chair where he'd thrown his clothes when he'd staggered home the night before, exhausted. He slipped into his boxers and picked up his dark blue trousers and then decided it was daft running downstairs at five in the morning in his work suit. So, tossing the trousers on the floor, he went to the cupboard and pulled out white tracksuit bottoms and a white T-shirt and ran bare foot to the bathroom. Job done, he hurried down the stairs. He could hear Arty making soft gurgling noises of contentment. No doubt delighted that he'd once again woken his parents from their much needed sleep.

"Arty, Arty," he said, kissing Rachael on the top of her head as he walked over to his grinning son in his high chair. "You'll be the death of me, young man." Arty gave a toothless grin and held out his little arms. "You know how to get round me," Daniel laughed, taking a small hand in his. "You smell lovely," he whispered, before turning to Rachael. "Been up long?"

"Half an hour. I hoped you wouldn't wake. Go back to bed, Daniel, I'll manage here."

Daniel dropped into a chair next to Arty. "I think I need to have a few words with our son, a large mug of strong black coffee and a kiss from you. No way can I go back to bed; duty calls.

Rachael made a face. "Is that a way of telling me you will be late tonight?"

"I'm working a hunch, love, so don't hold your breath."

★★★

Two hours later, feeling decidedly weary, Daniel arrived at police HQ as his watch read seven a.m. Walking into his office he was surprised to see Flower sitting in his chair. "You're in early," said Daniel. "Divorcee losing her allure?"

"Piss off, mate, nothing of the sort. I'm just a conscientious copper doing my job."

"And that entitles you to sit in my chair and go through my files, does it?" Daniel laughed.

"I admit I was searching for your casebook."

Daniel held out his briefcase. "Waste of time, Sergeant. It's in here. I'm curious; why did you want to see it so urgently?"

"I thought you might have the telephone number of that detective who was your sidekick in the East End, who you have always spoken highly of."

"And?"

"Well, Constable Andrews has asked me if you knew of anyone in the force who might have been working the East End area when Jack Carpenter was still around. You know you asked her to dig deeper into the circumstances of Carpenter employing Goodchild?"

"Yep, I remember."

"So what's his name?"

"Was Detective Jimmy Frost, dead two years. Prostate cancer. However, I do know of a long-retired sergeant who might be able to help. Before I moved here I used to have a drink with him after we'd gone off duty. It was a long time ago. He would be seventy plus by now but bright as a button. We meet once a year just to chew the fat for old times' sake. He was a young constable then, learning the ropes. He spent a lot of his early years in the East End. Wouldn't do any harm to try him. Dennis Flack is his name."

"You got the number?"

Daniel moved over to his desk and pulled the black-bound well-thumbed notebook out of his briefcase. "I think I have it here, if not I can ring Scotland Yard and they might be able to help, though it is some time since he retired. Just give me a minute; lots of old numbers here." Daniel flipped over a few pages. "Not here, but I'll look at home when I get back. I rang him several months ago to fix up a lunch, so bound to be in my telephone book. He was about to move but I've got his mobile. He's worth a try. I'll have a word with Andrews."

"I'm right here," said Constable Andrews, walking into the office with a smile on her face, and looking surprisingly fresh for someone who had been up most of the night going back and back over her investigation into Carpenter's past. "I'm doing as you asked, trying to find out how Goodchild came to be employed by Mr Carpenter, and the sergeant here said you might still have connections in the East End."

"We've just been talking about that and yes, I've kept in touch with an old sergeant called Flack. He might be able to help. Ah, good morning, Julia," Daniel said, stopping to nod at Julia Sullivan as she walked in. "Blimey, all on time this morning, aren't we?" he commented.

"I'm your PA, in case you've forgotten," laughed Julia. "And it's my job to be around when you need me. Even at the godforsaken hours you are all keeping at the moment. Coffee, everyone?"

Three heads nodded.

Daniel turned back to Jane. "I'll text you Flack's mobile as soon as I get home tonight. As I just told Flower, he's moving house so I don't know his landline number, but he's pretty good at answering his mobile – at least he is with me, as he knows it means a free pint or two," laughed Daniel. "Anything else interesting to tell me?"

"Maybe. Two days ago Goodchild was seen passing by Jack Carpenter's house quite regularly in her blue Volvo."

"How regularly?" questioned Daniel.

"I'm told that between eight in the morning until dusk she definitely passed three times. Could be more. She was driving very slowly. So yesterday I was at the house all day and sat at the window overlooking the lane for hours. She came past another three times."

"That's quite a lot of times," mused Daniel.

"Did she spot you?" Flower asked.

"No way would she have seen me through the glass. She never mentioned it when I called on her."

"You went to see her?" Flower asked.

"Last night. I confronted her. She confirms that she was driving the car."

"So what was her excuse?"

"That she wanted to make sure we were still guarding Mrs Carpenter. She was calm, welcoming and offered me a cup of tea. I said thank you but no – apologised for disturbing her again and left."

"Well, she certainly isn't very happy about our visits. What do you make of it?"

"I'm curious. Why is she so keen to see no harm comes to Mrs Carpenter when by all accounts she hates the woman, and she must know we wouldn't withdraw our surveillance completely, even though we are pushed for numbers. After all, guv, as you said a few days ago, cases can be solved by a hunch."

"Indeed I did, so I think it best if I ring Sergeant Flack myself. Sorry, Jane, but he knows me well and you will only have to pass on any information to me secondhand. You've done a good job, so please don't let this upset you."

Jane made no attempt to hide her disappointment. "I understand, of course, well I think I do, but I would have liked to have taken this enquiry to its end. It's what you asked me to do."

"I'm sorry, but I promise I will keep you in the loop. In the meantime, I'm asking you to join the team guarding Sophie Carpenter. Put yourself on the rota to stay in the house until she moves to London. You'll get overtime, and looking after that woman should broaden your experience if nothing else! I don't want her to be alone at any time. Please realise that this is not because I don't think you're a competent copper. Quite the reverse. I hold you in high regard. So just put it down to a weary careworn policeman at the end of his tether."

"Very well, guv, I think I understand."

Daniel wasn't too sure that Constable Andrews did understand, or held him in high regard any longer. *But then she probably never did,* he thought, as his door slammed shut.

Daniel watched her as she walked out of the office. "That girl will go far."

I agree," said Flower. "Sharp as a button and beautiful with it, but I wouldn't want to know what she's thinking right this moment. I think you've royally pissed her off."

Daniel gave a rueful smile. "I think you're right."

"Which brings me onto what I've found out about Tank Turnbull," said Flower. "He's run off to Spain; no way then that he could be doing these killings himself. His son Terry went with him, so I guess that takes them out of the equation, unless you think he could be paying someone to do the killings, and Jack Carpenter thinks that very unlikely."

"He's probably right, but let's not drop our interest in Mr Turnbull completely."

"Okay, I'll have a word with the Met. So, any more hunches, boss?"

"I'm working on it," said Daniel

68

Daniel stood at the edge of the cricket area and looked into the weak early spring sunshine. *A very welcome change in the weather,* he thought, wishing his luck would follow suit. It was some time since he'd been up to Jack's new development and he stared in amazement at the nearly completed site. There were men working everywhere. How Jack had managed to keep focused all these months Daniel reckoned was nothing short of a miracle, but then Jack had not got where he was today by sitting on his butt in a fancy office.

Daniel moved away from his car and started to walk across to where the portakabin had stood. He'd chosen to pay the site a visit on his own in the hope that it might jog his memory. Had he missed something on the day of the murder? Was there a clue staring him in the face that he'd failed to pick up on amongst all the chaos of that day? It was such a long shot that he was already thinking he was wasting his time, when he spotted Jack Carpenter standing forty metres away talking to the Mayor of Winchester. Given their last meeting, he was the last person he wanted to talk to. Turning quickly, he started to walk away, but too late.

"Hold it, Appleman," Jack shouted, saying something to the mayor before hurrying over to where Daniel stood. "I want a word with you."

Daniel braced himself for another onslaught he suspected was coming.

Jack's face was flashing warning signs as he poked a finger into Daniel's chest. "Don't expect me to apologise for our last meeting, Appleman, nothing has changed, unless of course you've come to tell me you have someone in custody."

Jack shook his head.

"Thought not. Well, I'll give you something else to think about. I don't like the way you're harassing those who work for me, especially my PA. I accept that you are growing desperate but that does not give you the right to order your officers to sniff around. You are upsetting me big time. Go away and look for the suspect elsewhere, for there is no way any of my staff would kill my children. Do I make myself clear? Anyway, what the fuck are you doing here?"

Daniel took a deep breath and gently pushed the offending finger off his chest. "Good morning to you as well, *Mr* Carpenter," he began, fighting the desire to turn and walk silently away. "To answer your last question, I came up here just to refresh my memory of the day we found your manager dead. It sometimes helps me to revisit a scene of a crime, especially when I'm still in the dark."

"Desperate, you mean," growled Jack.

"I'm never desperate – just sometimes mystified, and that's what I am right now."

"So you harass my staff."

"I'm only doing my job, Jack. I have every right to get my colleagues to question anyone I think might have useful information, or for that matter hiding information."

Jack snorted.

"Look, Jack, I want to find the killer as much as you do, so sometimes I upset people. To be frank I don't care – it's part of the job. So if you want an apology I'm afraid you won't get one. I cannot afford to ignore interviewing people just because it annoys you. I accept it seems improbable that any of them are involved but I have to be sure. Now, please don't let me detain you any longer. I expect the mayor has better things to do than twiddle his fingers while you shout at me, and I've got work to do as well." With that, Daniel quickly turned and walked away, leaving Jack with his mouth hanging open.

Not how you expect people to talk to you, Jack, thought Daniel as he reached his car. He smiled, feeling rather pleased with himself. He hated confrontation but every now and then it could not be avoided and he didn't care a fig how big a man Jack was in the community. In an investigation there could be no favourites.

★★★

Daniel greeted Flower with the crisp nod of a fellow copper. "I went up to the development this morning with the idea I might get a brainwave or something like that. I know quite a lot of time has passed since the murder but I wanted to make sure for myself that there was nothing I had missed, but I never got very far with what was a stupid idea because Jack Carpenter was there talking to the mayor. He was the last person I wanted to see, but he saw me before I could sneak away. He was still mad at me. Accusing me of invading his privacy and asking unnecessary questions about Janet Goodchild. He said I must be desperate."

"Well, he wasn't far wrong there."

"Sergeant!"

"Sorry, guv; so what did you say?"

"That in an investigation I didn't mind who I upset as long as it brought results."

"And?"

"I walked away. I was in danger of saying something I would regret."

"Best thing to do. Bit unfriendly of him though, when we are busting our guts to find the killer. I suppose you can't blame him. So, what next?"

"As you know, we suspect that the killer is close to Jack. I'm sure one of his staff is holding back some information that might help us, either deliberately or because they think it's not relevant. I know we've asked this question so many times that we are fed up with it but, as Jack said, we are desperate. However, I'm sure London is our key and no one is going to stop me digging. To start with I'm going to take a closer look at Goodchild. I may have too much imagination sometimes but I have a feeling she's not telling us everything. I'm pinning a lot on my old friend Sergeant Flack. I'm like a dog with a bone now and I'm not giving it up. All this may come to nothing but it's worth a try. Got a better idea?"

"I'm surprised you bother to ask."

***

Sophie was pacing up and down like a caged animal. Twenty-four hours until she left for London, hours that couldn't go fast enough for her. She never thought she'd be glad to leave the marital home with all its comforts and young available men, but events had changed all that. Life had become intolerable – constantly surrounded by police sharing her house and following her everywhere she went. She couldn't even have a pee without someone standing outside the door and she was feeling desperately frustrated. Her hormones were going wild. She'd pay a familiar Winchester club a visit. Who said you couldn't have a one-night stand at fifty? "Well, they don't know Sophie Carpenter," she said out loud as she grabbed her handbag off a table and made for the front door.

But as she put a hand on the door handle, a WPC by the

name of Libby Stuart put a restraining hand on her shoulder. "Sorry, Mrs Carpenter, you can't go out at this time of night."

Sophie angrily pushed the hand off her shoulder and looked daggers at the small WPC, who looked terrified. "Why the fucking hell not, young lady? You can't stop me. I'm bored, fed up with you lot constantly watching my every move. Jesus, soon you'll be coming into the toilet *with* me."

Libby held her ground in spite of Sophie's domineering attitude. It was more than her job was worth to let this rude half-pissed woman through the front door. Orders were orders and she was determined not to give way. "I'm sorry, Mrs Carpenter, but you mustn't go out. It is for your own safety. So please can we avoid an argument?"

"Argument! This isn't going to be an argument, young lady. I'm going out, and that's that. So step aside, before I clock you one with my handbag."

"You'll have to do more than that, Mrs Carpenter, to get me to move, and maybe it's the right time to tell you that I go to judo classes. So look at it this way. Tomorrow you will be on your way to London, out of danger's way. If you go out now you could well be dead and never get to London."

"Sod you!" screamed Sophie, turning away and storming off into the television room, grabbing a bottle of gin and a glass from a table before throwing herself into a chair.

Libby let out a sigh, brushed back her long blonde hair and realised she was shaking violently, but she felt good. "Where the hell were you when I needed you?" she complained to three male officers who appeared in the hallway.

"Just finding out what you're made of," said one of them with a laugh. "And what's this about judo classes?"

"Doesn't do any harm to exaggerate at times," was Libby's repost.

69

Daniel glanced nervously at his watch. He'd broken so many promises to Rachael since the first murder that he was determined not to break another one. As he walked out of his office he looked straight ahead, not wanting to be diverted by anyone, not even 'good night, boss, have a good evening'.

To his surprise he reached the station car park without a word being spoken to him, but not until he was driving out of the car park did he allow himself to breath more easily. "Yes!" he shouted, as he gripped the wheel, knowing that unless he had an accident he'd be home within the hour, and for the first time in several weeks he'd be home to put Arty to bed.

***

Rachael had decided on lamb cutlets for supper. She wondered whether he would like mashed or roast potatoes. She even had some sweet potatoes in the fridge but knew that Daniel was not too keen on them, although he would tolerate the odd one once in a while, providing they were covered in butter. She'd try them tonight. There was a bottle of Chablis Premier Cru cooling in the fridge and his cocktail glass and shaker were standing on the worktop. She was missing having him about in the evenings, especially since the birth of Arty, and they could bathe him together and Daniel would carry him to bed and and tuck him in. Soon he'd be reading him stories. *That is if there is ever time*, she thought. But recently, these precious moments were all too rare and she'd even found herself wishing that Daniel would retire and find a less stressful job. Some hope of that!

She kept looking at the telephone as time ticked by, fearful that it would be Daniel once again breaking a promise. Tonight she'd planned to return to the topic of a dog and finalise the decorating. And then – she drew in her breath nervously – she might even pick up enough courage to confirm her decision that she'd definitely be retiring from the force to become a full-time mum.

Fifteen minutes later she heard the front door open and her heart leapt into her mouth. He walked into the kitchen with a broad smile on his face. "Made it," he laughed as Rachael ran to kiss him. He held her close and wrinkled his nose. "That smells good, darling." And then spotting the cocktail shaker he gently pushed her away. "This isn't building up to that mutt thing again, is it?"

Rachael forced a smile. "I know when to bring that subject up, Daniel, and right now I think you need your Martini."

Daniel sighed happily as he moved to kiss Arty. "First things first," he said as he picked him up and drew him to his chest. "And how's my young man been today?" he asked, and was rewarded with a chuckle and dribble. How wonderful it was to hear his son laughing. He carefully lowered Arty back into his chair and, pulling out a tissue from a pack on the table, wiped the wet chin.

He judged it wasn't the time to tell Rachael that he might get a telephone call at any moment.

70

I drain the last drop of my Pinot Noir, smack my lips and control my breathing. This is it: the time has come. Time to bid Sophie Carpenter goodbye. After that, my life will become unbelievably exciting. I nearly wet myself thinking about it. I'm aware the risks are very high, and to stop myself having doubts about this last mission I think back to my violent times when a teenager. And I'm still fighting to keep my past from leaking into my system. I must control this or all will be lost. I'm aware that the devil still lives inside me and, given the chance, he would control me but I feel I'm stronger now than I was all those years ago. I look at my watch; still two hours before I feel it safe to move. I decide it is a good idea to bring my diary up to date. I have never missed a day since I was thirteen. One day, it will make interesting reading for someone – might even make a successful book. It might be a good idea to read back and see what a cruel person I used to be. That will remind me to be aware of how important it is to keep hold of my new persona and remind myself that the future will soon be bright. I pick up my diary from the table, it is heavy. I sink down onto the sofa and my hand is guided to a page I haven't read for years. I know I should slam the book shut. Too many memories might allow the devil to burst out within me but the page is like a magnet and before I know it I'm reading my scrawling writing. Not the neat writing of today.

We are on our way at last, leaving that dreadful man alone. My mother is in tears (only God will know why). My sister and I can't wait to get out of the house. Where we are going is more of a tip than the house we are leaving, but it will give us shelter and protect us from a violent man.

I rest my hands on the diary and flip the pages onto another year. How I'd hated my father. A drunk abusive man, who towered over my mother and terrified us all. I read on.

I saw the scissors on the kitchen worktop. I was filled with a deep loathing for my sister. Mother prefers her. She bullies me and takes what food we have from my plate. (Well, there was never much of that.) I know I've done wrong but the feeling of satisfaction I got as I drove the scissors into her flesh made up for the madness that followed. Result? Well, six hours later here I am sitting in a bus shelter, thrown out of my home (no doubt soon to be moved on by some fucking copper), wondering where my life is going to lead me. I have a suitcase, my diary and twenty pounds, nothing else. How things have changed since those walks on Brighton beach.

I let the diary drop to the floor. It is too painful to read further. The young offenders institute, the beatings, the solitary. The constant sexual harassment (and that's a polite way of putting it). Finally the degradation of living rough once I'd done my time and was adjudged fit to re-join the law-abiding community. Ha, that was a laugh. I think of the fights, the muggings and finally my joy of being reunited with my sister and watching her die.

I wonder what would have happened to the rest of my shitty life if I hadn't picked up the local paper and seen the advert. Once again I congratulate myself on making such a life-changing decision. And now, within the next few hours, I will have achieved my goal and be on the verge of another life-changing experience. I pick up the diary and turn to an empty page and start to write. I want whoever might read this diary in the future to understand my motives and realise that I'm no vicious killer, just someone ridding the world of trash, and realise I'm a hero. I write for several minutes before closing the book and replacing it on the table. I will write again as soon as I return. I move to the kitchen and wash my wine glass, walk to the bathroom, brush back my hair and tie it into a pony tail, wash my face and scrub my teeth. Then I change into my camouflage kit and move back into the kitchen where I pick up the knife and run a finger gently down the sharpened steel, and smile. I tuck it into my waist-belt. I head into the hall, where I put on my dark leather walking shoes. Then I stare at myself in the mirror on the wall. I think I look like a soldier about to go into combat. I flex my muscles, glance at my watch. One a.m. – perfect. Security will have wound down for sure. And whoever is left at the house will be fighting off the desire to sleep. I pick up my car keys and my night-vision goggles and move out of the flat. Three minutes later I'm in my car. I'm calm and focused. My mind and body are as one.

I drive slowly, watching in my rear-view mirror to be sure I'm not being followed. A new concern since the last visit from that WPC. I drive to within a mile of Jack's house and park in a lay-by. I start to walk. I know by the time I get to the house there should be only one or maybe two constables on patrol, the daytime shift having been stood down. (Big mistake, Appleman, but thanks.) This will make my task much easier. Two policemen fighting sleep will be a doddle. I laugh at the word *task*. Some people would have a violent word for it but I think *task* is perfect.

I'm glad it's not raining. A raincoat would have hindered me and rustled. I keep to the tarmac, ready to dive into the hedge if I see the lights of a car approaching. By the time I reach the bottom of the garden it is close to two a.m. I slip on my night-vision goggles. I see the gate. I climb over. I follow the same route I took the other night, congratulating myself at having persuaded Jack not to install CCTV cameras when he'd bought the house. I keep close to the trees, past the fish pond, past the summer house where I once watched Jack screwing Sophie. (At least I knew it wasn't love.) I feel sick.

When I reach the end of the garden I'm aware that I am about to begin the most dangerous phase of my mission. Okay, probably only two coppers inside, but I mustn't underestimate Appleman. There could be a third keeping watch outside. Impatient as I am, I decide to wait. I watch for movement, from a shrub on the right of the house. No movement, so no copper. I have to move to the left where the grill is. This will be risky as I have to pass all the windows that look out onto the garden. The adrenalin starts to pump I'm very aroused. My hand moves down. I moan and control myself. It's time to move. I drop to my knees and start to crawl past the windows. The last one before the grill is brightly lit. No curtains drawn. It is the kitchen. I guess this is where the police are sitting. No one in their right mind would want to be keeping the bitch company. My one advantage, I reckon, is that they must be bored, and drinking endless cups of coffee to stay awake. I'm tempted to take a look through the uncurtained window but decide that would be foolish. Only a few metres now before I reach the grill.

I freeze as I hear laughter. Jesus, where did that come from? I scan to my left, then to my right, then across to where the swimming pool is. I see no movement. It dawns on me that the laughter is coming from a television set in the kitchen. Steady, this is not the time to get jumpy. Once again I control my breathing and move to the grill. I reach out and tuck my fingers around the left edge. I hold my breath and send up a prayer to my guardian. The grill moves.

Sophie is as good as dead.

I lift the grill up and lower it carefully onto the grass. It is not my plan to come out this way. I readjust my goggles; I will remove them once in the house. There will be light from the kitchen and I will risk turning on the small light on the stairs, for a few seconds. I lower myself down into the cellar. My rubber soles make no noise as I walk across the concrete floor. I know I will leave a trail of dirt and shoeprints but I don't care. By the time they are found I will have completed my mission. Now, all I have to do is climb the concrete stairs to the door that leads to a passageway past the kitchen. I flick on the lights for a second to get my bearings. I feel my way up the stairs. As I suspected, the door is locked at the top so I reach in my pocket for Jack's bunch of keys which I took from his coat pocket earlier today. The third one fits the lock. The door opens silently. I move towards the kitchen, its door is half-closed. Shit! I freeze, deciding what to do. I drop onto my knees and start to crawl, holding my breath. No movement in the kitchen, only laughter. I'm shaking, I'm sweating but I make it past the door. Wow! Next I come to the door leading to the hall. This one is not locked and the hall is in darkness. That means Sophie has gone to bed. My luck is holding. I feel my way across the hall to the staircase, switch on the light and make my way towards Sophie's bedroom. Once I'm facing her bedroom door I switch off the landing light. I wait just in case the light has alerted the coppers. When I hear nothing my heart rate increases – I'm so close! I know Sophie's habits well. Upstairs about eleven, bottle of gin and a glass in hand. Lock herself in, and out to the world by twelve. But the lock won't keep me out; I have the key, Sophie darling, and soon you will be dead and I'm sure no one will shed a fucking tear. Once more I take hold of Jack's keyring and this time the first key works – I'm in. I stand still, hear her gentle snoring, blink to accustom my eyes to the dark. It is only minutes before I wake her and plunge my knife into her silicon, inflated breasts. My only regret is that I won't be able to see her eyes widen with fear. Oh what the hell – I find a wall switch. The room is bathed in light. I walk towards the bed I stand looking down at her sleeping form. I bend and shake her body; she moans: pissed out of her mind, no doubt. I shake again. She grunts like a pig and takes me by surprise as she sits bolt upright, her hands rubbing her face. "What the f…?" she mumbles. The knife nearly slips from my hands, so excited have I become. I can smell gin and sweat. I grip the knife with both hands and raise it above my head just as her eyes widen in terror. I give her no chance to scream. I strike at her chest. I feel it tear through her flesh. She makes a strange noise, falls back on the pillows but does not cry out. I strike again, with all my force. A spurt of blood hits my face – I lick at it and smile. "Die," I hiss, and strike again, then again. I'm awash with anger. I drive the knife in deep once more and then force myself to move away. No time to waste now, no time to watch the last drop of blood seep from her body, no time to cut off a relic of Mrs fucking Sophie Carpenter. I must make my escape. I'm as sure as I can be that Sophie won't be found until at least first light. No one will shed a tear and I will be thanked for ridding the world of an immoral, money grabbing bitch. I switch off the bedroom light, move out of the bedroom and close the door behind me. I creep back downstairs, knowing that the knife in my hand is leaving red droplets on the carpet, but what the fuck do I care? I can hear voices coming from across the hall from the direction of the kitchen; no one has moved yet. Last night as coppers, I'm thinking. Appleman will be incandescent with rage that yet again I have been a move ahead of him and this time I will be able to look him in the eye and smile with satisfaction. I edge my way towards Sophie's television room. I carefully push the door open, the room is in darkness. This time I do not risk switching on a light. I carefully make for the window. I flick back the catch: Jack has never bothered to alarm the house; once again I'm thankful he took my advice. I open the window and crawl out. I put my night-vision goggles back over my eyes and head back on the way I came. I drop panting onto the wet grass. Again I'm aroused. I control my animal urges. I push myself off the grass and move on.

My mission is complete I shout, "Thank you, God," into the dark sky.

★★★

I'm safely back at the car, not that I expected to be followed. When they find Sophie, panic will spread everywhere. Appleman will see the mud and the blood, and swear, but it will make no difference. My job is done. It won't take him long to know how I got in and out. No doubt he will wonder how I got in without his officers hearing me. Television, Appleman, television. He will be smarting, furious with his team and still no nearer to finding out who it is that is always one step ahead of him. Well, Inspector, you will soon know and your misery will be over. I can't wait to see his face. I start the car and drive away. My hands are shaking and smell of Sophie's blood. I take one hand off the steering wheel and suck the fingers. It only adds to my excitement. Once more I'm aroused but control the urge to stop and deal with the problem. Stupid me: there will be all the time in world for things like that. I join the main road and head back to my flat. I need to shower and tidy myself up. I'm finding it difficult to concentrate – the road seems a blur in my headlights. I curse loudly that I didn't bring a bottle of water. The adrenaline rush that I get when I kill always makes me thirsty. A car flashes me from behind. I realise I have strayed into the middle of the road. I quickly adjust. Lucky no one was coming the other way. I blink furiously, take several deep breaths and feel my heartbeat slowing down. I reach the outskirts of Winchester and breathe a sigh of relief – not far to go now. I park in my usual place and walk a little unsteadily back to my flat. Once in, I collapse onto my bed.

71

There were puppies rolling all over the bed, leaping, growling and tearing at the duvet. Daniel woke with a start, arms flaying wildly in front of his face. His mobile was ringing. It sounded like a puppy screaming. He reached for it and heard a familiar voice. "Morning, Danny boy, bit early for you am I?"

"Flacky. What time do you call this!"

"You used to be an early worm, Danny."

Daniel looked at his watch – "Yes, but five in the morning! I'm working on that case I told you about and have just gone to fucking bed."

"I think you'll be fully awake when you hear this."

Daniel rubbed his eyes. "Okay, but let me get out of here, don't want to wake Rachael."

"Okay."

Once in the spare room Daniel asked, "Still there, Flacky?"

"Yep, still here. You ready?"

"All ears."

"As you requested, I've been knocking on doors in the street where Jack Carpenter was brought up. My knuckles were getting a bit sore when I think I struck lucky. An old biddy, of indeterminate age, opened her door and glared at me. 'What do you want?' she asked suspiciously. 'You

374

from the old bill?' I assured her I was not, I was a journalist writing a book about the area and looking for characters that might be of interest to my readers. Well, that seemed to satisfy her and she whisked me into a filthy room and pointed to an even dirtier chair, whose springs were about to give out. Armed with a cup of tea she was soon in full flow. Oh yes, she'd known the Carpenter family. 'Diamonds the lot of them.' She was not so polite about her neighbours of the time though. A family called Goodboy. Two sisters, mother and father. Father was drunk most of the time, and abusive. Dreadfully disruptive family, she called them. Always fighting and screaming. She told me that eventually the mother and the two young girls fled the nest, leaving the father to die from alcohol, and no one in the street went to his funeral. Now this is where it became interesting and why I'm ringing you. It was local gossip a few years later that one of the sisters had died in a gang fight. The case has never been solved but word on the street was that the other sister was in a rival gang and had probably killed her. No love lost between the two apparently. 'That do you?' she abruptly asked. I assured her that that would indeed do me. So I finished my tea – which gave the name builder's a new meaning – thanked her and left. I was halfway back down the street to where I had left my car when I heard a shout. It was the old biddy waving a piece of paper at me. Curious, I hurried back. 'You might like to see this,' she cackled through cracked teeth. 'Forgot I'd still got it.' I didn't question this slightly doubtful explanation, 'Keep it,' she said, as she turned and headed back to her door.

Once I'd reached my car I took time to see what she'd given me. It was a twenty-three-year-old page from one of the local rags, full of adverts and small personal articles, two of which had been circled in red ink. One was a plea in the personal column for a Janet Goodboy to come home and pleading for anyone who might have information as to her whereabouts to get in touch, the last line reading, 'Missing you so much, baby. Your loving mum.' The second was in the wanted column, and guess whose name I saw? Your Jack Carpenter advertising for a secretary. And that got this old mind of mine racing and I just had a thought that perhaps the young woman who was suspected of killing her sister could now be Carpenter's secretary. A wild guess, I know, but to me it seems worth a bit more investigation. You know, change of name. Goodchild, Carpenter's secretary, right year, etc. Make any sense? Fanciful or worth looking into? You still there?" asked Flacky.

"Yes, sorry, just thinking."

"Got your interest, then?"

"Very much so. Can you email this to me now?"

"Sure."

Daniel gave him the address.

"And you might like to speak to Chief Inspector Rose Walters at Scotland Yard," continued Sergeant Flack. "She was involved in several gang murders around the time we are interested in. You might get some more info from her. I think she's close to retiring or might already have done so, but she's worth a try. I see her every now and then, so have a mobile number for you. She's an early bird like you used to be."

"You're a star, Flacky, always were. Do you know, I've had a hunch about this case and this may prove me right. I desperately need a break. I'll buy you an extra pint when we next get together. Do you remember what I used to say to you?"

"Don't expect too much from a hunch."

"That's right, but this sounds good. Now I must go but I'll keep you informed how we get on." Daniel broke the connection and rang Flower's mobile. A sleepy voice answered.

"Urgent, Paul. Get your arse down to the station pronto; I've got some info from Flack which we must follow up on."

★★★

Three minutes before six both men were in Daniel's office, wide awake and feeling edgy.

"Sorry about the hour but this couldn't wait," said Daniel. "Flack gave me some very interesting information which we must follow up urgently. You get some coffee and I'll make a call, then with luck we will make a move."

"No problem."

"Okay, keep your fingers crossed."

"And carry two mugs of tea?" joked Flower.

As soon as Flower was out of the room Daniel rang Rose Walter's mobile, more in hope than expectation, but much to his surprise it was answered after the third ring.

"Rose Walters?"

"Who is asking at this hour?"

"Chief Inspector Daniel Appleman. Hampshire police."

There was a pause on the other end of the line. Then, "Not young Daniel who had a crush on me?"

"The very one."

"Well, I'm sure you're not ringing me at this hour after so long to tell me that."

Daniel laughed. "No, afraid not, and sorry it is so early but this is very urgent."

"Okay, tell me."

Daniel explained, ending by saying, "And this old mate of mine told me you might know something useful. A long shot I know."

"That's a few years ago and my memory is not what it used to be but, to give you a quick answer, there were several unsolved murders with reference to rival gangs around that time. Almost impossible to prove who the killer was, but this woman you mention was suspected of one killing. Can't quite remember if it was her sister but what I do remember is that there was a girl named Janet Goodboy who led a vicious gang calling themselves *The Death Girls*. Before then she served three years in a young offenders unit. Another girl, who we assumed was her sister, belonged to a rival gang. I could try and find out more for you from the cold case files. I can still get access to them. Might take a little longer than no doubt you would hope but I'm retired, and I could try and find out if the young offenders institution is still operating. If so, I might be lucky and get a photo and fingerprints. Look, Daniel, I can't promise anything but I'll do my best."

A spark of excitement hit Daniel. "I'm not sure we have much time, but what you say is hugely helpful and backs up Sergeant Flack's story. I'll move on with what I've got and any information you can get will prove very useful at a later date if we have a suspect in custody."

"Will do, and good to hear from you. Good luck. Nasty case?"

"Very, and I fear my time is short before there is another tragedy. Thanks, Rose, I owe you one."

"Drink sometime maybe?"

"Maybe."

Daniel ended the call just as Flower walked through the door. "You look all buzzed up," he said, putting the two mugs of tea down on Daniel's desk.

"I think we've hit the jackpot, mate. Read this email from Sergeant Flack and then I'll tell you what Rose Walter's has just said. I think you will agree it is time to move, and move fast. I'm sure you will guess where to."

Flower rubbed his bloodshot eyes and took the email from Daniel. "Wow, this looks pretty damn interesting. Tell me what you heard from Rose Walters."

Daniel took a pull at his tea. "I'll give you the gist of what she said. The murder of the oldest Goodboy sister is still an unsolved case but from what she told me I think there is a real possibility that our Janet Goodchild is in fact the younger sister. Apparently the two sisters hated each other and the youngest did her best to do serious injury to the eldest twenty-eight years ago, for which she was sentenced to three years in a young offenders institution. A year after her release the eldest sister was knifed in a gang fight and died. No arrest has ever been made, but Janet Goodboy was leader of a rival gang known for their violence. Soon after her sister's death she disappeared off the face of the map, never to be heard of again. A lot of this ties in with what my old friend Flack told me, and what makes me take this very seriously is that Janet Goodboy was born in the same street as Jack Carpenter and, according to Flacky's old biddy, had a crush on him. So was it Janet Goodboy who answered Jack's advert for a secretary? Jack told me that he always tried to employ people from his area. It seems there's enough here for us to go and wake the saintly Ms Goodchild from her sleep. I have a good feeling about this."

"And if she is the killer, have you come up with a motive?"

"Love."

"Love?"

"Yes, love. We know that she has been in love with Jack for years, don't we?"

"So people say. But to kill his whole family. You've got to be a bit more than in love. Nuts seems a good word."

"Well, if she is Goodboy, she has a history of violence and abuse. Perhaps enough to make her unhinged."

"It still doesn't quite make sense to me," said Flower, "but it's certainly time to pay another visit to Ms Goodchild."

Both men were halfway out of the door when Daniel's mobile vibrated.

"Jane, good morning."

"Guv, it's Mrs Carpenter, she's dead. Murdered."

Daniel felt an icy finger run down his spine. "How the bloody hell has that happened? Where was security last night for fuck sake?"

"Constable Stuart and Constable Blacklock are in shock. I've just got here. I—"

"I'm on my way, Jane. Jesus, what a mess."

He broke the connection and looked at Flower. "Sophie Carpenter's been murdered. Right under our noses. Let's go!"

★★★

Daniel drove like a man possessed. "What the hell went wrong? The woman's been guarded day and night. How the hell has the killer got past our two officers? Shit! Short of Andrews sleeping with Mrs Carpenter in the same room or tying the poor girl to her, what more could I do? Keep her here in a cell – fat chance of that."

Flower shook his head. "I'm lost for words, gutted."

Neither spoke another word until Daniel braked to a halt outside the house and jumped out of the car. The front door of the house flew open and a very distraught Libby Stuart stared at them for several seconds before stammering, "Jesus, am I glad to see you both."

From experience, when he'd been a constable on the beat Daniel understood how she must be feeling, but he was in no mood to comfort her. "What went wrong, Constable? Did you fall asleep, forget you were supposed to be doing a job? For Christ's sake, woman, are you completely incompetent?"

Libby swallowed, fighting back the tears. "I, I don't know how the killer got past us."

"Well, they bloody did," snapped Daniel, striding into the house.

"Constable Blacklock and I have been in the kitchen all night, not a wink of sleep," said Libby Stuart. "All the doors to outside were locked. We never heard a thing until I took a cup of tea to Mrs Carpenter. Oh Jesus, there she was, the bed soaked in blood and knife wounds in her chest. I'm so sorry, guv, I thought we had all angles covered."

"Well, you didn't, did you?"

"No," said in a weak voice.

"One of you should have been sleeping outside the bedroom door. Surely you could have thought of that, after all I don't think you're idiots. And where is Constable Blacklock now."

"In the cellar. That's where the killer got in. There's a grill. Muddy footprints across the hall here and blood on the stairs leading to the television room window."

"Point of exit," stated Daniel.

"Yes, guv."

"Okay, you and Blacklock stay here and lick your fucking wounds. Sergeant Flower, Constable Andrews and I will go upstairs."

"I'm sorry, guv."

Daniel said nothing, just motioned to Flower and Jane and headed for the stairs. Once on the landing he stopped, turned to his two officers. "I'm as much at fault as those two downstairs. I should have given more advice. I knew Mrs Carpenter would be a target and I took my eyes off the ball."

"They should have used their brains," said Flower.

Daniel gave him a weak smile. "Well, we can't waste time right now apportioning blame. We have serious work to do. It looks as if my hunch might be right but I have always insisted on the meticulous gathering of facts. Hunches and personal antipathies might inform but must never be allowed to dictate the direction of an investigation. But this time—"

The sound of sirens cut him off mid-sentence. "Ah, the

team has arrived. Sarah will be with us soon." He turned to Flower. "I think Sarah and I can deal with this up here; you go and make sure this site is secure and start searching the grounds and surrounding area. It looks as if it will be a fine day. Hold the paramedics downstairs for a while until I give you the signal they can come up to the bedroom and take the body."

"Will do," said Paul, "but what about Goodchild?"

I have a strong suspicion that if she is our killer she will be on her way to Jack's and that's where I'm going once I've seen the body."

"Sort of claiming her prize," said Flower.

"That's the way I see it."

"You might need backup."

"I think it best if I go in alone at first. This may need sensitive handling. You follow once you've finished here."

"If you say so, but watch your step. You armed?"

"Yep."

"Okay then, but the sooner I get my team sorted the sooner I'll be with you."

"Fine. Ah, morning," welcomed Daniel, as Sarah Jones joined them on the landing.

"I've had better mornings," said Sarah. "Victim is Mrs Carpenter, I hear."

"That's right. Killed under our noses. I want a serious word with this killer. Right, let's go and see the body."

As soon as they walked into the bedroom the smell of death made Daniel shiver. He looked at Jane's white face. "Look, Jane, you don't need to be here. Forensic and I can manage. I think you need a strong cup of tea."

"Thanks, guv."

"It's never easy at any time to see someone who has been brutally murdered but you get hardened to the brutality of mankind – well, sort of. Make sure those two stumble bums downstairs don't fuck up any evidence."

"Will do," said Jane, silently thanking her good fortune at not being on duty throughout the night. She'd never seen the angry side of her boss.

Once Jane had left the room, Daniel and Sarah moved to the bed. They stood looking down at the bloodied body as if in silent prayer, which wasn't far wrong as far as Daniel was concerned. He was praying to a God he wasn't sure he believed in, to forgive him for the mess he seemed to be making. Never in all his years as a policeman had he felt so flat. At first he'd made the mistake of thinking this should be an easy case, but it had defied all logic, and he was swimming in a sea of mud, which was sapping his energy so much that he felt he'd soon drown.

Sarah sensed his despair but carried on with the job she was paid for. She could show her sympathy at a later time. "No struggle again, guv. Either she never woke up or she recognised her killer, who didn't give her time to put up a fight."

"Any idea how long she's been dead?"

"Not very long, I would say – she's not completely cold yet."

"Within an hour or two."

"About right, I would say." Sarah looked round the large room. The wall opposite the windows was lined with cupboards. "Boy, she must have had some clothes!"

Daniel nodded, his attention focusing on the windows. He walked over and drew the curtains and looked out at the immaculate garden looking so serene in the early morning mist. A complete contrast to the violence that had erupted in the bedroom.

As if reading his thoughts, Sarah came and stood beside him. "Looking at that you would never think that this peaceful place could ever be disturbed by such brutality."

"It happens," said Daniel turning away from the window. "I've seen it so many times."

"Our jobs leave us in no doubt that the world is a cruel place," replied Sarah.

"And talking of which, I must move. I must get to Jack Carpenter's house and give him the news."

"Rather you than me."

"It's a job I've never got used to but I must do this on my own. I need to admit mistakes, as well as everything else. You okay here?"

"Fine."

Daniel hurried out of the bedroom and on his way down the stairs he ran into a breathless Constable Blacklock looking very distressed. Daniel grabbed him by an arm. "You've woken up, have you, Constable? Well, that's very good of you and when you leave here I suggest you go to have your ears tested and carry on to an optician. You're a disgrace to the force, man. You've let the team down and I'll fucking well see you get the full wrath of DS Hollis. Now get back downstairs and bring the paramedics up to the bedroom and don't touch anything or you'll have SOCO after you as well."

72

Seven thirty, nearly there. My hands are really shaking now; this is the biggest day of my life and within an hour or two my future will be secure. I must concentrate on these last few miles; I cannot risk having an accident and the rush hour traffic is thick. I turn to a thought that has been bothering me for a few days now. I fear the presence of Francine. She and Jack have grown close, maybe too close, but I must resist the desire that is growing inside me to kill her. I must put up with her or plan her death for a later date if she becomes a barrier between my lover and me. The thought sends shivers down my spine – Jesus, this killing has got to me again.

With that thought in mind I manage to stay on the road and not lose my way. Every second, I'm getting nearer to my happiness. I can see Jack's beaming smile as I tell him Sophie is dead and that at last he is a free man.

The cottage comes into view; I slow down and drive past. No police cars, good. I'm still ahead. I do a U-turn and pull to a halt by the front door. I'm shaking like a leaf – I'm drunk with love and anticipation. I check my make-up in the car mirror, step out onto the gravel and smooth my blue skirt down. It is just above my knees and shows my legs off well. I run my hands through my hair, undo the top two buttons of my blouse, just enough to show the swelling of my breasts. Satisfied that I look sensual I walk towards the front door and press the bell.

73

Jack was standing by the the kitchen worktop waiting for the kettle to boil. He was dressed, like most days, in a blue suit, white shirt and blue tie. His black brogues were so shiny that Francine swore he could see to brush his hair in them. In fact she often laughed at his conservative way of dressing, sometimes even wondering if he only had a blue suit. He put one teabag in each mug, walked to the fridge and took out a carton of milk and heard Francine coming down the stairs. "Tea in here," he called.

She walked into the kitchen dressed in what she called her work clothes. A grey suit, skirt just covering her knees, a blue blouse and flat off-white shoes. "Thanks, Jack, I haven't got much time this morning as I'm off to see a lovely old lady living in Winchester, who I promised to visit before surgery this morning. She's dying. The cancer got her about a year ago and she's refused any treatment. Reckons she was on her way out anyway."

"I don't know how you can deal with something like that," stated Jack.

"It was hard for me to begin with, watching people with life-threatening illnesses, but you get used to it. If you don't it's time to quit." Then concerned she said to Jack, "You've lost so much weight, you look like a living skeleton. The tension is getting to you, isn't it?"

Jack put her mug of tea down on the table and gave her a weak smile. "You could say that, but it's no worse for me than for anyone else caught up in this dreadful situation. I just can't get the negative thoughts out of my mind. I feel as if the world is falling in around me. Why have my family been targeted? What have I done to deserve such punishment? Who can hate me this much? I don't care a fuck that my children disliked me, they did not deserve to be picked off one by one. And every day I think of Sophie, scared shitless wondering if she's going to be next. Thank the Lord she's going to London, but will she be safe there or will the killer follow her? Yes, I'm scared too, because I don't know how this is going to end. I would like to think that Daniel is close to wrapping up the case but I know that that is wishful thinking."

"Come here, Jack," Francine said, opening her arms to welcome him in. "Everything is going to be okay; we have got to be positive and trust the chief inspector."

"Always the optimist," Jack said.

"It's the only way to be. Living for years with a drunk mother taught me that."

They jumped as the doorbell rang.

"Who could that be?" queried Jack. "Bit early, isn't it, for visitors."

"Probably Cat. He gets more like a human every day. Prefers doors to be opened for him instead of using the cat-flap," Francine joked.

The doorbell rang again.

"Bit impatient, whoever it is," said Jack, walking out of the kitchen.

He turned the key and opened the door.

Standing with a big smile on her face was Janet.

Jack stepped back, surprised. "You're early this morning, Janet. Don't tell me there is more trouble up on the site?"

Janet smiled. "No, no. The opposite. I'm here to give you good news, really good news. Can I come in?"

"Yes, yes, of course. Francine's in the kitchen. Come on, she will make a fresh brew."

"I hate tea, you should know that by now Jack."

"Of course," said Jack cracking a smile.

As they reached the kitchen door Janet jumped in front of him, arms outstretched, blocking his way into the kitchen, thrusting her breasts towards him. "I don't want Francine to see this," she croaked. Then, taking a deep breath, she moved to within a few inches of Jack's face. "It's time Jack, at last it's time. Kiss me!"

Before Jack could move she'd wrapped her arms around him and pressed her body against his. He could feel her shaking.

"What the hell are you doing, Janet?" Jack gasped.

"It's time, Jack, time for us, don't you understand?"

Looking puzzled, Jack managed to manoeuvre his body away from her, but she immediately lunged at him again. But he was ready this time and sidestepped her. "Hey, steady on, Janet, what's this all about?"

Janet felt a bolt of unease pass through her body. This was not going as she'd expected. This was not how it was meant to go. She forced herself to remain calm. "Sorry, Jack, I was too direct; took you by surprise, eh? What" – here she almost choked – "I'm saying is that I'm yours. I have loved you for years and now that all the obstacles to my love have been extinguished we can live our lives together without the danger of being constantly attacked by your family. It's what you've wanted for years, Jack; don't repress your true feelings any more."

Jack had a terrible thought hammering at his brain. "God, Janet, what have you done?"

"Done!" she screamed, feeling she was about to lose control. "Done!" she screamed again, stamping her feet like a petulant child. "Done! For fuck sake, you stupid man, I've saved you from a life of hell. Your family are gone – dead, DEAD do you hear? I've rid you of your fucking sick, money grabbing family. That's what I've done. For you, Jack, all for you because I know you love me."

"No, no, I don't love you, Janet," whispered Jack, horrified by the thought of where this conversation was heading.

Janet's voice rose an octave. "It's time. Time at last for us to be together. I love you! Sophie is dead, do you understand that – Sophie is dead. And I know that you love me. All these years when you have been with that dreadful woman can be forgotten. We can be together now – forever, Jack, forever!"

Francine, worried by the sound of Janet shouting, hurried through the kitchen door, to be met by Jack frantically waving her back. Instead she froze, gazing at the obviously disturbed Janet.

Janet's mouth fell open. Then ignoring Francine she shouted, "I want you now, Jack! Get that fucking woman out of here."

"NO!" shouted Jack. "She stays here."

Francine continued to stare at Janet in amazement. "I think—"

"Shut your stupid mouth!" shouted Janet, waving at her violently. "If Jack wants you to stay then stay, but shut the fuck up. In fact, why don't you go back into the kitchen and leave us alone? You do not feature in my future plans. It's going to be Jack and me, understood?"

"What the hell are you saying?" Jack asked, managing to hide his growing unease.

Janet looked bewildered. "Don't you understand, Jack? There is no one in our way now. We are free to love each other

390

openly at last. Your children, and that bitch of a wife, cannot interfere from their graves."

A look of horror passed over Jack's face, as it dawned on him that this mad woman whom he had trusted with everything, including his life, was standing there boasting of killing his family.

"You killed Jenny and Harry," he gasped.

"And finally Sophie," Janet said triumphantly. "She's lying in her bed, blood seeping from my knife wounds."

"Please God, no," Francine cried out, reaching for the kitchen door to steady herself.

"Oh for fuck sake, shut up, woman!" shouted Janet. "You're becoming a nuisance. Yes, yes, I've rid the world of scum."

"Did you kill Timothy?" Francine whispered.

"It turned out to be a mistake, but you'll get over it, he wasn't right for you."

"You're evil," stammered Jack.

Janet frowned. This was the man who she expected to fall into her arms and thank her, not the one who was standing in front of her in shock. That's what it must be – yes, shock. No way had she so misjudged him. She shook her head as his words sank in. "Evil! How could you accuse me of that? I've killed for you – I've saved you from years of misery. I have offered you my love. You should be thankful that you had someone to protect you. People will thank me for what I have done. I will be their hero and you will love ME until the day you die."

"You're mad, Janet." Then fearing that he and Francine could be in danger Jack said, "Get out of here, Francine – the police, now!"

Bad move.

"NO! Stay where you are!" shouted Janet, slipping a knife out from under her dress and waving it at Jack. "I brought this to show you the blood of your dead wife. Yes, this was the knife I drove into your wife's silicon-inflated breasts. "

Francine vomited onto the floor.

Janet grunted in disgust. "Filthy bitch. And no need to call the police, they will be on their way to tell you your wife is dead. But I see a problem here, Jack, one that I thought might arise. She pointed at a white-faced Francine.

Fearing for Francine's safety Jack edged nearer to where she stood shaking. Taking hold of her hand he fixed Janet with a look of loathing. "You're crazy! I don't love you, Janet, I never have. Jesus, woman, what have you done? How could you kill so many innocent people?"

"Innocent! They hated you, they wished you dead. They wanted your money. They were making your life a living hell. I've saved you Jack, I've bloody saved you!"

"No Janet, you haven't saved me."

Janet's eyes went dark and Jack imagined he could see the madness radiating out of them. He had no doubt he and Francine were now in grave danger, which was quickly borne out.

Janet jabbed his chest with the point of the knife. A blood stain appeared on his white shirt. "You think I'm crazy! I'm not crazy. I've just saved you from a life of hell." And then she pointed a shaking finger at Francine. "It's you; I thought you might be in the way. You've come between us, you pervert. You're having an incestuous relationship. How could you draw Jack into your evil ways? You've tried to steal him from me." Then suddenly the knife was touching Jack's throat. "Well, you won't get him! I would rather kill him than condemn him to another life of shit."

"No, no!" screamed Francine, pulling away from Jack, and before he could react she was standing in front of him arms outstretched. "Leave him alone!"

"AAH!" screamed Janet and lunged.

The knife cut into Francine's body; she gasped and sank to the floor, her hands already covered in her blood.

"Now we are really free, you and me, Jack!" screamed Janet. "We can have a life together without trash getting in our way. Come on, take me now, Jack, it's just you and me. Come with me, love me, please, please! Now!" Janet ripped open her blouse to expose her bare breasts.

Jack let out a low growl and dropped down beside Francine and looked up at Janet, through eyes that were filling with tears. "Damn you, Janet, you have destroyed my family. I feel nothing but loathing for you. A mad unhinged woman!"

Janet moved to stand over him. She raised the knife. "I love you, Jack."

And then with one sweep of the knife she slit her throat.

In the distance Jack was aware of the sound of a siren.

"You're too bloody late," he mumbled, as he felt frantically for a pulse in Francine's neck.

74

Nine months later.

Rachael looked out from the bedroom window, watching Daniel walking across the field towards the house with their four-month-old Yorkshire terrier Avo trotting obediently by his side. They had christened her Avocado but Arty had soon turned that into Avo. She felt her son tugging at her trouser leg and bent down to pick him up, deciding as she did so that soon this was going to be an impossible exercise. Four months pregnant and already she could see the bulge when naked. As she held him tightly to her chest, the intoxicating smell of a freshly washed eighteen-month-old baby made her hug him just that little bit tighter. He was laughing as he seemed to do all day, and life would have been perfect if only Daniel could laugh again. She had a beautiful baby boy, another baby on the way, a dog, and new curtains and carpets, but that was not proving enough. She was learning very quickly that she needed Daniel back in her life. Ever since the horrendous outcome of the Goodchild case, Daniel had slipped into a dark mood, forever blaming himself for the failures. No amount of love or reassurance seemed to pull him out of his dark pit. Rachael heard the door close and braced herself for the normal broody, 'good morning'. She turned away from the window and made her way downstairs.

"Morning," mumbled Daniel, taking off Avo's bright red lead, before kissing Arty. There was just a nod to Rachael. If she hadn't been holding Arty she swore she'd have slapped his face. Instead she did her best to smile. "Big day today," she said with more enthusiasm than she felt. "You ready to go?" she asked, looking into his almost lifeless eyes. Where had the man she so deeply loved gone to? She braced herself for what she feared was coming.

"I, I, don't think I'm going to make it, love. The press staring at me, and that dreadful ACC smirking at me. Not to mention Jack Carpenter; how that man must hate me. No, this is not what I need right now."

Rachael reddened. "Listen to me, Daniel. It's nine months since all this happened. Do you really think that a man like Jack Carpenter spends all his time wishing you were dead or something? As for the ACC, well, that's plain daft. Not one person in the force has held you to account. DS Joyce Hollis and the chief constable have given you their full support, so does it really matter if one man blames you? You're a damn good policeman, Daniel, and too good a man to buckle under the pressure. As you well know, not everything goes a policeman's way every time. Okay, I admit the press were after your blood, but not now. There's more of that to be had elsewhere. So, the time has come to pull yourself together. You, I and Arty are fucking going this afternoon to applaud Jack Carpenter and shake his hand. And before you say another word, how about thinking of him? Look what he's lost. I tell you, Daniel, if you flunk it today I will go to Mum's until you can assure me you are back to the man I married. You are not being a good husband or father." Rachael stopped, short of breath.

Daniel stood very still for a few seconds, seconds which

Rachael felt were like an eternity. Finally, he looked up and smiled, holding out his arms. "Can I have Arty?"

With her heart pounding she passed him over.

Daniel drew his son up close to his face and kissed him. "Daddy will always love you and Mummy." With that, he handed Arty back. "Right, well, if we are going to be ready I suggest we have a quick breakfast, make a picnic and then you can drop me off at the station and you can head up to the site. I'll do my best to join you once the crowd has thinned. Okay with you, Rachael?"

There were lots of things Rachael could have said at that moment, some not so nice, but she threw him a smile and said, "Absolutely perfect." Then with Arty in her arms she turned to walk into the kitchen. There was no way she was going to show her tears to Daniel.

★★★

Ex-Constable Jane Andrews walked thoughtfully out of her parents' house and got into her car. As she turned the ignition key she couldn't help thinking how different her life was now. Once, she'd been so proud to wear the uniform and always felt a buzz as she neared the police station, but the aftermath of the Goodchild case had changed all that. "You're traumatised," her doctor had told her. Now, as she pulled out onto the main road, she thought of all the therapeutic sessions her mother had persuaded her to go to and the understanding her superior officers had shown her. "No bloody good," she'd eventually confessed to her mother. "I must resign." She indicated to go left and shook her head; that had been the saddest day of her life so far. And now here she was driving through Winchester to Jack Carpenter's opening ceremony, full of confused thoughts. How would her ex-colleagues greet her? 'Quitter' was a word that came to mind. As she drove slowly towards Winchester she knew that she'd done the right thing, and her new job working in a dress shop in Winchester was far less stressful and gave her time to work on her relatively new relationship with Rob Wilson, an IT expert, four years her senior, slim, wavy brownish hair and an infectious smile. That he towered over her didn't worry her a bit. She'd met him at a party given by a friend and from the moment he'd said 'hello' she knew he was the man for her. He was proving to be the calming influence in her life and she laughed at the thought that independent Jane Andrews was ready to be a housewife, longing to have children at some time in the near future. Nevertheless, as she drove into the site car park she felt a tug on her heartstrings as a well known ex-colleague waved at her. She knew then that she would never be able to completely forget the years she'd been a copper.

★★★

Mary Slater looked at herself in the bathroom mirror. It wasn't often these days that she wore make-up. Her friends at the shelter, as she liked to call them, didn't really care if she looked like a witch as long as they got their morning cup of tea. No doubt they'd miss her today, but that was tough, she had other things to do just for once. Francine had asked her to come with her to the opening of Jack's project. She nodded at her reflection and thought, *Not bad for a middle-aged woman,* then chuckled, *When have I ever fussed over my looks?* She moved out of the bathroom – picked up her bag from her bed and went downstairs to wait for Francine. *God, in all his wisdom, allowed a few miracles,* she thought, as she eagerly waited for the doorbell to ring. She was looking forward to shaking Jack Carpenter's hand and marvelling at his resilience. She hoped the whole of Winchester would be there to show their appreciation as she wandered into her kitchen and put the kettle on. A cup of tea was called for.

★★★

Winchester High Street was a heaving mass of humanity. Old couples, young couples, fat couples, thin couples, and all of various nationalities. *Quite a cosmopolitan town,* thought Francine as she walked painfully up from the Guildhall to the Caffe Nero. Two young men were attempting to play their guitars, and singing rather badly. She dropped a fifty-pence piece in their cap and was rewarded with a smile, before going back to singing off-key. A group of Japanese tourists were standing staring at them in amazement, their tour guide trying unsuccessfully to move them on. An old man sat with his back against a wall, his battered brown hat laid out in front of him, which made her think of the old man who had called himself Taffy. Bad memories still had a nasty way of surfacing most days, and today was going to be full of them. She looked up at the late August sun which was appearing over the city rooftops and rather guiltily wished she could be anywhere else but Winchester. She turned as she reached the cafe door and looked down the High Street, hoping that Jack might be on his way to meet her before leaving for *The Plot,* as he laughingly called it. She pushed open the door of the coffee shop and to her surprise and delight saw that the little table and the red fire extinguisher were still in place and unoccupied. She smiled as she walked towards the table, thinking that it was a miracle that she was still alive. It had been a close-run thing but, apart from the scars, both physical and mental, that would be with her for the rest of her life, she was back to normal. "But I'm lucky to be alive," she said to herself, as she settled into one of the table's chairs. She ordered a latte from a young, strikingly beautiful girl, who looked as if she'd be better placed as a

398

model, and settled down to wait for Jack, thinking that he'd changed so much since Goodchild's horrific death and not for the better. He'd aged ten years, his white hair was thinning, his eyes no longer sparkled and he'd lost so much weight that none of his suits fitted him. When she'd first set eyes on him in the Guildhall, a man full of dreams and energy, she would never have imagined that a man could change so much. Then, halfway through her latte, the man who occupied many hours of her dreams shuffled through the door, waved and came over. "Sorry I've taken so long but a few last-minute details needed sorting out with the mayor," said Jack.

"Not to worry, I was thinking how lucky I am to be here to take part in this special day. I don't know how many times I've thanked you for saving my life but I make no apologies for doing so. I wasn't ready to die, certainly not by the hand of that woman."

"You were lucky. The paramedics arrived just in time."

"It was God's doing."

"What?" said Jack, surprised. "I didn't think you had much time for Him."

"Well, now you ask, my beliefs have changed. Got time to listen?"

"Always time to listen to you. But first I'm in need of an espresso."

Coffee ordered. Jack said, "Okay tell me."

"You won't laugh."

"I've forgotten how to."

"Oh Jack."

"Sorry."

"This may sound a bit stupid, even rather weird, but I thank Him every day for allowing me to live." Francine stopped to take a sip of her latte. "You see, it goes like this. As you know, I have never been a great believer of that man in the heavens. I found church on the whole rather dull, the sermons unintelligible and the Bible, though a good story, seemed rather too far-fetched. But my recovery – a miracle, so my consultant says – has changed all that. Only a divine hand could have saved me, and I'm sure that that hand guided you to keep me alive until the paramedics arrived. And this belief has given me reason for living, and God, yes, the God I had never believed in, has come up trumps and persuaded me that I should carry on being a doctor and saving lives. I'm well aware, Jack, that probably the vast majority of an ever growing sceptical public regarding religion would scoff at me, but what the hell do I care? So there you have it. I'm not about to become a nun but I won't laugh when people tell me there is a God. Okay?"

"Fine by me."

"Do you understand though?"

"I'll give it my best shot."

Francine laughed. "I'll settle for that. Now, about today. You will enjoy it, won't you? I want you to feel proud of what you've achieved. Please do that for me. I know it may be hard but why not treat today as closure. It's nine months now, so time to start enjoying life again."

Jack shook his head. "I never thought I'd be sitting here with you, my only child. Only child, for Christ's sake Francine! My family slaughtered by a woman I would have trusted with my life. How, I keep asking myself, can I move on from that? So, Francine darling, you ask a lot, but I will try."

She knew that that was the best she was going to get.

★★★

Daniel fixed Arty in his child seat, put Avo in her cage beside him and waited for Rachael to lock the front door. He would have liked to be travelling with them up to the site for the celebrations. Well, that was what the press were calling it; he had another name for it. For him, and most of the Hampshire police force, it was not going to be a jolly holiday, as Cliff Richard once sang, or was it summer holiday? Ah well, whatever, it certainly wasn't going to be a holiday. The chief constable had ordered every officer to be on duty – he didn't want any security fuck-ups or drunk lads causing trouble. "And who better to oversee all this? You, Chief Inspector and DS Hollis. I know how well you work together," he'd said. Daniel had not agreed but she was one better than his nemesis the ACC.

★★★

Paul Flower stretched his aching muscles. This gardening lark was not for someone who hadn't the faintest idea of the names of any flowers, apart from roses, and as there were no roses in his new bride's garden he was tempted to treat every plant as a weed. He put the hoe over his shoulder and decided it was time for a much deserved cup of early morning tea, before getting ready for *the fucking awful day,* as his boss was calling it. He could hear Penny Howard, now about to become Penny Flower, humming as he walked towards the kitchen.

"Just rustling up a picnic, my beloved," she cooed, turning to look at the man she was marrying in two weeks' time. God, he was so gorgeous! Not a moment went by when she wasn't telling herself how lucky she was to have found him.

Paul pulled her close and landed a wet kiss on her lips. *Will I ever get tired of this woman?* he thought, as he felt desire cascade through him. But no time for that, he had work to do. He didn't want to let his mate down today of all days. He glanced at his watch, an hour, give or take a few minutes, before he had to leave for the station.

★★★

Mildred Turnbull eased herself into the economy seat on the Flybe flight from Malaga with a contented sigh, smiled at the man sitting next to her and pulled out her *Ideal Home* magazine. She stretched out her short legs and thought of Tank's fury when he came back to the villa and found her gone – not only gone, but with a shed load of his money. She was free at last; years of misery, slavery and violent sex was behind her. In a little under two hours she'd be landing at Southampton and then on a train to her beloved London and the Hilton Hotel in Mayfair. Already, she imagined she could smell the familiar aroma of the streets. Tomorrow, she'd ring a friend and they would go house-hunting for a small house, and maybe if they were not too tired pay a visit to Harrods and gaze at all the furniture she would buy. Then back to the hotel, and the bar, for a much needed port and lemon. Oh Jesus, the excitement of it all. The man on her right gave her another smile. "Like your hair, dear," he said leaning over to touch her hand. She felt a slight prick on her bare right arm, shrugged and scratched it. "Bloody flies," she said to the man.

"Shows they don't clean these planes properly," said her companion with another smile as he eased himself back into his seat.

Job done.

Mildred gave a sigh of contentment and closed her eyes. Time for a bit of shut eye before landing.

★★★

Tank's sides shook with laughter as he walked back into the villa. The Filipino maid smiled seductively and kissed him full on the mouth. Poor Mildred had had no idea that he'd had a spy in the villa who had heard her making plans. No one, Tank had assured her as he'd caressed the girl's soft skin, got away with such treachery. The old mare had stepped out of line and

402

would pay the price. Did he care? Not fucking likely, when he had a young nubile replacement. But then over her shoulder he saw a face he hadn't seen for a long time and had hoped never to see again. "Mickey!" he gasped, pushing the girl away. "What the fuck are you doing here?"

Mickey Dunn smiled as he pointed his Glock at Tank's fat stomach. "It's retribution time," he said, before putting three bullets into Tank's guts. He'd never forget the look on Tank's face as he sank to the ground.

And on the Flybe plane Mildred slept on.

75

By two o'clock the playing fields were crowded with families, friends and even the doubters who had opposed Jack's development from the start. The sun was shining, which it had stubbornly refused to do for most of August. Jack sat next to the mayor as the Daimler climbed the slight incline from Winchester to the site. They spoke little, Jack thinking about what Francine had told him in the coffee shop, and the mayor would tell his wife later that, "I never expected Jack Carpenter to be so uncommunicative. That man is suffering."

And suffering he was. He had a blinding headache and a pain across his chest. He was sweating, though the car was not hot, and he wished he could be anywhere else but about to stand up and give a speech, which more than half the audience wouldn't bother to listen to anyway.

There was some light cheering as the Daimler moved slowly across the pristine turf towards the cricket pavilion. Every now and then the mayor raised his hand, making Jack think that the man was enjoying himself more than he was. He cursed silently, unable to understand why he wasn't excited or feeling a wave of satisfaction as he looked out of the car window at the finished product. He could understand why people were thrilled but that didn't lighten his mood. "Look at me, I'm a wreck," he whispered.

"What was that, Jack?" asked the mayor.

"Nothing really, John, just nothing."

Yes, I am worried about you, and I will have a word with Francine as soon as this jamboree is over, the mayor thought, as the Daimler drew to a halt.

Before the chauffeur could open the back door of the Daimler, Jack was out on the grass. There were some things he never got used to and to be treated like royalty was one of them. He straightened his tie, made sure his shoelaces were tied and waited for the mayor to join him.

"This is it, Jack," the mayor beamed. "All this, your work, and look, thousands of people come to thank you. How does it feel to be a hero?"

"I'm no hero, John, just wanted to do something worthwhile for the area and the thought of thousands of houses going up here made me feel mad. As for the crowd, well, to be honest I don't think many really care about all this – the sun is shining, it's a Sunday and they want a good day out."

"No, no, Jack, you're totally wrong. These are Winchester people and they know when someone has done them a great service."

"Maybe, John." Jack sighed. "Could I sit down somewhere for a moment or two? I'm not feeling too well."

Looking with concern at Jack's pallor, the mayor took him by the arm. "We'll go into the pavilion. It's another half hour before the opening so you can have a drink of water and sit down. Before you have to face the masses," he joked.

Jack allowed himself to be led up the pavilion steps into the main area. There were rows of chairs where the dignitaries would sit while the mayor made his address and introduced Jack.

Jack slumped gratefully onto one of the chairs. He was

beginning to think he'd be pushed to stand through the mayor's speech and then reply.

He closed his eyes. The pain was getting worse and he felt sick. When he forced himself to open his eyes Francine and Mary were in the pavilion. "I don't like the look of Jack," Francine said to Mary. "I'm going to have a word with him." She hurried to Jack's side. "You okay?"

Jack did his best to smile. "I've felt better. I've a pain in my left arm and chest and I'm finding it difficult to breathe. I don't think I'll be able to stand for long."

Francine felt her heart miss a beat. Her experience was telling her one thing: Jack was having a heart attack. "Listen, Jack, I want you out of this chair and stretched out on the floor."

"I'm okay."

"Damn it, Jack, you're not! You're having a heart attack. Now let me help you out of the chair. You'll be fine if you do as I say."

The look on Jack's face was of startled surprise. "But the speeches—"

"Shut up; just do as I say." But before she could help Jack out of the chair he slipped off it and fell onto the floor.

Francine stared in horror at his white face staring up at her and heard his laboured breathing. "Jack, Jack, lie still. Help is on its way."

But Jack didn't hear her.

Francine fought back the fear that was threatening to overwhelm her. "Mary, Mary, we need an ambulance here – now – it's urgent! There's one a hundred yards from here by the edge of the cricket pitch. Run, run!"

Both Mary and the mayor flew out of the pavilion and Francine dropped down beside Jack. She tore at his coat, ripped the white shirt open and placed her lips on his mouth. When there was no response she placed her hands on his sternum and began pumping on his chest, head nodding up and down, up and down, like some mechanical bird. With every cardiac compression she was perfusing the brain, keeping it alive, but Jack did not respond. Reluctantly she drew her hands off his chest and felt for a pulse in his neck – nothing. It was not the first time she'd failed to revive a heart-attack victim.

She could not save him.

She lay her head on Jack's chest, mumbling all the time, "You can't do this to me."

Tears were almost blinding her.

The paramedics eased her gently away and Mary took her in her arms and led her out of the pavilion.

"He's gone, Mary," Francine sobbed, as they stood on the grass outside the pavilion. "I must go with him to the hospital. He would want that."

"And I'll go with you," Mary stated.

"I'd like that. I don't think I can do this on my own."

76

They sat on the grass watching the fish rise on the evening water. There was no sign of the fishermen, the only sound the whispering of the gentle breeze blowing through the trees that lined the riverbank. Soon the chestnut leaves would start to fall, heralding in the start of autumn.

Francine smiled at Mary and sighed. "That was lovely, Jack would have liked that, his friends there to say goodbye. Do you know, I doubt if he knew how many friends he had."

"You did him proud, Francine dear," said Mary, fighting to keep too much emotion out of her voice. "As you said, it was a lovely service and I think you were very brave to give the eulogy."

"I owed him that ten minutes. In spite of all the terrible things that happened after we met, he gave me a sort of love I'd never felt before. I can't really explain it but Jack made me feel loved, even special. And I think he loved me. He was not a man to pretend."

"I'm sure," said Mary. "And now, dare I ask your plans?"

Francine rubbed her forehead with both hands. This was a moment when she could have let her emotions rip – anger, resentment, despair, all of them would make her lose control and that was not on her agenda. When she finally spoke she felt eerily detached. "I never imagined it would be so hard to say goodbye to anyone, Mary. I've tried so hard to be decisive, to get my life back on track, to persuade myself that my life is here, that I belong to this community and this place, that life with my patients, many of whom I have grown fond of, is something I would need more than anything else. A sort of calming influence on my ruined life, as I see it. But my heart tells me otherwise and I feel I must follow my heart. So I will sell this house, give Cat to one of my patients who I know will give him a good life, and leave the practice." She gave a sad laugh. "Oh I know I have done this before and come back, but this time there is no life to come back to – only death. The ever present stench of death." Francine shook. "I can't live like that, Mary, much as I love this garden, you and so many other things that I know I should be grateful for, but I know I must move away and never look back. It's the most sensible move I can make."

Mary saw the sadness in Francine's eyes and knew it would do no good trying to persuade her otherwise. "You must make your own decisions but I will miss you, my dear friend, and so will the shelter."

Francine let out a long sigh. "My future lies unclaimed."